Praise for *The Point Man*

"I haven't read a novel like this since *The Exorcist.*"
—Robert Anton Wilson, coauthor of the Illuminatus! trilogy

"In *The Point Man*, Englehart never lets the absence of pictures slow his story."
—bookgasm.com

"Full of reach and astonishment . . . Few working writers alive have [Steve Englehart's] sense of sound and of scene."
—Theodore Sturgeon, author of *More Than Human*

"In a matrix of rock music, dizzy rock fans, the police, the Mafia, sex, betrayal, and innocent bystanders, the point man moves and performs his function. The magic is most magical, and enormous to boot, and the mystery and the tension will not release you. Or maybe this is enough: you'll like it."
—*Twilight Zone Magazine*

Praise for *The Long Man*

"Steve Englehart was one of the first authors I ever read. One of his Batman *Detective Comics* was the first comic book that ever scared me. With *The Long Man,* he proves that even thirty years later, he still has the ghostly touch. Immortals, alchemy, and beautiful revenge. I'm young again."
—Brad Meltzer, *New York Times*
#1 bestselling author of *The Book of Fate*

"Englehart, one of the best writers in comics, brings all his imagination and flair to this exciting tale of mystery, magic, and suspense."
—Max Allan Collins, bestselling author of *Road to Perdition*

BOOKS BY STEVE ENGLEHART

*The Point Man**
*The Long Man**

*A Tom Doherty Associates Book

The Point Man

Steve Englehart

A TOM DOHERTY ASSOCIATES BOOK / NEW YORK

This is a work of fiction. All of the characters, organizations, and events portrayed in this novel are either products of the author's imagination or are used fictitiously.

THE POINT MAN

Edited by James Frenkel

A Tor Book
Published by Tom Doherty Associates, LLC
175 Fifth Avenue
New York, NY 10010

www.tor-forge.com

ISBN 978-0-7653-2501-3

First Tor Trade Paperback Edition: March 2010

Printed in the United States of America

0 9 8 7 6 5 4 3 2 1

To Terry

Acknowledgments

Special thanks to Kent H. Jones.

foreword

The saga of Max August takes place across years, decades, even centuries, but everything must start at some certain time. Things are bound to have been different then, both for Max and for the world, because that's the nature of time—but in the moment, it was all just normal reality, and four-point-five billion people partook of it. Today, it's the difference in realities that fascinates Max more than the difference in himself, because each of his adventures is, in effect, a snapshot of its time, while he's an endless film.

So welcome to the world and the man of December 26, 1980, where the story that may have no ending has its very normal, but truly magickal, beginning.

In the Third Reich we have to forbid astrology. . . .
It is not for the broad masses.

—HEINRICH HIMMLER

Sometimes I can't help seein' all the way through.

—TODD RUNDGREN

Chapter 1

DECEMBER 26 • 7:30 P.M.

Barnaby Wilde was not his name.

BARNABY WILDE was what it said in block letters, in neon, above the plate window which held him.

He danced, his eyes tight shut, a faraway look in them, listening to Janis Joplin as she tore her heart out in passion and drugs. He was dancing in the window of the KQBU street studio under the eyes of an admiring crowd, but he was not a dancer. He was the disc jockey.

"Get down!" came from the multitude.

"Barnaby! Bar-na-BEE!"

"Sucker's all right."

"You asshole!"

He danced in the studio window, and he danced in the darkness of his mind, staring back down into Janis's eyes, as hazy as the room. She was riding the biggest wave in rock and everybody in the room knew it, most of them better than she did. He'd heard her do "Piece o' My Heart" at Wesleyan tonight, and he'd known she was unstoppable.

He was thinking about majoring in journalism, but only because he'd had to make some sort of choice and had no real direction. What he really was, he had learned since then, was a disc jockey. He'd sought out a show as a freshman for the same reason he'd sought out a poker game, used skis, and Marvel Comics: you came north to college to diversify. WESU had offered a folk show, Thursdays, 1 to 3. What did he know about folk? But he took it.

He became Barnaby Wilde, Rock 'n' Roll Requests, Fridays 8 to midnight. It played hell with his social life, but he didn't mind. The phones never stopped ringing. The February ratings had listed WESU for the first time ever; a college station was challenging both Hartford and New Haven. Barnaby Wilde was a Name in central Connecticut. And so he was invited to Columbia Records' party on the Wharf. And so, the moment came when he danced with Janis Joplin.

But don't get it wrong. When the dance was over, she giggled throatily and wandered off to find the bar. He went back to Nancy and they talked about the game against Amherst on Monday.

Still, it's memories that make the man.

Now, whenever Barnaby Wilde of KQBU San Francisco, weekdays 4 to 8, played a Janis cut for an oldie, he remembered her glazed eyes, and how her red hair flew in the green light. And, almost always, he danced . . . even if he did it in a street-front studio.

Some of the crowd on the sidewalk danced with him. Three guys in identical down vests did the Latin hustle. Two girls, not together, pressed against the glass like bookends, tits flattened, feet doing all the good moves. Barnaby's head was thrown back, his hips bobbed and wove with the horns. Janis started to scream in earnest, her voice out on the edge between artistry and hysteria. The drums were deafening, the sax afire. She rose, and she flew . . . and then she brought them all back home. A final four bars and the storm was past, leaving them all in the wake.

Barnaby brought his mike up as the echo died. "Janis Joplin, as if anybody needed to be told," he said, his tone warm and his words crisp, if slightly breathless. "The one and only-ever J.J.!" He punched the prime cartridge. "K-Q-B-U," sang the chorus, "thirteen ninety!" "Did you like that?" he called out to the crowd, opening the street mike for their "Yeahhhh!" "I mean J.J., not the jingle," he taunted, screwing up his face at them. They laughed. He punched up the next song. "I knew that you would! Hey, how was your Christmas? All right?" "Yeahh!" "All right! And the year-end Golden Greats keep on a-comin', with Barnaby Wilde on the Barbary Coast!" A lion roared: his trademark. The song's intro ended, and Hot Chocolate sang.

He flipped switches without benefit of glance; music swamped the small studio as his mike cut out. His hands moved across his control board like Elton John's on keys. Now they shifted his earphones to his neck, where they hung like a horse collar, and he swiveled toward the bright white box of cartridges Dymo'd "1966." The voice of his engineer rumbled in through his collarbones. "The Madwoman just called down."

Earl's voice was carefully neutral; he, too, was in the fishbowl. Earl had been an engineer since an engineer was somebody. It was he who had set up mikes for concert remotes from Chicago's Avalon, he who had invented the right mix to give the Lone Ranger's desert chases that windswept ambience. Up until the mid-60s, he had played the announcers' records for them. But now he sat on Sutter Street and made sure Barnaby Wilde kept to the schedule. He was way past his prime, and he hated his job, but he liked Barnaby Wilde, and he liked earning a living.

They both disliked the Madwoman.

Barnaby found his next cart and swiveled toward the side window, through which Earl was peering nearsightedly. He flipped his mike switch to "2." "What'd she want?"

"Didn't say. Just wants to talk to you when you're off."

Barnaby glanced at the clock: 7:38. "She's coming down?"

"No. You go up."

"Okay. At least it's not another memo." Both men laughed. "How was your Christmas, Earl?"

Earl lifted his skinny shoulders. "Ehh. Easier in some ways, with the kids all gone. But emptier, too. Less giving, and laughing, and mess." He shook his balding head. "Cost just as much, though. That didn't help. Somehow, with all the money I take out of this station, we're still on the edge of bankruptcy."

"I hear ya, big fella. Don't you wish somebody could explain—*really* explain—why money just ain't worth shit anymore?"

"Well, if they do, it'll be this week, when nobody's listening. This time between Christmas and New Year's is just dead air, as far as the world's concerned."

"A good time for coming around to fix my amp, though."

"I'll fix your amp, you poor doomed soul—if you're still working here after tonight. Hey, don't forget the McDonald's spot."

"No, I got it."

Barnaby stuffed a red-and-yellow cart, fresh from the agency, into his second player. Hot Chocolate was fading. Was Earl right? he wondered. Ohh, mama, can this really be the end at QBU? He took three deep breaths, fast, to shoot oxygen into his brain. Hell, no! Fuckin' A! He flipped his mike switch back to "1," reopening it to the world.

"Hot Chocolate—and gimme a hit o' brown sugar to go, too, m'man!" Dirty chuckle. "O' course, if you're one of those people who wants something a little more substantial in your mouth—something like two all-beef patties, special sauce, lettuce, cheese, pickles, onions, and a sesame-street bun—*well* then, listen very closely! Girls—?"

The girls began to sing, in their red-and-yellow voices. He noted the time, 7:40, in the log, and found the tag line in the black book for when they finished. "Remember, there's a McDonald's near you in Oakland, at 6623 San Pablo, and another in The City at 2801 Mission, especially for all you low riders—and don't forget to ask 'em for the brown sugar! Tell 'em Barnaby sent you!" The lion's roar. The Bee Gees broke into a croon.

Barnaby stood up and leaned forward, resting his palms on the console, looking out over the crowd. Earl, watching him, was reminded of a king surveying his realm . . . and Earl knew, as far as radio went, it was true. Barnaby Wilde was the AM King of San Francisco. With a high forehead fading into the first signs of a widow's peak, high cheekbones, large eyes which missed little, and the full mouth of a born talker, he looked the part almost too well.

Earl had known a lot of kings since Chicago—most of them very short-lived. This one wasn't.

The telephone rang in Earl's studio, and he answered it. Listened. Held it up to attract Barnaby's attention. He could have cut back in on the earphones, but then his sardonic grin might have been missed. Barnaby knew what that grin meant. He didn't usually accept calls during a show, but Earl always put this one through. Fuck! he thought wryly. He made a great show of reluctance as he picked up his own receiver. The crowd wondered. Earl patched in on earphones.

"Barnaby? Hi. This is Suzanna." Her voice managed to be low, husky, and tentative all at the same time. She had told him once she was sixteen; he thought it was more like fourteen. "I heard what you said about brown sugar. . . ."

"Could you turn down your radio, Suzanna?"

"Oh, sure." The crispness of his tone didn't seem to have registered. Or maybe, by now, she thought it was his normal manner of speech. The Brothers Gibb stopped overloading the line.

"Listen, Barnaby," she said, "I heard what you said about brown sugar, and, I'm not brown, except, you know, my *hair*, down *there*, but I'm having a party at my place tonight, an after-Christmas party, and I was hoping you could *come*. You know?"

"Come. Uh-huh." She was spaced, for sure; her voice wandered right behind her train of thought. With his free hand, he reached out for a Carly Simon cart.

"I had a dream about you last night," she went on, softly. "It gave me the idea, see? The earthquake came, right? The big one? It knocked down all the houses on my street. I sleep next to a window, so when everything fell, I was thrown clear, out the window, but the glass tore off my negilzhay. Actually," she tittered—there was no other word—"actually, I don't wear a negilzhay, but this was a dream. I was wandering through the streets with nothing on, and then I saw you. You came rushing over to me, and just then a great big crevasse opened up and we both fell in. You fell on top of me, Barnaby."

"That's amazing, Suzanna." Earl was rolling side to side in his chair, tears streaming. Some people on the sidewalk were pointing at the crazy old man.

"Well," the girl said, breathless at the memory, "the shock ripped all your clothes off, too—"

"I bet!"

"—and you were just lying there, dazed. I tried to see if you were hurt, but I couldn't move either . . . and then, you started to move, just your hand. Down between my legs. Just so slow . . ."

"Just a minute, Suzanna."

Barnaby punched the continuous cart again for the call letters, and opened the mike. "Don't forget: KQBU, in association with Bill Graham, presents Valerie Drake at the Cow Palace, 8:30 P.M. sharp on January 1st. Tickets are 10.50, 9.50, 8.50 and 7 bucks, and you'd better believe they're goin' like lifeboats in a monsoon. So get 'em soon, mon, at the Cow Palace box office, or by calling TELETIX. That's 415, T-E-L-E-T-I-X. Valerie Drake, one night only, New Year's Day—you figure it out. And here's some figuring music for you. Or music about figures. Carly Simon—!"

He picked up the phone. Maybe I should play "Misty" for her, he thought. But he said, "Listen, Suzanna, I've got to go." Earl signaled him: no! no!

"Wait!" she protested. "I haven't told you everything!"

"I know. But duty calls."

"But what about my party? My parents are gone till after New Year's, and we've got all the booze in the world. My dad will never miss it."

Despite himself, knowing he was nuts to give her any encouragement at all, he couldn't resist one question. "How many people will be at this blast, Suzanna?"

"Just us, baby," she answered, sounding suddenly more like twenty-six than sweet sixteen. "Just you and me, you know?"

"I know. Believe me, I know. But I can't do it, Suzanna."

"I'll come see you, then."

"I'm here every afternoon. Just be sure to keep your clothes on, so my boss doesn't raise a ruckus."

"Oh, you!" she pouted, and hung up.

Looking out at the crowd, Barnaby wondered how many heroic fantasies would shatter if they knew what he was really doing in here.

And how many more would be born?

He didn't know why he bothered to talk to her at all.

. . . Well . . . yes he did. As far from his plans as a date with horny jailbait was, those calls were still a mark of his success. The girl had never met him, but his voice alone, and the things he did with it, could get to her. Like every performer, he needed his audience, needed that response. The ratings told him he had it, but numbers were no substitute for live fans. Even spacy ones.

Or were there any other kind?

He hyperventilated for a full twenty seconds before going back on the air. The rest of his show went by like a dream, and then he was finished for another day. The crowd waved and broke up, scattering in all directions.

He picked up the program log with weary fingers and signed out. He had to think for a moment, his face slack, before he filled in the final line.

"Max August," he wrote.

Barnaby Wilde, you may remember, was not his name.

Chapter 2

DECEMBER 26 • 8:05 P.M.

Conscious of the sweat-stink under his arms, Max August went to see the Madwoman. *Her* real name was Madeleine Riggs, one of the new breed of broadcasters who had never been on the air. She had majored and Mastered in Business, and meant it; her official title was Corporate Liaison. Nobody had known what that meant when she'd arrived on her Fact-Finding Tour two weeks before, and nobody knew now, but she wore her authority with even more style than her Eastern fashions. She represented the owners, Northcliff, and she smiled all the time. Maybe there was a connection.

Nabbing a dry doughnut on his way through the remains of the Christmas party, he walked up one flight and knocked at the office she'd commandeered. He found her sipping a cup of coffee, seated behind the desk of the station's pre-Northcliff owner, who was now in Palm Springs playing golf.

Madeleine Riggs was a natural redhead, with blue-black eyes and a no-nonsense mouth, dressed in shades of green: herringbone jacket, tweed calf-length skirt, satiny blouse, cashmere scarf. The fedora that went with all that was carefully set on the windowsill. She could have been a knockout, Max decided, but the final effect was too studied. She looked like a mannequin, or a top-flight hooker. Of course, he never had liked her.

As he appraised her from the doorway, Madeleine was returning his gaze from behind her coffee's steam. She knew, in her crystal way, that this would be her toughest hour in San Francisco, despite the outward informality of it. She'd planned this meeting in every detail, right down to the after-hours time; it would be her own fault if she fucked up now. Fortunately, she never fucked up.

"Barnaby! Max! Nice to see you!" She smiled brightly, rising to shake his hand. She seemed to notice his stance for the first time. "Tired?"

"A little. You have something strenuous in mind, Madeleine?"

Her smile remained in place, but everything in it died. Turning her head away, she smoothed her skirt across her hips as if wiping her hands on it, and Max wondered if all his years as Barnaby Wilde had loaded his voice with more innuendo than he knew. But the replay in his head convinced him it was all in *her* head. So, he thought. It figures.

She sat down again, motioning for him to do the same. "Max," she said, "why did you play Janis Joplin tonight?"

"I wanted to. Is that why you wanted to see me?"

"The Joplin girl is dead, you know."

Long hours in the fishbowl were all that kept his face straight.

Not that he was a Janis groupie, whether he'd danced with her or not, but he'd never in his life heard anyone refer to her with such cheerful unconcern, either. How in touch with their music *was* this Corporate Liaison? A premonition touched him.

"She's a San Francisco tradition," he said. "Maybe a legend."

"There's no tradition in contemporary music, Max—just oldies, which this station has been playing all day. But I believe KQBU should be a Today operation. And that's what I wanted to talk to you about." She leaned back in her chair, her unbound breasts rising smoothly under the satin, her nipples tracing tracks he silently noted, waiting.

"Max, I was sent here from Northcliff to see what I could do to improve KQBU's earnings. I haven't passed the word before this because I didn't want to make anybody nervous; nervous people put on an act. I wanted to simply observe—the station's style, its competition, its managerial structure. And the types of people who listen to it. People are very important to me.

"Now I feel I've found the answer."

Her smile was back in sync, and Max felt his resentment beginning to grow. As the top-rated jock in the Nine Counties, he felt *he'd* found the answer already. It was an ego thing on his part, but that didn't bother him a bit, since egos are what make performers. What bothered him was the ignorance which must have shaped her "answer," and how it would clash with his ego. He was the one who'd be left to sell whatever idea she'd pulled out of her fancy hat.

But none of this showed on his face. He met her eyes blandly, and waited for her to continue.

"It's my job to find answers. That's what I'm being paid for. And, in all honesty, I intend to succeed," she said. "We all have to make names for ourselves.

"Max, the San Francisco market has become a crazy quilt. It used to be that KQBU, KFRC, and KYA were the only contemporary stations around, and since contemporary always takes forty percent of the audience, each of you had enough to get by no matter who beat who. But now there are stations all up and down the bay: Berkeley, San Rafael, San Mateo, San Jose. AM and FM. Not to mention new FMs right here. Most of them have followed a clear pattern: knowing they'll only get a segment of that forty percent, they shoot for a specific segment. Blacks go their way, gays go their way"—the smile twitched momentarily—"album lovers and disco lovers go theirs. Hell, that's democracy. But what's left for us, besides the death of a thousand cuts?" Madeleine Riggs reached into her cordovan purse and came up with a pack of Virginia Slims. She tapped one out, tapped it on a long thumbnail, and laid it in her mouth.

"Only music," she said, and lit up. "Much, *much* more music."

And at last Max knew where she was going. It came to him like the flash of her match.

"Computers."

"Very quick, Max. Yes, we've had great success with computers, in both Indianapolis and Salt Lake City. The music never stops, all day and all night."

Once more Max chose his words carefully. He was dueling with a dangerous child. "But San Francisco's a different market, Madeleine. This is a music city, and a people one."

"Computers are universal. Ex-hippies are no more immune to the times they live in than anyone else. This is the age of technology, my friend. Technology is what people want."

"Not disc-jockey people, Madeleine. They lose their jobs."

"In all honesty, yes, most of them. But not you."

Madeleine Riggs leaned back in her chair and regarded him along the thread of her cigarette smoke. That made him snap to, she considered, but her smile remained fixed and inviolate.

"The changeover takes place in six weeks; we'll install the Programatics in two. But I don't plan to stick around until then. I need someone here, secondarily as the voice of the station on the computer's tapes—and primarily as sales manager. As the Afternoon Drive man, you've been the real leader on this station anyway. You showed the rest of those hacks where to go, and how to get there. This just makes it official." Now her smile grew. "It's a hell of a lot of prestige, my friend. A solid stepping stone. Plus a pay hike from the seventy-five thousand flat you make now, to that and five percent of the station's revenue. That should come to one hundred fifty thousand total the first year."

Max was stunned, and this time he showed it. It was the last thing he'd been expecting. But perversely he retained his dislike of this woman. He could not be had so easily, or so quickly. He said, "Madeleine, I'm an air man. I like playing rock 'n' roll, live. That's why I became a jock." It sounded flat.

"I know. That's why we all got into this crazy business. But it *is* a business. Don't forget, you'll have more time for outside commercial work, as well."

Max tried to think. He put his hands, flat, on the desk before him, and studied them: the nimble fingers, the golden ring, the scar on the left thumb. They had controlled his fortunes up to now—they and his voice. On the air, behind a board, he was his own boss. But this offer was what he'd always worked for, wasn't it? He'd earned this offer, with his hands and his voice and his ego, day after day for nine years. He'd earned it in spades. And yet . . .

Not yet.

"I'll have to consider it."

"Fine. This is the 26th; would January 2nd, right after New Year's, be all right? I'd like to wrap this up."

"That's fine." He stood up and stuck out his hand. She shook it, smiling. Her hand was drier than his.

"Just one thing," she said. "When you're in charge around here—none of that Joplin girl, eh? I like life."

After the door had closed behind him, Madeleine picked up and sipped at her coffee—and found it cold. She drank it anyway. It hardly mattered, compared to the glow she felt inside.

She never fucked up. She'd hooked him good.

And all he'd seen was the bait.

Chapter 3

DECEMBER 26 • 8:35 P.M.

Max strode out onto the night-lit slope of Sutter Street. It was all but deserted now, though music still came from the outside speakers above the studio window, bracketing the new neon name of JOHNNY DARK. Nobody in radio was really named Johnny Dark, though hundreds of jocks had said they were. It was a house pseudonym, passed on from man to man, like Pope. Most of the newer jocks, especially on the sincere sound of FM, were using their own names these days, but in AM, in the 60s, it was more fun to think up a new one. Rick Shaw. Jack Robinson. Sandy Beach. Barnaby Wilde.

There was nothing wrong with Max August. But there was nothing particularly right with it, either.

Fun.

As he walked up the Sutter hill, turning his back on the Financial District, Max pondered the "crazy business" he was in. You had to be a little nuts to be a good jock, he thought. And you had to have a feeling for being young. But how young? And how nuts? What was wrong with a hundred fifty thousand a year? Shit, he was a capitalist.

His thoughts turned back to the Dallas-Ft. Worth ratings wars of 75, when he'd become so outrageous he'd made fools of the police on the air. That had raised a lot of hell. It had also raised his salary above fifty thousand dollars for the first time, because he'd won the war.

After that, the money had become unreal. He never had to worry about it any more, and he liked that, but it wasn't the money he had done it for.

Fun.

For the first time, fun and money weren't the same thing.

He turned to the left on Stockton, pacing as he'd danced, in the dark, and thought about his alternatives. From where he was now, he could go anywhere in the country as a top jock. It wouldn't be quite as much money as the sales manager thing, but he wouldn't starve. It would mean a move, but after sixteen stations in nine years, that was a minor inconvenience at most. It would mean a continuation of a life-style he'd grown very attached to—perhaps more attached to than he'd realized.

But for how long? How long until the people who actually *controlled* the next station decided on a change, and the problem arose again?

Here he would have security, and security was not to be sneezed at. Madeleine Riggs's voice played back through his ears, paraphrased: "Disc jockeys are no more immune to the times than anyone else." And it was just too damn clear that all the times had done since Max had left college was go downhill, with more of the same to come.

. . . . .

He'd been in basic training: six weeks out of college with a big B.A. under his arm, and running his ass off back down south at Fort Benning, when they'd pulled him aside for a little kaffeeklatsch. It was mid-August and hotter'n hell and nobody'd treated him human since they'd put him on the bus out of Miami a month before, so he knew right away there was a catch. "Somethin's *wrong*, man," he said to his bunkmate. "They *want* somethin'." And sure enough, they were offering him OCS. Avoid this two years of enlisted-man shit, they told him; sign up with us and be a lieutenant. O' course, we'll want six years from you then, and the rest of your life in the inactive reserve. Any time we need your skills, you'll get a letter, and you'll drop everything to ship out for Bumfuck, Egypt. But you won't be no fuckin' grunt. What the hell, you're goin' to Vietnam anyway, so why not go in style?

He'd smiled, and finished his Coke, and told them lightly, No, thanks. He hadn't volunteered *for* the Army, and he wasn't volunteering *in* the Army. Two years was more than enough already, thank you very much.

He'd kicked himself ever since, especially after he'd *got* to Vietnam.

. . . . .

He found himself standing in the corner of Union Square facing the St. Francis. It was quieter here, the traffic growl muffled by hedges. A droplet trickled across his cheek, and then another; the fog was coming in. It surprised him. Bogart and Hammett always found fog in their San Francisco, but it was fairly rare now. The weather was another thing that was changing for the worse.

All at once, something moved at the edge of his vision—something small and quick. He turned to see . . . but there was nothing. A trick of fog-shrouded headlights. It was cold out here.

A foghorn began tolling from the Golden Gate, warning the world of the unyielding land, muffled but relentless.

This way lies security, and power. Try to measure that against fun.

"The Joplin girl is dead."

. . . . .

Only two kids remained in front of JOHNNY DARK. Neither was dancing. It had a lot to do with the time; kids passed down Sutter Street from 4 to 8, and were passing out in some bar by now. But it also had a lot to do with Barnaby Wilde.

Coming out the front door just as Max reached for its handle was Chick Frommer, QBU's new engineer, a pink-cheeked blond kid with a face like the moon. Chick smiled as he caught sight of him. Max smiled back, professionally, but thought, Did I ever look that unformed? There were no lines in Chick's face. No character. Just eagerness and good will. Max stood in the fog, hand on the handle, for a moment more, feeling thirty years drop consecutively 'round his shoulders like iron horseshoes on a peg. But they didn't weigh him down; instead, in some way even he couldn't put into words—a rare event for a man like him—they confirmed him. He had withstood the storms and shoals of life thus far, and at last had some perspective. Something within him still felt like a kid . . . and yet he knew he was not, any longer. It was a good mix.

Madeleine was just turning out her office light. He walked up to her without preliminaries, giving himself no time to change his mind.

"I'll take the job," he said.

She smiled. "That was fast."

"I'll take the job, on the following terms." His face was deadly serious. "I understand that if I work for Northcliff, I work for Northcliff, and I'll take orders on station operations. But nobody—not you, or your bosses in New York, or anyone—is going to tell me what's popular in San Francisco, because it's my music sense you're hiring, or should be."

"I see," she said, her smile unmoving. "You're not one for mincing words."

"No. People are people, as far as I can tell. I don't kiss anybody's ass. If you want dutiful deference, you'll have to get it somewhere else, Madeleine."

Her mouth twitched. "That's fine with me, Max. I wouldn't have it any other way." The smile began to grow, and a new look came into her eyes. He couldn't quite define it, since he hadn't seen any looks at all there before. She held out her hand to him. "Shall we hash out the details over dinner?"

He looked down at that hand.

What the hell. He took it.

DECEMBER 26 • 10:30 P.M.

At Ernie's, over wine, lobster, and succulent filet, they hashed.

She was unexpectedly pleasant company, not at all the Madwoman he'd known in the office, and after half an hour, he found himself outlining his ideas on the new format to an interested and interesting woman, rather than his boss. He suspected it was his new status; she was clearly a power-tripper. Everyone at the station had remarked on the heat of her gaze in these past weeks, but it had been the heat of a laser crystal, unchanged at the core. Now there was a liveliness in her look, an unmistakable challenge, that Max had looked for since he'd first met her and not found.

"Damn it, Madeleine," he was saying, as the waiter brought their cherries jubilee, "the computer stations I've heard *sound* like computers. Two songs, titles; two songs, titles. That's what we have to avoid. I'm going to vary that as much as the machines will allow, and I want every concert we can get. We may not be live, but we'll be lively."

Madeleine leaned forward across the table, her smooth face thrown into high relief by the dessert's dancing blue flames. "So you'll go along with my computer idea, but try to hang onto as much of what you had before as possible," she said, laughing. "You're a stubborn man, Max August. And an anarchist."

"Shall we admit that I know more about rock 'n' roll than you do?"

"Rock 'n' roll, yes. Though I prefer the term 'contemporary music.'" She laughed again. "But I warn you: we're on the edge of something now, in the outside world. We've been drifting for a long time, and we need a change to give us new goals. Excuse the after-dinner philosophy—"

"No, go ahead."

"All right. I think, very simply, that we're on the edge between drifting and determination, and the era you're trying to hold onto, the era of 'peace and love,' was the era in which we began our drift. The free-format approach to anything, of which radio is only a small part, is soon going to be not only out of date, but actually distasteful."

Max could have argued with her, but leaning forward had put her breasts atop her crossed forearms, and right then, scooping warm fruit into his mouth, he was more inclined to admire them than settle the fate of the world. She noted his admiration with a secret pleasure.

"I couldn't do what I'm doing ten years ago, despite the vaunted revolutions and liberations," she said. "It's only now that I can do it, now that we're actually settling into the new reality. And I like reality."

"You know what I call New Yorkers?" Max answered amiably. "Reality junkies. You don't want *just* reality. You have to tie off a vein and shoot it up."

She nodded. "I'm a hard woman, Max, and I know it. I always wanted to climb to the top, and I'm going to; I'm not working for Northcliff because the nursing school was full. I put together my own investment service before I was twenty-five, and when the corporation wanted to buy me out, I leapt at the chance. In all honesty, this is a business for users, and people use people for a lot of low-level reasons: sex, revenge, self-protection—and one high-level reason, which is ambition. I respect ambition. It may be the only thing I do respect." She reached across the table and put her cool hand on his. "I'm using you, Max, because you're ambitious, too. If you do well, I do well; that's cold-blooded, but it's what we both want." She smiled suddenly. "I'd have had no use for you if you'd let me tell you what to play. That's why, in spite of my thoughts on the present and future, I like anarchists."

The single candle on their table sputtered, in danger of going out. Max said, "What about anarchists whose ambition might become climbing past you on that road to the top?"

"Let 'em try!"

He put his hand over hers. "What about anarchists whose ambition has become taking you back to your hotel room, right now?"

Madeleine squeezed his hand. "Let 'em."

At that precise moment the candle flame flared, throwing brighter glints into her blue-black eyes. Max raised his arm for the check.

DECEMBER 26 • 11:30 P.M.

They walked arm in arm to the Hyatt Regency, saying nothing. There was nothing more to say. The fog had descended like a blanket during their meal; buildings rose gray and ghostly around them, to vanish in the cotton-wool heavens. There was silence everywhere, and more in the great hotel.

The Hyatt Regency is San Francisco's most visually striking building. The twenty-story structure is a triangular pyramid, with two vertical walls and a third which rises in a series of steps to meet them. At the peak is a revolving restaurant/bar.

Inside, the hotel is built around one large open area, three hundred feet long, one hundred seventy feet wide, and one hundred seventy feet high. Each of the floors above the lobby level is like a terrace, extending out into that open space and ringing it. On the vertical sides, the terraces rise one above the other; but on the slanting third, each juts out farther than the one below. One of the vertical sides receives sunlight from a skylight in the roof, and great green plants hang from troughs along the outsides of the terraces' low walls to form living screens for the levels below.

On the lobby floor, there are full-sized trees, live birds, a babbling brook, and a mirror pool. Altogether, Max decided, it was exactly the place he would have expected this high-fashion lady to choose.

They rose in a hushed glass elevator, outside the walls instead of inside. They stepped out at the fifteenth level and walked quickly along the terrace, past the spectacular view, to her room.

There were still no words as they removed their clothing. Max dropped his rag-tag on a chair, while Madeleine carefully laid hers out on the desk. Her fedora came down last. Then she faced him, tall and lean, still unknowable, except for her eyes. They still burned with their own light, and now it was the light of promise.

Max took her arms, unexpectedly. He knew what he wanted, and knew how he would get it. He crushed his lips to hers. His hands tangled in her hair. Her knees loosened, and her weight pulled them toward the bed as he punched off the light.

In the sudden darkness he took her. Swift and deep, but pacing himself to make it last. Her breath spurted, first in gasps, then lower moans. Her claws raked across his back.

When he came, it was incredible.

Slowly, then, he rolled to Madeleine's sweat-slick side, ready to continue with her, but she rolled quickly after him. Her lips touched his chest, flicking down across the nipple and each rib. They vanished, then reappeared on his calf, and worked their slow way to his foot. And then, in the darkness, she was everywhere.

Hips, thighs, breasts, lips: from all directions at once. He felt his head spinning with her scent—not a perfume, but her own, individual aroma. He made no move to stop it. His only moves were repayment in kind, by turns caressing and cruel. She roused him again, set him straining up into the dark, and then she straddled him, sliding on with one smooth flow. She rode him, head thrown back, her body a slate silhouette against the deeper ebony of the room. She moaned again, and so did he. She was unbelievable, an unbelievable lover; who would ever have guessed it before tonight? She reached forward, grabbing both of his wrists in her hands, and pinned him to the bed as she rode him to the end. All at once she cried out, and his shout joined hers.

She collapsed across him in the aftermath, and he held her close. She nestled her face in his neck, her fine hair foaming over his rough cheek.

"You were wonderful," she murmured.

"That's back atcha," he sighed. "Madeleine, you are one hell of a bundle of surprises." He kissed the air above her warm neck, chuckling softly.

Gradually his breathing slowed and grew deeper.

Within minutes he was asleep.

. . . . .

She waited five minutes more, silently sensing the tension drain out of him, as each level of his consciousness surrendered to the night. He was taking the first plunge to oblivion, and each passing moment made it less likely he would climb back if disturbed. At last, when she was satisfied, she rolled smoothly away. With precise and graceful movements, she slipped from the bed and padded straight through the dark to the chair that held his clothes. Her right hand took hold of his jeans. She lifted them without the jingle of a single coin. Her left hand removed his keys.

She padded to the door and opened it; it swung with the ease of freshly oiled hinges. Two men were outside her room, resting against the terrace wall. One was old and bent, wearing a white suit; the other was much younger, but with hair prematurely white. Each threw a last look up and down the corridor as Madeleine surveyed the floors across the hotel's vast open interior. Finally the man in the white suit nodded briefly, and stepped forward. He took the keys from her hand.

Two minutes after closing the door, she was asleep in Max's arms. Smiling like a cat in cream.

Chapter 4

DECEMBER 27 • 3:00 A.M.

Short, squat, with features like mashed dough spread unevenly across their overly large heads, the elves were trudging earnestly through solid rock. There were both males and females, but neither by form nor by garb was it simple to tell them apart. Both sexes affected a variety of styles, from a variety of historical periods. Some wore modern cowboy hats and jeans, and one old fellow wore spats; but most chose to follow the example of their foreman, with his wide scalloped collar of moss green overlaying a simple brown shirt and leggings, his bright and shiny buttons, and his peat-colored shoes, large and squarish like his feet. Above his ears, very similar to an elephant's, he wore a pointed cap. He was at most eight inches high.

The elves' march appeared to have lasted forever, with forever as its goal. The column moved in weary but well-ordered unison as it wormed its way through the multicolored rock strata; nothing, not even the solid stone itself, seemed to excite the little creatures' interest. If one or another showed any emotion, it was not the ruddy cheerfulness of popular fiction, but rather a bullish sort of fatalism.

At length they came to a great space—not open, for they remained inside the rock, but filled with other elves, gnomes, and brownies nonetheless. There appeared to be two camps here, with each group facing in the opposite direction. The column led by the green-collared elf joined the group facing south, whose members nodded lethargically to the newcomers. A few hands were clasped, and here and there large-lipped sloppy kisses were exchanged. The brownies, generally smaller than the gnomes and elves, strained their thin necks to see.

Gradually the hubbub engendered by the new arrivals subsided. One very old gnome, crumpled from long centuries of command, then climbed awkwardly atop a vein of blue quartz, almost tripping over his long beard. He inspected the multitudes slowly, and the strata each group would be facing. Finally, satisfied, he raised his short arm. Each side began to march once more, in opposite directions, pulling . . . dragging . . .

EARTHQUAKE!

Max awoke with a start, and Madeleine sat bolt upright beside him. He reached out for her, saying "It's all right" in a professionally reassuring voice, almost without realizing it. He had been dreaming, something about rocks, and little creatures inside them . . . but the dream was already vaporizing, as dreams do. Now he was more concerned with any further shocks, and he sat there straining into the darkness, much as he had three hours before, only this time the stimulus was decidedly not pleasurable.

But mercifully the earth grew still.

A siren, far away through the fog and hotel walls, came to pulsing life; another, farther, joined it a moment later. That was all.

Max got out of bed, cracking his knees on the night table, and crossed warily to the window overlooking Market Street. The rising moon, just a glimmer in the rolling mist, showed him little. A stoplight far below changed from red to green; a car's headlights moved ahead. There didn't look to be any damage.

He felt Madeleine come up behind him. "Jesus H. Christ!" she said. "So that's a California earthquake."

He laughed, and was pleased to find that it was easy to do. "That was nothing; just a tremor. When we have the big one, you'll know it."

"You sound like you expect it any time." Her voice in the shadows was slightly breathless.

Max sat on the windowsill and patted a place in the pale light for her. She slid up next to him, their hips touching. He said, "It's funny, I guess, but you don't really *expect* it. It's like your New York muggers. Everybody who doesn't live in New York thinks it must be terrible to live there with all that crime—but New Yorkers take crime as a fact of life, so it becomes just another background noise. Well, here, it's the same with quakes. It's only you tourists who think of this as The City That Waits To Die."

Madeleine's face was a soft blur. "I've heard a lot of predictions, though. People say it's coming soon."

"I've heard that. *The Jupiter Effect*, and all . . ."

"Edgar Cayce . . ."

"Yeah, yeah." His voice was skeptical. "Edgar Cayce also predicted that China would become a hotbed of Christianity by 1968. I go to cocktail parties, too. But so far, no matter what the theories are, nobody *knows.*" He held her to his side. "Besides, the next one's supposed to hit L.A."

When she didn't respond, he said, "Listen, you wanna hear about fear? Eight years ago I went to Vietnam, and when I got to Long Binh for in-processing, I didn't know anything about anything. I could hear monkeys howling at night, and guys howling in the daytime, down draining the Saigon River and getting leeches on their legs." He laughed, with only a small professional boost, and was encouraged to feel her cuddle closer.

"See, I had never been that far from home. Flying across the

Pacific, I thought, man, the sky's gonna be red, and the dirt's gonna be blue, and everything's gonna be backward. That's stupid, I know; people were living there. But I just had no clear idea. Until one night I recognized the stars. When it's night anywhere, the sky is the same." He mimicked his younger self, putting it on for her. " 'Hey, wow, man, I recognize this! This is something from *home*! They sent the night sky right *over* here!'

"We were sitting outside watching a movie, sitting on sandbags, when I made this discovery. And right then, artillery started goin' off: *whomp whomp whomp!* You never saw fifty guys move so fast in your life. I mean, that place was *empty*. Everybody over the sandbags and calling, "Pile on, pile on," because you want people on top of you, 'cause they're gonna get hit first . . .

"And the guys that had been there two or three weeks are laughing their asses off, because it was all outgoing. It was *our* fuckin' artillery, and we couldn't tell the difference yet.

"Now *that's* fear: your first barrage in a war zone. An earthquake after that is nothin'."

She half smiled in the half-light, but said, "Still, there's no war on now." She shivered and hugged herself. "Everything else changes, but the ground is supposed to stay put."

Nice try, Max thought; no cigar. He ran his fingers through her hair. "Well, I can't pretend I like it, either. But believe me, Madeleine, most of the time there's only one way to feel the earth move out here."

Now she chuckled against his chest. "How terribly unimaginative, darling. I'm certain we can do better than that."

DECEMBER 27 • 10:45 A.M.

In the late morning, after reclaiming his flame-red Alfa Romeo Spider from the Sutter-Stockton Garage, Max headed back toward his home in the East Bay hills. San Francisco, as he rolled through it, seemed unaffected by the night's events. Thin but brilliant winter sunlight splashed each neatly kept building with bright color; the bay and the sky were both crystal blue. He passed the California Street cable car on Kearny, its bell ringing "Jingle Bells," and he thought, Every paradise has to have a serpent, so the fault lines are San Francisco's. But at least we have the paradise.

Like every Northern Californian, he was happily chauvinistic.

But once he'd swept up out of The City and onto the Bay Bridge, his thoughts quickly returned to Madeleine Riggs. She was very deep, that one. A challenge. Absolute cold and absolute heat coexisting in one achingly beautiful form. He smiled wryly as he remembered writing her off as a mannequin. The Madwoman. That was before he'd gotten past the facade, or known how far there was to get.

It's curious, he thought, that I used the Nam story to try to perk her up. I haven't talked about Nam for, I don't know, years. Not since I got back. But it just came out with her.

He decided that was enough along those lines, and turned the volume on his Blaupunkt up high. QBU filled both the Spider and his mind for the rest of the drive, through the flatlands of Berkeley and up Strawberry Canyon, to his house on the crest of Grizzly Peak. As he made the final turn onto his hilltop road, the entire bay, from Marin on his right to the Peninsula on his left, lay spread-eagled in the sunshine for his pleasure. It was so clear he could even see the Farallon Islands, small black bumps on the Pacific's razor-sharp horizon.

Looking right again as he slowed for his driveway, Max spotted Lisa Pierce, his next-door neighbor, trimming the pines which split the land between their two houses. Pulling up, he blew her a jaunty kiss. Lisa had married young, borne young, and gone to seed young, but her husband had bucks and she dressed to show it, even while working in the yard. She cared nothing for Max's celebrity, which is what made her his favorite neighbor. Not for nothing was his home a bay away from QBU.

Lisa wiped the sweat from her wide forehead with one gloved hand. "Max, you've been out tomcatting again," she said after one close look. "If it weren't subject to misinterpretation, I'd say you had cream all over your whiskers."

He laughed. "But I always come home to you, don't I, dear?"

"Always when I look my best, too." She glanced down at her fat knees, flowing from her Liz Claiborne shorts like cookie dough. "Ah well, if you can't help yourself . . . I suppose this means you missed the earthquake."

"Nope. Woke me right up, Lise."

"You were asleep? You're getting old." She leaned back gratefully into the cradle between two boughs. "The epicenter was right around here; a branch of the Hayward fault, they say."

"No kidding. I'd better see if anything broke."

"I lost two dishes. That was okay; they were dirty." She laughed at her own pretensions and went back to molding her trees. Max went up the steps to his front door, hurrying just a little.

The house he let himself into was decorated with a masculine simplicity only wealth and bachelorhood can ever achieve. The living room focused on a double-sized fireplace, with a strip of skylight running toward it from above, and a thick Persian carpet running toward it from below. There were matching natural leather couches on each side of the rug, and a large glass coffee table between them. Behind each couch was a picture window, one overlooking San Francisco and the bay, the other facing his backyard pool and his greenhouse extension. But the glass in the picture windows, as well as that in the coffee table, was photo-regulable at the turn of rheostats beside each couch; when Max was away, or wanted privacy, or just wanted to be free of fishbowls, he could darken the glass completely.

The need for this in the table was nil, but it made a good conversation piece, like the carving of a lion which crouched atop his fat African drum beside the front window. This was his one family heirloom, hewn from amber and inlaid with delicate pieces of polished woods for a mane. It was a good eighteen inches in length and in the right light could be mistaken at first for a cat. But the regal lift to the head, the massive power so subtly cut into the shoulders, quickly corrected that impression. The shadowed eyes peered back at those that watched them, disdainful of any danger. Its attitude, its purpose, was as clear as its crystal. This creature would have what was rightfully its own. That and no more, but that and no less.

Max went directly to the lion, to check that it was undamaged. Seeing that it was, he turned next to his Aiwa component system; another time he might have examined it first, but with the amp already blown, his family pride outweighed his music mania. Finally he walked quickly through the rest of the house, eyeing the shelves and ledges, and finding continued reassurance.

So he ended up in the kitchen, making himself a ham sandwich. Grabbing a cold bottle of Anchor Steam beer to go with it, he went out beside the pool and took off all his clothes.

On the far side of his yard, a steep cliff spotted with clumps of grass rose to a high terrace, but the house there couldn't see down on him. To his right, more of Lisa's pines blocked the view, and to the left, a high fence put up by less friendly neighbors did the same. He sat on the warm December concrete and put his legs in the cold December water and relaxed.

Max was in that phase he'd come to know from successive postpartum analyses: the beginning of the new affair. He had that tingle—and he couldn't hold the new lady from his thoughts for long.

Madeleine Riggs . . .

With women he cared for, Max was almost like his lion: he would have what was rightfully his, and maybe just a little more. He respected women, but they were objects to him, too, strange and mysterious; and he could be seduced. Still there had to be more than that—brains, and skill, and understanding—and, more quickly than ever after thirty unmarried years, there had to be love. Without that ultimate bond, Max could not linger.

Now he had a woman who could challenge him, both in and out of bed—and he had a tingle. It was a beginning . . .

Abruptly something danced at the edge of his vision. Something brilliant and clear enough to hook him out of his beer-, sun-, and sex-induced reverie. He flicked his narrowed eyes, and thought he caught the image of a tiny, nude girl, leaping like a dolphin on the bright waves of his pool, whose silvery laugh, like bubbles, trailed behind her in the air. But in half the time it takes to describe it, Max realized it was just a trick of the water and light. There was no girl there, just as there had been no animal in Union Square last night. It was just imagination.

His lips narrowed to match his eyes. This sort of fantasy was not like him. Long ago he'd learned to trust his senses; was that inner security finally being forgotten, as he gained outer security through the manager's job?

He shook off his thoughts irritably and looked at his watch. Earl would be here soon, and he'd have his first run at *being* the manager. One problem at a time; just like doing a show.

The doorbell rang.

DECEMBER 27 • NOON

"How're ya doin', Barnaby?" Earl grinned, a fisherman's tackle box hanging from his thin right fist, which poked from a heavily darned fisherman's sweater. Obviously December was not as warm for his old bones as for Max's. "It's your friendly neighborhood amp repairman."

"Shit, I thought it was the Ancient Mariner. Howdy, Earl. Come on in." But as Max, dressed again, stepped back to allow Earl's entrance, his face did not lighten to reflect Earl's mood. "Let me tell you the latest."

The engineer raised his skinny shoulders. "Oh," he said, "you must mean the computers." His grin grew as he shot out his hand. "Congratulations, Boss. If anybody deserved a shot, you did."

Max scowled. "How in the hell—?"

"The Madwoman told the morning crew. Came in, called a meeting, praised you in *very* glowing terms. Chick Frommer called me—"

"Shit. I wish she'd left that for me." He looked at his friend firmly. "You'll be staying on, of course; we still need engineers. As long as I'm in charge of that station, you'll be staying put."

Earl shrugged again, but gratefully. "I was hoping you'd say that, Barnaby—and I'm glad to accept. I don't mind telling you Fern and I would prefer to stay in this area, though we'd have worked something out if we'd had to."

"Well, you don't have to." Max threw one arm around Earl's stooped shoulders. "But it's all a long way from live remotes, isn't it?"

"Getting longer every year, and that's for sure."

The two old friends walked on across the room. "What do the jocks say?" Max asked as Earl began to unplug the amp.

"Oh, Granite's a little upset, him being the new man. But everybody knows job security's not part of radio, and they're glad for you. They know what you've done for the station." Earl's voice grew more confidential. "And everybody's relieved that the Madwoman's dropped the other shoe."

Max had to smile. The Madwoman had dropped more than her shoes since yesterday. But he said, straight, "I'll help everybody get settled in somewhere else, Earl. That's my first official policy. Miss Riggs wants the switchover in six weeks, but if anybody has trouble lining something up, I'll hold back to keep 'em working."

"You're a nice boy, Barnaby."

"Yeah, yeah. Thanks, Dad." Max turned toward the kitchen. "Now, do you want a beer while you work? Or will that muddy your concentration?"

"Barnaby, concentration is what I bring to QBU. Artistry is what I bring to your home; and for that, I may need several beers."

"You're on, big fella."

. . . . .

By 1:00 P.M. seven empty beer bottles were spread out on the kitchen table between them. Also between them, all the immediate problems Max was likely to face had been solved; and it was only then, as Earl slid the amp's rewired circuitry back into its black metal shell, that the engineer ventured the slightest hint of unhappiness. He hefted the Aiwa, its Japanese entrails half in and half out.

"Computers," was all he said.

"Now don't start on that, Earl," Max said. They both had a decent glow on. There was no need to spoil it.

"You know, Barnaby, KQBU's a good station already."

"We're eighth in the market. Without my show, we'd be twenty-fifth."

"Eighth, in the entire Nine Counties. And you agreeing to give up your show." Earl's lean jaw thrust forward, and his eyes were suddenly fierce. "Computers, Barnaby! On *radio!*"

"You say 'radio' like some people say 'God.' "

"So? I know machines. You think you're running them, but they always end up running you." He coughed. "Listen to an obsolete man."

"You're not obsolete."

"The hell I'm not. If engineers didn't have unions, we'd all have been out on our cans years ago. Barnaby—"

"It's been decided, Earl," Max said, and thought, So this is what it's like being the boss. He didn't like it, and pulled back almost at once. "I didn't do it. You didn't do it. We're both free to leave, but we choose to stay."

"I wish I didn't have to. I really do," said Earl intently. "But you're still young."

"Let's see if this thing works." Max lifted the amp from his hands and walked back toward the alcove. He deftly refitted the jacks, flicked switches and spun knobs, and music burst from the four wall speakers, loud and crisp and clear. He went to the front window to study the separation, not looking to see if Earl was following.

"You don't have to drown me out!" Earl had followed, forced to scream to make himself heard.

"This is how I blew the amp in the first place! This is the test!"

"What about your neighbors?"

Max tapped the window. *"Soundproof!"* But he went back and turned the system down. "This is my house, and I like my music loud," he said blandly.

"You're telling your engineer?" But Earl had gotten the message. Barnaby was a nice boy, but Barnaby was a prima donna at heart, and there were no two ways about it. He shrugged. He'd tried.

Max went back to the front window. He knew where Earl was coming from; it was where he'd come from for a long time. But it isn't like I signed a pact with the devil, he thought. The world is moving on all the time, and I'm just not content to sit in the past and be left behind. I want to accomplish things. (So then why am I so pissed off?)

His eyes wandered to the lion carving. The long-forgotten craftsman who made this would have understood, he felt. He picked the carving up, and weighed it in his hands. It was satisfying. Solid. Something that got made, not just dreamed about. Something—

Max stood so still that eventually Earl began to wonder. Earl scowled, but Max didn't turn to see. So finally Earl said, "Max?"

Max started as if he'd been shot. He shook his head and turned toward Earl as if seeing him for the first time. "Earl," he said slowly and with wonder, "this isn't my lion."

"Huh?" Earl came over and squinted at it. "Now what are you on about?"

"My lion had my uncle's initials, E.D.W., carved into the base, and this one doesn't."

Earl shook his head doubtfully. "Barnaby, I think this new pressure is getting to you. You remember that party you had for Granite last year, where I got a little tipsy and tripped over Fern's feet and knocked this thing off its drum? Remember that chip I put in it?" He picked the lion out of Max's hands. "There it is." Then he turned the carving over, and pointed out a dark scar on the left hind leg. "And there's the cigarette burn that was in it from before you even got it. Right?" He nodded sagely, happy to be able to get some of his own back. "I've seen this beast often enough. That's him, all right."

"Then where are the initials?"

"In there," Earl said, pointing to Max's head.

"Earl, I didn't dream them."

"So what are you saying? Somebody stole your lion and replaced it with a perfect copy, except for one major detail?"

"Maybe."

"Now, Barnaby . . ."

"Come on. I want to find out where they got in."

"Barnaby, really now . . ."

Rolling his eyes heavenward, Earl followed Max on a second inspection tour of the house, this time concentrating on the doors and windows. And, just as he'd expected, when they reached the last bathroom window and found it securely locked, it completed an unbroken series of unbroken entryways. "How about the chimney?" Earl asked solicitously. "Maybe Santa Claus did it when you forgot his milk and cookies."

"Hilarious, Earl. Truly sidesplitting."

The old man scowled and put the lid down on the toilet, then sat on it with extreme resignation. "Max, why won't you listen to reason?"

Max said, "I've had that carving since I was a kid. My Uncle Ed gave him to me . . ." He looked around the cramped room for a place to get comfortable and settled for leaning against the sink. "Uncle Ed was the family hero. He'd traveled all around the world, and not the way we do today; he'd done it at the turn of the century, in the days of McKinley and Teddy Roosevelt, when Americans could go anywhere, if they were up to it.

"By the time I knew him, of course, he was old enough to be my grandfather, and had long since settled down as the owner of a small hotel near where we lived in Miami Beach.

"I've told you about growing up on the Beach, with my dad managing several of the bigger hotels over the years. Uncle Ed's place was up in Hallandale, and that was a whole other story. When he'd decided to settle down, he'd bought a small inn with just twelve rooms. It seemed ugly and cramped after what I was used to, but it was perfect for him. It gave him a living income, it kept him busy, and his guests were mostly people he'd known in his travels, so they could reminisce among his souvenirs.

"On my thirteenth birthday he invited me to visit him. I had other things on my schedule for that day, including my first date with a girl named Janet Darrieaux; but I didn't want to hurt him, so I ran up on the bus around ten that morning. Get it out of the way early, I figured.

"I got off the bus and started across the street toward his inn, thinking about Janet and that night, when all of a sudden two guys came running out his front door, with my uncle right behind them. They were in their forties, and not too well off, but he was in his eighties—and still he was right on their tails. He grabbed one of them by his shirt and then tackled him, throwing his body into the guy's legs like a linebacker. The guy went down, and Uncle Ed took a hold on his neck, and the guy rolled over and flopped out like a beached whale.

"Meanwhile the other guy is hightailin' it toward me. I never even thought about *my* differences from him—age, size, or any of the rest of it. It was just Family versus Bad Guys, and I went running through the traffic toward the guy, cutting him off at the sidewalk. He had coins in his fist as he swung at me—I remember quarters spinning in the air behind his growing fist—" (And a second image flooded Max's memory for a moment: a tiny, naked girl, with bubbles of laughter).

"—and then he knocked me on my can." Max grimaced. "But having seen the blow coming, I had ducked automatically, and I wasn't quite out yet. I looked up from the sidewalk and flashed that he was still there, on tiptoe, straining to break into the traffic; that picture's as clear as the quarters. Not much else is. I went up after him and hit him, in the kidneys, and he came back at me with those loaded hands. A crowd was forming, and in those days they tried to help me. But this guy kicked his way free, and spun around toward the street again. But the recoil of his kick pitched him over the edge of the curb, and a cab knocked him flat. Two broken ribs, and his cheek and arm turned to hamburger. He started to get up, and then he finally gave up, his fists opening and the quarters rolling away.

"Not that you could prove it by me. I was just as flat as he was, though still on the sidewalk.

"And then Uncle Ed was looking down at me, his white fringe of hair stark against the blue sky; his face was very proud. I tell you, Earl . . . that decided a lot of my future life, right there. He treated me like a comrade-in-arms, instead of a crazy kid; checking me carefully for injuries before letting me sit up. Then he supported me like I was the old man, until I could make it on my own.

"The cops came, and Ed handed his guy over and made the charges—rifling the till. I had to keep telling myself that this was an eighty-year-old man; he was at ease, commanding, lucid—nothing like the senior citizens we had down in Miami. I was getting quite an education that day.

"Well, after the cops left, the two of us walked back to his inn. He took me into his rooms and poured me a snifter of Spanish brandy; 'Don't tell your mother.' Then he went and took the lion from its spot in the south window, where it glowed in the morning sun, and put it on the arm of my zebra-hide chair. He sat down on a carved stool in front of me, beneath a huge brown-and-red juju mask on the wall; the smell of the wide world surrounded us. I thought I knew what he would say to me then. But I was wrong.

" 'Maxie,' he said, 'this is the start of a new decade. I've seen a lot of decades come, and a lot of 'em go, and with this one, I believe I'll only do the first.'

"I told him, of course, that he was crazy; besides what I'd just seen him do, I knew that in Florida, things only get better. But he wasn't having any. He'd made up his mind.

" 'I want you to have this lion for your present, this year,' he said. 'He's inspired me for more years than I like to remember, and I know now he'll do the same for you. When you're feelin' down, just look at him. Try to get inside his head, and get the *feelin'* he's got, and it'll pick you right up. Right up.'

"Uncle Ed lit a thin cigar, and smoke filled the summer sunlight. 'Lions are kings, boy. Man likes to think he's somethin' better, 'cause he's got automobiles, and televisions, and puts satellites in space like those goddamn Russians, but he still don't know what the hell he's here for. Well, the lions I've met all know what they're here for. They're the kings of nature, and kings *by* nature, and if you can think like a lion, you'll do all right in this life.'

"Two months after that, he was dead."

Max turned toward Earl, his eyes somber and penetrating. "I have always tried to think like a lion, as much as I can. Maybe not a real lion, but the kind somebody carved out of amber and gave to him. I know the feeling Uncle Ed told me about—that very special kind of second wind. And I don't know why, or how, but I know beyond any doubt that that carving down there is a fake."

Earl shifted uncomfortably on the toilet seat. "But, Barnaby . . . since nobody broke in . . ."

"You don't believe me?"

Earl lifted his shoulders. "Hell, who knows?" But he was thinking about that chip he'd put in it—the chip that was still there. "I'd better get on back to the station. It's getting late."

The two old friends looked at each other across the tiled bathroom. Neither one really wanted to face the other down. And so, at last, Earl gave the ground . . . but that very act, as it often will, brought him to a contrary decision. He stood up, and his face was wise and kind. "Barnaby, really, I know what you're going through, with all the extra weight you're carrying now. And I don't mean to add to your problems; that's the last thing on my mind. But that is your lion. There's no way it could be anything else."

Max, too, was kind. "Then that sure makes it a mystery, doesn't it?"

DECEMBER 27 • 2:20 P.M.

And it remained a mystery. Max went over his entire house a third time after Earl had left, but found nothing. He spent twenty minutes in his greenhouse, kneeling gingerly on the thin board dividers marking out his plant and flower beds, scanning each pane of the glass walls behind them. And finding nothing.

When he finally climbed back onto the slate floor, he was absolutely certain he had not been burgled. The conclusion was as clear as Earl had made it: the lion in his house now was the lion which had been his the past twenty years.

And he really wished he could accept that conclusion. Just take the mystery and write it off as a trick of Anchor Steam beer. Under any other circumstances he would have done just that . . .

But not with this lion.

So he went back into the front room and weighed his options. It seemed he had only one. I've got a lot of people out there who'll help Barnaby Wilde, he thought. I'll ask them this afternoon whether anybody knows anything, and maybe I'll get lucky. At least I'll be doing something, and it can't hurt.

He was very wrong.

Chapter 5

DECEMBER 27 • 3:00 P.M.

At the station, the crew tendered their congratulations. Granite Reilly, the Midday Man, stuck his head out of the studio and showed only good will. Chick Frommer punched him shyly on the arm, grinning all across his face.

But Max, to their mystification, acknowledged it all abstractedly. Carlotta, the switchboard girl, had to call his name twice to make an impression. "You had an important message," she said disapprovingly.

"I'll get to it later."

"It's Valerie Drake's manager."

He paused. Then he sighed.

He was a professional.

The phone was answered on the first ring by a deep voice, expansive, with just a trace of a foreign accent. Max said, "This is Barnaby Wilde. I'm returning Mr. Cornelius's call," reading the name off Carlotta's memo.

"Oh, yes, Mr. August. It's good of you to be so prompt."

Max's eyes flicked to Valerie Drake's poster down the hall. She smiled ravishingly back at him past the frame of her lush, dark hair. "How's everything going for the New Year's concert?"

"Excellently, thank you. Bill Graham is always a gentleman. It is because of this concert that I called, you see. Miss Drake would be very much interested in a personal appearance on your program tomorrow afternoon. She has long admired your abilities. Would that be convenient?"

Would it? Max thought. "It would be more than convenient, Mr. Cornelius. I've long admired the lady, as well, and I appreciate her compliment right now. We would be honored to have her."

"Thank you. Shall we say seven o'clock tomorrow, then? You could save the final hour of your program for the interview."

"That would be fine. I'll look forward to it."

Well, well, he mused as he hung up the phone. Valerie Drake. He studied the poster more thoroughly, and with a new eye for detail. Beautiful women, he mused. Who admire me. How lucky can one man get in one week?

But then he remembered his lion, and the grin on his face left his eyes.

DECEMBER 27 • 3:10 P.M.

The door to Madeleine's office was locked when he got to it. He knocked, and her voice called out in quick response, "Who is it?"

"Max."

"Right with you, Max."

A drawer slid out and in; papers rustled. Then the door was thrown wide and she was standing there, smiling at him radiantly. As soon as the door had closed behind him, she lifted her head for a kiss. And she got it.

"So," she whispered a moment later, "how does it feel to be the boss?"

He looked her over before answering. Today she was wearing a soft-tied cream tunic, loose over her free breasts; a generously cut corduroy blazer; and tight black leather pants. "It feels fine," he said.

"I told the staff this morning."

"I know; but you should have left that for me. I know them pretty well."

She pirouetted away, her tunic ties flying as she crossed the room. "That's why I did it for you, Max. You can never tell how people will react to big changes, so I figured I'd take any heat. It was my decision, after all. But I'm glad to say everyone seemed pleased with your success."

She leaned back against the edge of her desk, hands flat behind her. The light from the window highlighted her coppery hair. "I called New York, and they want me back the day after New Year's, so that leaves us six more days."

"I don't know if I like that," he said.

"Neither of us has any choice, I'm afraid. These things are decided at the highest levels." She laughed gaily. There was nothing left of the Madeleine he'd thought he'd known before last night. "And we can do so much in six days."

"At least it includes New Year's Eve."

"Ah!" she said archly. "You're rushing things, my dear. One day at a time, please."

"Rushing things? After last night and this morning, all we can do is slow down!"

"God, I hope not." She took hold of her tunic with both hands and parted it to reveal her high breasts. "You have half an hour till your show, and I've missed you."

"You're insatiable!"

"The real me, darling."

But Max turned aside, opting out of this game for the moment. The events of the morning continued to haunt him, though he tried to take the sting out of it, for her. "I don't know," he said easily. "I may not be in shape for anything strenuous right now. Earl thinks I'm not playing with a full deck."

"What are you talking about?"

He put on his Rod Serling voice, still studying the wall. "Have you ever had something you knew to be true turn out not to be true?" he asked.

From across the room she matched his gravity. "Why, certainly, sir. When I was thirteen, I knew you could get pregnant if you took your clothes off with a boy watching."

And then all at once she was whispering throatily in his ear. "I'm still proving that wrong."

Max whirled. She was standing right next to him, hands pushing up her breasts. How had she crossed the room so quickly, so silently? He didn't understand, but as he started to ask, she offered his mouth her nipples instead, and it turned out his desire was still alive after all.

He accepted: first one—"Well, I'm not"—and then the other—"thirteen." Then he ran his hands across the smooth skin of her stomach. "I have a carved lion at home, only it's not really mine." Her stomach tightened; he thought from desire.

"I still don't understand," she said.

"Neither do I." He began to feel for the zipper on her pants. "I know my lion had some initials carved in its base, but when I looked today, they were gone."

"You must be imagining it, Max." She was loosening his belt, hurriedly.

"That's what Earl said. And all the accidental scars and nicks are right where they should be. But I know I'm right." He pulled her zipper down. "I'm going to ask my listeners to look out for it."

"Ah." She opened his jeans. "So somebody made an exact copy of your carving but overlooked a prominent feature. That's not very likely."

"I know. Again, that's what Earl said." He arched his back so she could slide the jeans down.

"And then there's the possibility that it was deliberate, to make you paranoid," she said. She let him lower her pants, and slip his hand into her panties. "You'd be dealing with a real lunatic, in that case."

Her crimson lips met his, hard.

DECEMBER 27 • 3:55 P.M.

Half an hour later, reluctantly, he left her. Walking downstairs to the studio, wiping his sweaty palms on his sex-scented jeans, he knew he was beginning to really fall. That tingle was beginning to burn.

He entered the studio, waved at Earl, and talked between songs with Granite, but his thoughts were behind him, in her office, and in front of him, outside the studio window. Because of her, and the changes she'd brought to his life, he'd be leaving this studio, and this already-swelling crowd, soon. In the midst of the tingle he felt a pang of regret. But that soon passed.

If his lion had been in there with her, he couldn't have felt better.

. . . . .

In her office, secure behind the relocked door, Madeleine Riggs stood stark naked, as Max had left her—but he would not have recognized her now. She was staring intently at a point atop her desk. Her hands were crossed on her chest, the fingers digging cruelly into the nipples. The cords in her neck stood out like the ribs in her side, and her back arched like a bow. Her lips were moving to a silent rhythm.

For over ten minutes she remained in that position. Only when the low-volume speaker near her desk announced more music with Barnaby Wilde, and a lion's roar followed, did she, gradually, relax. Her hands fell to her sides to hang limply. Blood dribbled from small cuts on her breasts and flowed red down their pale sides. She crossed to her desk with smooth strides, shaking some of the blood onto her stomach and thighs, and picked up the object at which she'd been staring.

A carved amber lion.

Turning it to read the three initials, E.D.W., she shivered with anticipation.

DECEMBER 27 • 4:10 P.M.

In a small, dark room in the Tenderloin, drag queens blared their trade with every elaborate movement. In a smaller dark room in the back, Charles Domenico lay rigid and afraid. He was young, just in from Detroit, black, straight. And broke. He'd had thirty-seven dollars when he'd left the Ford plant to hang his thumb out on I-90. He had less than thirty-seven cents now, two weeks on, and he hadn't eaten in sixty-two hours. He longed to leave this bar, but he had no place to go. He knew no one in San Francisco, the city with the Death Bridge. He couldn't get a job. The same hollowness in his heart that had driven him away from the Workers, those thousands of Workers every day in the endless plant, was with him here in San Francisco. Here in the bar. He couldn't face those other people. Any other people.

He'd come to the gay bar, terribly afraid, but more afraid of fading out like the morning mist. He had to eat, he said; he had to earn some money; could he sweep here, could he clean up for them? The head one—Elizabeth—had rubbed the other one's—Wendi's—slim hip as he thought it over. Charles was reassured. They weren't anything he would have to relate to. They were as alien as he.

This morning, though, the two of them had come to him, hair askew, and suggested . . . sweet Jesus Lord! He had told them no; he had cut them down. Coldly. They had gone. But not far; just outside there, in the bar. Charles had finished his sweeping then. He was done and wanted his money. But they said he would have to wait until they closed. No money now. Wait, Charles.

'Til later.

He couldn't leave without his money. He'd worked for it, and used up one of his few chances of contact to do it. He couldn't ever go back to a regular job and regular people. What on earth was he going to do?

"How're you doin', Charley?" The voice was evil, filthy with suggestion. "Keepin' it warm for us, hon?"

Charles stared with spastic fascination at the flimsy door. He couldn't lock it. Any minute now and it would swing wide, revealing those two painted men in their tattered heels. The two of them, against him alone. Two people, in the end, like all the other people surrounding him: thousands of them, millions, down every street, in every house. He could feel them more and more, closing in. There was no place to hide.

The door did not open. High heels clicked leisurely away. Charles remembered the Golden Gate Bridge, famous even in Detroit. "A Magnet for the Misguided," the *Free Press* had called it, and he had smiled. No; those folks had found what they'd been lookin' for. Tragically, he would be denied that. But he would not be denied.

He would work with what he had. There were matches in the scrub cupboard; tiny ones, paper ones, but he had ammonia to splash the room with. Opening the folder, he tore one out, and struck it with trembling fingers.

A flame burst from the match end, startling him. It was bigger than he expected. And it was growing. He dropped the match, backing away from it, but it didn't go out as he thought it would. The flame doubled in size, and doubled again. He tried to scream as he realized the craziness, but his throat was too dry. Only a wheeze, a squeaky thread, slipped out of his gaping jaws. The flame was the size of a rat, standing on its hind legs and sniffing the breeze. Now it was like a cat, with slanted eyes, and now a dog, a big dog, four feet or more in height, standing on the end of the tiny match and pointing its snout at Charles, sniffing him. Flames within the flame crawled like snakes. They twined around each other. They clustered. They grew thicker, and more coherent. Then there was no longer a dog there, but something else. Something Charles did not want to see born.

Charles kept his eyes on the tiny match. It was not consumed.

He heard a voice, like the hiss of burning logs. "Charlesss."

Charles Domenico lifted his head. He didn't want to. This contact would be the worst. He willed his eyes to close, but the lids were pulled back stuck, beyond his feeble control. They hurt him. His eyes looked into those of a man, made of flame, dancing on the edge of his match.

The creature was human, but just barely: a gleam in his creator's eye. He glowed red-orange, with features of a deeper crimson: great noble eyes, without lids; a jutting nose, thinner at the tip than at the bridge; a cruel mouth, sultry and sulky. Heavy masses of orange-yellow hair flowed back from a high brow, darting and curling in tangled waves till they mingled with the beard below and crested on his broad shoulders. His body was slim and tightly knit, entirely devoid of harsh angles, except for the genitalia.

As the corners of the tiny room caked with grotesque shadows and smoke, the flame-man spoke with Charles Domenico.

In the bar the jukebox blared; Elizabeth and Wendi heard only Valerie Drake's distorted soprano. But Charles heard Heat and Light. The flame-man told him things he alone had always known, and other things at which he'd only guessed. Charles nodded, intent, oblivious to his former needs of food and freedom. And at the end the Light told him what must happen next.

Wendi looked up in surprise when Charles stepped from the back room five minutes later. The young black was wearing Elizabeth's raincoat, his hands thrust deep into the black plastic pockets. Wendi smoothed the short hair of his evening's companion, and slid off the stool to confront him.

"Charles," Wendi said, the gruff undertone not lost in his throaty purr. "Charley, I told you to wait in the back room."

Charles shot him. A flame-man sped from the barrel into his hot pulsing heart, just as the Light had promised.

Wendi staggered backward, but kept his balance on his heels. He clutched at his left breast, unbelieving, and ripped it away in a trail of crimsoned rubber. A short bark broke from his lips, and then a spray of blood. He fell forward across the table, its legs exploding under his weight; they both crashed to the floor.

Valerie Drake's record ended. Elizabeth screamed, and came up from behind the bar with a sawed-off. Charles was waiting for him, as if he'd practiced this—as if he knew, or had been told. He shot the bar queen once, precisely, between the eyes. Another flame consumed its prey. And then Charles Domenico fled into the street, stuffing his gun back into its plastic pocket.

He ran up Larkin Street to Sutter and turned right. He had many blocks to cover, but he moved easily among the rush-hour crowd, no longer trembling from hunger, no longer afraid, exultant, patient. It took him twenty-five minutes. A police car, siren blaring, shot across Sutter as he neared his goal, but it didn't slow for him. He felt he was invisible. He was in this world, but not *of* it. Never again, *of* it.

When he saw the crowd outside the disc jockey's studio, he was momentarily slowed at the thought of inching his way through their heaving solidity. Some of them were dancing. But then, in the flick of someone's butane lighter, he received his resolve anew. He saw it clearly, in the Great Light.

"Pardon me." He smiled shyly, but veiled his eyes as he entered the crowd. No one should notice him. No one should scream as he passed. He was nothing, and nobody. To them. 'Til he showed them the Light.

It took him five minutes more, but finally Charles emerged into the open space before the disc jockey's window. Girls were dancing there, and some boys. Some black, most white, some yellow. Charles hadn't known very many yellow people, but he watched the news sometimes. He would be on the news now. They would shove things in his face and ask him, "Why?" And he would tell them.

The disc jockey finished a record, and smiled at him, talking about a lion he had lost, asking for help. The fire-man told Charles that he couldn't allow that. The DJ pushed a button and the speakers belched a lion's roar and Charles pulled out his gun again. He took hold of it in both his hands and pointed it at the bastard's smile and then the fire-man deserted him.

One moment he was with Charles, behind him and inside him, burning in the secret heart of death—and then he was gone. Charles shook with the chill of desertion; a moan escaped his blue lips. He pulled at the trigger with shivering desperation; he knew he would miss and he did miss. But even if he'd had fire of his own, he would not have hit Max, because Max, sitting pretty in the wide window, had suddenly felt a burning light, a golden glow, a glow he'd known too well in Nam, and he'd known he must move *now* and think later. Without hesitation, without consideration, Max threw himself to one side and down as the safety glass starred and sang.

And Charles had no time to aim a second time; nor was he sure he wanted to, when the people in the crowd were turning round on him, while others ran and others screamed, and a brother chopped his arm and he fired off at random and hit a man and got hit in the face, and he yelled and he laughed and he yelled and he laughed and he laughed and he laughed and he laughed.

Until he cried.

Chapter 6

DECEMBER 27 • 7:15 P.M.

Max was in Madeleine's office when the two homicide inspectors arrived. Domenico's one shot had buried itself in the corkboard ceiling; its worst effect was a slight ringing in Max's ears, which was already starting to fade. By rights the patrolmen who had taken the hysterical madman in tow were all that was needed to cover the crime, but some people have more rights than others, and Barnaby Wilde was one. The inspectors said they wanted to settle this one personally.

The chief inspector's name was Hamoto. Since he was Japanese, those who met him felt badly about thinking him inscrutable, but that's what he was. He was nearing forty, and wore a genteelly aging suit, immaculately pressed and tailored to his two-hundred-plus figure, with a discreet white button-down and black bow tie. There was one square inch of black hair below his lower lip—something like Hitler's upper lip—and the entire effect added up to something reminiscent of Charlie Chan, which made those who talked with him uncomfortable, which is what he wanted. In his kind of work, it helped.

The other inspector was younger, and more stylish. His hair, a warm brown, was blown dry and razor cut. Gray wraparound sunglasses curved out from it. His three-piece suit was expertly tailored, and his watch had a gold band. Hamoto introduced him as Inspector Hardesty; the set of the younger man's mouth made it sound appropriate.

"A union card on the assailant shows him to be one Charles Y. Domenico, of Detroit," Hamoto said as he found one of Madeleine's modern office chairs and worked his girth down into it. "A good look in his eyes shows him to be one of the walking wounded."

"Wounded? Did the people in the crowd hurt him, Inspector?" Madeleine asked. She seemed to be having trouble paying attention, but she was once again the Corporate Liaison, every coppery hair in place, and Max, even after the shock of his experience, thought she looked like a good thing to live for. But that wasn't the main thing on his mind.

Hamoto smiled inscrutably at Madeleine's question. "No, ma'am. I meant that Mr. Domenico was one of the hundreds of people we get every year who are here to go down for the third time. I don't know what it is that gets them, but they come."

"Then you don't think I meant anything to him in particular?" Max asked.

Hardesty, standing behind Hamoto's chair, his big hands gripping its back, slowly swiveled his head in the DJ's direction. "Why do you ask that, Mr. Wilde?"

"August," he said tersely. "My real name's Max August, Inspector. I ask that because, well, it's the second strange thing that's happened to me today. And"—his face was resolute—"there may be a connection between them."

"Hmm?" murmured Hamoto with a rising inflection. "Tell us."

"Oh, Max," Madeleine interrupted, her voice a study in amused common sense, "you're not going to bring that lion into this."

He gave her an ironic grin. "That's exactly what I'm going to do."

"Lion?" echoed Hardesty. Max turned his head back toward the two policemen's watchful eyes. All three of them missed the sudden movement of Madeleine's mouth: a drawing back of her scarlet lips, and a flash of ivory teeth.

"This morning," Max began, "I discovered that a family heirloom, a carving of a lion, had been stolen, and another substituted in its place. The new one is exactly like the original, down to some scuff marks it's picked up over the years, except that some initials on the base are missing. The best explanation I can come up with is that the thief was engaged in altering his fake to look like the original when he was interrupted."

Hamoto asked, "Did you report this to the police?"

"No, I . . . well, I'm sure it's a duplicate, but my engineer was just as sure it was the same carving."

"Then there's some doubt?"

"Not in my mind."

Hardesty asked, "What was the connection between your lion and Charles Domenico?"

"Just before he shot at me, I made an announcement over the air to ask my listeners for help."

Hamoto sucked on his underlip hair. "And you think, then, that Domenico stole your lion? Why? And why would he try to kill you to keep that fact quiet?"

Max spread his hands. "I don't know. I haven't the foggiest idea. But there is a connection, I'm sure of it."

"Well, Mr. August," said Hamoto judiciously, clasping his hands across his wide belly, "it seems a little farfetched to me." He tilted his head, his eyes opening a fraction wider. "Don't get me wrong, sir. We'll investigate this carving's disappearance, and if Domenico did have anything to do with it, we'll find out. But I'd be less than candid with you if I held out much hope in that direction. I don't believe the man's capable of actions as coherent as you describe." He rocked forward in his chair, found the point of balance needed to escape it, and rose ponderously to his feet. "It's more likely to be simply a coincidence."

"That's what I'd think," offered Madeleine.

"One thing, though," said Hardesty, consulting a small notebook. "Domenico was talking about a fireman when he was taken into custody. Does that mean anything to you, Mr. August?"

Max shook his head.

"You, Miss Riggs?"

Madeleine looked at him in surprise. "Me, Inspector?"

"In shooting at Mr. August, he could have been attacking your station instead of the one man."

"I see. But no, I don't know any firemen. I'm just a visitor in San Francisco." Her smile was winning. Behind the sunglasses Hardesty's eyes were hidden.

"Oh, yes," said Hamoto, loosening up just a little, "my daughter loves your show, Mr. August. Could I get your autograph for her? She'll kill me if I let you go without it." He began to rummage through his inside coat pockets. "I must confess, it was part of the reason I came myself this evening."

"Columbo did that much better," said Max with an edge to his voice.

"Oh, no. Really. This is outside the realm of the case."

"I can see that," said Max. But he took the inspector's pen and paper, and wrote, "To—"

"Eileen."

"—Eileen. All my best, Barnaby Wilde."

"Thank you," said Hamoto as he carefully tucked the autograph back in his coat. "She'll be thrilled."

Shaking hands all around, the two men left. As soon as they were out of earshot, Madeleine looked at Max knowingly and said, "Bureaucrats." Then, "Well, are you ready for dinner?"

Max shook his head. "Not tonight, lady. Even if nobody else believes me, I believe me, and I'm going to keep on the trail while it's hot."

"What trail? I thought you said this Detroit character was your man."

"The inspector said it wasn't probable. He may even be right, since nothing today has been probable. But I want to check out another little idea I had."

"What is it? I'll come with you."

Max grinned, his eyes alight. "No, Madeleine. I don't think you and this suspect would get along at all."

Madeleine's eyes hooded. "Oh, yes? Well, give her my regards." She came around the side of the desk and clasped her hands behind his neck, lightly, her body close but not touching. "Seriously, darling: don't waste too much time on this wild goose chase. That's what it sounds like to me, and we don't have all that much time for ourselves. If you finish before midnight, come see me." Her eyes, too, were alight. "Promise."

He lifted her arms free gently and kissed each palm in turn. "It's a date," he said. Then he kissed her lips.

Madeleine remained standing where she was as he left her. Her hands stole up to massage the burning cuts on her breasts, and she frowned, thoughtfully.

Chapter 7

DECEMBER 27 • 8:35 P.M.

Max rolled down 101, headed for Hillsborough, down the peninsula. Patty Hearst had lived in Hillsborough, like plenty of other bored little rich girls, and one of them was the infamous Suzanna. She'd offered him her address many times in the past months, and at last he planned to take her up on it.

That was the extent of the trail he was following. He had half an idea—that if Domenico were too far gone to have pulled off the theft, maybe the culprit was somebody who could *pay* for Domenico and others to do their thing. Couple that with a fact—that he knew of no other person so fanatically devoted to getting some part, any part, of him, as Suzanna Ward. Max would be the first to admit that the case was flimsy, but he didn't have to defend it in court. Better to grasp at straws than just go down without a struggle, he figured.

He was only now, with this long stretch of straight highway ahead and QBU's oldies in the background, coming to grips with being shot at. In Nam he'd been shot at a lot, and had shot back a lot; that time was almost a decade gone. This afternoon, after the world had exploded in his face, had seemed like a dream, and most especially after the cops had turned their interests more toward autographs than assailants. He'd been unable to sort out his feelings then.

But now, alone in the darkness, he found a comforting realization about gunplay: just like riding a bike or learning to swim, if you've learned it once, it's never strange to you again. The fear, and the thrill, and the basic choice between them, remains absolutely untouched by time. As does the golden glow of certain knowledge, when all your senses come awake and alive. He smiled grimly. He'd been wrong to think he had lost his touch.

Strange people with guns wouldn't stop him for a minute.

. . . . .

After Long Binh, his unit had been sent to Dao Tiang to take over from the ARVNs. Dao Tiang had been one of Michelin's largest rubber plantations before the VC disrupted their operations. Michelin himself had had a large mansion there, called by the arriving Americans the Big House; like everything else on the plantation, the Big House was now a wreck.

The ARVNs had taken to living in big holes they had dug in the marshy ground, six feet by eight feet and covered with scrap tin and dirt. They crawled back and forth in trenches. Everything was covered in the bright orange of rust.

The VC had an R & R center six miles away; the Americans knew it was there, but they could never find it. Charlie, coming in, would take whatever mortars he had left and lob them into Dao Tiang base just to get them off his back. A fun place.

But these were the problems of the Headquarters and Headquarters Company. The 112th Light Infantry Brigade, which included Max, set up shop thirty miles east of the Big House—still on Michelin's land, but not so's you could tell. They put up some buildings out there, little more than hooches, which were never again tended to during the entire year Max was stationed there. The 112th was 11-Bravo—foot soldier—and they had no time left for niceties. Their base was a place to rest up, get drunk, get fucked up, or—if you were willing to risk the AWOL charges—to slip into town and get fucked for real. Often the 112th would go three months without coming in at all; three months without a shower or a shave or a change of clothes. It was miserable, but after a point, like everything else in this man's army, it became a laughing matter. You just learned which people to stay upwind of.

The first week out, Max went through three fire fights, and the rest of his problems were minimal.

DECEMBER 27 • 9:50 P.M.

The night sky was clear as Max neared Suzanna's address. There was no moon, but the stars were out in force. He had plenty of light as he cruised down her street, and he had no trouble finding the discreet numerals etched on a boulder in her front yard. A rambling mini-mansion sat well back from it, peaceful and prosperous.

A dry wind was blowing in from the bay, slipping up under his light jacket. He picked his way as quickly as he could across the flat, white-painted stepping stones which dotted the lawn, and pressed his thumb against a button which brought soft chimes.

From upstairs came an answer, indistinguishable. There was the sensation, more than sound, of someone hurrying down interior stairs. Finally the light above him came on, and the door opened on a chain. A girl with mussed blond hair, a purple mohair sweater, and dirty tight white jeans peered vaguely out at him.

But she was at least twenty-five.

"Excuse me," Max began in his best voice. (Shit! She never mentioned that her sister was here!) "I'm—ah—looking for Suzanna—"

"Barnaby!"

And with eyes as wide as a child's at Christmas, she flung herself into his arms.

He was staggered, both literally and figuratively. "What—?" he tried, already knowing full well what was what. "Suzanna?"

"I knew you'd come. I knew it, I knew it," she murmured, her mouth nuzzling up under his chin. Her breath was vermouth and orange soda.

He looked up and down the street. There was no one in sight, but a curtain across the way opened and closed. Hastily he staggered across the threshold with her still hanging on his neck. She was a full-grown woman; there was no ignoring that fact. He kicked the door closed behind them, and gingerly pried her loose.

She was pretty, dangerously so, but her blond hair had been

streaked with a bottle too long ago, and the roots were not only dark but dirty. Her eyes were hazel, and slightly askew, so she looked at him and past him simultaneously. It was not the vermouth that had done that; it was her natural state. Her mouth was heavily made up, and smeared now after her greeting. She had a white zit.

Not far below, her breasts were packed tightly into her undersized sweater.

There wasn't one chance in hell that she was fourteen.

But her voice was the one he knew. "You sly, sly man. You put me off and put me off, but I knew you'd come in the end. Welcome to my Christmas party." She scampered away to a massive antique cabinet and threw back its door. "What'll you have?" she called as she stood aside to exhibit row after row of bottles. "Daddy's got bourbon, gin, vodka, vermouth, rum, snapps—"

"Schnapps," he corrected automatically; then held up his hand. "Nothing, thanks, Suzanna. I just came to—"

"Oh, you'll *come*, never fear." She winked at him with childish bawdiness. Then she started to unbutton her sweater. "I've been just dying for this moment." She sighed.

"Dammit, Suzanna, cool off! I only—drove down here to ask you a question." It sounded absurd. All his facts, if you could dignify them with that title, were fucked. He no longer knew what he was doing here.

But Suzanna knew what she was doing. "Have a drink afterward, Barnaby. Oooh, I'm gonna drink *you*!" She was stalking him.

"Suzanna, have you been in my house?"

She stopped; the aroma of soda pop and sweat hung heavily between them. She looked at him half curiously, half exultantly. "Don't I wish!"

"Suzanna—!"

"I never have. Never ever ever. Never."

Well, that was just about that. Now all his problems resolved themselves into one: how to get out of this mess with his reputation intact. He had no illusions about what would happen, even in good old San Francisco, to a DJ caught frolicking with a fan. Forget the new job, and the money, and the bright unsullied shine of a winner.

"Okay, Suzanna. It's been great, meeting you at last. You know the number." He turned toward the door, but his feet slowed and stopped as he saw two large tears spill from her eyes—eyes that never left his face. There was something eerie about this girl, as if the fourteen-year-old who called him was the real Suzanna, and she'd only borrowed this older body for the night.

Max felt as if his mind were turning to quicksand. Since eight o'clock yesterday evening, his entire world had sunk from sight, to be replaced with another, almost identical, yet lacking the owner's initials. Max August had been a disc jockey, a dancer, a man who controlled his own life as easily as he'd controlled his studio board. But now, Max August was a sales manager, a romantic, a theft victim, an attempted-murder victim—and a man whose world had turned twisted.

Suzanna said, "I saw you with that redhead, Barnaby."

Max's eyes narrowed. Was *this* real? "When?"

"Last night."

Max released his breath in a long, low sigh. He hadn't known he was holding it. "Where?"

"At the station. And the restaurant. And the hotel. I followed you."

"All night?"

"Yes, I did. You sat on the other side of the restaurant. You wouldn't come to see me, and I told you I'd come see you." Her resistance had vanished. The words poured out in a flood.

"And then, when we went to the hotel?"

"You had your arms together. You went up one elevator, and I went up another. It's easy to see out of those glass cages. And you two weren't watching anybody but yourselves." The tears were running down her smeared face, but her gaze remained fixed on him. "I went and sat on the stairs, waiting for you to come out, Barnaby. I had some coke with me, and some cherry brandy. I waited a long time. And then two men came."

A thin smile slid onto his face—the smile of a hunter whose prey has finally been flushed from the woods. His eyes never left her as, very gently, he asked, "What two men?"

Suzanna looked down at her jeans, but she seemed to have lost interest. Her head came up like a limp doll's. In a strange way it was as if they had consummated something, after all. "They were looking around like they were hotel detectives. One of those guys threw me out of Jim Morrison's hotel once with my girl friend, Judy. I don't see Judy anymore. He was at the Ramada Inn . . ."

"Suzanna."

"I'm sorry. I never mean to get lost," she said in a small voice. She started to play with her hair, rolling it between her thumb and fingers.

"The men . . ."

She nodded. "They looked like the house detectives, so I hid where they couldn't see me. One had white hair, and the other had a white suit. The one with the suit was old. They walked up outside *her* room, and stood there a long time. Other people came down the hall, but they went into other rooms. The men just stayed. And then *she* opened the door."

"Madeleine? The redhead?" For once in his life, Max could hardly get his words out. The quicksand was growing deeper—hungrier.

"She was naked," Suzanna said in a dull voice. "She looked at the other floors across the way, and they checked the hall again. They still didn't see me, though. And then she handed the old man some keys."

"You're making this up," he snarled.

"I am not! I've followed you before. I can do whatever I want!" Her chin was up; her hands bunched into little fists.

"What time did this happen?"

"I don't know. I don't worry about time." She giggled suddenly, as if the impulse had sneaked up on her. "I was pretty drunk. I'd finished my bottle, so I'd done some more coke, but it was wearing off, and I had to drive home and not wreck the car, because Daddy said he'd be really mad the next time. So I had one more snort and left. *You* weren't leaving."

"Yeah. Can you describe these men?"

"I already did." She was beginning to squirm. The older look crept back into her eyes; she covered her breasts with her hands, in a mockery of modesty. "And I'm not putting out any more for free."

"Just tell me this, then—"

"No."

"Just this. What happened to you, Suzanna? Why do you act this way?"

Slowly she dropped her hands to her side again, and slumped down into the couch. It was as if he'd cut her strings. "That's a dirty story," she said so softly he almost missed it.

"I'd like to hear it," he answered just as softly.

She didn't look up, but began to recite in a dull monotone. "A long time ago, when I was real little, I got into all sorts of things. Drugs. You know. Mommy and Daddy were pissed, but they're always pissed. I had an old man, then; his name was Jingo. And I OD'd on bad acid." She sighed. It was such an old story. "I was in a coma for three weeks. Oh, I'd done PCP, too. I don't know anymore. The doctors said I was like Peter Pan. When I got better. Never grow up." Her head rose, while the rest of her body remained in place. Her eyes glistened, but there were no tears. "People don't *have* to grow up. There's no fun in that, is there? You haven't grown up, have you, Barnaby?"

Chapter 8

DECEMBER 27 • 10:45 P.M.

Max's car burned up the freeway in the night. The emptiness of the route seemed to mock his speed, spewing out endless stretches of bayshore, drive-ins, and squat office buildings, each with its own parking lot. Across the bay, the lights of Oakland and Alameda leapt among the low hills, paralleling his run. The sky held paler reflections deep down in its star-dappled gray. The bay was black.

A thousand questions nagged at him, all born of one mother: Madeleine. If he had thought he was fucked before, it was nothing to now. Madeleine had given his keys to the two men? Was that how the substitution was accomplished? And then the keys brought back before he awoke? Or was this just another well-lit blind alley, with another surprise twist at the end? Madeleine's voice, a voice he knew so well now, in so many intimate ways, replayed in the darkness of his mind. "And then there's the possibility that it was deliberate, to make you paranoid."

And: "You'd be dealing with a real lunatic."

Lunatic? No, that he'd never believe. A clever thief, yes; that he could believe. One who liked to fence with words. One who could move across a hotel room—or an office!—with stealth and speed. If this were true, she'd been laughing at him the whole time. He set his full lips in a thin line. She wouldn't laugh last.

The lighted clock overlooking the last city exit read 11:15 as he sped down the off ramp into the darkened Embarcadero. He ignored the stop light at Mission, and the one on Market, nearly driving a cab to the curb. He screamed hard right into the Hyatt lot.

Stalking across the huge lobby, he looked neither right nor left. A couple in the shadowed bar recognized him and called greetings over a combo's cool jazz, but he was no longer a part of that world.

He slowed only when he came up outside Madeleine's room. ("If you finish up before midnight, come see me.") In a funny way he was calm; he had his footing, and a direction again. If this was the end of the manager's job, he was prepared. The lion came first. It was his, and no one could steal it, no matter what she offered in return.

And if she has the lion on her, she'll be in no position to fire me! he thought.

Jaw tightly set, he knocked on her door. There was no response.

"Madeleine? It's Max." This time, he heard something move in there. And, faintly, the sound of wind. But no one came to the door.

"Madeleine?" He took hold of the knob. Then he turned it.

And all at once it gave, the door flying open on its hinges, pulling him forward, off-balance. A roaring blast of wind hit him, sucking at his clothes and hair. He caught himself on the desk, straining to see in the half-light coming in from the hall, feeling the quicksand again, holding on.

He made out a shape in the shadows, a massive, hulking thing. He couldn't make sense of it. It was too big for a woman, or a man.

And then he saw the eyes.

They were pale half-moons, unmistakably alive, and even as he realized with sickening clarity that no two of them made a pair, he understood also what the shape was that held them. It was a cloud, a slate-gray storm cloud, brimming with those lidless eyes, inside the room. The wind was spawned in its churning depths, to return at rising speeds. The thing was a living vacuum!

Max's fingers lost their hold on the desk. He lurched across the room and lost his footing. As he fell across the cloud, lightning leapt in a small, brilliant arc to his hand. He choked back a cry. The stench of charred flesh was flung arrogantly into his face.

He threw himself sideways, using the gale's own centrifugal force to help him, calling up all his old skills, the ones he hadn't used in so long. He hit and rolled, grunting to absorb the impact. His arm cracked against a chair. Carpet fibers caught in his bleeding palm. He went on over, kicking a wastebasket hard against the wall, but coming up again, on his feet and loose. He spun back around, dropping into a balanced crouch.

The cloud had become darker. The storm was building in it; more lightning licked along its edges and glittered deep in its depths. The wind was blowing harder; a sudden gust slammed the door, plunging the room into total darkness except for the lightning. There was a sound like coming thunder.

This can't be happening! he thought furiously. This is impossible! But the cloud was still there, and the gale was growing stronger. Lightning lashed out at his eyes.

He thought again: all right then! Let's beat it, whatever it is!

He feinted to his right, toward the door, but the cloud rolled to block his path. It hovered just above the carpet, rising higher than his head, and all the eyes stared unblinkingly at his efforts.

He bent quickly and scooped up the wastebasket. Heaved it into the cloud's center. Sparks burst in an explosion, cutting the darkness like burning bees. Metal shorted it! Elated, desperate, Max searched the gloom for other weapons, but could see only the bed, the desk—the copper ashtrays? He scooped up three of them, moving back between the bed and the desk. The cloud made no move to follow him.

He skimmed one ashtray at it, and a satisfying shower of sparks answered him. Fighting the wind, he stepped up onto the bed; the mattress rocked beneath his feet. Now the cloud rolled toward him, and he threw the second ashtray. He jumped to the floor, trying for the doorknob. But the gale took him with unexpected fury, holding him motionless, dragging him back. Furious, he fell headlong into the mist, feeling its raging power at full force. His body arced; lights spun behind his eyes; his nerves sang; his urine broke; his breath was snatched away.

He went black, feeling as if he'd dropped into an endless, burning abyss.

And in the last moment he heard Madeleine's voice, screaming all around him, three words:

So long, sucker!

Chapter 9

DECEMBER 28 • 11:10 A.M.

There was gray daylight in his eyes when he came to. There was a stench of burnt carpet in his nose, and nodules of the carpet itself. There was a roaring in his ears, like the scream of the cloud-thing, but fainter, as if it were somewhere nearby but no longer on top of him. He thought about caring, but couldn't.

He thought mostly about coming to. It wasn't what he'd expected to do. He'd seen Death in Nam, known Death, dealt Death. He knew the pearlescent Grin, those teeth always the same under the mask. There were teeth in that cloud, all right; the lightning and the eyes were the new mask. He was meant to have died.

Instead he came to sucking charred rug balls up his nose.

He brought one hand up beside his head, once-limber fingers painfully outstretched, more carpet caught in their blood-crystal wounds like black flies in amber. He pushed down against the pile, no longer experimentally, gaining strength with each new moment of the knowledge of life. Pain laced along his arm and through his shoulder: warmth. He rolled to his side, and his face came free of the carpet, and after that it was almost easy. He sat up and leaned back against a wall.

The room looked like hell. Wherever the cloud had touched down, blackened char remained. At two points it must have brushed the wall. The television had exploded and was lying on its back like a fat man disemboweled. The picture window was fused, and the sunlight coming through it came diffused. It gave the wreckage a spectral glow, a mockingly painterly purity.

Max, too, looked like hell, but his purity was found only in his pain. He choked back a grunt as he worked his way up the wall to his feet, refusing to give her the satisfaction. There was no doubt in his mind who'd done this. Madeleine. The Madwoman.

The bitch.

Somehow—*somehow*—she had controlled that . . . thing. . . .

He walked fairly well to the bathroom, holding himself taut and erect. He washed his face, his hands, his blistered torso, forcing his skin to flex and break. The cold water felt good, but he'd need some professional care. There was a deep burnt trench across his forehead, just above the eyes, and his left hand was split and scored. Most of the rest of him hurt, but he could live with it. He *was* living with it, and that was the bottom line.

DECEMBER 28 • 1:05 P.M.

When Inspector Hamoto came back to his squad room after lunch, he saw Max August sitting stiffly in his visitor's chair whistling "Light My Fire," and he stopped in mid-stride. No expression crossed his face, but his shoulders straightened and his thick chin came up before he crossed into Max's field of vision.

"First, let me tell you that Domenico was involved in a bar shootout half an hour before he shot at you," Hamoto said without preamble as he lowered himself into his wide wooden chair. "I had *thought* this meant that you were a random target, Mr. August. But tell me."

Max laughed softly. His forehead and hand were now professionally taped and gauzed, and other wrappings wound invisibly under his fresh shirt and pants. Though the day was still cool and cloudy, he was wearing loosely tied tennis shoes over the dressings on his feet. With a dose of Empirin and codeine in his stomach, he was feeling not too bad. Not that what he felt like mattered to him. "I got a clue last night, Inspector. A girl, a fan, named Suzanna Ward. She's been after me to 'get to know her better,' and it occurred to me that she might have stolen my lion. I was wrong, but as it turned out, she had been following me the night before last, when I'd been out with my boss, the lady you met yesterday, Madeleine Riggs. Suzanna told me she'd seen Madeleine Riggs give my keys to two men. They were—"

"Wait." Suddenly Hamoto was rising from his chair like a sounding whale. "I'll be right back," he said, and walked quickly out of the room.

Max sat and watched him go. His brow began to furrow with his puzzlement, but the burst of pain made him think better of it. He knows something about this, he thought. I thought I'd have to buck-and-wing to get him to buy my story after his notable lack of interest yesterday, but he's been working.

Ten minutes passed, while the squad room around him came

to afternoon life with male banter and shouts and the shuffling of paper. Then Hamoto reappeared, and at his side was Inspector Hardesty, an unlit cigarette in the corner of his mouth and an open matchbook in his hand.

He bent low, close to Max's ear. "Would you mind coming into the interrogation room, Mr. August?" he asked with leaden emphasis. Max looked into his blank gray glasses, then around at the squad room. He shrugged and stood up.

They walked across the steel-gray linoleum to a cubicle formed from the corner of the larger room and two other walls made of green steel and dull wire-mesh glass. The desks in the squad room were also green steel, but in the interrogation room the decor was strictly Philip Marlowe modern. A scarred and peeling orange table squatted beneath a hanging light, surrounded by four cigarette-burned straight chairs. A chipped Mr. Coffee rested crookedly on a rolling tray with only three wheels. A dented wastebasket lounged in a corner where someone had kicked it. There was nothing else in that cubicle except the smells of smoke and fear, and although Max could look out at the bustling room beyond, he knew that no one else, cop or criminal, would ever witness what went on in here.

He took the chair closest to the entryway. Hardesty sat down opposite him, the shadows from the overhead lamp long on his hard face. Hamoto poured out three steaming cups of coffee, handed them around, and sat down next to Hardesty. Max sipped his coffee. It was lousy.

Hardesty ignored his cup, as he continued to ignore the unlit cigarette in his mouth. It bobbed up and down as he spoke. "Inspector Hamoto has informed me of your statement thus far. You don't have to repeat it. Just continue from where you left off."

Max took another sip of his coffee, pretending to savor it, taking his time.

"Would you like a stenographer, Hardesty?" asked Hamoto.

"No." Decisively.

Max began to understand that here, too, things were not as they had seemed. He put his cup down, and began.

"Miss Riggs was seen handing my keys to two men . . ."

"How did she get them?"

"I assume she took them from my pants."

"You weren't wearing your pants?"

"No. We were in her room at the Hyatt Regency."

"You didn't tell us that before."

"Why the hell should I?"

"He's right," said Hamoto.

Hardesty ignored him. "Go on."

"We had gone to bed," Max said flatly. "We had fucked each other. I went to sleep. The men, I assume, went to my place and stole my lion, then returned. Then, last night, after I heard about this, I drove back to Miss Riggs's hotel to confront her. But when I entered her room, I ran into something I can't fully explain. It was some sort of creature, a living thundercloud, full of lightning and eyes. I know"—he looked each of them full in the face—"this is even harder to believe than my feeling about my lion, but Suzanna's testimony substantiates that story—and you're looking at the results of my meeting with the storm cloud." He held up his bandaged hand.

"I haven't said no," said Hardesty. "Tell me everything you can about that cloud." He took the cigarette from his mouth and held it between them. He thrust it forward three times as his eyes bored into Max's. "Every-fucking-thing."

"You're not with the police, are you, Hardesty?"

"I'm asking the questions for now."

So Max went through the scene again, from the moment the door blew open to the cloud's final words. He left out only the sensation of tottering on the edge of eternity; he didn't like to think about that and there was enough to his story without complicating it.

When he'd finished, Hardesty got up from his chair and came around to him. Without warning, he flicked his cigarette past Max's ear and, as Max reacted, stabbed his fingers into his bandaged hand. The DJ gasped in pain and came quickly to his feet.

Hardesty backed off, hands low. "Relax . . . relax. I had to check, didn't I?"

"There are other ways. Call my doctor."

"I like my evidence direct. I'm funny that way." Hardesty reached inside his jacket and came out with a shield pinned to his wallet, holding it so Max could read it plainly.

FBI.

"We're working on your boss lady, Mr. August. That's why I played my charade with the inspector yesterday: to look in on her, not you. It was a good chance to get close, instead of trailing her from a distance like I've been doing for the past three weeks."

Max looked to Hamoto. Hamoto shrugged and looked back at Hardesty. Gingerly Max sat down. "What's she done?"

"She's a Russian agent."

"Come on."

"KGB."

"Madeleine?" Max shook his head. "What game are you playing now? No Russian agent can control storm clouds."

"You'd be surprised."

"Hardesty—if that's really your name—*I'm* the one with the funny story."

"That's what you think."

Hardesty got up and walked to the door of the interrogation room, examining it to make certain it was shut. Then he bent and picked up his discarded cigarette from the floor, and stuck it back in his mouth, still without lighting it. He brooded out through the chicken-wire glass at the routine of the squad room beyond and frowned at the proximity of two uniformed bulls telling each other jokes with lots of hand motions. "You know those guys, Inspector?"

"Yes."

"Yes?" But he turned back around. He pulled his cigarette pack from his jacket pocket and held it out to Hamoto, who took one, and Max, who shook his head.

"You don't smoke?"

"Not cigarettes," Max answered steadily.

"Sure." Hardesty nodded shortly. He sat down.

He seemed, for the first time, to be having trouble deciding what to do.

But then: "Mr. August, I want you to understand that in any case less urgent than this one, I not only wouldn't be telling you this, I wouldn't be talking to you at all."

"I do understand."

"I hope so." He took a deep breath. "Okay: the story begins in the 1950s; you're old enough to remember at least some of what they were like. We had the Cold War, so-called. Korea, Berlin, Hungary; the hydrogen bomb and Sputnik. The bad old days.

"But in '62, that all culminated in the famous Cuban Missile Crisis. 'The other guy blinked,' and the Russians backed off. We had Détente. Cultural exchanges. SALT treaties." He took out a Cricket lighter, but it was an absent gesture. He spun the striker wheel without pulling the butane release. "What we had was shit!

"The Russians have never backed off. They were just content to let us think they had, while we got our ass chewed up in Vietnam. They didn't have to do a damn thing to us while we were doing it to ourselves. But ever since we pulled out of Saigon with our friends hanging on our choppers by their fingertips, the Russians have come back out of the closet—so far out that people have actually begun to notice." He snatched the cigarette from his mouth in a sudden, brutal gesture. "And that's just the context.

"So: it was 1959, and we were in a war. And somebody in Washington got the bright idea of trying a new way to communicate with submarines. See, there's no way to talk to a sub when it's underwater; there wasn't then, and there isn't now. Radio won't penetrate water. But, thought this bright boy, what about telepathy? Now, in 1959, nobody really took that too seriously, but there were no limits to what we'd try then, so they tried this. And amazingly, it worked. A little. But not enough to satisfy either the science boys or the brass. In the end they gave it up as a bad job.

"But then the French got hold of the story, and printed it to embarrass us. And the next thing we knew, Dr. Leonid Vasiliev, chairman of psychology at the University of Leningrad, proud possessor of the Lenin Prize, released a statement that the Russians had done it all twenty-five years before. Right? The usual crap.

"But then we started to get word that Dr. Vasiliev had been put in charge of a special new laboratory, specializing in parapsychology." Hardesty showed his teeth. "Now, what do you know about shamans?"

"Don Juan, you mean?"

"Who's that?"

"Don Juan?" Max blinked. "Carlos Castaneda wrote a bunch of books about him—a Mexican sorcerer."

"Never heard of him." Hardesty was impatient. "I'm talking about the Russians. Shamans originated in Siberia, according to the books I've read; this 'Don Juan' must have learned his trade from them. Some people call them Russian witch doctors, but actually they're the original parapsychologists. They could heal, but they could also levitate and talk with other shamans in their minds. They danced themselves into a frenzy and walked on fire. This made them the Russian holy men.

"Russia has always had a weird side; a hundred years ago, it was common to talk of her 'mystical soul.' Russia loves the shadows. Her natural governmental policy, either under the czar or the Supreme Soviet, has always been to avoid actual war if possible, and conquer through deception and confusion. Bribe your friends, bribe your enemies, lie to both and let them devour each other—then assimilate what remains. That's the Russian Way.

"The country's had more than its share of out-and-out mystics. Most famous, of course, was Rasputin, who influenced the Czar after he cured his son of hemophilia. He could also influence women so they'd jump willingly into bed with him—and this despite his being as ugly an old bastard as you'll find. But before he became 'the Mad Monk' of the Russian Orthodox Church, he was a shaman, straight from Siberia.

"His enemies shot him, but he survived. Then they poisoned

him, without effect; shot him again, twice, without stopping him; and finally beat him unconscious. Then they dumped him through the ice of a river, where he finally drowned.

"Then there was Gurdjieff, and Madame Blavatsky, two Russians who started mystical movements that still exist today. Gurdjieff looks benign, in retrospect, but he *was* a spy in his younger days. Madame Blavatsky is a little harder to figure; she claimed to be in touch with dead 'Masters' of the past, who fed her information.

"And more recently, there was Wolf Messing, who was born a Pole but fled to Russia after the Nazis annexed his homeland. He worked as a stage psychic, but when Stalin got interested in him and tested him, he proved he had real powers. There's a story that he robbed a bank for Uncle Joe by just willing the teller to hand over the money. Messing went on to become a star of Russian entertainment—sort of a psychic Bob Hope.

"Messing died six years ago, but almost from the beginning in 1959, he worked with Vasiliev and his successors; the doctor died in '66. In '63, after the famous Cuban Missile Crisis, the Kremlin ordered top priority for its military—and for the 'biological sciences,' which include parapsychology—with special emphasis on espionage use. The results of their military program are only too obvious. The results of their psi work are, naturally, not.

"But today there are twenty-eight centers for psychic research in Russia, with a combined budget of one hundred thirty-seven million rubles. Their nerve center is a place called Academgorodok—'Science City.' It happens to be located in Siberia."

"You're telling me that Russia's not a communist conspiracy, but a mystical one?" Max's eyes were beginning to glaze over from this deluge of information. He thought about a sip of coffee but rejected that. "I'm sorry, Inspector. I don't doubt that Madeleine has some special power, maybe even parapsychological. But this network of scientifically trained wizards operating out of the ancient home of the shamans sounds more than a little paranoid."

He didn't add that he had long believed the FBI's paranoia over

Martin Luther King, Jr., had led J. Edgar Hoover to have Dr. King killed, and that CIA paranoia over John Kennedy's intention of pulling out of Southeast Asia and abandoning the agency's bills-paying smack traffic had led to Dallas, and then the war. Those were just his opinions, picked up over the crumbling years since; they could have been paranoia, too. But the net result was that Max trusted the FBI very little, and still less when it came to conspiracy theories.

Hardesty's face was calm, but he knew exactly what Max was thinking. He'd seen that look in other people's eyes till he was sick of it. You wish we'd get out of your life, he thought grimly. You wish we'd stop trying to stay on top of things, and then everything would settle down. Well, believe me, you bastard, I'd love to try it. I'd love to just sit back and watch what happens to you without our protection—sit back and watch the decay come on even faster, while you go under at the hands of the Syndicate or your goddamn Russian girl friend. But I won't. Because I can't. Because I'm just dumb enough to want to save this fucking country, even if it saves you, too. And because I need what you've got in order to do that, I'm going to keep you happy—at least, until I'm through with you.

"Mr. August, I do not think all Russians are in a mystical conspiracy, or even that all Russians are mystics. I do think it's a talent which comes easily to people from that part of the world.

"Let me tell you some of the people Academgorodok has tested and approved—people that we know about.

"Nelya Mikhailova. She can move objects by looking at them.

"Yuri Kamensky and Karl Nikolaiev. They communicated telepathically between Academgorodok and Moscow, a distance of two thousand miles.

"Vladimir Raikov. He hypnotizes people and brings out what he calls reincarnated personalities.

"Rosa Kuleshova. She's blind, but she can see with her fingers.

"Nikolai—"

"Okay. I hear you, loud and clear." Max picked up his coffee cup. "Can I have some more?" he asked Hamoto, who had been sitting silent and unmoving during this entire colloquy, watching the two of them with his inscrutable eyes.

"Sure. I'll make some fresh."

"That'd be nice."

"Mr. August." Hardesty would not let up, now that he'd started. "The Russians have been learning what all this is about, and working with it on a practical basis, for twenty-five years. This storm cloud of yours, which sounds to me like mental energy made visible, doesn't surprise me at all. It only gratifies me, as another confirmation of what's going on."

"Do we have people to fight back?"

"No. We do not. We're working on it now, of course—now that we've decided to worry about them again—but we're years behind. America has only two major centers: Duke University, in North Carolina, and Stanford, down the road. That's it. We still don't really *believe* it, you see. There's no commitment. There's just me and a handful of others, who are supposed to keep tabs on their psychic agents in a thoroughly nonpsychic way."

"Agents like Madeleine Riggs."

"Exactly. Her real name's Aleksandra Korelatovna, by the way."

"I'll call her the Madwoman, thanks. A rose by any other name . . ."

"Is still full of thorns!" Inspector Hamoto stood watching his coffee machine, his broad back to them, but his voice choked with anger. The others looked up at him in surprise.

Hardesty jerked his head. "What's eating you?"

Hamoto turned around. His thick jaw was outthrust. "What a city this is! I've been a cop for seventeen years, and do you know what we've had to deal with in that time? All the usual shit of any modern city: murders, rapes, felonies in all shapes and sizes. But since this is San Francisco, we get all the weirdos, too. All of them! Charlie Manson, the Zebra Killers, the Zodiac killer, Sara Jane Moore, the SLA, Norman Kemper the cannibal . . . who else? The Chowchilla schoolbus kidnappers. The People's Temple. Dan White.

Dr. Steiner. And now, at last, psychic Russian spies, who could have picked anywhere in the whole wide world."

"I can get someone else assigned to this case," said Hardesty, unimpressed.

"That doesn't solve the problem. Mr. August is still entitled to this department's protection." The coffee was ready; he poured a cup and handed it to Max. "But I don't have to like it."

"Like he says, they could have picked anywhere, Inspector," said Max, turning back toward Hardesty across the table. "But they didn't. They picked here, because they picked me. Why is that?"

"It beats the hell out of me, Mr. August. I was hoping if I told you what I know, you'd have the answer to that."

"Well, I don't." He sat back and thought for a moment. "Is the Northcliff Corporation, her employer, a Russian front?"

"Not so far as we know. They bought out a business she was operating—"

"She told me."

"Okay. But we don't think they knew what they were getting. She was using them to expand her cover."

"When did they buy her out?"

"October."

"Only two months ago? Was QBU her first assignment for them?"

"Uh-uh. She's a very busy woman. As I say, the FBI'd been onto her for a little more than a year. Our friends"—the word wasn't really distasteful in his mouth; more like something that has lost all its taste after long chewing—"in the CIA picked her up when she entered West Berlin in November of last year. One of their operatives was strolling by the wall late one night—that's not so unusual, since it meanders across the entire city, and it's a favorite way for Berliners to get off by themselves—when this man happened to look back and see her standing all alone there. She attracted his attention for two reasons—well, three—but the two relevant ones were that there was nothing abutting the wall at that point but a large and vacant lot, so it was unlikely she'd come from the Western side. And, though he didn't put this in his report, he later told me that he had the impression—the *feeling*—that she was just settling down to earth. Landing. But not as if she'd *jumped* from the wall. She was landing softly." Hardesty shrugged. "The light was bad, of course."

Max just looked at him. Hamoto pursed his lips.

"On the basis of her sudden appearance alone, the CIA kept tabs on her," Hardesty went on. "Her papers were in order: an American tourist from New York. She left Germany and went back to the States, where she stepped right into the presidency of a company—an investment service, Atlantic Coast Counsel—a small but going and apparently legitimate concern since 1959. The CIA was certain she had not been associated with ACC before, so they brought us in. We watched her informally, a low-level tag, and never once found her engaged in even the suspicion of espionage. What she did was make some spectacular predictions during the year, attract the industry's attention, and cozy up to Northcliff's advances.

"Significantly, her story at that time—that she had run ACC for the previous *three* years—was never questioned on Wall Street. Several Northcliff competitors and three government regulatory agencies looked her over, and nobody called her on it. Since the CIA's not always right—and less so with each passing year—we might have believed her, too . . . if it hadn't been Northcliff she was joining. When she went on board with them, we decided to dig a little deeper, and I went back to the agency's man in Berlin."

At long last, Hardesty lit his cigarette. He took one quick drag and began to speak again, driving on to the end in bursts of smoke.

"She got a good slot in the corporation, at least partially by charming the chairman of the board. She got the title of Corporate Liaison, a sort of independent appraiser of Northcliff's various holdings—and right away left on assignment to London. It seemed way too soon for someone who'd just started, so we asked the Brits to keep an eye on her. Naturally they fucked up. We haven't the slightest idea what she did or who she met while she was there, or even if she stayed in England. I picked her up when she flew back on the sixth of this month, and after a week back in New York, she came here."

"To steal my lion—and make a fool out of me." Max shook his head wearily. "Who are her two accomplices?"

"We don't know. They're new to the picture."

"And you don't know where she is now?"

"I wouldn't be here if I did. I thought the inspector was wrong when he asked me to listen to you today; I thought she was settled in till after New Year's." Hardesty looked at the wall above Max's head; it was an apology.

Max remembered asking her for a New Year's Eve date, and her reply: "You're rushing things, my dear." He sat forward in his chair. "I thought she was settled in, too."

"Until I heard your story, I still had no hard evidence that she was one of the Russian psychics. The local agent-in-charge has other, more normal cases, and I couldn't push for a twenty-four-hour tag . . ."

"So he came to us," said Hamoto. Every time he spoke, it came as a surprise.

"And you couldn't spare any men, either?" Max asked him.

"We have the same problems." Hamoto's inscrutability had returned, but it was like moss overlaying deep waters. "We lacked even the background the inspector's laid out. I told you before, we're all tired of the crazies. Charlie Manson claimed to be a magician, too; it appeared he could talk with his girls across distances, through walls. I suppose I didn't really believe in Inspector Hardesty's Communist Mind-Benders. Frankly, I still don't really believe in them . . . any more than I believe in your storm cloud." Max opened his mouth to protest, but a fat, flat palm arose first. "I believe that you believe it. But I think there's some other explanation—some rational explanation. Hypnosis. Drugs."

He stood up ponderously. "I'll cooperate with anything the inspector suggests now. I don't have to believe to do my job. And now that we have evidence that something is going on, I'll be able to spring a few men. One of them will be your bodyguard."

"Thanks just the same," said Max, "but I don't want one."

"The inspector's right, Mr. August," said Hardesty. "Until we know why Aleksandra went after you, we can't be certain she won't try again."

"Maybe so, but I don't want a bodyguard." Max looked from one to the other, his face set. "What could a bodyguard have done to help me last night? Not a damn thing. And all one would do now is slow me down." He smiled. "I've always liked to work alone."

"But, Mr. August," said Hamoto, "you see now what you're up against—what we're all up against. This case requires a concerted effort. We're already working on your lion, and we'll put all our efforts into locating Miss Korelatovna; as will, of course, the FBI. Don't get the idea that we'll lay back on your case, or fumble it. We won't." He leaned forward on the battered tabletop. "You just keep on playing those records—keeping my daughter and all the other kids in this city happy. That's all you have to do."

Hardesty leaned forward, too. "This is what we're paid for. We'll get her."

"How?"

"Don't worry," said Hamoto. "We will."

Max laughed shortly and stood up. "May I go now?"

Hardesty stood up opposite him. "Sure. Go ahead. And if you don't want a bodyguard, then no bodyguard; I guarantee it. Anyway you want it, Mr. August, I'm inclined to let you have it—right up to the end. Right up to when you find out you need us, and we're not there."

. . . . .

After Max had gone, Hamoto reached into a drawer and pulled out a phone. "I thought you were following her last night, Hardesty," he said mildly.

Without turning, Hardesty said, "I was."

"But she got out of the hotel."

"Yes, she got out of the hotel. So I have to take a piss once a night. You've never lost a tail?" He lit another cigarette and drew on it harshly. "I want a tail on *him* now, Inspector."

Hamoto was already dialing.

Chapter 10

DECEMBER 28 • 2:20 P.M.

Top down, chill wind good on his bandages, Max drove through the streets of the city, just to be out and around. His hands and feet did the work automatically, never intruding on the images which spun just as smoothly through his mind—images he'd never expected to see, or wanted to see, again . . .

. . . . .

In the 112th, "Point Man" was a job that rotated. Everybody had to pull it sometime, and everybody who hadn't pulled it so far felt the same sinking feeling when his number came up. You were picked to go out in front, all alone, charting the path for the rest of the squad, or platoon, or company, or even the sixteen hundred men of the brigade. You. Alone. And if there was anything else out there—VC, tiger, land mine, booby trap—you were going to be the first one and the only one to meet it.

The first time Specialist August's number came around, he found he was *very* unhappy about it. Fire fights are one thing: your blood is up and your odds are down, with so many other guys around you. Point Man is another thing altogether. But it's not as if you have a choice. Everybody gets picked sometime. When it's your turn to do it, you do it. That's how the Army works.

But despite these continuing rationalizations, he was still sweating nickels when the platoon broke for dinner that night. It was going to be an all-night movement, lasting until late the next morning, because they were headed for a landing zone. The moon would be a little past full, coming up two hours after dusk and staying up till dawn, giving almost too much light for Max's taste.

After eating quickly, he sacked out for the two hours, no longer amazed at what conditions he could sleep under. When he woke up, he felt new and refreshed; but then as the time to head out came closer, the little worries of any trip began to crowd his head. Have I got everything? Do I know where I'm going? He didn't want to get started and find out he'd forgotten the one thing he needed to survive. There would be no going back.

Everybody tried to give him something for luck: a rabbit's foot, a four-leaf clover sealed in plastic, the wife's underwear. He refused them all, not wanting to entangle his own luck out there, but dragging out the process, drinking in the concern, no matter how obliquely demonstrated.

Finally, however, the command to move out came down, and he couldn't delay any longer.

The sounds of the night were louder than they'd ever been as he walked out alone into the moonlit unknown.

At first he was constantly looking back over his shoulder, to see how far ahead of the others he was. He was supposed to stay in sight, but on the flats, that could be anything up to half a mile. He kept going over the hand signals in his mind: get down, come ahead, stay put. Anything else, and there'd be no need for silent signals.

Every few minutes he stopped to listen and look. He noticed, not laughing, how funny it was the way things fooled you. At first you think you see movement, and you know it's really not. You think it's probably the blind spot in your eye, but you don't dare take that for granted. Then, finally, you think you really do see something, and you freeze, and you concentrate on that one area, and you try not to become paranoid about what's going on over *here* while you're looking over *there.*

But nothing happens either place, and the guys are closing in behind you. So you move on.

And as you keep moving on, these sensations start to turn familiar. You realize you're still in the same damn jungle as before, and you start to regain your personal rhythm. Everybody in Nam had a rhythm, somewhere outside himself. You could never predict it before the fact, but you could easily feel it in action, once you learned how.

Rhythm was going out and killing all day, firing off everything you owned, and coming back with a full patrol. Rhythm was going out the next day to take a piss and having your brains jellied. It was nothing like a personal thing, though personal men died every day. It was part of the unit, the commanders, the territory. Some days you just knew you were all right, whatever happened. And other days you just prayed.

That night, beneath the jungle moon, Max began to learn the rhythm of the Point Man. He began to worry less about what was going on, or even what could go on. He began to think, hey, I can handle this. I'm not as afraid as I thought I would be. This ain't too shabby.

And after a while he began to get into the beauty of his solitude. For the first time in weeks, maybe even months, he wasn't surrounded by other men. Nobody was telling him what to do. He could go to the left; he could go to the right. He could run. He could slow down. Whatever he alone wanted to do.

And after a good long while, he began to get very aware of who he was.

In those last hours before dawn, he was never more aware; his senses had never been so keen. He felt each one of his hairs grow. He knew, to the smallest fraction, how much air he was inhaling. What its scent was. How its direction had shifted since his last breath. How it sounded through the trees.

In the moonlight he could see every detail of his surroundings and he could see them on the grand scale. He could see how he was a part of it all, and how he could survive it. He knew what to do, without thinking. Notwithstanding all the drugs he had taken before that night or since, he had never felt so completely wide awake, and he wondered, why can't I feel like this all the time? Why can't I always have this golden glow?

And he knew that now that he'd known it, he would volunteer for this feeling again. From that night on, in his heart of hearts, he would always be a Point Man.

Chapter 11

DECEMBER 28 • 3:20 P.M.

The window at QBU was boarded over, though incongruously the neon name of GRANITE REILLY flamed above it, and the Supremes sang out from its sides. There were just five kids and a dog standing by.

"Hi, Barnaby!"

"Hey, what happened'a you, man?"

He waved with his bandaged hand but continued through the front door. He didn't want to talk.

But the people inside were expecting him.

"Max! What the hell—?"

"There're cops here. What's going on?"

"What's this about the Madwo—Miss Riggs?"

He waved them off. "I've got to check out the situation myself, and then we'll have a quick meeting. Tell everybody five minutes to four." He smiled meaninglessly and turned his back before anyone else could get a word in.

Carlotta turned to Chick and shrugged. "I told you. Bosses are different."

"Nah! Not him!"

"You'll see."

Max found a cop outside Madeleine's office. "Turn up anything?" he asked briskly.

"Nothing, Mr. Wilde," answered the cop. He was young, but

his face was already world-weary. "They turned everything inside out."

"Okay if I go inside?"

"Sure. Inspector Hamoto said you were allowed."

"That was nice of the inspector, in my own station."

Max closed the door firmly behind him, crossed quickly to the desk, and rifled the drawers. One after another they were all empty. He called for the cop.

"What was in these drawers?"

"Nothing. I told you."

"She had papers."

"They were gone when we got here. The whole room was as clean as a whistle."

But when, Max wondered, did she clean it out?

He lifted the phone and asked Carlotta to check the night book. She found no listing for Madeleine Riggs.

She hadn't come in. Then she'd cleaned out yesterday afternoon. Knowing *then* that she wouldn't be back? Even though we'd fucked right on this same damn desk, and I walked out as dumb and happy as a newborn pup?

Or—did she, in fact, come in last night? Without the night man knowing it—or even seeing her as one of the people whose name does appear in the book?

The psychic aspect of the situation was the killer. How could he know what was real? Either way he read the facts, she had those powers he couldn't account for.

Unless she had planned to leave yesterday in any event. In that case—since (Max assumed) she had called Domenico to come kill him—she would have had to come up with another plan after Domenico failed. But then, wouldn't she have insisted on staying with him, rather than leaving it to chance that he'd come see her?

Or was she so absolutely certain he'd come?

And then, the final question: why, after all that, hadn't she killed him? Why had she left him alive?

And the answer: how could you know, when she made up the rules?

Some of the rules, he reminded himself with an angry shake of his head. She's still human. I know that for sure. And I can make a few rules myself.

If the Russians have new techniques at their command—techniques developed in labs, not shawl-hung gypsy tea parlors—then they're techniques other people can get a hold on, Max thought; and he thought back to his first readings of the devil doctor, Fu Manchu. Fu's tricks had seemed so perfectly evil to a young boy caught up in the book, but quaint when he put the book down. The Science City of Siberia might be as far away as the Mandarin courts of old Cathay, but that was their only similarity. In the real world . . .

Max picked up the phone again and punched up a 212 number, New York. It was 3:40 here, 6:40 there; but against all the odds he caught Harry Spencer in his office.

"Max! Good to hear your voice, scout!" Spencer's voice was unmistakable. Before signing on as Northcliff's radio VP, he'd done years of Pepsi commercials. "How's the new sales manager? Miss Riggs sent us a glowing report, you know. Congratulations."

"Thanks, Spence. It's completely deserved." He laughed easily, scratching at the returning itch in his bandaged hand. "I've got a little problem to report, though."

"Ah, no, Max. We've been having an end-of-the-year happy hour, all afternoon. No more business today."

"But you only drink Pepsis, Spence."

"Would you please be serious."

"All right," Max said, "I will. But just remember, you asked me." He took a deep breath. "The multitalented Miss Riggs has gone missing on us."

Spencer snorted. "Nuts. I thought it was serious. That's just her style. Here today, gone tomorrow. A busy little bee, that's our Miss Riggs. Tomorrow or the next day, I'll get a memo telling me she's in Tulsa or some other damn place. Of course, that's if she's still troubleshooting my department. If she's moved over to farm feeds this month, I won't hear about it at all."

"You mean she doesn't work under you?"

"Ha! She works under the Old Man exclusively. And I mean *under*, if you catch my drift." He paused. "That's just between us."

"I hear ya, Spence. I can believe it. But it's important I get in touch with her. She caused a little trouble at her hotel before she left, and the cops are looking into it—"

"Trouble? What kind of trouble? Why cops?" Spencer's voice had lost its banter.

"A bar bill. Some broken furniture. Nothing I can't get the cops to cover up; they'll do it for me. But I want to talk to her, Spence. I'd appreciate anything you've got."

"Sure, scout. Just a minute." The phone clicked onto hold, then came off again after a second. Spencer said, "I like a man who keeps his head, Max. Thanks," and then the voice of Pepsi was replaced once more by Muzak. A minute droned by, as only a minute of Muzak can.

After another one Spencer was back. His voice was different, like a Pepsi gone flat. "Max, I'm afraid I . . . can't help you with this, after all. I've been reminded that our executives' private lives are confidential, even to a station sales manager. I'm sorry." Pause. "Very sorry."

His words were clear, and so was his tone, to someone with years of radio experience. As definitely as if he'd been standing there with them, Max knew that Spencer was no longer alone in his room.

"I understand, Spence. Don't worry. I'll handle the cops as best I can."

"Better handle them good, Max. That's one of the things managers are there for." But Spencer's voice was relieved.

"Sure, Spence," Max said. Then he added, "Take care of yourself."

DECEMBER 28 • 3:55 P.M.

The meeting with the staff was correspondingly brief. The police had just left, leaving everyone abuzz and confused. Max laid out the barest of the facts, enough to lightly hold together if you didn't put too much weight on them, sketching a woman who ran all around the country and had run this time just a shade too fast. There was probably nothing to worry about—in fact, we're just as well rid of her, right?—but the police were poking their noses in anyway; you know how they are.

Then he turned to his bandages, telling them of his new five-dollar Safeway hibachi and his three piña coladas before trying to light it up. Everyone laughed, and similar experiences were recalled. Only Earl seemed worried, but he said nothing. Then the meeting was at an end, and things were back to normal. For the others.

DECEMBER 28 • 4:00 P.M.

It was not so easy for Max, and it got harder. Blocked off in an inner studio, a mirror image of his usual bailiwick, he could have been doing his show from Saturn instead of Sutter Street. He missed his cues constantly and, worse, had to fight to keep the cynicism from his patter. In the little time he had between the songs and the spots, he couldn't think of anything more useless to him now than those songs and spots. He wanted to be outside and free.

Just after sundown Barnaby Wilde came riding in on the fade of Country Joe's FISH song and challenged any other maniacs out there to do their worst. Earl's eyes popped at that one.

The phone calls followed. Short calls, nasty and brutal; long calls that would have been longer had not Earl shut them off. One of the advantages of having the largest audience in town, Max mused with dry satisfaction, was the number and variety of special-interest groups involved. As Hamoto had noted, the Bay Area was well stocked with psychos, and overflowing with antihero-worshipers.

At 6:35 Earl put a call through that was different from the others. It was Suzanna.

"Hi, Barnaby . . ." She was in her little-girl phase again, and he could barely hear her over his music in her background. "I wasn't sure you'd want to talk to me anymore."

As a matter of fact he didn't; but Earl hadn't known that. Max felt sorry for her now, but, at the same time, she was the clearest exemplar of all that oppressed him this evening.

Still he tried to be gentle. "We're getting a lot of calls now, so I can't really talk, Suzanna."

"You still haven't found your lion, have you? Didn't that red-head help you?"

"No, she didn't. She's disappeared, too. I really have to—"

"The pigs came to see me today, Barnaby."

"The pigs. Yeah. I figured they would. And you told them everything you told me?"

"Talk to the pigs? Are you kidding?" All at once her voice took on that coaxing purr. "I only open up for *you*."

"Oh Christ, Suzanna—!"

"Barnaby . . . I know where she is."

"Suzanna, don't play games."

"I'm not." She was pouting. "I can help you if you come see me. Don't you want to come see me?"

His face was tight. "I would if you had something. But I don't think you do."

"Then I'd better hang up. Good-bye." But she waited on the line.

And finally he said, "Okay. If you do have something, I want it. But if you're lying to me . . ."

"Meet me tonight, Barnaby. Meet me—at the bandstand in the park."

"Golden Gate Park? Why there?"

"I used to hang out there, with Jingo. It's more my home than this ritzy dump. And you won't have so far to drive. And we'll be more alone." Her mood had swung to bubbling excitement; her words ran over each other. Max didn't want to argue with her, but he put his foot down hard.

"Okay. I'll meet you at the bandstand at 9:30 sharp. I can't make it any earlier, because I have to get some dinner first. I haven't eaten all day."

"We could eat dinner together, like you did with her."

"No, Suzanna. Nine thirty or nothing."

"And you'll be nice to me if I help you?"

"We'll talk about that when I get there." He hung up before he could be drawn into promises he wouldn't keep. He took three quick breaths. Then he flipped his mike switch to "2."

"Earl, how'd you like to take a ride out to Golden Gate Park tonight, after dinner?"

"Barnaby, you need to get some rest. I'm telling you—"

"I have to meet somebody, Earl. And I need a chaperon."

"You?"

"It's your friend Suzanna."

"Ah." Earl straightened in his chair. "Okay. But only if you'll go straight home afterward. Promise me."

"Great."

Max turned off his mike, and reached for his Empirin while he considered Suzanna Ward. But her face kept slipping into that of Madeleine Riggs. Conniving goddamn women, he thought sourly. What next?

Chick Frommer stuck his head in the studio door. "Valerie Drake is here," he said.

Chapter 12

DECEMBER 28 • 6:50 P.M.

Max groaned. He'd forgotten all about Valerie Drake and the interview he'd so eagerly accepted in the good old days of yesterday afternoon—just blanked them both right out. He quickly flipped his switch back to "2."

"Earl, did Granite promo Valerie Drake?"

"Everybody did, Barnaby. Except you."

"Swell."

The door opened behind him, and he stood up as the lady entered, followed by Chick and, Max assumed, Mr. Cornelius. Max's mind was racing, he felt boxed in, and his smile was glittery and hard; but it was at least one consolation that Valerie Drake, down off the poster and into the flesh, was almost breathtakingly beautiful. She had long, wavy hair, almost black with deep auburn highlights, which hung heavily to the middle of her back. Her eyes were large and wide-set. A thin, fierce nose served to point the way to her wide and generous mouth below. She was wearing a pink body stocking running neck to toe, beneath a simple ink-blue wraparound and tight denim jeans. Her feet rested easily in four-inch spike heels. She gave Max an answering smile as their eyes met, and she hugged herself. "Whooo! Why is San Francisco always colder than it should be? Do you have any brandy?"

"It can be arranged. Hi. I'm Max August/Barnaby Wilde." He shook her hand and turned to Chick, hoping hearty efficiency could compensate for everything else. Hadn't Cornelius said she admired him? "Run down to D'Angelo's," he told the boy, "and get Miss Drake some Courvoisier VSOP."

"Valerie," she said.

"Valerie it is."

"What happened to your head and hand?" she asked, reaching

up to touch his forehead lightly. "My God, you look like you fought for your honor and won."

"I've never won a single one of those fights," he said, but didn't elaborate; he was tired of lying about it. He pulled out a chair for her, then looked to her manager, but he'd already found a seat in the back corner.

Mr. Cornelius was an older man, maybe sixty-five, but the lines crisscrossing every inch of his chiseled face were so fine that from a distance he could have been mistaken for fifty-five. He held himself easily erect, even while seated. His suit, cut in up-to-the-minute European fashion, was pitch black, almost nonreflective in the studio lights. His shoes, of polished leather, were also black, as was his wide string tie. His shirt was midnight blue; his hair gunpowder gray. Sitting silently in the corner, he seemed content to be just what he looked like: a shadow.

It was his star who held the spotlight. "I'm so happy to be on your show, Barnaby. You'll make my New Year's show a sellout."

"Not me. You've done that all by yourself."

"Oh, I've had help. Haven't I, Corny?" The man in black raised his eyebrows but said nothing.

Max checked the studio clock. "It's five of seven. We break for news on the hour, and then we'll start right up with you."

"That'll be fine." She looked around. "It must be frustrating working in an unfamiliar studio. I hope I won't be in your way."

"That'd be hard for you to do, to me or anyone else. No, I'm finally getting used to this place. Just stop me if I try to cue your knee."

"Oh, I don't know . . ." She gave him a look like the one on her poster and laid her own hand on his knee. His reaction, though he successfully covered it, was one of annoyance, and surprise at his annoyance. She was being pleasant enough, and she looked better the longer he knew her. But it didn't take long to realize that even more than with radio, he really had had his fill of manipulative women today.

He turned to the end of the record to cover his thoughts. "Not too long now, San Francisco! Not too very long at all! Comin' up in just a shade under ten mi-noo-tos, the hottest lady in America today, and let us not dwell too long on the sociological implications of that! A QBU exclusive on your very own crystal set: Miss Valerie Drake! So call your friends and neighbors now, 'cause it's later than you think."

He punched the lion's roar, brought up the Beach Boys, flipped off the mike, and turned back to her. She was examining his board with a professional eye.

"I heard about your fan from Detroit yesterday. Do you get that kind often?"

"After some of the calls I sparked this afternoon, I'm not sure. But I think it only happens when the moon is in the seventh house, and Jupiter aligns with Mars."

She inclined her head. "Are you into astrology?"

"Oh, God, no. That's from *Hair.*"

She laughed, musically. "I know that. But I'm always on the lookout for fellow weirdos." She leaned forward, raising her slim hands before his face as if to frame it. "You're a Leo, with—a strong Mars. Conjunct or rising." Her dark eyes flashed from their depths, a moment only, like ripples on a pool by moonlight. "Probably rising."

Max pulled a face. Valerie touched his knee again. "You don't approve?" she asked.

"It's not that." He laughed abruptly. "I'll believe anything today. It's just that—I met another woman recently who quoted me earthquake predictions."

"I see. Well, not to worry. I'm not into astrology all that heavily. It's just something I picked up somewhere, something to play with."

"Good. I want to stick to rationality today."

"Rationality it is. Corny, did you bring my horn-rims?" The older man again only raised his eyebrows.

Max said, "By the way—I am Leo. How'd you know?"

"The light in your eyes. The other factors in a chart can modify it, but generally the Leo influence feels like a radiating sun. In your case—"

"That doesn't sound like something you just picked up."

"No," she said. "It doesn't." And she smiled, unexpectedly, enigmatically. And yet warmly, as if her secrets were meant to be shared, in good time. For the third time her hand found his knee.

This time he moved it coolly away.

. . . . .

When it came time to go live on the air, however, things started off more smoothly.

"So, Valerie, you're doing a show to kick off the New Year, January 1st, 8:30 P.M. at the Cow Palace. Is this the start of a longer tour? I haven't heard of any long swing."

"It's not, Barnaby. No, I've been recording in Marin for several weeks, and I wanted to party with the people first crack out of the new box, so we set it up."

"Try out your new material, something like that?"

"Sure."

While charging the people ten dollars and fifty cents to watch you practice, he thought. But he said, "You have a new album coming out any time soon?"

"This spring. But I don't really keep track. I just sing, and let other people take care of business."

"That must keep a lot of people busy. These days, of course, popularity in one field generates business in all fields. There's your poster, your perfume, your doll, paperback books. Maybe even movies. But you don't take credit for all that?"

"Well, some, I guess." Her tone was light, but her eyes were puzzled. "I like to entertain."

"Who gets credit for your voice?"

"Ask my father." She laughed. "No, I'll take that one. I don't think I was born with much of a voice, really. I've had to work on it very hard. I could always hear in my head what I wanted to get out of my mouth, but I had only a certain range. But you work, and you work, and now I think I've got what I want.

"The record company goes nuts when I say I'm not naturally wonderful, because they swear it's not true, but I know who I am."

God, this is useless, he thought. "Do you enjoy who you are?"

"Very much. I always have. I think that's the best thing I have to offer people—more than my poster or my perfume. I just enjoy living, and if people want to hook onto that, I'm more than glad. We can use all of that we can get in this world."

"Amen," Max said Solemnly. "And speaking of today's world, is there any danger involved in a woman putting herself in the spotlight, out on the road? Do you carry a gun, for example?"

She looked him up and down before answering. "No. I don't need a gun. I can protect myself without one."

"How's that?"

"Now, Barnaby, if I told everybody, I wouldn't have the element of surprise. Telling you would be pointless."

Pointless, he thought. Yes. Do the interview, the inner view, Valerie, without ever letting anything slip. Tell us your voice was bad, but only in regard to its being perfect now. Otherwise, what's the point?

This is just like the Madwoman, he thought bitterly, as he stared across three feet of dead air at The Star's bright wide eyes. Laugh. Sing. Bare your breast. But always for a *point*; one you don't share with us peons; and that is that you're climbing on us. You're asking us to bow down, to take what you give and believe that we've known you, while the Real You is phoning it in, from somewhere far away.

You're a phony, Valerie Drake. It's the name of the game. Stars have to shine. And if we let ourselves be blinded by the light, we'll never see what's behind it: the human being, with warts and scars and a voice that *still* needs a wall of electronics to really make it.

I know Stars. I am one, in my way. But I'm sick to death of this bullshit.

And still, the professional within him tried to keep it alive. He said, "What do you feel when you're up on the stage?"

"Oh," she answered, "it's the closest thing I know to sex. It's just me and that great beast called the Audience, and half the time I can't see any of the individuals in it clearly. And there's all that energy flowing between us."

"You sound almost like a mystic."

"Who, me? Oh, no."

"But you're into astrology."

"Not at all." She gave him a hard look, her first one. Stay off this subject.

"Don't be shy, Valerie. You guessed my sign, just like they do at the singles bars."

"That's just a game." Her lips were tight, but she kept her voice light. "I like to play games of all kinds."

"What sign are you?"

"Just like at the singles bars? Why don't you guess?"

"I don't know astrology. I just ask questions."

"Right. And I sing songs."

"And you sing for the people?"

"Yes."

"Are you sure it doesn't have *something* to do with you?"

Earl was looking wide-eyed through the window, trying to catch his attention. He did, but he couldn't hold it. Valerie Drake, sweat suddenly beading on her forehead, had a lock. "It pleasures me," she said bitingly, "just like it does them."

"And you go home rich?"

"That's the dream, isn't it: a life that you love, that makes a lot of people happy? Of course"—she was talking past him now, to the unseen audience throughout the state—"you can get too much of any good thing. Remember that song Janis Joplin did:

Oh Lord, won't yew bah me a Mer-say-dees-Benz?
Mah fren's all drahve Porsches! Ah mus' make aymends!

Remember that?"

"I sure do. You do Janis very well, Valerie. Did you study her when you were starting out?"

"Sure. Her, Linda Ronstadt, Bonnie Raitt—I *love* Bonnie Raitt—Bessie Smith. Even Billie Holiday, even though I usually do more uptempo tunes."

Max was merciless. "And where did you find yourself among all those voices?"

Valerie's eyes narrowed almost to slits. "Well, I think I can show you, Barnaby. Find 'Love Has No Pride' on my latest album." When Earl, next door, had done so, she continued. "Thank you, Barnaby. You handle my records so skillfully." Max nodded curtly to Earl, who could hardly bear to look at him, and the song began.

As soon as their mikes were closed, Valerie stood up. "You piece of shit! I was told this was going to be a friendly session. I was told you were a friendly guy. I don't have to put up with this crap."

"It's just that I like Bonnie Raitt songs better by Bonnie Raitt."

"Well, listen, asshole, Bonnie Raitt is still a cult act, and I'm the Grammy Award winner. You may think you're gonna get some scoop on Valerie Drake for your little local audience, but it doesn't work that way. I'm a Star, buddy. I earned it, and I'm keeping my image come hell or high water. You got me, man?"

"I got you, lady. I got you as a plastic rip-off. You take other people's songs and play sex kitten with them." He mimicked her. " 'To hell with content; content I can buy for ASCAP rates. What I need is to know when to smile, and how; when to cry, and how; and when to close my eyes and remember lost loves—and how!' " He stood up, too. "You're all on the outside, and I'm sick and tired of people like you!"

She was screaming. "You're right I'm on the outside! I'm up on the stage—not hiding behind other people's talent in this fucking box! If it weren't for people like me, you'd be cleaning toilets in Tijuana!" She spun away from him, knocking over her chair with a crash. "Corny, what the hell am I doing here?"

For the first time during this entire encounter, her manager stirred in the corner. "Sit down, Valerie," he said mildly.

"The hell I will! You told me this was a good opportunity for me!"

"For all of us, Woman. For all of us." He stood up himself but without Valerie's violence. In the white studio light the edges of his black-clad form cut sharply against the browns of the cork-board background. He stood unmoving, his face in the shadows, his hands at his side.

"Mr. August," he said slowly, "I can help you find your lion."

Chapter 13

DECEMBER 28 • 8:10 P.M.

Slipping under the Dragon Gate, Max, Valerie, and Mr. Cornelius entered Chinatown. In San Francisco, unlike other Western cities, that quarter lies in the city's heart. There the Oriental influence is more pronounced and more accepted, and to work in the city is to cross through the neighborhood regularly. Certainly Max, with the QBU studios just one block away, knew Grant Street like the back of his hand.

And yet tonight it was strange to him . . . as strange as the scene in his studio. The three of them walked under alien banners, whipped by winds channeled down through the narrow canyons, and inhaled an avalanche of odors. Down the hill, past the irregular shapes of lesser buildings, the Transamerica Pyramid rose white and perfect and no less alien.

Mr. Cornelius forged ahead like a thirties' ocean liner, stately and proud, and black against the night-lit waves of crowds. Moving now, there was a tangible decisiveness at the older man's core, which only became apparent through his contrast with other people. Max wanted to ask where they were headed, or at least smooth their passage with some small talk, but Cornelius's steady progress precluded that. Max would have had to shove people aside to catch up to the man who touched no one.

Valerie Drake walked between the two of them, but Max had nothing to say to her, nor she him.

He wondered if he'd been right to ask Earl to let him go alone.

At Washington Street they turned uphill. Signs clustered around them, red, yellow, gold, and green. Sound turned in upon itself, full of horns and voices in exotic tones, either lower and more rounded, or higher and more wire-ribbed than English. Small eyes watched from behind curtains in endless windows of filigree and brass, learning.

Just as the older man's uphill pace was beginning to quicken Max's breath, they turned again, into an alley which snaked far back toward a single dim light. One other naked bulb marked the halfway point; on the street-front side of the left-hand building, a sign read "Yung Family Benevolent Society" in small English and large Chinese. Strung between these three points was only winter's chilly darkness.

Five yards into the alley, silence suddenly descended, as the street noise remained on the street. Mr. Cornelius had not slowed, but Max slackened his own pace and fell back.

"Lost your nerve?" asked Valerie nastily, turning to look at him from the shadows ahead. Her manager continued on into the deeper darkness, but she stopped and stood, her hair back-lit by the mid-alley bulb. "Afraid the boogie man'll getcha?"

"Not afraid," he said calmly. "Just using my head." Then he added, "I've seen a boogie man."

"Corny knows," Valerie answered succinctly. "Though why he cares is beyond me."

"There's a lot that's beyond you, isn't there?" Max answered with elaborate concern, but inside him, her first words, "Corny knows," were still echoing. Just who is this guy? he wondered for the tenth time, and, looking toward the end of the alley, saw the man in black standing tall and still beneath the final light. All but his gray hair and the tips of his ears were in shadow.

Valerie turned back toward her manager. "Make up your mind, Born-to-be Wilde," she flung over her shoulder as she crossed the median circle of illumination and stepped into the farther dark.

Max flexed his hands, stretched his back, wished he had a gun, and followed.

As he passed through the median light, a sharp squeal snapped his head to the left, and he jumped forward into concealment, crouched and ready, his mind hardening itself against onslaughts. But facing him was only a narrow window looking in on a dimly lit warehouse, where three old women in purple aprons were making fortune cookies. Their ancient machines, rattling and shrieking, served them precut dough which they folded around their messages, scooped from a community bowl before them.

The image of the Three Fates did not escape Max's notice.

Mr. Cornelius's voice drifted down along the alley. "They were the daughters of Night—and all but ignored in their own time. It took Shakespeare to paint them large enough for us."

"Funny," Max said levelly, straightening up. "They don't look British."

"Come along, Mr. August," answered Cornelius with a hint of amusement. "I promise, I'll explain everything."

So Max turned and followed his host and hostess through the door at the end of the alley . . . and entered a restaurant.

. . . . .

The restaurant was small but bright, with waiters in the baggy white jackets of waiters everywhere, and a sizable number of patrons who were mostly but not exclusively Chinese. Max, taking it all in, felt vaguely disappointed.

They were given a reserved table in the far corner. "Why don't we order first?" asked Cornelius. "I'm famished."

"It's your show," Max said. He had only one favorite among Chinese food, sweet and sour anything, and he fell back on the pork.

Valerie, on the other hand, began her order with questions about the waiter's family and his cat, before turning to a selection of dishes Max didn't recognize. And Cornelius did his ordering in Chinese.

Watching Cornelius in action, Max could only liken him to one of the great defense lawyers, Belli or Bailey or Foreman, whose every action was dramatized but completely effective. The man was confidence personified, and it was not a show. Max would have seen that at once, as he had with Valerie. No, this was one of the rare, few men who are perfectly at ease in any environment, whether obliged to melt into the background while his star held center stage or to take the stage himself.

Max, no stranger to confidence himself, began to brighten up simply sitting in his company. Now it was Valerie Drake, the Star, whose turn it was to fade.

"So you can help me find my lion, huh?" Max asked as the waiter brought their tea.

"I can."

"Do you know where it is now?"

"I can find out." Cornelius turned to Valerie, who was watching them both intently, her chin resting on tented fingers. "Woman, why don't you tell Mr. August what exactly it is that I do. I think it would sound less biased, coming from you." The word *woman*, in Cornelius's mouth, sounded not the least bit demeaning; rather it had the ring of respect about it, an acknowledgment of differences among equals. And it had the unmistakable ring of someone who has earned the right to use it. Max, having assumed Cornelius old enough to be Valerie's father, marked that ring carefully.

"Well," she said. "What it is that you do . . ." She sat back and rubbed her chin with one hand before looking toward Max with cold eyes. "For publicity purposes, and casual encounters, we call him my manager. But he could more accurately be considered my . . . wizard."

"Wizard," echoed Max, his tone flat.

"Wizard. Yes. You remember the Maharishi, of course; the guru the Beatles went to India to see?"

"I remember him. He followed them back to the West to become the Colonel Sanders of meditation."

"That's right." She was doing what she'd been asked, but without unbending any more than she had to. "The Beatles had gotten their success act together, and they decided they wanted to get their heads together, too. They went looking for a holy man, and they liked what they found, and they told their friends—hell, they told the whole world—and pretty soon more people made the pilgrimage, and then more, and then some more. After an astoundingly short time, most of the rock scene was into higher consciousness—"

"—or drugs."

"—or drugs. But that was always true." She looked down her nose at him. "The point here is consciousness. People learned it was there—that there was something more to life, let alone music, than met the eye or ear. So it got to be hot for a while. And then something new came along, and the vogue died away. But the knowledge of consciousness had been introduced. It was still available if you wanted it. And some people still did. Not, now, for itself, but for the benefits it could bring to their careers."

"I don't get it."

"I'm sure. But just think, okay? There are guys around who *know* something. They do astrology, Tarot—maybe they read babies' entrails, I don't know or care—but they *know.* And what does any manager do if not *pretend* to know? Is Country coming in or going out? Will people be buying records or attending concerts? Am I better suited to large halls or small clubs this coming year? That's what you have to *know* to stay on top, and the wizards can tell you."

Max sat back, his face showing disgust. "Miss Drake," he said. "Mr. Cornelius. I can believe in ESP. Psi power. Mental energy. Yes. But knowing something before it happens? *Knowing* the future? No, I don't think so. That doesn't compute."

"All *I* know," said Valerie with a note of triumph, "is that Corny's been right for me, every time. I wasn't so sure of him either, when he took me on, but look where I am today. I'm a star, whether you like it or not.

"And I'm not the only one. Mick Jagger has a wizard. So does Rod Stewart. And Johnny Carson was supposed to have been—"

Max held up his hand to cut her off. He stared at her, and as far as he could tell, she was sincere. This was not an act like her public persona. That had been a good act, but he had seen beneath it. What he saw and heard here was a woman who really believed she worked with a wizard.

Mr. Cornelius said, "Now what would you like to ask *me*?"

Max stuck his hand out, palm up. "First, let me see some identification."

The man in black lifted his shoulder and dug into his hip pocket, coming up with his wallet. He opened it to reveal a thick slab of currency, in American green and other colors; from behind that he removed a faded green document, which proved to be a West German passport. Inside, a photo with an ironic smile balanced the data on Heinrich von Nettesheim Cornelius, Köln. Sixty-seven years old. Unmarried. Riffling the pages, Max saw nearly thirty entry stamps, mostly from the U.S. The passport was two years old.

"To be perfectly accurate, my name is pronounced Kor-nay-lee-oos," said the man in black, "but a man as traveled as I must learn to adapt to prevailing standards. 'Cornelius' is acceptable."

"You speak English very well."

"And French," added Valerie. "And Spanish, Portuguese, Mallorquin, Swedish and Danish, Hebrew—" She was interrupted by the arrival of their waiter with their food.

While Max looked at his watch, thought of Suzanna, and reached for the rice, Cornelius waved off his protégée's enthusiasm. "I have a facility for systems of logic. Languages, mathematics, physics . . . astrology. There is nothing exceptional about my facility, or any of these systems."

"Keep talking," said Max.

"Astrology is the oldest science," said Cornelius quietly. "From the moment of creation of the cosmos, be it by way of God or the Big Bang, each individual part of it has exerted an influence on every other, as Newton proved. The distances between the parts has become, in some cases, unimaginably great, but the equation holds for all that. The Moon, at a distance of two hundred thirty-nine thousand miles, still exerts a pull on the liquids of the Earth. The pull of Mars must be much less, and yet it must exist. And at whatever strength, this pull will be the same for everything on this planet. This remains the case for each planet in turn, all the way out to Pluto.

"People have known these principles for more than thirty-two thousand years of recorded history. It is only in the past three hundred years that Rationalism has declared itself exclusive on this world, and denied all that cannot be measured in its scales. I shall not bore you with a recitation of Rationalism's repeated discoveries that one reason it could not measure something was that its measuring devices were inadequate; the seemingly unending litany of benign substances suddenly found to cause cancer is but the most recent.

"But please understand me. I do not dismiss Rationalism. To be certain of facts is the only way to advance. But to believe one knows the answer before the testing is completed is the worst sort of blind faith."

Cornelius paused to eat for a moment before continuing, working his chopsticks as if born to them; Max, using his pair more deliberately, had consumed more than half his meal already. Valerie Drake ate unhurriedly, her left hand out of sight toward her wizard's leg beneath the table. As far as she was concerned, Max no longer existed.

"Our ancestors knew, through simple observation, that certain positions of the 'moving stars' above them in their clear, brilliant nights coincided with specific events," said the man in black, laying down his utensils and picking up his thread of thought with equal ease. "The conjunction of Venus and Mars meant passion; that of Jupiter and Saturn meant the beginning of an age. Moreover, since most of the stars did not move, and thus provided a background against which movement could be measured, the place in which a conjunction occurred was found to amplify the meaning.

"It is a cliché of modern drama to show the ancient astrologers making foolish predictions; in fact, they and their art would have been quickly discarded if their advice had proved useless to those who employed them. Thus the Egyptians, Babylonians, and Chaldeans based their entire societies on astrology. Thus the magi—which means 'astrologers,' though all church-approved translations before this century refused to admit it—found a messiah, by following the stars.

"Let us skip over, however, the recitation of events which occurred when man *believed.* Rather let us see what has been measured in our own Scientific Age."

"Not so fast," said Max. "You tell a spellbinding story, but it's not as if people just up and changed their minds on astrology for no reason. For one thing, from what little I know, astrologers had always said that the Earth was the center of the universe."

"And so it is, for someone on Earth. The effect of the Sun on us remains the same no matter who is circling whom, and it is effects of which we speak.

"Now, one of the Sun's major effects is measured by its sunspots. These dark patches on the face of the day star are the most violent explosions in the unimaginable nuclear reaction which keeps us all alive. When the Sun increases its activity in this manner, recognized changes occur on this planet. Rational Science has linked sunspot activity to mass death through epidemics, the amount of albumin in blood serum, the water level in lakes, industrial output, migrations, Liberal governments, and the vintage years for Burgundy wines.

"Ah, but what causes these sunspots in the first place? Well, Dr. John Nelson, while studying the factors which affect radio signals for RCA, discovered that sunspots occur when the planets of the solar system form hard angles—ninety- or one-hundred-eighty-degree angles—to the Sun. In other words these planets, which science says spun off from the Sun, still affect their source through their movements, even as their source affects them."

"But still," Max said, "there were those two hundred scientists who signed a statement a couple of years back, saying there was nothing to astrology."

"There were one hundred eighty-seven," said Cornelius, "and

after they made their backgrounds as nonastrologers clear, there was only one proper reply to them—the same reply Sir Isaac Newton offered Edmund Halley, the discoverer of the comet bearing his name. When Halley asserted, on the basis of Common Sense, that there was no validity to astrology, Newton answered, 'Sir, I have studied it; you have not!'

"And that is what I say to you, Mr. August. I have studied it, and I know that it works, just as anyone who studies it comes to know it. If you now engage me to investigate the disappearance of your lion, I can undoubtedly help you find it."

Max looked at his watch again; it was five after nine. "How?"

"A study of your birth chart will tell me the factors likely to afflict you. A study of the time of the theft will tell me which factors were operating then. And there are other analyses I can perform. It will then be clear as to the reasons for the theft and the eventual outcome of it. I shall even be able to provide data on its current location."

Max swallowed a burp and shifted himself on his chair. His answer was direct. "Thanks, Mr. Cornelius. But no thanks."

Valerie said, "I knew it."

"So you did, darlin'," Max answered equably. "Though I must say, Mr. Cornelius, that none of what you've told me sounds beyond belief. Just beyond what I need. I've got my own plans for finding my lion and the lady who stole it, and I can do that best alone."

"Even if your opponent has extraordinary powers?"

Max's eyes grew colder. "So my opponent does," he said softly. "And so, to hear you tell it, do you. She's a psychic, you're an astrologer; other than that I don't know of a dime's worth of difference between you. So why should I risk it?" He pushed his chair back and took out his wallet. "You come highly recommended"—with a mock headbow to Valerie—"but I'll pass."

"I told you, Man," snorted Valerie. "Mars rising always works alone."

"I didn't disagree, Woman," replied Cornelius urbanely. "And yet Mr. August now has the option of accepting my offer at a later date, which he would not otherwise have had." He took a card from his billfold before him—a business card, pure indigo blue, with only his name calligraphed in white. He took a pen from inside his black jacket and wrote on the card, in white ink and a fine, old-world script. "My number in San Francisco," he said. "I can be reached there at any hour of the day or night, should you need me." As he spoke the last four words, the confidence in his eyes became a meaningful force. Max pretended not to notice; he didn't like lawyers' tricks.

"Thanks for the introduction to this restaurant," Max said, laying a ten-dollar bill on the table. "The food was excellent."

Cornelius handed the money back to him. "This was my treat," he said as he caught their waiter's eye. "Emerson, Mr. August is leaving us. Please bring him his fortune cookie."

"I'll pass on that, too," said Max, and he left.

Chapter 14

DECEMBER 28 • 9:15 P.M.

When Max pulled his Spider to the curb in front of QBU, he found Earl, arms akimbo, leaning back against the building and watching the sky above Sutter Street. So, too, was Max. When he had walked through Chinatown an hour earlier, the stars had shown in a clear December sky, but the stars were gone now. Heavy clouds were crawling in across the city's hills; the great television tower on Twin Peaks was no more than a febrile twinkle. A wind had sprung up, and it was turning cold.

Max didn't like those clouds.

"How was your dinner?" Earl asked, folding himself into the Alfa Romeo's passenger seat. "Mine was real boring, thank you very much."

But Max seemed not to hear him. "The clouds really came in quickly, didn't they?" he muttered, and took the Spider out of there with a squeal. Earl looked at him with exasperation, ready to set his increasingly abrasive friend back on his heels in earnest this time; but after that one look, he decided on the better part of valor.

"The weather is terrible everywhere," he said as equably as he could. "The last ten years, everybody's seen it. The East Coast has those terrible winters, Europe has the droughts. And here, you know, we used to have sunshine from February right through November, with rain the other three months; but this week was all sun, until just this morning when it turned gray. Then it cleared up at sundown, and now it's getting worse again." He hoped that would settle the boy down.

"Why is the weather so screwed up, do you suppose?"

"You're askin' me? Well, I've heard all the theories: the ozone layer being destroyed, sunspots increasing"—for some reason Max shot him a hard glance, which made him stumble—"uh, the pollution causing a 'greenhouse effect,' making the planet heat up. And then I've heard just the opposite: that now that we're taking the pollution *out* of the air, we're letting the Earth cool off. In short, Barnaby, like everything else, nobody knows. Situation Normal, All Fouled Up."

"Do you think *somebody* knows? I mean, *really* knows?"

"Well, I heard where RCA can predict the weather a little—"

"You heard that? Where?"

"Hell, I don't know. Really, Barnaby, I just read it somewhere. Engineers get a lot of time to read." Earl opened his window and breathed in the rushing air. The tiny Spider was rocketing over the roller-coaster ride of Fell Street toward the park, all but alone at this hour. The sky seemed to be lying on top of them. "Do we have to go so fast?" he asked.

Max smiled for the first time. "Bear with me, big fella." But he didn't look around, and he didn't slow down.

They went into Golden Gate Park on Kennedy Drive, slipping through groves of tall trees. Soon they came out by an open green, and there before them were the clouds again, now massed so thickly that they looked like molten lead—dark, but flickering with sullen light. QBU, always on, began to play a Stones oldie, "Gimme Shelter"; as its dark and eerie wail spun from the speakers, Max let out a bitter curse. "Damn him! I told them not to play that!"

Oo-h, the storm is threat-nin'
My ve-ry life to-day!
If I don't get some shel-ter,
Ooh yeah, I'm gon' fade a-way!

Max reached out convulsively and snapped the station off.

"Max, what *is* the matter?" Earl demanded, but Max made no reply.

Earl's face showed pain. He'd never seen his friend so keyed up, and he didn't like it one bit. He tried to tell himself that he was an old and cynical man, who had seen it all over the years—but darn it, Barnaby Wilde was too good to be acting like this.

Thunder rumbled through the heavy air and the asphalt beneath their tires as they took the final turn toward the bandstand. They had seen no one in the park so far, but suddenly Max stiffened in his seat and sat forward. "Look!" he said. "There she is!"

Suzanna saw them at the same time. She was alone on the road past the bandstand, under a streetlight which revealed clothes as tight as the night before; she wore no coat, despite the chill. Max was only five minutes late, but her relief at finally seeing them was clear. She raised one arm in an awkward, girlish greeting.

"*That's* Suzanna?" Earl asked, staring.

Max floored the accelerator. The fear was creeping up on him, the fear he could not name: the emptiness of the park, the clouds, the unnatural clarity of the night air just before the storm. He wanted her inside, off the street, out from under the falling sky—

And at that moment, with a blue-white explosion that all but threw them off the road, a hellish bolt of brilliance blew Suzanna Ward away.

Tires screaming, Max came down hard on the brakes, and the Spider went out of control. They spun three times across the asphalt, nearly rolled up on two wheels. Earl was yelling, grabbing the handles, the dash, anything. Max hung with the wheel. They spun one last time and went into the grass.

The lightning flared again. The girl's body was not far away. Max threw open his door, tore his seat belt free, jumped out. Only one thought filled his mind now, the one that was branded there: the girl with her head thrown back in a wide-eyed spasm of scream, her hair flaring with discharge, her fingers clawed and clawing the enveloping fire. Blue spots danced through his vision as he ran to the spot where she'd stood. He was moving on instinct, exactly as he had in the Madwoman's room, exactly; he felt as if he'd been the one to be hit. There was still a screaming in his ears: a siren, or perhaps himself. Yes, himself. But it was all in his mind, not his throat. The scream was the scream of silence.

He got to her, knelt beside her. Her body was scorched and charred. Her eyes were open but fused and white. There was no blood. He moved as the war had taught him, not thinking or needing to think. He leaned down to give her resuscitation, and his nostrils were filled with the stench of roasting flesh. He knew that smell too well.

She whispered into his mouth, "Barnaby?"

He had thought she was dead. "I'm here, Suzanna. It'll be all right."

She didn't hear him. "Barnaby?"

He held her close, her absurd adult body like a child's in his arms at last. She understood.

"Man called. Said he wanted to . . . give your lion back . . . but you'd be mad. I could help you. Help me." She sighed. "Meet you here and take . . ."

"What is it, Suzanna? Take me where?"

But she had died.

Thunder blasted from all sides; it was artillery, and not too far away. And then, in its fading rumble, came the worst of all. Even as Max poured his breath into Suzanna's dead and stinking lungs, he heard, within the thunder, velvet-soft and mocking laughter. A man's laughter, incredibly vile.

Incredulous, he threw his head back, face to the sky, searching, daring the clouds to strike at him. He saw dark shapes there. Eyes. And from them black bile poured straight down at him, striking his face and smearing his sight.

Rain.

Rain, thick and dark. The clouds had burst, and the pagan lightning danced. Massive bolts arced from one low horizon to the other, spinning a spider's web of brilliant and crystalline evil. The madness was encircling him again.

. . . . .

They'd been moving toward another landing zone, and Max was Point Man, volunteer. It was daylight that time, just after noon, and it was raining softly. The jungle was alive with sounds, mysterious but familiar, just before all hell broke loose behind him.

He spun back, his M-16 coming up, but the ambush was already complete.

They let me go by! he thought wildly. They let me pass to get the whole platoon! He went running back full out, to aid and assist—but it was fruitless. Thirty-five Americans had followed him into the trap, and the last of them were falling like sacks of sand beneath the withering crossfire of some fifty VC in the hills to both sides. Some of the VC must have died, too, but not enough. There were fifty of them still alive, and Max. Alone.

He thought of rushing into that fire storm like John Wayne, blasting wildly, taking out as many as he could before he died. But that wouldn't do any good, and with a bitter swallow, he knew it.

Instead he turned and ran like hell, remembering the song they'd heard introduced just that morning: "Gimme Shelter." Some of them had crossed themselves, and known.

. . . . .

A form blotted out his upturned, brimming vision. It was Earl, tugging at him, urging him to his feet. "She's dead, Max," he was saying; a fact Max knew. But this moment was between him and the force that had killed her. Beyond the dark head with the worried eyes, the clouds still churned and snarled, and the laughter was still echoing. "Do you hear that?" Max asked and answered, "No, of course not." He felt himself coming to his feet, the girl still in his arms, his face still toward the clouds. His eyes burned with overflowing rain and he shut them, or thought he did, because the sight of Suzanna dying and dead in his arms remained. Earl was talking, steadily, urgently, telling him they had to leave, they had to go, they couldn't stay here with a dead girl, it was no good for a man in Max's position.

"I can't just leave her!" Max shouted into the wind. He stumbled forward, toward the sheltering bandstand, the girl dead in his arms, and steaming. The rain wouldn't wash her blistered stench from his nostrils. He had to lay her down where it was dry. Earl was pulling at him, and Max said something he himself didn't understand, but his friend's touch fell away. Max went on alone, upright, ready for a second lightning bolt but knowing he would be spared.

He laid her tenderly on the bandstand stage, sweeping back her tangled hair from her saddened face, feeling the loss of that addled but vibrant mind under his hand, the forehead just skin and bone now, a death mask. He arranged her on the stage, folding her hands together, tugging down her skirt, straightening her sweater, closing her eyes, wiping her dry.

Earl was behind him again, and in the silence of the bandshell, out of the elements, Max began to hear him. He was still talking about leaving, over and over, providing reasons, thinking of the future; and in one sudden shift, time and space reset themselves like fractured bones, and Max knew that in the real world, the one that was still here now, his friend was right. There were police, and FBI men, and Northcliff and QBU, and the Madwoman and her friends, all claiming parts of him. And there was the girl on the stage, dead. In some other world she might now be bound for glory. In still another world she, and he, and the evil of the clouds might be forever timeless, resolving themselves and already resolved. But in yet another world, this world, San Francisco and the Year of Our Lord, there were resolutions still to be made.

He turned back to Earl. "Okay."

Chapter 15

DECEMBER 28 • 9:55 P.M.

Outside the park, from a phone booth at Oak and Masonic, Max had Earl call the cops, anonymously. He was afraid they'd recognize his voice, and he hated being afraid. He wanted to grab the phone and tell them, "I'm Barnaby Wilde, and Suzanna Ward died because she loved me, so the KGB could slap me down." But like that faraway morning in another dirty war, it wouldn't have helped. He had to think beyond the moment—whatever that meant. He didn't know.

Earl, climbing back into the car, said, "You did the right thing, Barnaby. The police will take care of her, but you can't trust the police to take care of your reputation."

Max said, "Just give me a minute, okay?"

"No. Not okay. Put this hunka junk in gear, or else let me drive. You're coming back to my house, right now."

Max lifted his head as if coming awake, or seeing his friend for the first time. He felt slow and stupid and washed up. It was all he could do to nod.

DECEMBER 28 • 10:05 P.M.

The two men entered Earl's house furtively. Like Max's idea of space and time, the bonds which joined these two had broken and reset, but neither was at all certain how. And as in Max's bathroom, neither wanted to really know. It was enough to have crossed the open street and be out from under the sky.

Beyond Earl's skinny shoulder, through the neatly kept entryway, Max saw a small sitting room and a small woman asleep therein: the engineer's wife, Fern. Her mouth hung open, the thin jaw to one side, as she breathed in and out, about to snore. Her hair was up and so were her mule-clad feet, pointed toward the softly speaking television. An old blue robe covered her. Earl moved on ahead, across the room to awaken her, and Max saw that the room wasn't so small, after all. A huge Christmas tree settled deep into its red and green support base filled one corner, its bushy branches hung with beautiful metal balls and figurines and strings of popcorn. The shawl-draped couch had been pushed away from its deeply indented accustomed place, and the TV squatted in front of the record player. Tightly patterned wallpaper was covered with framed photographs, of younger Earls beside other young men before street-front call letters: WMCA, WCFL, WXYZ, KMOX. The smell of good food hung over all.

Fern came awake reluctantly, yawning and scratching, until she saw her visitor standing irresolutely in the hall. Then she shot a sharp glance at her husband and sat up fast. "Max! Goodness gracious—please come sit down. Earl, why don't you offer the man a drink? You must both be cold. And some of the Christmas ham—"

"Now, mother," said Earl, kissing her cheek. "Barnaby and I have some things to talk over, so you just run on up to bed." He turned off the television. "That's a rerun. They always show reruns the last week of the year."

She looked him in the eye, and something passed between them. "Okay, pappy," she said. "Never argue with the media. Isn't that what they say, Max? Are you sure I couldn't make you a ham sandwich? It's a real good ham."

"No, thanks, Fern." The jock tried to return her smile and couldn't quite. "I'm okay."

She gave him a quizzical appraisal, but said only, "All right, boys. The room is yours. Way past my bedtime, anyhow." She looked the room over quickly, then left, her mules clacking. "Good night, Max," she called from the bottom of the stairs.

Earl waved a hand at the sofa as he, too, left the room, coming back two minutes later with two mugs of coffee—cream in his, Max's black, as always. He settled down facing Max along the couch, balanced his mug on his skinny knee, and spoke firmly.

"Okay, Barnaby. Now you tell me everything that's bothering you."

"You wouldn't believe it."

"I can try. We've gotten through a lot of rough spots before now, son."

Max gave in. "Earl, I don't know what's happening to me."

"That's not like you."

"You bet it's not!" Max's head came up, his face bleak. "I never met a situation yet I couldn't solve, one way or another. Not even in . . . Nam. But I can't get any sort of grip on this."

"You don't think the girl was struck by accident, do you?"

"There. You see? No, I know you don't." He paused, backed up. "Earl, I don't *think* it was deliberate; I *know* it was deliberate. I know it because I'm the only one who's seen it all. The rest of you—you, Hardesty, Hamoto—you've only seen parts. You were right beside me tonight, but you only saw part of it. And you didn't *hear* it at all, did you?"

"Hear it? Hear what? That's the second time you've asked me that."

Max turned his head toward him, his eyes powerful, probing. "What would you say to me, honestly, as a friend, if I told you—dammit, I *am* telling you, that I heard laughter coming down from the clouds after Suzanna died. What would you say?"

Earl hesitated, licked his lips. He felt a sinking feeling. "I would say—"

"Never mind. I can see it in your face."

"Barnaby, I don't know. It sounds crazy, sure—but I guess anything's possible now."

"The FBI says it's psychic power."

"I don't follow."

"The FBI is in with the cops on this case. One of their agents laid it out for me this morning. Russia has psychic secret agents, and they're behind all this. He gave me lots of facts; I could follow it. ESP. Mind over matter. Illusions.

"So okay—so they have extra weapons. But they're still flesh-and-blood people. They have their limitations like the rest of us, and in a fair fight, I'd go up against them. In Nam I went into full-fledged jungle warfare just as dumb and raw as you can imagine. But I learned. In its own way it was the same in radio. If you really want to succeed in anything, that's half the battle, right there. So no matter what they threw against me, I was willing to give the Russians my best shot and take my chances. That's the way I am." He shook his head. "But now I just don't know."

"Are you saying you'd have gotten killed over this—this carving?"

"Not just that. It's . . . what it must be like to be raped. You live in a world with a sense of boundaries; there are public places and private places. One of those private places, as corny as it sounds, is your house. Somebody breaking in and taking something you had put in your own room, on your own table, safe—it grates on you, like a paper cut. No matter how many times you feel it, you can't feel it without a shudder—and you can't live without feeling it again and again.

"It's a violation, that's all. And it's ten times as bad when it's your trust that was violated. I was falling in love with Madeleine Riggs. I trusted her. I took her to bed. And that means something to me. Now I can't think of her without wanting to break her face. It's just that intense. I don't want her dead, but I don't want her running free, either. I want her in the slammer, and I want my lion back in its room." He drained his coffee in a gulp.

"But how can I do any of that if I can't get a grip on her, or her friends? Maybe I can get a line on her, but what is it I'm really getting into? The KGB was responsible for that lightning bolt tonight. Maybe they were responsible for the whole storm. You see, I don't know. Despite what I've been told, this has gone far beyond ESP. It just keeps getting bigger and bigger, and I'm getting lost."

Earl sipped at his coffee. He rolled it in his mouth. He put the mug back squarely on his knee. "Do you think the FBI was lying to you?" he asked finally.

"No, I don't. I think the guy was talking straight; it cost him too much to do it—just like this is costing me. But what if the FBI is in over its head, too?"

Earl looked at the cluttered room. He couldn't find what he sought. "Are you suggesting magic, or something?" he asked quietly.

"Or something. I *think*."

The looks on the two men's faces were full of pain. Earl wanted to help, more than anything else in the world. Barnaby Wilde was like a son to him, the son he and Fern had never had, and sons should be helped when they've run out their string. It didn't matter that the son sometimes caused him grief. But there was nothing he could do.

Nothing.

A car drove by outside, the shush of its tires in the rain a familiar sound gone bad. Max sat up. "Earl, I'm going to stay out of circulation for a while—away from you, and the station, and anyone else who might suffer because of me."

"Stuff and nonsense."

"I mean it. Call Cassidy after I leave and have him take my show for the next week. Let Northcliff take care of the managing, if they want. I'll handle my own problem by my own self."

Earl looked at Max's face. Max looked back. This time, they knew each other perfectly. "All right, Barnaby," Earl said, chewing his lip. He couldn't think of anything else. Max August stood up.

The two men walked across the close room, out into the night, and stood on the concrete front stoop. Wet leaves scuffed and skittered around their feet. A dog barked.

"You really heard laughter in the sky?" Earl asked quietly.

"Yes." Pause.

"Okay." Pause. "Okay, then." Earl stuck out his hand, and Max took it in both of his. "Good luck to you, Max," Earl said. "Very good luck."

"Sure."

Chapter 16

DECEMBER 28 • 11:05 P.M.

The drive back home was endless. Dead air. He reached for the radio but didn't finish the motion. It had to be dead air now. The rain smeared the windows and he let it go. He wished he liked cigarettes.

He'd been wrong to involve Earl; all he'd done was show the old man that he couldn't help him, and that was cruel. Whatever the problem, Max should have handled it himself. That's the Point Man's job.

But there was no golden glow anymore. No sense of vibrant life.

Just dead air.

At last, he wheeled up onto his street. His porch light hung alone among its neighbors, a phony golden glow winking through the windshield's film. He pulled up and got out and trudged toward it. The sky did not strike him dead, or even sound its thunder.

But when he opened his front door, he saw wet footprints in the foyer.

And a smile spread across his face.

Because they were real.

His smile tightening, he stepped firmly across the threshold and closed the door behind him. He flipped the light switch, and when nothing happened, he laughed.

But something small skittered over the tiles past his feet.

And right after, something large vaulted out of the shadows and threw him to the floor.

Max felt it coming, as only a soldier from a shooting war could. There was the soft grunt of breath, the miff of folding cloth; the total containing a message as sure as the fly ball the outfielder knows just how far to run in for. Max's arms were already coming up to shield his face as the man piled into him, and he fell with both legs high, letting his back take the brunt of the impact, loosing his breath to absorb it. There was no fear, and a surprising amount of pleasure.

He brought his knee up hard, and was rewarded with a blast of hot breath and saliva. The man brought his thighs together to protect himself, but Max's knee was still there, and he used it now as a lever to lift the man up and over his head. There was more pleasure in the sound of the man's head impacting the tiles, and Max was already moving, getting back to his feet, almost laughing out loud.

It was only his continuous motion that saved him. A shot broke the darkness, aimed where he had been. Max had a split-second impression in the moment of the gun's flash that the man behind the gun had white hair.

Max lashed out and caught the gun hand in a solid grip. The two men went down and rolled across the floor, crashing painfully into the wall. Max tried to beat the gun from the white-haired man's hand, smashing it against the tile or the wall, but his opponent had recovered his strength and was fighting with unbridled ferocity. Neither could clearly see the other, though Max's eyes had accustomed themselves to the dark. They were lost in a primal world of scent and sound and force.

Max's left hand was bleeding beneath its bandages, and slippery; the white-haired man ripped his right hand free savagely. The jock had concentrated his strength on the gun hand, and this would cost him, because White-hair's stiff fingers went straight for his throat. Again blind movement saved him; the fingers struck his jawbone instead, a near miss, but with enough force to drive his head back hard against the wall. Stars and streamers exploded in Max's eyes; for a moment he went blank. But some deeper level of his brain kept control, and his grip on the gun hand stayed solid.

Now Max went for the other's throat with his teeth. White-hair howled in sudden pain and threw himself backward convulsively.

By twisting his entire body, he finally pulled both hands free, and then was gone in the darkness.

Max wasted no time in following suit. He ducked silently into the living room and dropped down behind the far couch. Now each was hidden from the other . . . unless, thought Max, White-hair could see psychically. Involuntarily he ducked his head, though he knew that was useless if his fear were true.

But no sound came from the foyer, and Max raised his head once more. He could still see very little, but he could make out the familiar details of his room. He breathed through his mouth as he scanned his field of vision. This was another trick he'd learned in war: you look straight ahead, unblinking, while slowly turning your entire head. The result, an almost subliminal knowledge of shapes that didn't belong, came from the sides of your vision, where your night sight was strongest.

Any sign . . . any sign at all. He felt the bulk shape of the other couch, the paler gray block of window, the angular profiles of the stereo components in their alcove. There was little cover for a man.

As he turned his head back again, staring at a point beside the entryway and watching the entryway itself, something made a quick move toward him. The breath stopped in his throat, but he knew it wasn't his man. It was too small, and too fast. A quick dart of vision directly toward it lost it; he moved his eyes back to one side and it appeared again.

It was crouched just inside the room, very small, but stocky and powerful. Max felt it had large ears, like an elephant's, out wide. It stood on low, thick legs, and looked from right to left in unconscious mimicry of Max. Its gaze passed along the couch at cushion level, below the heights where Max's own eyes looked back. It was searching, but not anxiously or malevolently. At times, as Max's retinas tired, the little creature vanished for a moment, but there was no doubt in Max's mind that it was really there. What it meant was something else.

Abruptly the creature lunged across the room toward the alcove, moving like a gopher or a chipmunk, with swarming speed belying its bulk. As it passed in profile, the elephant's trunk Max had expected was not to be seen. Its face remained no more than a blunt oval, with just the hint of nostrils. As it neared the high cliffs of the stereo system, it raised its left arm sharply.

For the first time Max realized it was a Point Man. Other shapes, crowding and elbowing, came through the entryway behind it.

Watching their dark mass among the gray patterns of his peripheral vision, forced to look anywhere but straight at them, Max August also knew fear for the first time.

And the next instant he was thrown face-first against the couch.

His head rebounded and fell; his body followed. Just before he struck the floor, he caught onto the couch and knew clearly:

(sapped by White-hair)

(didn't see him come in)

(will kill me if I go under now)

He gritted his teeth and rode out the impact with the floor. His right hand came up like heavy meat and blocked the gun butt arcing toward his eyes. The butt instead glanced off his forehead, ripping the burns just an inch above the fragile nose bridge whose collapse would have driven bones into his brain.

He forced himself to strike back, thrusting one open palm past the length of White-hair's arm against the chin beyond. He saw the shadowed head snap back, but a follow-up blow with his other hand missed, and the gun detonated over his left ear with an immediate pain such as he had seldom known. He curled himself up and forward, driving his head into the other man's chest to throw him back, to protect his own head, and to seek the relief for his ear that comes only from contact with other flesh. White-hair fell to his side, Max grabbing again for the gun.

Now the mysterious creatures reappeared, scrambling to the top of the couch for a better view. The gun went off a third time, a useless blast that ripped a chunk from the ceiling and sent plaster pelting down on them all. The creatures started, but held their ground, pointing at the two men.

Max got hold of the other's gun arm, but he was still recovering from the blows he'd taken. White-hair's strength was unfailing, and with his free hand he tore at Max's hair. The trench in Max's forehead was split wide, spilling hot blood into his eyes. Max's grip on the gun arm held firm, but as he was pulled backward, the gun—just another dim shadow in the night—was moving slowly, inch by inch, to point full in his face.

The little creatures were leaping from the couch, crowding in for the denouement. Max had no time to think. He stopped resisting the gun hand and yanked it forward. As it rushed past his head, he bent the wrist backward and pried the gun loose. Or almost. The gun went off a fourth time. The flash lit their faces yellow-white.

Max rolled to one side, blind and choking on cordite.

The white-haired man spouted blood.

Max kept on rolling, beyond the edge of the couch. As soon as he was shielded, he wiped his eyes clear and spun back. Incredibly, White-hair was already on his knees, blood spreading like a dark storm cloud across his chest, yet still moving, still trying to get up with that brittle drunken energy of the man who won't admit he's dead. He still held the gun in his hand, and the hand had not yet dropped. Max watched spellbound as he wavered . . .

. . . and then White-hair turned the gun toward himself, and pulled the trigger again!

The shot was as loud as the crack of doom, but this was not the end. Max could see the toll the impact took on White-hair's loosening frame, but still he did not fall. No, he did not fall, but pulled the trigger again—and then *again!*

And in the instant that the seventh shot tore through heart and lungs, all the lights in the house snapped on. Max suffered one terrible instant of eye-searing agony, and then saw his foe clearly for the first time. He was still on his knees, still holding the gun—and his face was split with a wide and gleaming *smile.* His eyes were wide open, stretched with smoke and pain, and looking directly back at Max. The man stared at him, stared deep into him, smiling, smiling . . . until those damned eyes rolled up and back, and his body toppled like a house of cards.

His head struck the floor with a carpeted thud, and he smiled into eternity.

Max gagged.

Turned away.

The returning silence was the sound of the grave.

Chapter 11

DECEMBER 28 • 11:15 P.M.

It took more than a minute before Max could force himself to confront what lay before him.

Standing there finally, looking over the smiling dead man and the pools of matte gore soaking his expensive Persian rug, he thought, It's been a long goddamn time since I saw a man die. And longer still, since I came so close to getting wiped myself. All of White-hair's muscles had gone slack when he died, including his involuntary systems; his bladder had opened, as had his bowels. It was ugly, and the more so because it was out of its time.

No matter, reflected Max dully, how accustomed to slaughter you get in the fuckin' jungles, no matter how many mornings in a row you get up and move out on a Search and Destroy—you spend all the other mornings, before and after, getting up from your warm bed and reading about death in the *Chronicle*. Your problems today are the time spans of records, and logistics is getting women into bed, and it is not the same, no way, no matter how you like to tell yourself it is. No matter if the skills still work . . .

The sight and the stench overwhelmed him. He turned toward a wastebasket and threw up.

When he had finished, he felt much better. His mouth, like his burns, was bitter and hot, but his mind was clear. He went to the bathroom to rinse, to put on fresh dressings, and to pop more Empirin. He skipped the codeine; he dared not slow down.

It looked as if he had won this one. But had he? The man's self-destruction, his smile—the scurrying, half-seen little creatures—what did they all add up to?

Max returned to the main room. The windows were darkened, as they always were when he was out of the house. The house itself was soundproofed. Therefore this struggle could not have attracted attention. But White-hair had shot himself. There had to be a reason for it, something Max wouldn't like. Was he to be framed for murder? It was all he could think of, yet it seemed oddly mundane for the people he was dealing with.

But maybe the Russians had slipped up for once. Even if White-hair had been here before, he'd have had no reason to learn about the special windows and walls. So there could be people—police, FBI—waiting nearby to be roused by the shots.

There was one way to find out.

But first Max looked for the creatures. He searched all around the room, but found nothing, not even with the edge of his vision. Were they invisible in the light? More unanswerable questions.

Worry about the tangible problems, he thought. First, turn out the lights. He went through his house, flipping switches, and didn't worry about how they'd come on. Sometimes, just after he'd plunged a room into darkness, he heard the scrambling of little feet behind him, but he didn't look back.

When he returned to the living room, he took a deep breath, and held it while he knelt beside the body to search its pockets. He found a Marlboro box with twelve bullets inside, and a newly cut set of his house keys. Beyond that, there was nothing, and that included the obligatorily absent clothing labels. The white-haired man was still smiling, and his eyes were still wide open. As he had with Suzanna not an hour and a half before, he pressed the eyelids shut; and now he pressed the smile into a frown.

After that he picked up the gun, still warm to his touch, and reloaded it chamber by chamber. Then he walked out into the night, to see who might be there.

Fog engulfed the hilltop and was growing thicker as it snatched at his body. The rain had slackened, but the thunder was still rumbling. It seemed to be only thunder.

The fallen pine needles in his front yard made a silent cushion for his boots. He moved quickly among the trees but found no one. Then he went along the side of the house, through the narrow walkway between his house and the fence. It was very quiet in that corridor. Only the fog.

The backyard was empty near the pool, but he couldn't be so certain of its further reaches where beds of flowered ground cover, whose daytime blooms folded in upon themselves at sundown, flowed in black waves toward the trees. The steep, rocky cliff seemed to shimmer. The fog touched them all, and joined them all together; it seemed to Max that a footfall anywhere the fog reached would reach his ears, as well.

At that moment he heard a footfall clearly—and not from a distance, but from the eucalyptus shadows just off to his left.

He whirled on it, gun ready and even eager. A sharp voice responded. "Hold it right there," it said. Max knew that voice. Hardesty.

Still he kept his gun at the height of a man's midsection. "What are you doing in my backyard, Inspector?" he asked coldly.

The fog boiled outward as the FBI man stepped forward. He, too, held a gun, aimed at Max. Then, from behind his broad back, came another man, an Oriental, but not Hamoto. This one was Chinese. His hands were empty, but the look on his face said he could take care of himself.

"Put the gun down," said Hardesty clearly, but Max held his ground. "I could shoot you for trespassing, Inspector."

"You'd have a witness."

"Not if I shot him, too."

Hardesty laughed, considered, and lowered his weapon. With just a slight exaggeration of the movement, he reversed it and replaced it in a belt holster over his left hip. The raincoat he wore slipped easily aside to let it pass.

"You," snapped Max at the Oriental, "come up beside him, where I can see you."

The man did as he was told. He stopped just behind Hardesty's left shoulder, and the two of them stood there quietly, waiting for Max's next move. Nothing showed in either of their faces; they were alert but not hair-trigger. Well trained.

Max lowered his gun. "Okay," he said disgustedly, "nobody's going to shoot anybody. But I still want an answer to my question."

"Why do you suppose I'm in your backyard, Mr. August?" said Hardesty. "I'm keeping an eye on you, and anyone who might come to visit you."

A chill ran through Max's tall frame, a chill he could not for the life of him control. But it was dark, and it was cold, and the tendrils of fog made everything seem to move. Hardesty, at least, appeared not to notice. "We followed you, August—from your station to your dinner, to your meeting with Miss Ward in the park. We saw your touching concern for her, your noble phone call. Why'd you go to see her, August?"

A jock has to speak while he thinks. He may not *say* what he thinks, but knowing which direction to jump, without hesitation, must become automatic or he's through. And Max was thinking that if Hardesty and his friend had been *behind* him, then they hadn't seen White-hair get in, and they didn't know he was there now. He said, truculently, "I'm still looking for my lion."

"Inspector Hamoto and I asked you nicely to get off that."

"So you did. But I didn't."

"You left her to die, huh?"

"She was dead before she hit the ground."

"So you say. Why'd all the lights go on a moment ago?"

"Who's your friend?"

"I'm asking the questions."

"In my backyard? Have you got a warrant?"

Hardesty avoided that. "He's in my line of work. He's interested in the KGB, too. Why'd the lights go on?"

"Gung hay fat choy," said Max.

The Chinese frowned. " 'Happy New Year,' Mr. August?" he said over Hardesty's left shoulder, with precise pronunciation and a gravelly accent.

"Well, well," murmured Max. "The FBI is recruiting outside the country nowadays."

"Mr. Xin is an ally," said Hardesty, and the way he said it made it clear Mr. Xin was not Taiwanese. "But I'm in charge."

"America and the People's Republic, together against the common foe, and all in my backyard," said Max, after a rich moment for the implications to sink in. "We haven't been friends all that long—not long enough for our secret services to be working together in joyous harmony—and yet here you both are. I guess this case *must* be top priority."

"With you as our best lead."

"Best lead, or only lead?" Max was pushing hard; he couldn't afford to give up a single inch, not with the secret he was hiding. "Is this all you've got going?"

"We're making progress."

"What's the scam on my dinner partners, then?"

"Heinrich Cornelius and Valerie Drake? They're clean as far as I know. Why? Do you suspect them?"

"I hardly know them. That's why I'm asking you."

"And I'm asking you, for the last time: why did your lights go on?"

"I was checking a fuse."

"At this time of night?"

"I'm a night person. I sleep mornings." Max was getting cold. "I'm going inside."

Mr. Xin said, "We, too, are cold. As long as our presence is no longer unknown, will you invite us inside, as well?"

"Like hell," Max answered; and then came up with a reason. "I don't know much about the law, but I know if I invite you in, you're in to stay. And I wouldn't put it past you two to search the place."

"And find what?" asked Hardesty ironically. "This?" He dug a hand into his raincoat pocket and brought out a plastic bag of dope and three packets of cocaine.

"Are you planning to plant that on me, or smoke and snort it yourselves?" But Max knew that stuff, all right. It had come from his bedroom.

"Your nose isn't squeaky clean, August. I found this this afternoon, and I can bust your ass any time—for this, for leaving the scene of an accident, and ten other things. Don't think I haven't considered it—or that your reputation and connections with that stooge Hamoto would save you if I did."

A wave of unreasoning anger swept Max, and his eyes flicked involuntarily toward his house. It was only a reflex; the next moment he looked back again, intending to launch an all-out offensive . . .

. . . and felt an uncontrollable shiver twist him instead.

Mr. Xin was standing quietly behind Hardesty's *right* shoulder.

The fog was undisturbed.

Max stared at the Chinese face. The light was too bad to be certain, but he thought he saw Xin smiling back—smiling, even as the white-haired man had done. With eyes that were deep and mad.

Max met those eyes unflinchingly; Hardesty was forgotten. "Good night, 'gentlemen,'" he said slowly and coldly. "May you both freeze solid before we meet again." And he turned on his heel.

Only he knew how close he was to the edge.

DECEMBER 28 • 11:52 P.M.

Reentering his house, Max locked the door well and considered his position. He felt like a germ under a microscope, but he'd been damn lucky. If White-hair's death had been set up as a frame, it had fallen apart, with Xin and Hardesty kept outside.

But this was only a temporary respite. The KGB was after him in earnest; first with a brutal warning, and then, somehow knowing he wouldn't heed it, attempted murder, with a fallback frame in case their killer failed. Or—*was it the KGB and the FBI both?* Or, he wondered bleakly, was it even that logical? What if the two blows back to back were just straight terrorism? *"You'd be dealing with a real lunatic, in that case."*

Nothing they did fit any of the rules he knew. It was all quicksand. He had to think, but—

From the living room came a moan.

Every hair on Max's body lifted, like a thousand crouching spiders. He felt the gun in his hand. It felt archaic. There can't be more, he thought.

The moan came again, more insistent.

Max pushed off from the door like a swimmer, and went to the living room entryway. He looked down where he'd left the corpse.

It wasn't there.

Instead, at the end of a wide, wavering path of gore, like some gigantic snail, it lay on the far side of the room. And it was grinning again. The chest, dark with blood, was smeared with long, thin streaks. One hand lay outstretched, the forefinger extended, the tip dark with blood, as well. On the clean cream wall, a single word was written.

NAUGHT.

Outside the thunder cracked the sky, and from those heights—or from the depths of the dead man's chest—Max heard again that subtle laughter. Confident. Mocking. And mad.

"You'd be dealing with a real lunatic."

Max felt it was he who was mad. The man was dead! he thought wildly. He has to have been! Max spun around with his gun, facing down dark corners. I can't handle this—there's no way—! And there's not going to be any way! I have got to get someone to help me!

But who . . . ?

Who . . . ?

DECEMBER 28 • MIDNIGHT

He found himself standing by the telephone. As he realized that, he stepped back. It was probably tapped. But he didn't dare leave the house unattended, to go to another phone. He went ahead and dialed.

Valerie Drake answered on the first ring. "Speak to me."

He spoke past her, keeping his voice low. "This is Max August. I need to talk to Mr. Cornelius. It's urgent."

"Hello, Max." She was distant but relaxed. "We were expecting your call. He's on his way."

"Let me talk to him. There are people watching my house."

"Sorry. I mean he's *literally* on his way. He left ten minutes ago."

"What are you talking about?"

"Don't worry. He knows what to do." And with that, she hung up.

Chapter 18

DECEMBER 29 • 12:21 A.M.

The doorbell rang.

Max came up off his chair instantly, and moved to answer before his caller could ring again; but he kept the chain on as he cracked the door. The gun was warm in his hand.

It was Cornelius. He was wrapped in swirling fog, and looking back at Max with reassuring intensity.

"Get in here quick," Max said. "I don't want you to be seen, if possible." He slipped the chain and stepped back; Cornelius swept in and pushed the door shut in silence. He had added an opera cape to his all-black ensemble, and it looked not only right, but natural. And—he looked somehow younger. "This way," said Max, but the visitor held his ground.

"Mr. August," he asked seriously, "why do you want me here?"

"That's what I want to show you. I'm in a hell of a mess."

"Certainly, but why *me*? What made you decide to trust me, after all?"

Max spread his hands. "Well, for one thing, you're the only one I know who looks even remotely like he can help. But for another—if you were part of the opposition, you wouldn't have used Valerie Drake to make your contact. At least"—he paused—"that's my gamble."

Cornelius smiled. "Just so it wasn't a whim."

"A whim? God, no." But now it was Max's turn to hold back. "How did you know to come here, before I called you?"

"I thought Miss Drake did an excellent job of explaining my methods this evening."

"But that was about rock, and long-term planning. Not spur-of-the-moment surprises."

"This was no surprise to me."

"You mean you did send that guy?" The gun came up.

"Of course not." Cornelius was contemptuous. "I merely meant that I knew my enemies would strike twice during the evening, and that you would be in danger. When I judged the events had transpired, I came to view the results. Now, let me see this 'guy' of whom you speak."

"Your enemies," said Max. And there was a lot more he wanted clarified. But having asked for help, he decided to let Cornelius get on with giving it. "Come on," he said, turning toward the living room.

Cornelius moved toward the corpse as if drawn to it magnetically, and squatted down Indian-fashion beside it. He turned the head to provide a better view of the face, studied it, and then ran his fingers over the contours as if he were blind. Max stood beside them. "Do you want to hear what happened?"

"Certainly. I am always interested in details."

Max told him everything, starting with Suzanna and ending with Mr. Xin in the backyard. When he'd finished, Cornelius stood up easily, fixed Max with his clear blue eyes, and asked, "Did the white-haired man have a large, black dog with him?"

"Dog? What about Mr. Xin—?" Max clenched his fists; the night was too far gone for him to keep being surprised. "No, no dog. But he did have those little creatures."

"Well, one lives and hopes," said Cornelius, with what seemed to Max a touch of sadness. "I didn't truly expect it."

"You lost a dog?"

"I did—and not, I should add, one of stone and wood. But it was many years ago." Cornelius looked down at the body again. "Your assailant's name was Hamish Rhymers."

"You knew him?"

"We had met. He was only a tool."

"A tool? Shooting himself four times—smiling—crawling across the floor after any other man would have died? Some tool!"

"Yes. Well, I believe he *was* dead, in a clinical sense."

"How many senses of death are there?"

"None."

Max scowled.

"Relax, Mr. August. We have work to do here. Every bit of evidence regarding this incident must be expunged from your home. Do you have any spackle?"

"Spackle? I guess so."

"Then repair the holes in the ceiling, and any you find in the walls or flooring. Scrub off every trace of blood, except in the rug, which we shall take with us when we go. Gather up every shell casing, and any other debris. Now, do you have a basement?"

"No."

"Someplace with enough dirt to bury a body?"

"Aren't we taking Rhymers?"

"I meant your body, Mr. August. It was what Rhymers was planning to do with you."

For the first time in hours Max smiled. "I think you'll find what you're looking for in my greenhouse. You go back down the hall and it's your last left. But don't turn on the light. I'll get you a flashlight."

"I won't need one."

The man in black swept away down the hall, and Max set to work on his tasks. There were only three holes to repair; all the others were in the body. The blood was harder; it had soaked into the grain of the wood, but hard scrubbing eventually took it out. And the gun didn't eject shells, so there were none to gather up. Although he was depending on the man, Max found that he liked Cornelius's not knowing everything.

When he was finished, he stepped back to the foyer for a final surveillance of the scene . . . and found Cornelius standing there silently among the shadows.

"Christ! Don't do that!"

"My apologies. Are you finished?"

"I guess so."

Cornelius gripped his arm with fierce urgency. "Are you finished?"

"Yes!"

The older man relaxed his hold. "I confirm it. I have watched you. Now come see what has become of your greenhouse."

"Mr. Cornelius—"

"We do not have all night. Come."

"Mr. Cornelius." Max's voice was steel. "I am not a schoolboy. I spend a lot of my time entertaining schoolboys, but don't make the mistake of equating me with them. You offered me your help, and I need it, but I won't be ordered around for it. We work together, or we don't work at all."

Cornelius spread his hands at his sides and moved his head in a half bow. "Your point is well taken, Mr. August. I have not worked 'with' anyone in years, and am perhaps a bit rusty at it. Again, my apologies. But when we are well away from this house of death, I shall be pleased to explain myself; so for the moment, won't you allow me to continue?"

That's one hell of an apology, thought Max wryly. But he had gotten it on the record. "Just so we understand each other."

"We are beginning to."

They went back to the greenhouse side by side, and in the gray light filtered through its glass walls, Max saw what he'd expected: a seven-foot hole where his tomatoes had been. But the marks along its edges weren't the wide, smooth marks of a spade. They were narrow, ragged, and busy, as if an army of chipmunks had done the work. Or—

"He had to have brought the gnomes for a reason," said Cornelius.

Max digested that in silence. Just then, through the walls, he saw a figure move beneath a pine. He nudged Cornelius.

"He hasn't sensed us. I've made certain we've presented no center." He pulled Max back into the hall. "We are almost done."

DECEMBER 29 • 1:10 A.M.

Once more in the living room, Cornelius set to work pushing the second couch, the one that had not borne the brunt of battle, to one side; it left an area some ten feet square. "Bring the body into the circle," he said in a voice untouched by his exertion, and Max couldn't help but be impressed by his stamina; he really looked, now, no more than forty. Max, at thirty, worked up some sweat hauling the rug and its contents across the room. Hamish Rhymers felt as if he'd become heavier as time passed; he'd certainly become stiffer, more awkward to move. And worse to smell. Max dumped him unceremoniously in the center of the open space and stepped back.

"I'll ask you to seat yourself within this area," said Cornelius. "I shall be making my drama around you." Max was struck by that phrase; he wasn't sure what the older man meant, but as a jock he liked the way he played with the language. Breathing shallowly, he took a seat on the floor beyond Rhymers's outflung hand, open like a beggar after alms.

Mr. Cornelius took a cane from a pocket in his cape. It had a head of well-handled gold, the hawk head of the Egyptian god Horus, which the man in black unscrewed smartly. The body came away to reveal a long, thin sword. "Now," he said, "make no disturbance until I have completed my work."

Max began to understand, if dimly. Cornelius turned toward the back of the house and stepped slowly forward, four times. He squared his feet, raised the hilt of the sword with both hands—and drove its point into the flooring below, his shoulders cracking with the effort. Then he dropped his hands and the sword stood quivering like a living thing.

Max made a mental note that he was facing east. It might be important.

Cornelius raised his right hand so that the forefinger touched his brow. He took a deep breath, squared his shoulders, became very still—and then, with a kind of heavy vibrato that reminded Max of the buzzing wind in a forest of redwoods, he spoke one word: *"Ateh!"*

Cornelius dropped his hand straight down. *"Malkuth!"*

Then up again, to the right shoulder. *"Ve Geburah!"*

And then the left shoulder. *"Ve Gedulah!"*

Finally the left hand came up to join the right, and they came together in the center of the cross that had thus been formed, just above the breastbone. *"Le Olahm, Amen!"*

Cornelius dropped his hands, and paused. When he was prepared to continue, he leaned forward and plucked the sword from the floor. Held it out at arm's length, its tip just higher than his head. Drew a pentagram in the air.

"Je-ho-vah!"

He drew each syllable out, without inflection, until the last of it ended with the voiding of his lungs.

He walked partway around the circumference of an imaginary circle, his sword held before him to carve the route, until he was facing the south. He stopped and drew another pentagram. There was a subtle difference between it and the first one, but Max, fascinated, couldn't tell what it was.

"A-don-ai!"

Cornelius moved on to the west, where he stood a long moment before continuing. His head turned slightly. He seemed to be listening. But at last, he drew a third pentagram. It began from a different corner, Max saw.

"E-he-yeh!"

Then he went on around to the north. The flash of his sword was especially savage now, as it traced the final figure.

"Ag-la!"

And finally he completed the circle, returning to the spot where he'd begun. He drove the sword back into the wood at his feet. Max had to admit he was impressed—enough to cast a furtive glance at Hamish Rhymers, to see if he would rise again. Cornelius was utterly serious. He could have been alone in the room.

And he was going on. Still facing the east, he stretched both arms upward and outward, the elbows bent at right angles and the hands bent back, as if he were supporting some great weight. In a lower key, and more softly than before—as if he had attracted the attention of whomever he had spoken to—he said, "O wise Angel! Ruler of the Tempest, Guardian of the element of Air, be present!"

Dropping his hands, he walked a quarter of the circle once more, and faced the south. He raised his hands and touched first the thumbs, then the tips of the gathered fingers, to form an upward-pointing triangle.

"O Lion! Ruler of the Solar Orb, Guardian of the element of Fire, be present!"

Max sat forward at that, but Cornelius was already moving on. In the west he extended his arms, then brought them back to touch the thumbs and fingers in front of his chest. This time the triangle pointed downward.

"O Eagle! Ruler of the Fragrant Abyss, Guardian of the element of Water, be present!"

Then he turned back to the north. There he put his right foot forward and stretched out his hands, the right one upward and forward, the left downward and back.

"Black Bull, horned one, Ruler of the Dark Land, Guardian of the element of Earth, be present!"

Finally, as before, he returned to the east. He stood there silently, his hands loose at his sides. Gradually he seemed to swell, his back arching, his head coming fully erect, his arms curving, the hands up and open as if carrying something. At last, when he was all but up on tiptoe, he abruptly threw his arms out straight in front of him, the palms turned away from each other, and yanked them apart as if opening curtains. His breathing was coming in rasping gasps. With that same sudden frenzy he snatched up the sword before him and marked out a new pentagram in the air—reversed from the ones he'd drawn before. Then he went quickly to the south and drew another reversed figure; and again to the west; and again to the north.

When he'd come back to the east, he spun toward Max, looking over his head at the full circle and the room and executed a series of dazzling two-handed movements with the sword, ending abruptly with the blade once more in the floor.

"It's done," he said. "No one will gain anything further from this house. Let us go, and quickly."

"You couldn't have said sweeter words," said Max. He bundled Rhymers in the blood-soaked rug with his box of spackle, his rags, and his used burn dressings, and dragged them all to the door. Cornelius opened it as Max reached his side, and took the front end of the rug. They went straight out into the fog.

"Do not look back, or to the sides," said Cornelius under his breath. "Do as I say and we will not be seen." Max just nodded.

And no one did stop them, or voice an alarm, as they went down the steps and out the drive. Pine cones cracked beneath their feet, but the sound was heavily muffled. It was just the reverse of his feeling before, that all sounds carried in the mist.

Waiting for them a half block away was a black Volkswagen van, its motor idling and its lights out. As they approached, the side door slid back noiselessly, and Max saw the beautiful face of Valerie Drake framed by the filtered half-light of the streetlamp.

She bent down and helped the two of them lever the body into the van's interior, before Max and Cornelius followed.

The door could only be closed by slamming it, so Cornelius knelt and held it to as Max clambered over the body and the singer slipped back to the driver's seat. Still with her lights off, she let out the clutch and the hand brake, and they rolled smoothly onto the slope of the boulevard. Only when they'd gone three blocks without a sign of pursuit did she let in the clutch, and Cornelius slammed the door.

"Now the die is cast," said the man in black.

Chapter 19

DECEMBER 29 • 1:40 A.M.

At the wheel sat one of the most glamorous women in show business, with her body encased in the maroon marshmallow of a down jacket, her dark hair covered by a print scarf, and her eyes sharp on the rearview mirrors. In the back of the van her wizard crouched beside a corpse, with only the right edge of his youngish face lit in the pale reflections from the windshield. And on the far side of the corpse Max coughed once and said, "You gave me a story earlier tonight—both of you. It sounded acceptable at the time. But this has nothing to do with astrology. I've also been told that this is a communist plot, run by psychic spies—but it's gone far beyond anything I'm willing to grant to that, as well. I've gambled that you know the truth, Mr. Cornelius, and you've promised to explain—so now's the time."

Valerie Drake said, "Yes, Grasshoppah—what is Truth?" But Cornelius shushed her gently, affectionately, while keeping his eyes on Max. His right eye glittered.

"Mr. August—or may I call you Max?"

"Max is fine." Quit stalling, he thought.

"Max, now that we are at our leisure"—he waved a hand ironically at Rhymers—"I shall certainly explain. It is, after all, your lion which has brought us all together, as you've surmised."

"Your spell, or whatever that was, mentioned a lion—"

"Quite so. Understand, I did not enjoy dissembling at our first encounter this evening—although I am, in fact, Miss Drake's wizard, and an excellent astrologer—but I knew you no better than you knew me. Moreover the average person—which you, in this regard, may consider yourself without doubt—is not prepared by his average life for the knowledge I possess, nor for the code by which I live. You would have laughed, even with your experience of last night.

"But you will not laugh now. Your innate common sense will find no other explanation to fit the facts. And I insist upon your examining all the facts—including what I'm about to tell you—for as I've said once already this night, it is through facts alone that one comes to know truth. Only when you *know* what you *know* will you—or I, for that matter—be satisfied."

"That's my credo anyway," said Max shortly.

"Hold on," said Valerie from the front. The van turned left and tilted suddenly as it left the hilltop road for the long, sharp drop toward the flatlands by the bay. The two men readjusted their positions, and Cornelius cleared his throat.

"Let me begin," he said, "by confirming that you are, in fact, confronting the KGB. In a sense. More accurately, you are confronting a single man, named Wolf Messing."

"Wolf Messing?" Max reached back what seemed a long way for that name. "According to what the FBI told me, Wolf Messing is dead."

"Dead?" echoed Cornelius, laughing. "No, not *dead*—devoutly though it may be desired."

"But he must be in his eighties. If psychic power comes from the mind—"

"The mind does not age, Max; it only matures. The physical *brain* can be rendered impotent by the physical body, but the mind, never." He paused. "And the body can be taught to live, as long as necessary. I, myself, will be one hundred and eleven years old this Virgo . . . September."

Max's eyes were learning the gloom in the van. He could see, now, the fine-lined, chiseled face in the shadows, the flash of powerful eyes. Forty? Sixty-five? One hundred plus? He sat back on the wheel cover, bracing himself for everything to come.

"This is a war between Messing and myself," said Cornelius, still crouched, untiring. "A war between wizards."

"I . . . think I guessed that."

"Of course. You are not stupid. I am a wizard in actual fact. I was born in Germany, one hundred and ten years gone, and for the past ninety-three years I have walked the path of the occult. I have mastered the decay of my tissues, far more completely than has Wolf Messing. It involves attunement to the larger tides of forces which sweep this planet. By itself, this is the way of the mystic: attunement and no more. But a wizard goes beyond that, and uses the forces which surround us to reach his own, reasoned goals.

"There is an ancient saying: 'Nature unaided always fails.' Humanity, like anything else, has its purpose, and humanity's purpose is to act as an overseer. Humanity alone of the forms of life on Earth has the power to regulate all the others. Humanity alone has a higher mind; this you learned in grade school, eh?

"The wizard, then, seeks to use his mind fully, to know his own mind, so to speak. He finds that planets actually do influence individual lives. He finds that humans can indeed communicate telepathically across space, and across time. He finds that rituals, and music, do put one in particular frames of mind. He finds that there are drugs which have more far-reaching effects, and then he finds he can go beyond artificial means to achieve the same effects.

"In short, he learns the ways of another reality, a larger reality—ways that are both clear and permanent. Naturally he remains a part of our reality, to all appearances an ordinary man like any other, but his knowledge comes from all reality. He trusts not fantasies, though he meets many in his mental explorations. He trusts only facts, and logic, and he does not deny any of the facts he finds. Then, like all other men, he acts as an overseer, but in a much larger environment."

Cornelius reached into a compartment behind the passenger seat and withdrew a Thermos, from which he took a long swallow before passing it on to Max. It was pure mountain water.

"There have always been wizards," Cornelius continued. "In almost all cases, they have chosen to obey the ancient aphorism that the four duties of an occultist are To Will, To Dare, To Know, and To Remain Silent. Wolf Messing follows few rules, but he follows this one. You have heard of his stage acts, his legendary performances for Joseph Stalin. You have not heard what he does for the State today."

"You're wrong there," said Max. Even if Cornelius hadn't warned him to do so, he would have studied the other man's story carefully. Here his familiarity with combat and with bullshit worked together. "Messing was a honcho at Academgorodok."

"Honcho?"

"Boss," said Valerie, not looking around.

Cornelius nodded. "But he was not *a* boss, Max. He was, and is, *the* boss. Dr. Vasiliev was only an administrator." For the second time since midnight the man in black raised his opinion of this young disc jockey. He was sharp, and well informed.

Cornelius returned to his story. "Messing controls the growing network of psychic espionage emanating from Moscow. It is an arm of the KGB, with all of that ministry's support capabilities. Moreover he heads a small interior cell, composed of fellow wizards—or shamans, as he prefers—who have worked with him a minimum of seven years. Some of these people were selected through the aptitude tests given all children at the age of six, and have studied with him almost all their lives. Aleksandra Korelatovna is one of these. Hamish Rhymers was a lower-level psychokinetic—someone able to receive input and energy from a controller." He added, with distaste, "He was also, like his master, a defector, though in his case from Scotland. His controller tonight was the double agent, Xin. A lovely crew."

"Does Hardesty know about Mr. Xin?"

"He should, but he doesn't. To him, Xin is the Chinese expert in *countering* the Russian psychics—Hardesty's opposite number." Cornelius snorted, an eminently European sound.

"Messing's goal, of course, is the goal of his masters: the subjugation of the world to the single Soviet will. The success or failure of that drive will be the main theme of the remainder of this century. The West has begun to recognize that fact, but would rather not; its leader, America, is a Cancerian nation, and always waits to be attacked before arming itself. Thus it has gotten itself far behind the Soviets in all aspects of warfare, including psychic warfare. It has fallen to those individuals who understand wizardry and who oppose the goals of the Soviets to counter Messing's threat. I am one such, for I have seen totalitarianism twice in my time."

Cornelius smiled. "Now, this is not as quixotic as it might sound. I am Messing's superior in wizardry. I have lived longer, and I have practiced longer. Despite the best efforts of his cell over the past six years, since I first countered one of his plots, I—and those whom I have chosen to protect—have remained unscathed.

"Wizardry, to reiterate, is literally in the mind of the beholder. The proper frame of mind is essential for success, and though anyone can learn what that frame of mind is, the ability to make use of it varies from person to person. Messing's students, his military apparatus, the Wolf himself—none of these, singly or combined, can best me."

Max blew air softly through his teeth. He respected self-confidence, but he was leery of too much—in someone else. This guy could be slingin' it by the shovelful, he thought, and I'm sittin' here with my tongue hangin' out. I'm not a fuckin' Moonie, even if I did ask for his help.

Max looked out through the front window to get his bearings. They were driving north along the bay, through the Richmond warehouse district; this was certainly not their destination. Most likely they were headed on to Marin, where Valerie had said she'd been recording.

He probed a little. "You say you're one-hundred and ten, but you look half that because of your wizardry. And Messing is in his eighties, but he looks most of that because he's not as good."

"Yes. He is good, but not *as* good."

"And does he ever wear a white suit?"

"Always," said Cornelius. "It was his trademark, on the stage."

"Well, son of a bitch. Aleksandra's other friend at the Hyatt." Max sat back and smiled, almost tenderly. Another loophole filled. More quicksand made solid. He looked curiously at Cornelius, in his all-black outfit. "The bad guys wear white, in your expanded reality?"

"We are wizards, not cowboys," replied the other with a touch of asperity. "We wear what we please."

"But what is wizardry? That's the sixty-four-dollar question, isn't it? Is it like magic?"

Cornelius snorted. " 'Magic' is a debased term. It can mean anything. 'Sorcery' is better, but it sounds too much of the Arabian Nights. I prefer 'wizardry,' which means, 'the work of the wise.' "

"Fine. But what is it?"

"I am trying to tell you." Now the man in black sat back, taking his weight off his legs for the first time. He took another drink of water, and stretched, making sure he was comfortable before beginning again.

"It is held," he said at last, "that there are four modes of existence, on whatever level, and that these, for convenience, may be called Fire, Water, Air, and Earth. I say for convenience, for these four Elements are not merely their manifestations on this level of existence. Obviously, fire, water, air, and earth as we know them cannot be the basis for all creation. But this is what the wizard means when he speaks of them:

"Fire is the *principle* of activity. Water is the *principle* of attraction. Air is the *principle* of interaction. Earth is the *principle* of inertia.

"Consider the principle of activity in the anode of a battery, and the principle of attraction in the cathode. What you have between these two is a closed circuit, an interaction—or an open circuit, and inertia. In a computer there are millions of these possibilities, and all the wonders of a computer are accomplished by a long series of such possibilities, some of which respond by completing the circuit, saying Yes . . . or by not completing the circuit, saying No. Yes/No, Yin/Yang, it's all the same. It's called binary logic. With binary logic, and the computer in which to use it, we obtain answers."

Cornelius leaned away. "This eternal four-fold conception is basic to the Western tradition of wizardry, whether one follows the pagan branch, or the Judeo-Christian branch.

"In the pagan tradition the four Elements were represented, quite simply and unselfconsciously, by the four gods in the agricultural life: sun, rain, wind, and soil. In pagan rituals the main implements are the wand, the cup, the dagger, and the pentacle.

"In the Judeo-Christian tradition the divine name of the One God, Yahweh or Jehovah, is spelled with four letters, IHVH. There are then four lesser names, which I used in my banishing ritual at your home. In Christianity itself the four gospels continue the pattern; Mark is vigorous and without extensive interpretation, John is mystical and profound, Matthew is for the instruction of converts, and Luke brings it all down to basics.

"Meanwhile, in the Chinese system of the Tao, we find Yang, which is activity, and Yin, attraction. Along with Lesser Yang and Lesser Yin, these combine to form the trigrams and hexagrams of the I Ching. And in all other philosophies, the fourfold nature is to be found; though as a Western man, specializing in the Western tradition, I shall confine myself to the terms I know best."

The van was slowing now, pulling up to the row of toll booths blocking access to the Marin bridge. Valerie handed the uniformed woman at the only open toll booth a dollar, and the recipient's eyes acknowledged that she knew with whom she was dealing; but a lot of stars live in Marin County. Then they were on their way again, sweeping across the magnificent serpentine structure through lessening fog. They were gaining the shelter of the headlands.

Cornelius continued as if there'd been no interruption. The

idea that the toll taker might have seen Rhymers seemed never to have entered his mind, though it had run past Max once or twice. "In wizardry, again," said the man in black, "there are the four cardinal precepts: To Will, To Dare, To Know, and To Remain Silent. And there are two more groups of four to which I now wish to direct your attention.

"First, there is the matter of creatures in the lesser realms—elementals, or, more commonly, fairies.

"There are creatures of Fire, called salamanders (not our physical lizards, but beings who live in and tend the flames); creatures of Water, called naiads; creatures of Air, called sylphs; and creatures of Earth, called gnomes."

Max nodded. "They're what I saw tonight."

"Exactly. And it was through their control of the cloudlike sylphs that the Wolf and his protégée have attacked you twice."

"I think I'm beginning to get this," murmured Max, mostly to himself. Once again he saw the gnome with his elephant ears and his stocky legs, crouched in the entryway. Something began to tug at his mind.

"Elementals," said Cornelius, "are elementary; they are the principles of which we've spoken in their lowest form. Elementals have no will of their own. Salamanders want nothing but activity, heat, and destruction. Naiads are beautiful, sensual, and hypnotic. Sylphs are always changing: spiritlike one moment, cloudlike the next moment, a breeze the next. And gnomes are always at work. Because they are the slowest-moving, gnomes are seen more often than any of the others, and therefore are known throughout our world, as brownies, elves, leprechauns, pixies, gremlins, or simply the little people."

"Wait a minute," Max said. "That's sparking something. I think I saw a naiad in my swimming pool yesterday. And I had a dream about gnomes the night before—just before the earthquake."

"That earthquake," said Cornelius, "was a result of the shift in the balance of forces when the Wolf took possession of your lion."

"All right!" said Max. "The lion!"

Chapter 20

DECEMBER 29 • 2:15 A.M.

The Volkswagen took the Stinson Beach exit, so it was headed either for the ocean or up Mt. Tamalpais. Either way, the smooth straight ride of the freeway was about to turn to switchbacks, and Max looked again at their almost forgotten passenger lying wrapped in his rug. Max never got carsick, but he thought it best to crack a vent anyway. He wanted to keep alert now.

Mr. Cornelius reached inside his black jacket and brought out a black silk pouch. He pulled its strings to open it, and removed a deck of cards, from which he selected one. He held it out in the darkness. "Have you a light?"

Max flicked his butane, and saw that the other man held a Tarot card. The Wheel of Fortune, it said. In the center was a turning wheel, like a playground Ferris wheel, with monkeys climbing around on it. In each corner, watching this activity, was a different head: a bull, an angel, an eagle . . . and a lion.

"These are the symbols for the four principles. The bull is Earth, the angel Air, the eagle Water, and the lion Fire." As Max snapped off the lighter and sat back again, Cornelius said, "Listen now to a tale of history.

"Some eight hundred years ago, in the declining half of the twelfth century, the city of Fez, in northern Africa, was the intellectual capital of the world; it had replaced Alexandria, after its destruction by the Arabs. In those days learning was restricted, not by Science, but by the Church; by coming to Africa, it was possible to avoid the Inquisition. Wise men from all parts of the known world passed through Fez, and thus, the wisdom of all known cultures was blended there.

"In the year 1200 a grand conference was held, at which the wise men—the wizards—sought to create a synthesis of all they knew.

For an entire year they refined the various doctrines their cultures had taught them, seeking universal truths; it is this process which the alchemists among them called 'the transmutation of lead to gold.' At the end of the year this conference had achieved two notable results.

"The first was Tarot, which detailed the concepts by which life is lived, in pictures so that language would be no barrier to the student . . . and so that this system could be hidden from the eyes of the Church under the guise of a harmless fortune-telling game, or even our familiar deck of playing cards. But a Tarot deck is, in fact, a rule book for the fourfold reality.

"The second result of the conference was the creation of four talismans. They were carved by the most skilled craftsman of his day, Octavius Morgenus, a genius with a feel for wood and stone like no one else . . . ah, but you know that. His first opus was your lion.

"But understand," said Cornelius. "Morgenus created an eagle, as well. A beautiful creature, of koa wood and aquamarine. The raw materials had been brought from the ends of the earth by the wizards, in preparation for . . . let us call it what they called it: their Summation. At the dawn of a new century. At the dusk of the old.

"Morgenus carved suppleness, and power, and beauty into that eagle. He carved the fierce eye, and the protective wing. He carved the contradictions and the spellbinding glamour that the bird of Jove must have. And he created the magnetism of which I speak, when I speak of Water.

"Then he turned his knives to the angel. Tall, thin, bewinged. Like smoke caught for just a moment in the random but definite shape of a man. It seemed to move in the woodcutter's hands, as if to escape the world of form altogether. He revealed it from limba, and holly, and quartz, and it was the image of Air.

"Then, lastly, he brought forth a dark bull. From red oak and black diamond he made a rough, rugged beast, with horns held low. Only the tilt of the head betrayed the calculated subtlety of the work. Depending on how the light fell upon the eyes beneath the thick, overhanging brow, the viewer could assume the bull was eating . . . or preparing to charge. This was Earth.

"These were the four signs of the Summation. The Tarot was a book, carried by each wizard as he left Fez, which would preserve the Ancient Wisdom for the next eight hundred years. But the talismans were to preserve something more than even wisdom. They were to preserve the world itself."

Cornelius stopped and wet his throat again. Then he handed the Thermos across to Max and waited for his questions. But for the moment Max was content to just listen. He handed the Thermos back silently.

Cornelius continued. "Only two hundred years before the Summation in Fez, until A.D. 1000, mankind had yet been in the Dark Ages. It had been a grim and brutish time, unimaginably squalid. Humanity had lived through it, yes, but there was very little pleasure in the living. Even then, in A.D. 1200, the Renaissance and the first flowering of an *ordinarily* higher existence were more than a century away.

"This was a transition time. And these wizards, seeking a better future though none would live to see it, oversaw the creation of these four symbols as powerful reminders of the larger reality. A wizard is still a man, and even the most enlightened spends much of his time lost to himself, unaware of anything save the immediate world, even as you or I. The only difference is that a wizard finds ways to remind himself of the larger world, as often as possible. Those talismans were to show any who beheld them what heights had been reached in Fez, and what could be reached again.

"So when the Summation ended, and the wizards left Fez for their myriad homelands, the four carvings went with four of them."

Max cocked his head. "Why wouldn't they leave them in a temple or something?"

"Useless, to world travelers," replied Cornelius. "No, Max, those talismans marked the true shape of the world. They should be in and of the world! They went where their possessors carried them and whenever one such met another wizard in some distant byway, he passed it on with an account of his observations and adventures, as a runner would pass on a torch."

"But wouldn't they run the risk of the carving being destroyed or lost?"

"There was too much energy involved. A wizard with a carving would be too aware to make such mistakes." Cornelius smiled across the shadows. "Even a nonwizard such as yourself, who did make mistakes, was driven to rectify them."

"But that's not wizardry. That's just the way I am."

"And that's the way the wizards were, as well." Cornelius braced himself as they took a sharp curve; they were definitely headed upward. "For four hundred years the carvings crossed and recrossed the world, passing through innumerable hands. In that time the Magna Charta was signed, the Renaissance began, printing was invented, and a completely new half of the world was discovered. Then, in 1600, the talismans were brought together again—this time in London, which had assumed Fez's mantle of the center of civilization. The number of people attending this regathering was far less than the number of four hundred years previous, despite the intervening rebirth of enlightenment; one, because although the carvings had remained intact, some of the wizards of Fez had died without passing on the history of Fez; and two, because competition between the several enlightened countries had begun. It was politically impossible for, say, a Spaniard or a Masai to enter England.

"This latter topic occupied much of the gathering's time. Some who were there saw only ruin in what four hundred years had wrought. What good was the growth of society's bounties, they asked, if society itself placed them beyond reach? But others answered, What good is man's free will if he does not face ever-greater challenges?

"It was a serious debate, but it was never resolved, because these people were part of their divided time. The glory of Fez could not be recovered, and the wizards split apart, into four groups. Some wished to continue seeking an ever-freer world, while the remainder wished to use their power to bring the world to heel. And in each of those groups, there were those who would act, and those who would dream.

"I shall not burden you with the history of the past four hundred years. It is only important to note that very soon, the year 2000 will be upon us. And that will mark not merely a new century, nor even a new period of four hundred years. The year 2000 will mark the beginning of a new Millennium—a period of one thousand years. And if you think, after all I have told you, that that means nothing, that it will be a time like any other time, then you are not the man I now believe you to be.

"In the year 3000 B.C., life for the mass of humanity was as absolutely disposable units, in the power of an unimpeachable leader. In the year 2000 B.C., humanity gained stature, as laws for the ordinary man's protection were codified. In the year 1000 B.C., humanity began to assert its self-interest, in opposition to the still-potent totalitarianism. In the year 1, the possibility of personal transcendence entered the human mind. In the year 1000, enlightenment dawned.

"In the year 2000, another new era will begin. I believe it will involve this world's emergence into the solar system, as humanity gains an even grander scale of being. But Wolf Messing believes it will see the final triumph of totalitarianism.

"This is the reason he and I are at war. We each have the power to shape the future, and one or the other must win.

"And at the moment it is I who must overtake him. In preparation for the new Millennium, Messing has set his cell on an all-out quest for the talismans. He has already succeeded in obtaining the angel and the bull; now he has added the lion. The eagle alone remains. And though he is naturally my inferior, the possession of all four carvings would awaken power within him which would test mine to its limits."

"But the way you're talking," said Max, caught up at last, "it doesn't sound like you have until 2000 to stop him."

"Indeed I do not . . . because our material reality never changes overnight. Even a great catastrophe, like the murder of a world leader, or the use of an atomic bomb, sets up a series of waves which affect reality for years. The events of the year 2000 will not occur in a vacuum, out of touch with what has preceded them. If all the forces of reality are flowing in one direction at that time, not all the wizards of Fez could do anything to stop them.

"I say again, the way of the wizard is to utilize the forces which already exist. The war for our future reality is being fought now. And Messing pursues a scheme to change the course of our lives very soon. If he is not stopped, he could succeed; and the events of the past would seem as nothing compared to what would lie ahead.

"This, then, is the truth you have sought."

Chapter 21

DECEMBER 29 • 2:45 A.M.

When Cornelius stopped speaking, it was suddenly very still inside the car. Max realized that it had begun to rain again. The drops were fat and heavy, rattling hard against the van sides and the roof. Could be some sleet in there, too. He hadn't noticed.

He bought himself a moment by looking out the front window. Valerie was still driving, and still quiet. He wanted to say something, but wasn't sure how to begin. His mind was digesting, sifting, looking for flaws but not finding any. It's all possible, he thought. It could be. The view through the windshield showed only cliffs and drop-offs.

Max looked back. Cornelius was waiting. Max said, "This Wolf Messing, and Aleksandra Korelatovna—they *are* real people, right?"

"They are."

"Only they know more than I do."

"Yes."

"And I—anybody—could learn what they know?"

"Yes. But it takes time."

"I'm willing to devote my time."

"Thank you, but I'm not willing to devote mine. The Wolf must be kept from the fourth talisman; that is my only responsibility now."

Max frowned. This wasn't what he'd expected. I thought my joining his cult would be the first thing he'd want, he mused. "What about your responsibility for Valerie's fabled career?"

"It is planned for the next six months." The man in black raised a hand. "You misunderstand me, Max. I explained the basis of Western wizardry to bring you into the picture as it is, not to burden myself with a student. I could not allow you to die, simply because you had inherited the lion of Fez; but all I am offering—certainly all I expected you to want—is protection."

"That's not enough, now. Not after seeing the whole picture. You can always use an extra man, even if it's only for the hand-to-hand stuff. I'm a good fighter when I know what I'm fighting."

"As in Vietnam?" said the other man, with soft meaning.

"What about Vietnam?" Max held his voice in check, but his eyes narrowed in the gloom. Instinctively he began to breathe through his mouth.

"I studied you thoroughly, Max, when I learned I was to meet you."

Max's voice was low. "If you've got something to say, say it."

"It's not germane. You will do no fighting for me." Mr. Cornelius raised himself with his arms and brought his legs back underneath him, resuming his crouch. "You are coming to my house, where you will be safe. Or you are getting out of this van and proceeding as you had been doing. Now which is it?" The older man's voice was impartial, but now suddenly impatient.

Max laughed, not quite sarcastically. "I am coming to your house, where I will be safe," he said. But hidden by the darkness, he thought, We'll see, old man. We'll see.

The van slowed suddenly, as the gate which blocks access to the top of Mt. Tam loomed up in the thin mist before them. Valerie stopped a foot in front of it and got out. A wad of keys sparkled in the headlights; the gate swung wide. She climbed back in and drove past it, then went back and relocked it.

Max had taken the time to study her. Now, as she put the Volkswagen in gear again, he said, "Valerie, besides the success, what's in this for you?"

She pushed a damp strand of dark hair back from her eyes, but kept them on the road. "Haven't Jane Fonda and Marlon Brando taught you anything?"

"The causes they push aren't as all-encompassing as this would have to be. And they're known for what they're into. You're not. Most of our argument tonight was over the mere mention of astrology, which turns out to be just a drop in the bucket."

"Well? *People* magazine doesn't own the copyright to my life. Wizardry doesn't fit my image, and I'm not fool enough to forget that, even if you are. If Jimmy Page wants to own Aleister Crowley's old house in Scotland, he only adds to Led Zep's notoriety. But Valerie Drake isn't after notoriety."

"Who's Aleister Crowley?"

"An Edwardian wizard." She took her right hand off the steering wheel and reached back to touch Cornelius's shoulder with that same casual affection Max had noted at dinner. "But," she said, "my manager doesn't like me to talk about this sort of thing at all."

She looked back at Max, just for a moment. "Listen, I guess you're not such a bad guy. I know the strain you were under, which I didn't at the time. But you have to realize that, for me, my 'fabled career' comes before everything else. You can't fuck with that and get away with it."

"I hear you," he said. "I'm sorry." Then he laughed. "I can hardly believe that interview was just tonight."

"I can. I didn't do half of what you two did, and I'm beat."

She swung the wheel sharply to the left, and they jolted off the narrow pavement onto an even narrower dirt path, running around the side of a great slope. Most of the clouds were below them again; six inches to the left and they'd join them. They crawled along for several minutes, with dying thunder rumbling up from below, and then Max saw the shape of a house, framed against the gray skyline. There was a low crescent moon above it, beside two bright planets.

When they rolled to a halt in a turnaround, Cornelius stretched and said, "Welcome to my home, Max."

"Enter freely, and of your own will," said the jock.

DECEMBER 29 • 3:00 A.M.

The three of them stepped out into the grip of a cold wind. They were high up, nearly to the top of the twenty-six-hundred-foot peak, and there was little natural cover. The house, a few steps above them on the slope, had almost a Victorian feel to it, though no Victorian was ever so large or so far from others of its kind. And Max could make out certain concessions to the mountain, such as picture windows and sundecks. Victorian sundecks? he thought. Somehow it worked, but he didn't feel like figuring out how.

Mr. Cornelius came up beside him. "I shall be involved in my work from the time I arise until the late evening, so you will not see me during the day. Please consider this house your own, and, once you awaken, Valerie will direct you to whatever you need. Sleep as late as you like, because I assure you we are safe from the Wolf, and the cloud."

"One last question before you go," said Max. "If I talked to Valerie after you left your place in the city, and then she came to get us in the van—how did you get to my place in the first place?"

Cornelius placed his forefinger beside his nose, and winked. "By taxicab," he said, and began to laugh. "Come on inside, Max. We'll call this a day."

Chapter 22

DECEMBER 29 • 12:10 P.M.

When Max awoke, it was with sun in his eyes. He had slept strangely, unconscious and yet not, his mind turning over and over. For some time, as dreams measure time, he had been aware of a warm glow beyond his eyelids, but only when his bladder demanded it did he let himself come to. He needed his recuperation, and liked it.

In the bathroom off his bedroom he had the feeling of being down in the Keys again. There was that familiar unfamiliarity with his surroundings; the openness, airiness, and leisure. Toiletries were laid out beside the sink, along with a small bottle which read, in Cornelius's script, "Balm of Gilead, Elder & Yarrow. For Burns." Max tried it on his forehead and it felt all right, so he spread it to his other wounds.

Back in the bedroom he explored a long wall closet looking for his clothes. Instead he found a selection of clothing for all occasions, from hiking to formal wear, in small, medium, and large. He selected a large terrycloth robe which covered him above the knees (might as well act like a vacationer), and went out to the Victorian sundeck beyond the bedroom's sliding glass door.

The deck turned out to be stained redwood, with enough vertical slats in the railing to provide the proper cloistered air. The view, however, was anything but cloistered. Sunshine swept across the vast grasslands of the mountain, down to the Pacific and out as far as the eye could stand to see. The weather had turned perfect again after its night of rain and oppression; there was not a cloud in the sky.

As Max had suspected, Cornelius's house had the slope all to itself. A small flock of wild deer far below were the only living creatures in sight. The sun was just past the peak of its low winter arc, off to his left, so he knew he was facing west. Somewhere down below, then, must be Stinson Beach and Bolinas; and the dark bumps almost hidden in the glare of the horizon were the Farallons.

Looking down from the deck, he felt again the reality of the wizard's thesis of polarity. There, almost invisible but there, were the lines between sea and sky, between sea and land, between land and himself. He saw his right foot and his left foot. Right hand, left hand. Which are reversedly run by the left brain and right brain; one does logic and one does emotion. Everybody's heard that. He asked himself what, of all Cornelius had said, hadn't he heard? It's not so much a mystery as a commonplace now.

But God! does it sound weird to say so!

He sat down on a deck chair. To think of wizardry as *real.* Just another commonplace tool of life . . .

If Cornelius was right, then wizardry was no different from nuclear physics, or politics, or anything else that a few people knew but most didn't. A war between wizards would be no stranger than a war with killer satellites and nerve gas. Both could kill you just as dead, and the nerve gas would probably be more frightening.

So what must it be like, to be a wizard? Cornelius seems pretty normal, but then, the normal we've got today is a far cry from all previous normals. What about someone like Merlin, who dealt in Great And Cosmic Truths when everyone around him was a peasant? How warped would that have made him? How had he gotten by?

Cornelius claimed that wizardry's been around for thirty-two thousand years; and it's had to have been hidden all that time. There had to have been very few men involved in it, out of the masses, and out of all those years. But today—? How many more could get in on that game in the 1980s?

If there are cycles of history—if things don't just happen, but have some kind of meaning—then what's the meaning of the mind expansion, the consciousness raising, that all of us went through? My generation was the focus for all that, and we're the largest generation around. We'll be a decisive factor in the world throughout our lives.

And we'll be in charge at the time of the Millennium. . . .

Max sat up and shook off a chill. Well, I'm in charge of *me now*, he thought angrily. And even if this didn't make as much sense as it does, it would still make more sense than anything else did yesterday. I've got my feet back on the ground again, and I know where I stand.

He got to his feet. It was time to get on with the day.

DECEMBER 29 • 12:40 P.M.

As he reentered his room, classical music began to swell from the other side of the house, so he went in search of its owner. He had never cared all that much for classical, but he realized he liked what he was hearing; and when he found the room it was coming from, he realized why. He was facing a music man's dream.

Six six-foot Hill Plasmatronics speakers—two against the front wall, two against the back, and two standing guard beside a group of deep-cushioned chairs in the middle of the room—were glowing purple as they worked; their mid to high frequencies came from passing an electrostatic charge through suspended helium molecules. Each speaker, with its own helium tank, was wired into a single ADS-10 Digital Time Delay to give the proper concert-hall ambience, and the source of the music was one of four matte black Nakamichi 680ZX cassette decks. Arranged beside these in a mammoth oak étagère were two Bang & Olufsen 4004 turntables, a McIntosh amp, preamp, and tuner, and a Studer A-80 twenty-four-track reel-to-reel. This was getting into studio equipment, and, yeah, there were six Neumann mikes standing to one side like ushers at a wedding.

Fully one half of the étagère was taken up with records, and the Keith-Monks Record Cleaner to care for them. What does a wizard listen to? Max wondered; and was fascinated to see that the answer was Everything. Or almost. He saw the Beatles, and then Lennon, but no McCartney. He saw Simon & Garfunkel, but then only Garfunkel. He saw Beethoven, Cab Calloway, and Elvis Costello. Judy Garland, Grateful Dead, and Gustav Holst. Turk Murphy, Pavarotti, and Steeleye Span.

The part of Max that purely and simply loved music was overwhelmed. He stepped back to take it all in once more, and for the first time saw the glass door in the wall beyond the hallway door through which he'd entered.

On the outside deck Valerie Drake was lying nude in the sun.

She lay on her stomach across three viridian cushions, head turned to one side. Her hair rolled across her face like a wave, covering all but her scarlet mouth, and as she breathed softly in and out, a loose strand bobbed and floated in the sun. Her body was slim, but now Max could see the barest hint of muscles across her back and shoulders. Holding a stage is not soft work, he thought. And he thought, well, she knew I'd wake up sometime.

He pushed the sliding glass sideways. At the sound of it Valerie raised her head languidly, and reached up to push back her hair. Seeing him step out into the light, she said nothing, but reached back deliberately to tie the strings of a viridian bikini top Max hadn't seen against the plush cushions. Then, arching her back so that her now-confined breasts rose into view, she reached down toward her hips. Viridian drawstrings lay to each side of her there, too, and a crescent of viridian cloth lay between her tan legs. With one practiced motion, she tied the three pieces together, and suddenly she was respectable.

It didn't make Max lose interest.

He went over to the redwood railing and hitched up onto it, facing her. His own robe made him no more legal than she. As she rolled to her side and sat up, he caught her scent on the breeze.

He said, "If we're just going to stare at each other, let's bet on who blinks first."

"I don't gamble," she said matter-of-factly. He felt none of her interview hostility, but neither did he pick up overwhelming joy. As if going through the motions, she said, "Did you sleep all right?"

"Yes, thanks." He took a breath. "Listen, I do want to apologize for baiting you last night. You say you know what I was going through, but I shouldn't have taken it out on you. I was an asshole."

She smiled. "You were, at that. But you're forgiven." She adjusted the top of her bikini, idly. "Corny would say that you've got to be something before you can be something else, but he doesn't always make sense."

"He made sense to me."

"So you believe him? You believe in wizardry?"

He answered carefully. "I'm willing to look at it. I'll believe it when I know for sure, like he said. But I haven't heard anything unbelievable so far."

Pause. She was still working on her suit, getting it just so.

He said, "Are you a wizard, too?"

"Me?" She finished her task and straightened up. "Nope. Oh, I know a couple of tricks, to help my work, but I really don't have the time. I'm a singer, is what I am."

"Like he's an astrologer?"

"Like I'm a singer." Her dark eyes flashed in the sun. "Don't you ever learn?"

"Hey! We're not on the air now. And I'm not going to sell you out to the *National Star*, either. Have Cornelius check my horoscope for you, if you think that. I'm sure he's got one, somehow."

She relaxed. "No. Okay. I don't think you'll sell me out. But I don't think you understand me yet, either. You take 'Barnaby Wilde' as a sort of joke, something to play around with, like you play around on the air. But I live Valerie Drake morning, noon, and night. I'm the wholesome Queen of Rock, always, and I'm very good at what I do—both the rock part and the Queen part. But it only takes one small crack in the facade before the Big Exposé, and a week after that, every mag and rag in the Western world will be reporting the Inside Details." She shrugged. "Once the bubble bursts, you can't get it back again."

"After the way Cornelius talked about Cosmic Reality, and forces affecting the next thousand years, it doesn't sound like you and he would have much in common."

"Max, Corny was a wizard long before he met me. And for all I know, he'll be one long after I'm dead. But like he said, we've all got to live in the world, too. He doesn't want to get out of touch. More than that, he wants to be right on top of things. So he works in music, which provides him access to the top nongovernmental circles in the world."

"Why not governmental circles? Why not advise the President?"

"Freedom of action, of course. And freedom of thought. Do you really think he could get more done through a bureaucracy?"

"No, I guess not."

"You're damn right not. Now, as for me, I want to be Valerie Drake, superstar. I don't give a fuck for power, but I give it all for money, and position. So I get the best manager ever born." She looked him straight in the eye. "And there's one more thing we both get out of this. We get each other."

"Uh-huh. I thought I picked that up."

"You're shocked, right? Younger woman—"

"And older man, a hundred and eleven next Virgo. Valerie, after what's happened to me lately, it'd take a lot more than that to shock me."

She nodded, then slid smoothly off the cushions and knelt beside a cooler. "Want a beer?"

"Yeah."

She handed him a Grenzquell and took one for herself. It is really hot out here, Max thought. The thin air up this high really lets the sun shine in. The crisp German beer made sweat pop out on his arms, and he loosened the robe around his torso. Valerie, too, was covered with a thin sheen of perspiration which glistened as she stood up and slid back onto the cushions, pulling her knees up and hugging her legs beneath her waterfall of dark hair. She looked gaminlike, delectable.

"Is that really true?" Max asked.

"Is what really true?"

"He's really a hundred and ten?"

"Yes. He is."

"That's a miracle in itself, as far as I'm concerned. No matter how he explains it. Who even lives to see a hundred and ten, let alone . . ."

She laughed for the first time. "Even science doesn't say your tissues have to wear out, anymore. It's just that most people won't give up some idea they had of themselves in the past. They want it to be 1900, or 1940, or 1970, so they're out of sync. They make themselves old by definition. But Life is happening Now."

"That sounds like something a Punk Rocker would say."

"Okay. Both punk and wizardry are antibullshit. But the kids don't have enough experience to really understand what they're saying. Now and nothing else: that's the point of punk. It's not the point of wizardry."

She stopped speaking for a moment, her lips pushed out in a moue from the weight of her head on her knees. When she opened her mouth again, the ease of the past few moments was half gone. But, Max noted with silent satisfaction, it was still half there.

"I'll stay with the Now, Max," she said. "I'll trust you like Corny trusts you, and put last night behind me—and we'll talk like the friends I think we both want to be. But God help you if you ever put any of this out to the public."

Max drew himself up, and raised his right hand for an oath. "I swear never to put out," he said, and gave her the Boy Scout salute.

She had to smile, but there was a watchfulness in her eyes. And still there was a need for trust there, too. In that moment she became enormously more complicated than the woman Max had known up until then, and he felt a surge of something more complicated than anything he had felt. His face grew solemn. "I won't tell," he said and bent forward to listen.

She said, "I was a Punk when Corny found me. Rainbow hair, razor blades, the whole bit."

Max looked doubtful. "You?"

She straightened her shoulders, as if sloughing off a great weight. "I come from Louisville, Kentucky. When you talk about desolation, for me, Louisville is it. Block after block of wide, empty streets going nowhere, flanked by tall, empty buildings, all deco on the outside and blank on the in. The sickening smell of fermenting sour mash over everything."

"I know the place. I did six months there in . . .'74. It didn't work out between me and the PR man's wife."

"I left there in '74. I had help. My stepfather raped me." Her eyes were bitter cold, remembering. "I got on a bus a week later and went to New York. I got a job. It was bullshit. One night me and my girl friends went to CBGB, and that summed it all up."

She stopped talking again, and Max said nothing, though his mind was awhirl. Poor lady! No wonder she didn't want this known.

She looked up at him. "Have you ever been into Punk?"

"Not *into* it, no."

"No. Because your generation had better things to do."

"My generation? You make me sound like an old man."

"You're in your thirties, I'm in my twenties. You grew up in the sixties, and I grew up in the seventies. That's a big difference. Your generation had a war to fight against, and big Injustices to fix up. You had Heroes and Villains. But what did we have? Nixon and disco. The collapse of the West, followed by a vacuum.

"That's why nothing ever lasts. There's always new people, young people, full of energy. And they don't know about your grand design for peace, or for war. They have to find things out all over again, for themselves. And if you say no, they'll roll over you."

"And then after they've rolled," said Max, "somebody even newer will roll over them."

"Sure. That's why I say that Punks didn't see the whole picture. But neither does anybody else.

"Me, I quit my straight job and started singing with pickup

groups in the Village. Finally I got in with a group called Jampakt, which played pretty regularly at the Club Ded, down on Sixth Street. I did that for a year."

"Under your own name?"

"No. I called myself Purina Dog Ciao."

Max laughed. "I heard of you! That's the kind of name you have to remember."

"I know." She grimaced. "That's why it's so hard to cover up now. But that's where I met Corny. He came in one night and called me over. I was real unimpressed with his fancy black clothes, but the first thing he said to me, before he even said hello, was: 'Valerie Drake, we both know you have talent. You lack polish, but in the past month, you have thought more and more often about how far you could go. I am Cornelius. From 1968 until yesterday, I was personal manager to—' " She stopped, and fluttered a hand. "No, that's not my secret to give. Can I have another beer?"

"Sure," Max said. He was fascinated by her story. Unconsciously, even though she was still hugging her legs, she was acting out each part as she came to it. A Punk strut by a seated woman had just become one of his favorite visuals.

"Well, anyway," she went on after a healthy swallow, "Corny'd been with someone very impressive . . . or so he said. I went and made a few phone calls, and he not only checked out, but the people I called were very impressed with him. 'Genius' is what I kept hearing. 'So why haven't I heard of him?' I kept asking. 'He's only tight with a few people,' they said, 'but with them, he's very tight.'

"So I went back, and he gave me his astrologer rap. He said he'd train me according to my strengths, step by step. He's very into details, of course; he never asks for faith. I could see how it would go, and it made sense.

"At the end I asked him, 'What do you get out of this?'

"He didn't bat an eye. He said, 'Money. Freedom. Power. You.'

"I almost laughed. I'd been expecting something like that. But—I didn't laugh. I looked him in the eyes, instead, and knew him for what he was. A real man. A real *person.* I knew he was proposing something far more important than a one-night stand—something more important than marriage, for that matter. I don't know how to explain it any better than that."

"I hear you," said Max. "Go ahead."

"I said yes to him that night. And I've never regretted it. With Corny's advice and training, based on both our instincts and his readings of the larger forces, I became Valerie Drake, the superstar. I take no shit, and I've got what I want, at last."

Max looked down at her. It was very hot. "I don't know if I like the moral."

"You don't have to. A lot of other people adore the result, whatever the moral. Valerie Drake, superstar, is a fine example of American womanhood, and I am Valerie Drake, whatever else I may be."

"Okay. I'm not one to preach."

"Hell, no! Not after selling out to, of all people, that bitch Aleksandra."

"I didn't sell out to her. I was being pragmatic, but I had plans." It was the truth, but even in his ears it sounded like a lie.

Valerie nodded solemnly. "Well, that's yesterday's news, too. Doesn't seem to matter much now."

Max got himself a second beer. "Do you know Aleksandra?" he asked.

"I know of her. Corny's told me a lot. She's sharp, and very sexy."

He ignored that. "She's also going to be very sorry."

"What do you mean? You're not still thinking about that, are you?"

"If you want to know the truth, I've never stopped."

"But that's nuts. You're safe now."

"Look, you be true to yourself, and I'll be true to me. She and Messing scare me a little, yes, but so have a lot of other things in my life. Someday, with or without your wizard, I'll learn what I need to know to take her, and then I will. That's all."

Valerie's mouth twisted in a crooked line. She seemed to be arguing with herself. She seemed to decide, then drew back. . . . But finally she asked, slowly, "What would you say if I told you you could see their base of operations from here?"

Max pushed himself off the railing. "What do you mean?"

She stood up and pointed down the hill, out into the ocean. "There," she said. "Messing's base is right out there."

He followed her aim. The sun was lower in the western sky now, and, black against the golden water, the Farallons lay shimmering in the haze.

"Nobody lives on those islands," Max said, but it sounded hollow. (Where does a wizard live? Anywhere he wants.)

"He stays on the north island when he's in this area. He was there until he took your lion, and he'll be back after New Year's."

"But he's not there now?"

"No."

"What about Aleksandra and the rest of his KGB contingent?"

"They stay together. They're all in Brazil, looking for the carved eagle."

Max turned her toward him. Her skin was smooth and warm. "Then why isn't Cornelius down there, too?"

"Why bother? This is Messing's western base. He'll be back, and Corny will know. Otherwise," she added, "Corny'd have to run around Brazil, not knowing where he's going, and that could cause all sorts of accidents."

"But why does Messing live where you can see him?"

"He doesn't know where *we* are. Corny told you, he's got the guy covered. He's saving this surprise for when Messing's done his work for him." She drew away.

"But he'll have all four talismans then. That means great power."

"At the right time. There's some sort of blowoff coming, and the power won't do him any good until that time. Corny just has to hit him before that." Her eyes flashed. "Shit! It's not my war! I'm just telling you what he's told me, and I wasn't supposed to do *that*!"

"But—"

"But! But! But!" They were getting into their argument phase again.

Max began to pace back and forth on the deck. This was a whole new ball game. Valerie watched him intently, without wanting to be seen in turn. She was breathing heavily.

Finally he turned back on her. "Where's my lion? With Messing or on the island?"

She hesitated. He could read the answer in her suddenly troubled face. "And there are no guards?" he asked.

Her voice was intent. "Not human guards. There might be something else. But I didn't mean for you—"

"It'll be a piece of cake."

"Max, don't be an idiot. You'll blow Corny's plan."

"Maybe. But Messing'll be missing three of the four talismans when the payoff comes. I'm surprised Cornelius didn't think of this himself."

"He did," Valerie said bitterly. "He did think of it. But the island's all high, steep cliffs." She was very angry. "He couldn't make a climb like that."

"Well, I can. I can pay him back for saving my ass, and contribute a little something to the pot myself. It's about time." He reached out for her. "I know there'll be danger, but there always is in war."

She would have none of it. She wrenched away, her hair swinging brilliantly black against the endless sweep of blue sky, and her hands in tight fists. She went to the far railing and looked south along the coast.

Max stood where he was. He was sorry to have hurt her, but his debt to the Madwoman went back farther. First due, first paid.

Without looking at him, Valerie said, "Do you remember your time in Louisville, in '74?" Her voice was strange.

"Sort of, yeah."

"I used to listen to you then. You were my favorite DJ."

"You're kidding."

"Cut the crap. You know you were everybody's favorite."

He smiled. "Well, okay . . ."

"You did a rap one night, just spontaneous, about having ridden the *Delta Queen* that afternoon up the Ohio. You talked about the rhythmic pulse of the paddle wheel, the hiss of the flowing water, the smells and the colors along the banks. Do you remember that?"

He smiled again, this time ruefully. "No. I'm sorry. I wish I did." He really was sorry. "I've said a lot of words since 1974."

Still without looking at him, she said, "You made going somewhere sound like the best thing a person could do. That's when I decided to go to New York, instead of fighting my stepdad." She lowered her head and sighed. "Go. I'll help you."

She came over to him, her face weary. "Corny has a boat, the *Poseidon*, anchored at the Bolinas Rod and Boat Club. I'll get you the keys for it, and for the van. You've got clothes in your closet."

"Will this get you in trouble?"

"Not if you're successful, I guess. Anyway, he won't be out of his rooms before ten tonight. You should be back by then, and you can face him."

She was so close to him then. He put one hand on her waist. But she turned away again, looking at her watch. "It's nearly one thirty. You've got less than four hours of daylight. Or maybe you should wait for tomorrow."

"Tomorrow's a long way off."

She nodded and walked away from him toward the sliding door. As she slid it wide, she looked back at him over her shoulder, her hair masking all but her eyes. Classical music thundered. Then she went inside.

Max wanted another beer. His throat was very dry.

Chapter 23

DECEMBER 29 • 1:45 P.M.

As Max drove the Volkswagen back onto the federal road, he saw San Francisco spread out below, very clean after yesterday's rain. The yellow-green hills this high up, all but barren of trees, gave way lower down to dark green pine forests, steeped in shadows; then more barren hills spilled out like tumbled bedspreads toward the city's spires. The Pyramid, as ever, dominated all its brethren. A hawk drifted slowly somewhere in between.

There was little traffic on the narrow road. A small blue TR-7 driven by a jaunty gentleman with cap and thrusting beard. A pale old Chevy from New Mexico filled with girls passing a joint. Three cyclists, side by side. It was a good day for a drive.

There was a Weather Report tape in the van's Nakamichi. Max punched it up, and the wail of the saxophones filled what turned out to be twelve speakers. One in each door, front and rear; high, mid-range, and low. Acoustically perfect, of course. He turned it up.

Then he turned right at the ranger station, away from the road which had brought them up from the valley the night before. This direction would take him down the far side of Mt. Tamalpais, toward the ocean towns. Appropriately the way became darker and damper. Trees sprang out and up from the steep slopes to block the sky. Ferns hung heavily from their trunks, and moss swaddled every rock like damp diapers. The air grew thick.

Purina Dog Ciao! Who would have guessed that? But she's still got some problems she hasn't been able to put behind her. Number One, the fixation on her career. Though I'd probably catch a touch of that if I were that big, and had a past to hide, he decided.

But her second problem's the biggie: fear of men. Her stepdad did a terrible trip on her with that one. No dating that I've heard—

just one older (*much* older) man. Cornelius and her career tie together as one big substitute for the risks of a normal social life. And now there's me, right in the middle of that. "Your generation," huh? Yeah, "my g-g-generashunnn!"

Well, I'm not as old as Cornelius.

The trees and the moss huddled closer.

Max began to take a look at them. Not as background, but as something worth looking at. Some *things*.

This could be spooky, he thought. Everything else—rocks, too?—alive. Trees and rocks as individuals. Millions of them. Billions.

And their little helpers, the gnomes. Leprechauns scampering through the grass—that grass right there. Sylphs riding in the clouds, and naiads diving like eagles into lakes and streams—and swimming pools. Salamanders dancing on the end of every single match.

It was cold in the shadowy valley.

How does Cornelius do it? he wondered. Can you really get used to a world like that, with no private spots all your own? He remembered his other times as the Point Man, and the cleansing solitude. He shook his head.

Around the next bend sunlight splattered through the trees against the windshield, and soon he came out of the forest. A few minutes more and he came 'round the last hill to see the coast sweeping northward in a perfect arc. Once more the sun was warm on his left side. Two hawks burst suddenly into his view, chasing a smaller bird. One of the hunters spun into a right-angle turn and dove, but its prey dropped simultaneously, and the three of them vanished beyond the ridge without a death.

A gate by the side of the road was draped in pine boughs and red ribbons. Oh yeah, thought Max. Christmas.

DECEMBER 29 • 2:40 P.M.

Bolinas was a one-street town with older, rundown buildings, and the hippiest people Max had seen in years. Big eyes peered out from under loose-knit caps and long bangs as he asked directions from a strolling family. A horse was tethered to a dingy white garage behind them. The grocery had a two-story false front. Tall trees hid the afternoon sun; it was cold and damp again.

The Bolinas Rod and Boat Club sat near the far end of the street, where the land fell away and the pavement kept on another hundred yards atop a causeway. Some ten to fifteen boats were at anchor in the harbor alongside, riding a rising tide. The building itself was a showbox set on pilings; inside, the big, rectangular room was empty, save for a herd of old brown display tables and one drowsing guard.

Max walked directly toward him, his footsteps echoing off the blank walls. The guard, a baggy-eyed kid about nineteen, dropped his chair back onto all four legs, but kept his head hung low on his chest, just as it had been. His eyes watched Max's shoes.

"Can I help you?" he asked lugubriously.

"I'm taking the *Poseidon* out. I may need some gas."

"Nah. He keeps it full." He did not seem interested. "You're Barnaby Wilde."

"That's me," said Max pleasantly, but his eyes grew hard. "Did Mr. Cornelius call ahead?"

The kid finally looked up. "Nuh-uh. I know your voice."

"The curse of radio. You don't want an autograph, do you?" Max was deliberately keeping it short.

"Well, I—nuh."

"Okay. What tricks are there to getting out of the harbor?"

The kid dropped his eyes again. "Well, once you clear the shore, all you can do is head for the Duxbury Buoy. That's the southern boundary of the Duxbury Reef. Just stay to the left of it. Do you know how to clear the channel?"

"Only on the radio."

"Huh?"

"Never mind."

"Oh. Oh, I get it. Well, watch the breakers. If they're breakin', that means there's a reef. When you see 'em, watch for a lull, and then count seven more waves. That'll be the next lull, and that's when you move out."

"Sure. I used to know that, back in Florida. Anything else?"

"Nuh. Just—" He gestured vaguely, almost raised his head.

"An autograph?"

"Yeah."

"Sure."

. . . . .

Max had grown up on boats, so the *Poseidon*'s only surprise was its luxury, which wasn't so surprising. Cornelius never skimped and here he had a Cruisers' VeeSport 26 with twin turbo'd 350-cubic-inch MerCruiser engines. It was a beautiful boat, white and golden tan, with every imaginable option from a remote-controlled spotlight to the ubiquitous Nakamichi audio system. But Max liked the MerCruisers best. They would cover the twenty-three miles to the north Farallon in twenty minutes.

He rode the swell over the submerged Bolinas barrier and shot out into the gray green of the ocean. The weather was good, cold but clear, and he could see the peaks of the Farallons easily; out from behind the trees, the sun was still strong. Surf ducks bobbed and honked as he passed, and their cousins, the sea gulls, paced the *Poseidon* on its way.

He knew little of the Farallons. The three islands were another federal park, like Mt. Tam, but reserved exclusively for animals. Sealers and egg collectors had all but exterminated the wildlife before the feds took over at the turn of the century; only an occasional scientist went out there anymore, and then only to the southeast Farallon. The north Farallon, seven miles away, was never visited. It would make a perfect hideout.

Max hefted Rhymer's gun in the pocket of his windbreaker and savored the adrenaline in his system. He wondered what he'd find when he got to the island. The way the *Poseidon* was skimming across the waves, he wouldn't have to wait much longer to find out. He laughed happily and settled back to enjoy the ride.

Chapter 24

DECEMBER 29 • 3:20 P.M.

Clouds of gulls drifted heavily around the spires of the north island as the *Poseidon* approached, and flocks of ducks dotted the pearlescent water. The stink of ammonia from their dung was intense. Max cut the engines and let the boat's inertia carry him in while he reconnoitered, but saw nothing that looked immediately promising. North Farallon was half a mile long and a third wide, yet without a shore or any inlet large enough for the VeeSport—just lunging peaks, like the clawed fingers of a drowning god, stark and black in the afternoon light. The lowest peaks were a hundred feet high; the tallest a hundred and a half.

Max could have circled the island in five minutes, but decided to be as circumspect as he could. He went up onto the pulpit and dropped anchor forty feet offshore, working it until he was damn sure it had caught. Then he stripped off his clothes, each move deliberate and quick to generate the maximum warmth. He tied the clothes in a bundle, which he held atop his head with one hand, and slid over the side into the Pacific.

It was so cold he felt as if he were having a heart attack. His chest went rigid with pain, and his head, though he kept it above water, began immediately to ache. But he could stand it as long as he had to. When he neared the cone he'd picked out as the easiest to get ahold of, he held back, treading water with his feet and free hand, until the seventh wave came by. It swept past slow and swollen, and he rode it in to his goal.

The rock was slippery with spray and dung, but he wanted out and he got out, clambering stiffly up into a notch that was little more than a foothold between the spires. He noticed that his hands and knees were scraped and raw again, but he couldn't feel them. He knew he would in time. He began to dress.

Birds scattered at his awkward movements. There was an endless variety of them: gulls, auks, and many others he couldn't name. A black bird with a striking, white-tufted head and a brilliant orange beak through which the sun shone watched him impassively from the higher rocks. A sharp bark brought Max suddenly around, but only in time to watch a bewhiskered sea lion slide languidly into the surf, leading his flock. Another Point Man.

Fully clothed, Max wedged himself in his notch and leaned out over the water, looking up. The island looked like it would fall apart at the first good wave, but there was no sign of any other peril. A tight smile crossed his face as he took hold of the rocks with his bleeding hands and began to work his way upward.

The climb was tough and invigorating. The rocks, after years of catching the full force of Pacific storms, were deeply pitted, but their steepness made the going slower than Max would have liked. The sun was beginning to dip in the cobalt-blue sky above him, and he pushed himself as fast as he could to beat it.

Still it took nearly half an hour before he reached the top. He pulled himself over the final boulder and sat down to catch his breath. From here he could see a broad, uneven basin, coming down off the insides of the many cones. There were gullies where water had worn its way, and smaller peaks here and there among them. Nests dotted most of the high points, and nesting holes dotted the land. Grass spurted out wherever it could get a grip.

But there was no sign of Wolf Messing—no sign at all. Max would have to search, and there was only an hour to sundown.

During that hour he covered the basin from one end to the other, but had no luck. He soon eliminated an aboveground structure—nothing was big enough to be its disguise—but if there were anything hidden beneath the rocky ground, it eluded him. It was not so large an area that he couldn't push or pull each likely boulder, trying to get it to move, but none did.

As it became harder to see in the gathering twilight of the basin, he began to have serious doubts. Good Christ, he said to himself, maybe this was a trick. Maybe Valerie, or Cornelius himself, is working for Messing. Maybe Cornelius wanted me out of the way for some higher reason of his own. Maybe Cornelius *is* Messing.

But none of that sounded right. He was sure Valerie had been straight with him. I was wrong about the Madwoman because I wasn't looking for it, he thought, climbing back to the rim of the basin for another survey, but I'm not wrong about Valerie.

But then, where is Messing's hideout?

When he got to the edge, the sun was just going down over the vast, open horizon which filled his vision. He could see so much, he could see the curve of the world. The sun had grown gigantic, like an overripe orange about to burst; and then, as it touched the edge, the air layers compacted it, turning it into an accordion, a soup dish, a crown. Finally there was only a thin line of molten metal, and when that, too, vanished, the high clouds that had begun to stream out of the west took up the changing colors. A breeze came up, stronger than before; the warmth of the day began to fade almost at once.

That's the edge of the world out there, Max thought. The edge of the planet.

Some other planet was twinkling back at him, low in the darkening sky. I wonder which one, he mused. I wish I knew. Especially if it's pulling on me.

He looked around him with an exasperated sigh. Who knew? The sky above him was marvelously clear, already beginning to overflow with stars; only the lights from the city, twenty-three miles behind him, had kept their area policed. There was no moon—there wouldn't be any until the middle of the night—and that would work to his disadvantage, because he was there to search, not to spy. But he did not plan to go home empty-handed. If his lion was anywhere on this pile of rocks, it was too close to take a miss on.

He pulled a flashlight from his jacket pocket and started back down into the basin. And as he did so, something caught the corner of his eye.

There was something huge and dark standing where before there had been only peaks. Keeping it on the edge of his vision, Max could tell that it was lighter than the surrounding rocks, more angular. If it would move, he could get a better fix. But it didn't move. And then he finally recognized it, and knew why.

It was a castle.

Once he understood that, the details of it became chillingly obvious. There were towers, turrets, crenelated walls—even a pennant flapping in the evening breeze. The narrow slit eyes of its windows looked back at him, cold and direct.

He shifted his own eyes then. The castle vanished, and all that remained was a series of irregular peaks, black against the star-spangled sky.

He looked away, and it reappeared.

An elemental castle. A fairy castle.

It pissed him off.

He'd finally found what he'd come for, but it might not do him any good. Could a man enter an elemental castle? And if he could, what would happen if he ever once looked straight at it?

Cornelius, he thought, you didn't tell me about this.

Well, there was enough starlight for him to get to it without his flash, and he slipped that back into his pocket. Then he bent and rubbed dirt on his face and hands; without that, there was more than enough starlight to make him shine like a silver dollar.

He went in fast, in quick bursts—from this rock to that mound, and wait for any reaction. From the mound to another rock, and wait for any reaction. Quick and Quiet, that was the motto. In the beginning he took care to stay low, so he wouldn't block the stars; afterward he bent or rose as the landscape demanded.

But as he moved along the gullies, he became aware that he hadn't gone unnoticed after all. Something was pacing him, just off to leeward. Or was it only to leeward? Poised and listening, he thought he heard scuffling to windward, too, all but hidden in the burr of the breeze.

Max took three deep, openmouthed breaths, to shoot oxygen into his brain, and flipped a mental coin. Then, coming up with the full force of his straightening legs, he threw himself into the gully on his right. His hands were outstretched, his fingers clawed—and they were nearly broken as they came down hard against bare stone. There was nothing there. But the sounds moved mockingly down the shadowed depression. And others closed in from behind.

Spinning around, he saw *something* there, something—

Of course! The gnomes.

Max snorted in disgust as he recognized their elephant ears and their stocky bodies. And they did resemble the creatures of his dream the night of the earthquake. They were wearing clothes that were a cross between medieval peasant garb and Indian buckskin. Fringe hung from their short arms. One of the females had her arms wrapped around what looked like a tiny rock, carrying it protectively.

Max watched them, and they watched him, with bright piggy eyes. He found he could look at them more directly before they vanished, probably because he was gaining experience, so he reached out a hand to touch them. But they surged backward, too shy.

Now his eye was caught by something else among the rocks, and it was no gnome. It was glowing, with a hauntingly opalescent light, above the path he had abandoned. For one bone-chilling instant he thought it was another storm cloud, but then he saw that it had no bulk. It was only a glow, dancing in the air.

It reminded him of a will-o'-the-wisp, the swamp gas he and his friends had chased through the swamps as boys.

Was this a salamander?

Whatever it was, the glow was an eerie sight on that moonless night. It swung to and fro as if searching for something, then steadied itself and started to flit down toward the man crouched in darkness. Crystals in the stones sparkled at its coming; flat shadows from the rocks bowed low in its wake. Max could not break cover, or outrun it over the uneven ground, so he waited where he was, tight-lipped.

Four feet away, the salamander glided to a halt. It bobbed slowly, up and down, up and down, though it could not fail to see him if it had eyes; Max thought he saw a primal face in it, like a jack-o'-lantern's. But then it turned aside, and moved past Max, to vanish among the boulders. The shadows flickered, and all was darkness once more.

Max sat back on a stone, his knees cracking in release, and breathed a long sigh. The gnomes continued to watch, jabbering excitedly, six feet to either side.

After a minute Max stood up, slowly, so as not to spook them again, and turned back toward the castle. He felt that he was safe among the elementals; if Cornelius was to be believed, they worked only on levels below that of humanity, unless directed personally by a shaman. These were just the island's natives, going about their business.

The rest of his journey was uninterrupted. He could see the castle much more clearly now, and there was neither light nor movement to indicate any inhabitant. He ran the last twenty yards to a side wall, and took stock.

Each individual stone in the wall was distinct, though seen as if through a saffron haze. Very cautiously Max put out a hand; it went through the haze feeling nothing, but the wall itself was solid. Under his fingers it began to steam. He could smell the settled age of it, the dank minerals. It was as cold as the grave.

Drawing back, he surveyed his position. Behind him the starlit basin was empty of men, though small shadows moved from rock to rock now and then. To either side the wall ran some fifty yards before turning corners, and only then did he realize it wasn't vertical. In fact, it slanted inward at a pretty good angle.

Clouds began to move in from the sea. The air was very moist.

Max moved through the yellow gloom toward a small door near the rear of the castle, much less elaborate than the massive portal gracing the front. Once a rock shifted beneath his boots and clattered across several others, and he froze in mid-stride, waiting. For two full minutes he heard nothing but the wind. He went on.

The door felt like oak under his touch, though it, too, steamed. The lock on it had once been strong but had weathered badly. No one had bothered to oil it against the salt air. An elemental castle's real only to the elements, Max thought, not to people. He pulled his flash from his pocket again, and, shielding it with his free hand, bent to examine the lock more closely.

It would be easy to force.

He forced it.

There was no sound, just a sudden jerk as the metal tore free of the wood, and the door moved back in his hand. He remembered the pine cones that didn't crack when he stepped on them, and he doused the light.

Well, good luck, he thought.

Everybody had said that to everybody in Nam. It meant just what it said, though it had long since lost all meaning. It meant that this was it: back to the war. 'Bout to toss them dice just one mo' time.

Well, good luck.

He pushed the door open, a block of old ice, and stepped quickly through and to the side. He didn't want to be a silhouette. He waited. Heard nothing. Put his finger and thumb in a circle over the flashlight's lens, and flicked it on.

The thin beam swept across a thick but well-worn rug, spread wide across the interior stone flagging. The rug was made up of fantastic designs, but he'd look at them later. He probed the corners of the room with his light, poking past heavy tapestries and stone columns. Unused torches thrust from blackened holders. A great wooden table dominated the far side of the chamber, flanked by many chairs. At the near end of it stood—

A man!

No! Broken teeth—bloodied hair! The nose and eyes black holes!

A corpse!

But Max had been expecting something, and this wasn't even original. He'd seen it too many times in the movies, let alone in the person of Hamish Rhymers. "At least this ain't no fuckin' cloud," he heard himself say softly as it began to stumble forward, and he ran out to meet it.

He didn't want to risk a shot in case anything else were here, so just outside of striking range he stooped to lay the light where it would show what was to follow; then stood up and drove his fist deep down into its pulpy belly. It staggered, and its arms were flung wide. But then those arms were flung forward again, and grabbed Max like clammy vines. Max managed to wrench one hand free; it came loose in a spray of fetid flesh.

Caught in the upthrust of the stark yellow light, the dead man was grotesque beyond belief. It used its decomposing head to batter Max's without regard for itself; the remaining bridge of its putative nose spread out across its face, but it didn't stop. Neither did its grip on Max's arms slacken; the inner layers of muscle and bone were still strong. The light on its eye sockets gave it a look of anticipation.

Max kneed it in the groin and felt something give, but it didn't weaken the arms. Gritting his teeth, he reached forward with both hands and began to tear the stomach apart. It didn't help. With a roar he began to smash back at the head with his own. Its flesh and hair flew in all directions, but it didn't loosen those arms. Again and again Max struck.

Then, at last, almost suffocated in the evil pus which covered his face, Max felt the bones of the skull give way. He struck once more, and the give was much more noticeable. But he couldn't beat the thing to death with his own skull, and the arms still would not let go.

He threw himself backward, pulling the corpse off-balance after him, until he came up against a stone wall. Using it for leverage, he brought his knee up again, higher and harder, while he continued to rip with his hands. In three strokes he had cut a swath from its legs to its breastbone. Now the wall behind Max held him as he drew both his legs up into that cavity, placed his boots flat against what remained of the dead man's rib cage, and kicked out with all his remaining strength. His legs tore through the thin bones, and as the spine snapped, the chest collapsed and the arms went slack.

Released, Max fell to the floor.

Half-blind from the slime which still filled his eyes, the sight he retained red and swimming, he rolled to one side. The corpse was still on its feet, though there was little recognizably human above the hips. The head had fallen into the open chest cavity, and the arms were splayed out at strange angles from the middle of the bent back. But it staggered madly from side to side, still searching and still hungry.

Above him on the wall Max saw one of the unlit torches. He tore it down and touched his lighter to it; it exploded into smoky flames.

His eyes were wild as he shoved the torch into the dead man's chest cavity. The liquescent flesh sputtered and crackled, then caught with a rush. Still staggering in blind frenzy, the thing became its own torch.

Max laughed out loud, a harsh bark. No final crawls for this one, he thought. The Wolf loses another slave. He sagged back against the wall, limp with relief and triumph, to watch the corpse's dance of death with proprietary eyes.

"It was not alive," a voice said.

Chapter 25

DECEMBER 29 • 6:30 P.M.

Max came up off the wall like a scalded cat. Something was in the far doorway, all right, but it wasn't a man, or a corpse. At first he couldn't make out what it was, but then the torchlight of the reeling horror caught that corner and he saw a black dog—the largest, most ferocious dog he had ever seen. Its head, even lowered in warning, was as high as his own waist. Its hot gray eyes held the gleam of near-human intelligence, anomalous and terrible above the sharp canine snout. And it had no right hind leg.

But the voice, thick with Slavic accents, was not the dog's. It came from the deeper darkness behind that crouching beast.

"When physical form dies, astral form lives on. Form of crude elemental, bereft of purpose. You call them ghosts."

"That was no ghost," said Max roughly. He felt for the gun in his pocket and found it; there was no longer a reason not to.

"You are a shaman, then?" said the voice. "You *know*?"

Max's throat was dry, but he forced his voice not to show it as he pulled his gun and aimed it at the shadows. "Messing?" he asked, cold and hard.

The "ghost" collapsed in its final spasms, the rotted teeth clattering out across the stones in all directions. The stench of it was everywhere. It lay on its ruined back, arching high like a splintered bow, until some bubble trapped inside exploded. Scraps of bone and plasma hurtled hard against the far wall; the bone slid back again, steaming.

"Wolf Messing?" asked Max.

"I am he."

Max fired into the darkness.

Immediately the dog leapt at him. Max had time for three shots, dead on; the dog did not react. Max was thrown back under the great paws, the hound loomed above him in the dying light, and he knew he had no way to hold those gleaming teeth from the arteries of his throat—not at any time, and certainly not so soon after the last fight. To his surprise, however, the dog seemed satisfied to have taught him his lesson. It sniffed him, nosed him, and then backed off, studying him, again with that air of intelligence. Finally it padded back to guard the door; the gun had skidded far out of reach.

Max sat up. "Okay, Wolf," he said shortly. "Let's get on with it."

From the shadows a man stepped forward, and light appeared

inside the room—the same saffron light as before, but now bright enough to dazzle for the first few moments.

Wolf Messing was an old, old man, bent low above a gnarled cane and yet dressed in top hat and tails, cut from durable white cloth. A scarlet-lined white cape curved around him, from his hunched shoulders to his thighs, giving him the look of a mushroom; his hat sported a scarlet band. It was the exaggerated outfit of a stage performer, from another era and another clime. His face was somewhat like Albert Einstein's, with the same thick mop of hair, though Messing's was unnaturally brown. Thick wire-rimmed spectacles rode low on his bulbous, bloodshot nose, guarding the tiny black eyes above; but those eyes held a piercing, almost hypnotic force. The mouth was a derisive slash. His nails were impeccably manicured.

After he had cleared the doorway, another person entered behind him. This was an old woman, fat where Messing was thin, eyes dull and rheumy where Messing's shone. She wore the typical peasant scarf and tent skirt of the steppes and huddled close to Messing's bent left elbow like the dog should have but didn't. She was simpering blankly, mindlessly.

The old man looked deep into Max's eyes and said, in a voice both thick and loose, "Decay is coming. In the end as in the egg: naught." It was a greeting, an introduction, and a polemic, all in one.

"Film at eleven," said Max. But inwardly he was cursing Cornelius up and down. Damn you, you bastard! You think you're so fucking omniscient! And you don't even know if the guy you claim is your inferior is in Brazil or on your doorstep! You son of a bitch, if I get out of this—!

"So glad you know my name," said Messing. "So hate introductions, and other tedious chores conventions require. Oh, but do you know my wife?" He said "vife." Inclining his head toward the old woman, he lifted his bushy brows.

Max said nothing.

Messing grinned widely. "A man who too hates introductions.

A man after mine own heart." He lifted one wrinkled hand from the ferrule of his cane and clutched at his chest. Blood suddenly exploded from between his clenched fingers as he wrenched his hand away. "Here it is."

Max took a step back, astonished. Messing exploded into laughter, his small frame all but bouncing up and down on the floor; without his cane to lean on, he might well have fallen over in a heap. He held up his "bloody" hand, palm out and shaking, to show a spent plastic bag.

Max said, "Hollywood stunt men call that a cackle bladder—a chicken bladder filled with fake blood. It must have wowed 'em at the Kremlin in 1939."

Messing's laughter was high-pitched, and getting very loose around the edges. It continued in what seemed uncontrollable spasms for another moment, and then broke off as abruptly as it had begun. "Ah, Californians. Live too much with fantasy, Herr August. You have no dreams left."

"I'm learning all the time."

"Not enough." Messing challenged Max with his eyes again; his moods were clearly mercurial. "Come into my parlor," he said, turning back toward the door.

Frau Messing and the dog waited for Max to pass, then brought up the rear. She said something that must have meant "Don't walk so fast," because her husband slowed while she bolted the door behind them.

The room they entered was as dark as the one they'd left, until Messing brought the lights up. He might have had a radio-controlled device on his person; or maybe he could do it psychically. Max wasn't going to sweat the small stuff. Six people, four men and two women, sat in chairs arranged before a small stage. Their heads were up and their eyes open, but they didn't move or look around. The Madwoman and Mr. Xin were not among them.

The room was decorated in a chaos of styles: Russian, Japanese, Egyptian, western American, and others, probably Balkan, which Max couldn't name. The tapestries were also of varied styles, but with a common motif: knights and dragons. The dragons were winning. The windows were intricately cut stained glass, fairly dirty. But the centerpiece of the chamber was a great wooden waterwheel, turning with the flow of a small stream which ran along a trough at the base of one wall. It was not a traditional waterwheel, having only enough vanes to keep one in the stream at a time; generating power was not its function. Instead other vanes divided its interior circumference into four quarters, and these vanes supported four revolving platforms. As the wheel turned, the platforms turned to remain horizontal, and this was necessary due to the four carvings which occupied them: a bull, an angel, *the* lion—and an eagle.

The complete set. Despite his attempt at control, this time Max's face fell.

But fortunately Messing didn't notice; he was talking to his wife. "Narda," he said sharply, and continued in his native tongue, pointing toward the dog. It leaned toward him, and Messing spoke to it in a lowered voice; his manner was not as much like master to pet as it had been with his wife. The dog seemed to answer his words, nodding, inquiring, growling its pleasure. Its eyes sparkled as they turned toward Max and measured him. Its tongue licked Messing's hand.

Frau Messing called from her corner of the room and raised her arm; the shaman acknowledged her brusquely. He laid down his cane and straightened himself, then climbed purposefully onto the stage. Two strong spotlights pinned him from above as the old woman pulled a lever; his suit, his teeth, and eyes all gleamed. The six people in the chair remained unmoving.

Messing took a deep bow, and then another, throwing his arms wide as if to receive the applause of millions. The psychic Bob Hope. His eyes swept the audience of nine in the room and went on beyond their heads; only then did he look directly at Max. He pointed to the wheel. "The traditional concept of universe. Four elements which make the great cycle of life are shown: bull for Earth, eagle for Water, angel for Air, lion for Fire."

"I know all about that."

"I doubt it very much."

Max wanted the subject changed. He knew he wouldn't enjoy this one, and it might well be leading to the quicksand.

"Why did you leave the initials off *my* lion?"

Messing smiled. "For quicksand, Herr August."

Somehow Max forced himself to sneer. "The mind reader, huh?" He waved a hand at Messing's shining outfit. "There's no biz like show biz, is there, Wolf?" But it was pure bravado.

"I love this apparel, yes. Presents me in the manner to which I am best known: a Star. In this country—if I were known in this country—a Superstar. But would you like brandy?" He took up an ornate antique decanter from a prop chest at his side, and reached for a pair of crystal snifters.

"I'll pass," said Max.

With apparent regret, Messing poured a healthy dollop of golden liquid into one snifter alone, and raised it to his red nose. "You know not what you miss. Drunkenness is divine madness." He took a small sip, rolled it around his mouth before allowing it to slide down his throat. He exhaled with a satisfied sigh, and his hypnotic eyes sparkled. "Ah, madness." He smiled a crooked smile as his wizened face took on color. "Never have I warmed to vodka. And this despite my Polish birth."

"My heart bleeds for you. But I'd rather hear how you made this castle appear, and become real."

"Pfagh! It was always 'real.' Your friend so wants people to understand shamanism; he will have explained levels of reality."

"What friend?"

"Come now, Herr August. You cannot hide thoughts from *me*."

"And what are you doing here?" Max continued doggedly, just as he'd done against Hardesty, just as he'd been doing for days. He knew the question was inane, but inane questions were all he had left. Messing's knowledge of Cornelius, and Max's relationship with him, was another blow to his expectations; he could only keep slogging forward.

But Messing kept tripping him up. "I never have left, save for the night I captured your lion. I am on this island eighteen days now; fortunately I have but two remaining."

"And then what?"

"And then I flee the collapse of the Western world, along with many others too." His smile was brilliant, toothy, a stage smile to be seen in the back row. "You know of me, yes? Greatest star in all the Russias?"

"I know that you're going to die very soon."

Messing took his left hand from his glass, pointed it at Max, and crooked the first and fourth fingers for the traditional evil eye. Something struck Max on the bridge of the nose, so hard it drove him to his knees, his eyes streaming, the pain a raw nerve. He tried to get back up and face it, but a new surge threw him to his side, writhing.

Messing said, "I was born in the territory of the Russian state, in the hamlet of Gora Kalwaria. I was abnormal from the earliest times. Memory, a phenomenon. Knew the Talmud by heart at six years of age, and this caused our rabbi to seek my admission for religious training. But I refused to go, quite stubbornly. Then one evening as I returned home in the chilled midwinter twilight, a gigantic figure appeared to me on our front steps.

" 'My son!' it said to me. 'From above, I am a messenger to foretell your future. Go to the school! Your prayers will please heaven!'

"I felt struck by lightning."

"Yes," said Max, "I know the feeling." He pushed himself away from the floor, and levered himself into a vacant chair, weakly.

"Yes . . . struck by lightning. Nonetheless I do not take orders." Messing spoke into his brandy snifter. "At eleven years, with less than a ruble, I sneaked aboard a passing train and tried to hide under a seat. The conductor, of course, caught me out, and, with what seemed the total weight of all authority in the world, demanded my ticket. I knew not what to do . . . yet I hesitated not at all. I held out a worthless piece of paper, from the floor beneath the seat. Looked deep into his eyes. Put all of myself into willing that he would accept it as my ticket.

"He held the paper in his great hands, turned it over and over. I continued to exert force with my thoughts. He turned the paper one last time . . . and then he punched it. Handed it back and said, 'Why are you under the seat? Get up! Within two hours we will be in Berlin.' "

Messing laughed in gleeful remembrance and took another swallow of his brandy. His face was very red now. His wife was sitting at the end of Max's row, behind the unmoving spectators, placidly knitting; the dog lay by the waterwheel, watching Max with its demonic eyes.

"In Berlin I worked as a messenger in the ghetto, but there was little money in that. One day I fainted from hunger while crossing a bridge and was taken to a hospital where they pronounced me dead. No pulse, no breathing, my body was cold. I was taken to the morgue. But fortunately a medical student who was seeking cadavers for his experiments that night found a faint heartbeat, very irregular, returning to me.

"When I awoke, three days later, I was in the care of a man I shall call Herr Doktor Abel. He was a psychiatrist and a neurologist, very interested in my cataleptic abilities. Soon he discovered my other abilities, and so he encouraged my mind control." Messing was rolling now, as if he'd told this tale a hundred times. Max saw that he had the long words down too pat; he'd learned some parts of this English version phonetically. A man who liked to be thought a world-class star must be ready for the world.

The thought of stars brought Valerie's face back before his mind's eye. What would she do when he didn't return? How soon would she alert Cornelius to his absence? And would it make any difference?

But Messing was continuing. "When I turned thirteen, Herr Doktor Abel introduced me to my impresario, Herr Tselmeister, who found for me work in the Berlin Panopticon. I played a corpse.

Enter the clear crystal coffin Friday evening, before the stupid crowds, and lie, unmoving, cataleptic, until Sunday evening. For this I was paid all of five marks a day.

"During the weekdays, I wandered the Marktplatz, attempting to overhear the thoughts of the passers-by. Oft I heard not only their problems, but the solution to their problems. I told them, and began to become truly famous. Herr Tselmeister changed my act.

"During the war, age sixteen, following a performance in Wien—Vienna—I was invited by Albert Einstein to visit at his apartment. And when I arrived, he had a second famous guest: Sigmund Freud. All of us had achieved already great fame, but Einstein was almost childishly interested in my abilities, in the manner he was interested in all. Freud was merely curious; for this, he wished to have charge of an experiment. Of course, I agreed. He proposed to send me commands, to see if I might receive them. He supposed this difficult, if not impossible; I knew it simple.

"And so Freud sat to one side of Einstein's clustered room, and I to the other, while the professor observed quietly, stroking his thick brown moustache. Freud began concentration, his brow deeply lined: I felt him, as the feeling of a radio receiver which is slightly out of tuning. You see, he was pushing too much in the incorrect manner and interfering with himself. But I caught him! He thought, 'Go to the bathroom cupboard and pick some tweezers. Return to Einstein, and pull out from his luxuriant moustache three hairs.'

"I picked the tweezers, but only asked the professor if I might pull out the hairs. He laughed, and agreed. Freud was very angry."

Messing stopped and waited for applause. Max sat silently, as did the six others; their continued immobility was beginning to be the most unnerving part of this whole macabre scene. Who the hell were they, and why didn't Messing ever acknowledge them? Frau Messing laid down her knitting at the far end of the row, and began to clap enthusiastically. The black hound began to bark.

"Danke, danke schön." The old man smiled, nodding toward the entire room. "Well! Thereafter I toured in the world, all six continents. In 1927, I met Mahatma Gandhi, who also tested me to satisfaction. I believe you know, Herr August, of my later escape to the Soviet Union, where I worked with Stalin. But you do not know, no more than others, that I had 'retired' because of boredom with these tricks. Telepathy is not different from ice cream; to partake every day for twenty years makes it distasteful, no matter how others may yearn for it. I began to show my boredom. After the successful conclusion of the war, I was called increasingly into question.

"In privacy I continued to work with the highest authorities, but the Party goal was to turn Russians away from superstitions toward dynamic rationalism. It was officially announced by the philosophy department of the Soviet Academy of Sciences that I performed my 'tricks' by . . ." He hesitated, searching for the words; couldn't find them, but went on smoothly, ". . . well, if a man wants for me to turn to the left, he will unconsciously shift himself in that direction, and I will notice. Through the 1950s this was printed on all my program booklets. Not until 1957, the change in the Party line, did this cease. But in those years I had used my private access to the leaders to gain access to the largest collection of occult literature outside of the Vatican.

"Ah, that causes blinking, my cool friend. Yes, yes, the Vatican and the Supreme Soviet are both quite interested. The Catholics amassed their collection from their persecutions, and it was the same when the Bolsheviks overthrew the Czar. Everything to the storehouses! There it remained, until I gained access.

"Since then I have had one quarter of a century of intense study, and all the support I could wish. For the masses, of course, there can be only mass goals; thus the state-run research at Academgorodok. But for the person, I, Wolf Grigorevich Messing, have mastered arts far better than those limited goals. The State now is where I was sixty years gone, eavesdropping on the minds of peasants. They begin to love ice cream, while I dine on . . . cherries jubilee."

"And now you vill dine on me?" asked Max with all the irony he could muster. The pain in his face was almost a memory, and Messing was a very old man. From her end of the row Frau Messing simpered sweetly, and Max looked her way, simpering back, striving for misdirection. Then he flicked his eyes back toward the shaman, measuring the distance between them. The muscles in his thighs tightened—and a fat, damp hand dropped purposefully on his knee. He jerked, and spun to look behind him—but saw, instead, Frau Messing, big as life, in the flesh, sitting directly next to him, eyes not rheumy but bright, and hard, and laughing. Eyes like those of Mr. Xin, and Hamish Rhymers.

But then those eyes were just the eyes of a senile woman once again, and the woman's wrinkled hand was lifting unsteadily from his leg. She simpered benignly into his staring face, and that hand kept rising and picked her nose.

Max could hardly breathe. Now the quicksand was everywhere.

"Heroics have had their days, Herr August," said Messing with magnificent fury, "but courtesy to my wife has not. I am him who will crush the world, and you, like your FBI, and your so-good friend Cornelius, are pawns. Less. For pawns have function, and are subject to rules. But with me, there are no more rules. Decay is coming! In the end as in the egg: naught!"

He stomped to the edge of the stage, out of the crossed glare of the twin spotlights. Now he was backlit, his mane of hair a chaotic halo, his face double-shadowed as he bent over Max. "And decay has already come to you, Herr August," he whispered venomously. "You will remember Ia Ngu province, the morning of 5 September, 1973?"

"You haven't made a bit of sense since I got here," said Max bitterly. "I don't know what you're talking about." But he couldn't keep the truth from his eyes.

"You know," said Messing. "And I know. There you are, yes—advancing with your new company—in a long sideways line, so no American would shoot accidentally another." He raised his wrinkled hand to his forehead theatrically; but there was nothing theatrical about what he was saying. Max lay pinned to his chair, looking up at those two withered lips about to recite his innermost secret—the secret he had spent a third of his life trying to forget. The secret of his black soul. "Now you come into an open area. A hamlet lies ahead. Sandal tracks are well marked in the mud. A few crops nod in the wind.

"The Vietnamese freedom fighters attack as you enter into the open. You Americans return fire. The battle is short, then the Vietnamese run toward the hamlet. Some Americans rise and run after; others lie where they fell, dead robots. You run after, Specialist August.

"As Americans enter into the hamlet, people come out from their huts as they have learned to do, slowly, defenselessly. Do not run away; Americans will think it is freedom fighters. Do not run toward; Americans will think it is freedom fighters. Merely walk, slowly, hands empty. Americans will search, and pass by.

"But now, someone shoots an old woman. Someone else shoots a child. A man screams, and a dog barks, and someone shoots it, also. And you, Specialist August—"

"You bastard," said Max very softly.

"No. *You* bastard." Messing chuckled wetly. "You murderer! Was it"—he stared hard at a point just above Max's eyebrows—"thirteen? Yes, a fateful number. Thirteen helpless civilians. You shoot them as they stand. No"—he stepped back into the spotlights, and his arms were raised in triumph—"you are no hero, then or now. You are merely another of many American murderers, with guilt deeper even than the world believes. The Army court-martialed one lieutenant only, but never touched the rest of you. Ha! For you, for America, heroics have had their day."

He snapped his fingers sharply, and the hound shoved Max with its great black head. "Get up, Herr August," said the old man. "Get up and come into your cell, where you belong."

The sextet sat quietly, but Frau Messing applauded in Max's ear.

Chapter 26

DECEMBER 29 • 7:45 P.M.

Max followed the little man up a flight of tightly winding stairs. It was hard to say how high they climbed, because Max frankly didn't care, but even so it seemed the stairs extended farther than any tower he'd seen from outside.

The passageway grew more and more claustrophobic, until, at last, they came to a small, circular landing, outside another towering oaken door. This door matched none of the others in the castle; it spoke of India, with an intricate mandala burnt deep into its facade. There were no torches in the tower, but the saffron light followed the shaman. Max realized finally, dully, that it was like the light in your mind when you're stoned.

As opposed, now, to what?

Calmly, deliberately, Messing bent over the door's handle and worked something hidden from Max's view. The door swung open, and the shaman motioned Max into the cell beyond. Max went and the door closed with a solid thud behind him.

The room in which he found himself was a bare, seven-sided cubicle whose ceiling bore the same mandala as the door. There were no chairs, no bed, so sink, no toilet; just the same cold, flat stones for the floor and walls, with one narrow slit in one wall to let in air. Looking out, Max saw a thin swatch of dark sky and darker sea. The lemony light inside the room was not nearly as bright as before, now that the shaman was gone.

Mechanically Max began to test the stones for hidden panels or loose joints, but after an hour of labor, he'd found nothing. Then he turned his attention to the door. It was a massive slab, of a single piece, with square sides and bottom and a rounded top fitting precisely into the matching masonry. Heavy iron hinges were attached to the wood with thick spikes, and hinges and spikes were further joined by solder. The only tools he had for working at the door were his keys, which weren't much; but he took his most pointed one and began to chisel around the hinges. It was hard work, and his fingers and wrists frequently cramped, but rather than resting he kept on, working his way past the pain, minute by minute and hour by hour. But in the end, try as he might, he couldn't continue to work his way past the memories.

It's memories that make the man.

He saw again all the deaths in Vietnam, theirs and ours, a year of deaths. Each one played back behind his pained eyes in slow and deliberate detail, as slow as his progress on the door. And each time he saw another one die, with a clean drilled hole, or with a bloody, sucking cavity, he remembered how he felt on the morning of September 5, 1973, and he heard the evil banshee wail of "Gimme Shelter" . . .

. . . . .

Hiding, for six days, after the ambush of my men. Alone in the treacherous jungle, trying somehow to get back to base. Under cover all the time. Moving whenever I dared, not often, low and slow, feeling, groping, tight, 'cause I didn't know where they went. But I was the only one who could tell what happened. And finally I did get back, and we came out with a force, and found two men still alive, six days later, buried under the rancid bodies. . . .

The war, and blowin' people away. It's a power trip, and that's all it is. You really kinda stand up after a while, and you're pissed off: you're not an innocent anymore, and goddamn these fuckin' people. And it doesn't matter who they are. It doesn't matter in the slightest. They're Vietnamese, you're in Vietnam, you'd rather be back drivin' your '57 Chevy up and down U.S. 1 and bein' nice to everybody. You didn't ask to lose your ideals but you've been pushed around, you've been told what to do since forever, your girl friend wrote you a Dear John; you don't have the support of the people at home, which is pissin' you off; you say, Goddammit, fuck it, man! *Brrrrttt!* You're gonna win the war all by yourself, right then and there, that's gonna be it. And you just don't flat out give a fuck; and you know that you can do it. It makes it all that much easier to squeeze the trigger and just flip the clips; and flip the clips and flip the clips until somebody either knocks you down or tells you you're crazy or there's nothing left to shoot. And you have absolutely no remorse about it.

Because a lot of times, we would draw fire from an area, and you can't fire back. "I know; I know we're gettin' shot at, guys, just keep down, you can't shoot over there because that's a sacred burial ground, and if we shoot into that area, we're not gonna get the support of the regional chief; or the village chief; or the mayor. And I know Joe here just lost half his leg, but that's a no-no. . . ."

The helplessness. And the hopelessness. Sittin' down, havin' lunch; you don't sit together, the closest guy may be fifteen feet away. And you're talkin', it's quiet, the voices carry. He's leanin' against a tree, eatin' a can o' chow. And you hear a report: crack! And everybody, whew! flat on the ground. Except for the guy you were talkin' to. He's just sittin' there, and you're yellin' at him, "Get down!" Cause a lotta guys freeze, they don't respond to anything. Till a medic walks over and picks off his helmet, and he'd got half his head in there. Then the blood starts flowing. And the guy just sits there. I thought he was frozen, but nah, he's *dead*. And you look around and you wanna do somethin' about it; I mean, we were just havin' a simple conversation. Whether you knew 'im or not. He's a G.I. Joe from Podunk, Oklahoma, and he was a good guy, and somebody blew 'im away, well, where is the son of a bitch? Nowhere to be found. It just makes you wanna, you know, it makes you wanna kick ass. You know that's not the answer. "We don't do that." But—

And then thirty-five guys, just the same. With two to lie there for six days and get eaten by bugs and lizards. And you, the Point Man, left alive. Why? To make it add up somehow. To make it feel like it came out even . . .

Ra-ape! And Mur-der! Yeah! Yeah!
It's just a shot a-way. It's just a shot a-way!

RA-APE! *MUR-DER!!*
It's just a shot a-way! It's just a shot a-way! Yea, yea, yea, yea!

His watch read 5:15 when he struck the metal in the door. He had gouged out a hole eight inches long and two deep along the edge of the hinge; but then the key he was using began to rasp, and the feeling ran up his whip-strung tendons to the back of his pounding skull. He tried to force his way deeper, chipping away at the sides of the hole, but there was no mistake; the interior of the door was a solid sheet of steel. He had worked himself into such a one-pointed trance in his hours of excavation and memory that it took a good two minutes for the enormity of his discovery to sink in. Then he simply dropped his ruined keys back into his pants pocket. His face was empty.

For seven years, he thought, I've tried not to remember that day. For most of those years I wouldn't even talk about Nam. I wouldn't see *Apocalypse Now.* I told people, if they pressed me, that I was just a grunt like a lot of others. And God help me, I was.

So I thought I'd lose myself in Barnaby Wilde, the rich and crazy jock. Become a new man, in a world where we make war no more. And I succeeded. I finally lost myself so well that I got to thinking I could go back to being a Point Man, and leave the bad times untouched.

But it was only a dream, all along. The guy who's been running around saying I'm the prince of the city, I think like a lion—that's not a real person. The real person is a not-too-bright jerk from south Florida who went over there and killed a lot of people for no reason that really stands up. And I might as well admit it. "We *don't* do that," and it sure didn't even the score.

I've had it on my conscience every single day since. I told no one.

And both Messing and Cornelius knew.

What the hell am I doing, trying to play with the wizards?

Outside, the moon was high in the sky. It was a thin, sharp crescent, like the blade of a guillotine; some star sparkled below its arc. The sun could not be far beyond; it was no more than two hours to dawn.

What did Cornelius do when Valerie told him? Max wondered, over and over again. He no longer hated the man in black. How could he? With his eye on the moon, there were moments when he found himself expecting the two of them, Cornelius and Valerie, to come swooping down on broomsticks from the stars, blasting Messing and his island with multicolored rays from their palms . . . and other moments, immediately following, when he thought them both to be children, not at all the people to stand against a shaman with the entire Soviet State behind him.

The ebb and flow of it made him sleepy, at last, and he took a deep breath to clear his head. But his head wouldn't clear. He shook it, and then pounded it twice with the palm of his hand, sharp blows, and still his eyelids grew heavier and heavier. A stab of panic might have followed; he was too far gone to know. He saw the masonry flowing around him, and some of it rushing up to meet him, and he couldn't tell if it was wall or floor. He hit, he slid, he came to rest, and looked at his own feet some distance away, through lids that were not quite closed.

Beyond his feet the door swung open. He knew that was significant; he could see the hole he had made. He watched it swing. And he watched who entered the cell behind it.

It was Madeleine Riggs. She was dressed as a houri, the maidens of Moslem paradise, all hanging silks and swirling lace sewn with pearls. Around her ankle was a clasp of crimson jewels. Her thin brows were arched ingenuously over her blue-black eyes, her scarlet lips parted with excitement.

As if caught in a bubbling stream, she was dancing; surrendering to a power greater than her own. The colors of her skin changed with every movement, now pale, now dark, now rosy and verdant and lavender. It came to Max, from a distance, and late, that some of the colors which played through her form were not visual at all, but sensible only as heat. Challenging infrared, cool ultraviolet, and the blue from the depths of the night sky, all these and more highlighted her movements, and she spun and whirled and danced closer.

She was the essence of lust.

He didn't want to respond, but he had no choice left. The rage and disgust which screamed out in some small dark cavern of his mind had no contact at all with the muscles and glands of his body. He had loved this woman once; he hated her now. But his body still responded with love.

She danced like a gypsy in hell, and he lay on his back and watched her with hollow eyes. She came to dance over him, smooth legs outstretched until her bare feet touched his hands. He wanted to grab her ankles, pull her down on him, but could only watch as she flaunted what he saw there, offered and withheld it, and laughed with delicious power. Only the man who could take her could have her, and Max was not that man tonight.

She bent forward, ripe breasts hanging loose beneath the gaping lace, and reached for his belt. With one sharp sweep, she undid it, and her warm fingers felt beneath his waistband, to find and take the clasp. She pulled his pants apart, pulled them down his useless legs, and freed his manhood. She bent down above him, her eyes looking into his—and without transition, without break, she was lying on top of him, her weight warm on his chest, her hair red spun silk across his neck—her eyes looking into his from inches away. Like Frau Messing's. Like Mr. Xin's. Like Hamish Rhymers's.

That same look of forbidden knowledge.

"Some have studied with him almost all their lives": Cornelius.

"He had the impression she was just settling down to earth": Hardesty.

Max might have gone mad then. Terror overwhelmed him as he stared into those mocking eyes, unable to move a muscle. She smiled at him, as she had always smiled, and slid down along his chest, her breasts like silk, to take him between her sharp white teeth. Her tongue was hot and moist.

In less than half a minute he had climaxed, agonizingly.

She stood up and produced a silver chalice. She held it to her mouth and disgorged what she had taken. Then she raised the cup in a toast, a salute, and Max saw the most truly evil smile he had ever known. One bare foot rose from the floor to caress the side of his face, and then she spun away, gaily. She turned, she wove, and danced away out of the room. The door swung shut behind her.

And Max fell cursing into sleep.

. . . . .

But even his dreams brought him no peace. On all sides of him, he saw once more the trudging gnomes and the sparkling naiads, now joined by powerful men of fire and whirling storm clouds with hundreds of hungry eyes. Each one moved to hidden rhythms, and in the distance, directing them, oblivious to Max's slow protests, Wolf Messing stood tall in the glare of the spotlights. Applause came to Max like the cracking of earth, and the sodden crash of underground waves.

And yet . . . also there, but unseen, unseeable, was an amber Presence, a golden glow always somehow just beyond his grasp.

Chapter 21

DECEMBER 30 • 7:00 A.M.

The horned moon, high and pale in the eastern sky, bathed the slopes of Mt. Tamalpais with its light. In the black shadows of the tangled trees, eyes glinted suddenly, before five slender deer bounded out onto the softly whispering grass. For the next hour they alternately grazed and listened, covering much of the open field which sprawled some two hundred steep feet below the lone public road. But an observer, had he been there (which was unlikely), and very keen (unlikelier still), might have noticed that the deer didn't graze over one wide swath of the field—a swath twenty-five feet wide, and four times that long.

But even a knowledgeable observer, watching that swath from the sides of his eyes, would not have seen anything else.

In a roughhewn room cut from the solid earth of the mountain's eastern slope, with an eastern wall which seemed a hundred-foot window overlooking San Francisco and the moon, the corpse of Hamish Rhymers lay spread-eagled on an alabaster slab. Cold, unmoving, the body and the slab were set in the exact center of a triangle cut in the earthen floor; the grooves that marked the figure were filled with sulfur and ashes. Rhymers's feet pointed toward one of the triangle's tips; his head faced the flat side opposite. Beyond that, at the point where another tip would be if a second triangle had been added, two black candles sputtered and smoked.

The actual tip of the triangle touched a circle, cut and marked in the same way as itself. The circle was also marked in another manner: a bank of heat lamps built into the earthen ceiling above it threw their warmth and their low red glow precisely inside it. In the circle the air was tropical; in the triangle it was chill.

In the circle Cornelius and Valerie Drake, both nude, stood side by side, chanting. Their song had first been heard on Earth over thirty thousand years before. It had no words, this song—just sounds, harsh and guttural, so low that each of the two living bodies in that room actually vibrated with the effort of producing them. Microphones set into strategic corners picked up the sounds, and fed them back through advanced electronics and six hidden speakers until the entire chamber thundered with them. Cornelius and a thousand harmonious voices sang the despair of the dying; and Valerie, nearly falling beneath the hammerblows of her echoes, sang the pleasures of life.

Some thirty feet away a fawn nuzzled his mother's ear as she tore at the fruitful grass and kept a wary eye on the silent lights far below. The wind fitfully ruffled their coats.

A circle marked out by candles surrounded the smaller circle and its triangle. The two black candles beyond the corpse were part of it, as were three more black candles—one across from the first two, and the others at right angles to these. Four more white candles stood at the halfway points between the blacks, for a total of nine. They had all been lit at midnight, when they had been a foot tall and half a foot thick. Now they were guttering, near to dawn and extinction. The moon in the sky to the east was growing dim in a rose-gray sky.

The chant was coming to an end, ascendant and more forceful. Valerie's eyes were glassy, her breath short, and her brow streaked with sweat-soaked hair. Cornelius, with his thickset, fifty-year-old body, stood solidly, holding control, though no one else could guess what his fortitude cost him. The chant was a command: arise! For seven hours the wizard and his woman had been working for this moment, raising themselves to a fever pitch through ritual, wine, and song. Anything that could exalt them, ancient or modern, had been utilized by the sure hands of the older man. And now these two were no longer human. Now they were multitudes, massed in eternity, and living for one thing alone: the raising of Hamish Rhymers.

Now nothing on Earth could deny them.

On the alabaster slab in the chill triangle, the corpse began to stir, like a man in the midst of a bad dream. Valerie's eyes grew wide and haunted, but her lover's reassuring hand gripped hers tightly. One of Rhymers's hands came up, the palm dead white and the back a sullen red where the dying blood had collected. Then the head rose on its stiff neck, cracking the rigor mortis, and a low sigh was pressed from the unyielding chest. One eye opened, glittering strangely like cheap glass. The other remained closed, glued shut with blood and mucus.

Cornelius gave Valerie's hand a heartening squeeze and walked forward to the edge of the circle of heat. He raised his hands and called out, "Rhymers!" in the same deep voice he'd used to banish the white-haired man's presence two nights before. "Rhymers! What hath transpired with Max August?"

The corpse sighed once more. It turned its eye on its master with a jerk. Its hand fell back to the slab.

"Rhymers! I adjure thee most solemnly: speak!"

"Taken . . ."

The voice seemed to come not from the body, but from the entire triangle. Valerie struggled to see it more clearly; she felt there were alien shapes whirling 'round before her eyes. But her wizard saw the clear form of the dead man's ghost, standing spare and spectral to the left of the earthbound body.

"What hath transpired?"

"Don't . . . don't bring me . . . dead now . . . the tunnel . . ."

"Speak, and I shall grant thee release. Speak quickly."

"Messing . . . waiting . . . knew he came on island . . . don't . . ." The head trembled and shook; froth formed at the lips. "Waiting . . . like a spider . . . waiting . . . let him enter . . . the castle . . . tested . . . with a ghost . . . impressed . . . don't make me . . ."

"Speak!" Cornelius threw a glance out his window. Dawn was very near.

"Impressed by his courage . . . not his knowledge . . ."

"But he did not slay him? Answer me!"

"No . . . Messing . . . holds him in the tower . . . Korelatovna took . . . his essence . . ."

Valerie pressed close to Cornelius. "Does he mean—" she began to whisper, but the microphones threw her words back at her like a scream. She held her tongue.

The mikes didn't capture Hamish Rhymers. "Messing will . . . leave him to rot . . . in invisible castle . . . funny . . . fun . . ." His hand came up again, in supplication. "Now. Release . . ."

But Cornelius was inexorable. "Have the Wolf's plans been altered?"

"No . . . no need . . ." A rasping noise crawled from Rhymers's throat; Valerie realized with horror that he was laughing. "He will destroy you . . . Cornelius . . . this time . . . he will win . . ."

"Who is on the island?"

"Messing . . . Frau Messing . . . Korelatovna . . . psychokinetics . . . the dog . . ."

"The dog? The dog is there?"

"Release me . . . Cornelius . . ."

The sky was crimson now; sunrise was less than a minute away.

"And all four talismans? The Wolf hath all four?"

"Release me . . . release me . . ." The head began to snap from side to side. "Release me . . ."

"The four talismans?"

"Yes!"

"Go then. I do release thee." He drew a figure in the air with his hand. "And I do thank thee for thine attendance, o shade. Return unto the night whence thou hast come."

The sun rose over the eastern hills.

Cornelius sat down abruptly on the earthen floor. Valerie, her eyes no longer glazed, but very, very tired, started to walk out of the circle, but her wizard's hand caught her ankle in a grip of iron. She looked down at him dully, then at what she had been about to do. She bit her lip. "Sorry." She shrugged.

"We shall close the circle after we've rested. Here, sit by me."

But she remained standing. "You knew all along, right?"

Cornelius regarded her frankly. Even now, drawn and sweaty, Valerie Drake in the nude was a sight no man could ignore, but it was her eyes he sought with his gaze. "You refer to Messing's presence on the island."

"You're damn right I refer to Messing's presence on the island. You told me he was in Brazil. That's what I told Max."

"I thought Max should meet his adversary."

"But you lied to me, Man."

"Yes." He stood up, with heavy grace. "I am your wizard, Woman. I do for you what you cannot yet do for yourself."

"But what about Max? What are you going to do for him?"

"Max is on his own. Max has always been on his own."

Valerie dragged clawed fingers through her tangled hair. "I can't believe I'm hearing this. You promised him protection."

"Yes," Mr. Cornelius said. He rubbed his hands on the backs of his thighs, then raised them high and wide. "We shall close the circle now."

Chapter 28

DECEMBER 30 • 11:45 A.M.

Max August awoke with disgust in his mouth.

He remembered nothing of his golden dream, but everything of his seduction; and in the thin light and salt breeze of the morning, as his rage battled hard with his helplessness, he kept wanting to throw up. Madeleine! he thought furiously. Damn! Of all of them, why her? And of all ways, why that way? Was it just humiliation—or was it more?

He realized belatedly that his hipbones hurt from sleeping on the stone floor; the sockets felt as if they'd been fused. He climbed to his feet, unsteady and aching, and still feeling desperately tired. He reached out for the slit of the window, and thought, It must have been more than simple humiliation. But what, then? Why don't I ever know why she and Messing do what they do? Why does everybody know something I don't?

But then he frowned. And sneered. At himself. I thought I did know—thought I'd gotten it all figured out. Each time I've gotten through a tight space in the past—what is it now? four days—I've told myself that *now* I knew what the game was. Madeleine messed me over, so I'll track her down; Madeleine's a witch, but I've got a wizard friend; she's got a wizard, too, but they're all in Brazil. . . . And besides, I believe in wizardry now, myself.

Yeah, I believe. But what good is that if I don't act like it? If Messing had invented a gun to cause cancer, okay; easy. Happens all the time. But if he's doing "magic" . . .

"Shit!" he snapped out loud, and thought, I'm just going around in circles. I went through all this yesterday morning. Yeah, it's weird to believe, but now I believe. Just stood there on the deck and looked down at my hands and said, Gee, it's almost a commonplace. And then came right out here. Why? Because wizardry may be real, all right, but in somebody else's world. Not in my world, out under the sun on good old familiar Mt. Tam, with a girl whose poster's on the wall at QBU. Nah, wizardry's for the old men, at night, and hey, I'll be sure to look out for it then. But meantime, back here in the real world, how's about a little search-and-destroy while the magic men are away? That's what we do where I come from.

Max began to pace, as that thought brought up the memories of Ia Ngu again. But now they didn't seem so devastating, and he knew why. Yesterday he *had* been reliving Vietnam, so the sudden revelation of his Vietnam guilt, coming on top of his facile, ignominious capture, had been a crushing blow. His world, as he continued to think he knew it, split apart.

But this morning, with *a* world still here, with the old world not gone but just discredited, he realized one simple, salient fact: Vietnam is the wrong war.

I can't deny Ia Ngu anymore, he thought flatly. But it's not what matters today. I've got to lay it aside—*not* bury it—while I fit myself out to fight the war of the wizards.

Because if I don't, I'm going to die.

He looked at his watch. It was just noon. A good time to start living.

DECEMBER 30 • 12:01 P.M.

He sat down, his back against the wall below the window. Sunlight from the midday sky pierced the slit at a sharp angle and played on the back of his head, a small but welcome comfort after the cold, uneasy night. He watched the rest of its rectangle on the floor beside his tight fingers and tried to get the feeling he had in his studio, where he was in control. The roar of an airliner came down in waves from the sky outside. Could he be only twenty-three miles from home?

Cornelius had said that wizardry was in the mind, and if there were any way to beat the wizards, it was in his mind, Max now knew. His body might be burned and battered, but his mind, after so many years live on the air, was still sharp; so, having no other hope and a quiet room to work in, he proposed to let his mind have a run for the money. Just let it run loose through the things he'd been told by Cornelius, by Messing, even by Hardesty, and see if it could find a way out.

He took three quick breaths, and began.

Okay, he thought, I accept what Cornelius told me; even Messing admitted it was right. There's a whole other side to the reality we take for granted, and the rules we know are only half the rules. People can communicate mentally. There are levels of consciousness, which follow a fourfold system. Each of the planets, and everything else in the universe, exerts a pull on every other thing. Everything is related.

So then . . .

. . . a good part of wizardry must be just knowing those relationships. Knowing all the rules. Not just *accepting* telepathy, but finding out how it's done, and doing it yourself. Not just reading about astrology, but understanding it. Anything the human mind has found out once can be found out again, and wizards are just the guys who keep looking when the rest of the world looks away.

Okay, but . . .

But the world—this world, the one that looks away—*is* still playing by *half* the rules; and they *are* real rules. To be a wizard, you have to look at the other side of reality, but you have to be clear about what you're seeing when you do. Just going "Oh, wow" is no help. You could be tripping on an illusion. And letting someone else do the looking, to tell you what's there, is just the Moonies. You have to be your own judge, with all the responsibilities that entails.

You have to be your own Point Man.

Max smiled at that, and then held the smile, amused that he could be smiling after the hell of last night. Madeleine, he thought wryly, by making me feel even worse than I already did, you may have done me a big favor. You took me all the way to the bottom, and there's only one way to go from there.

Well. So far, so good. But knowing all the rules is only part of wizardry. There's To Know, To Will, To Dare, and To Be Silent. The fourfold system. So you have to Know, and Will to do something with it, and Dare to do it. And then Shut Up, so you can judge what actually happened. Turn the noise down and look at it rationally.

Being rational about the irrational—that's the key. If you're only irrational, you're just crazy, like Domenico. And if you're only rational, then you're just a bookkeeper. Either way, you've only got half the world.

It was beginning to come together.

Are there talismans, or aren't there? Cornelius and Messing both say yes; no doubt, a conference full of scientists would say no. But what they say doesn't prove it *to me*. Even if I were to *want* to believe, after all this, I couldn't *know* until I'd used one myself. And if I never did, then the only honest thing to do would be to keep an open mind. But if I did use one, then I should accept what happened. I might want to Be Silent about it, for political reasons, but it'd be self-defeating to try to fool myself.

Honesty. There's another key word. Be rational about the irrational, *and* the rational. If you lie, you confuse what facts there are; then it's no wonder people don't know what the hell is going on.

Honesty and rationality, he thought, add up to nobility. And that's what I always got out of my lion.

There was no longer any sense of passing time in Max's mind; just the sense of passing thought, like the waves over which the *Poseidon* had surged, each wave flowing seamlessly into another. Sometimes the next thought had come to him earlier; sometimes there was no visible connection to anything he had ever thought in his life. But he was gradually gaining a feel for the ocean.

Sometime in the midafternoon he realized that he'd been hearing voices from outside his window. The sun had gone over the tower, and his east-facing slot was now pierced only by the wind, whose whistling song had disguised the sounds of voices almost totally, at first. But now that he stood and strained to hear, he could make out a chorus of both male and female tones (the silent spectators, back among the living?). Whoever they were, they were far below, in the courtyard at the base of the tower, and they were chanting fervently.

> Thee I invoke, the Bornless One.
> Thee, that didst create the Earth and the Heavens.
> Thee, that didst create the Night and the Day.
> Thee, that didst create the Darkness and the Light.
> Thou art Osorronophris, whom no man hath seen at any time.
> Thou art Jabas . . . Thou art Iapos . . .

It went on, the words troubling and strange, but Max had heard enough. He turned from the window, and the smile on his face was wide and hard.

He had his answer.

There was at least the chance of a way out.

Somewhere in this castle is my lion, he thought; a talisman of incredible power. And I have to do just what they're doing: try to communicate. Try to make the connection that has to exist between my lion and me.

His smile grew harder. He didn't really know what he meant, exactly, but he knew that he was right.

So he sat down on the stones again, rested his back against the wall, and began to concentrate on his carving. There was probably a sacred lotus position for this sort of thing, but he didn't know it. Neither did he know any spells or lion chants; thinking would have to do. Attunement, Cornelius had said. The way of the mystic.

At first it was all very deliberate and conscious. The connection must have something to do with the connection he had already, the feelings of pride it had always evoked. He tried to concentrate on that, and nothing else.

Soon, though, all this conscious activity grew stale, and Max had to fight to stay with it. Each time he caught his thoughts wandering away, which happened more and more frequently, he forced them back; he had never known how hard it was to think of just one thing, even for a few seconds. His D.J.'s mind was sharp, all right: too sharp. But, at some point, he realized from one distant corner of his mind that he hadn't been wandering for a while. And he saw that, even then, the bulk of his thoughts remained primarily with the lion.

He was finding the levels of consciousness in himself.

He began to see the lion, very clearly. It grew to fill his mind till he could see it from all angles. He saw the burn scar, and he saw the initials. He studied its face; he examined its color. He could see it in some elemental jungle, padding through the tall, saffron-colored grass, its head up, eyes bright, and tail swinging. The damp heat of the jungle lay over it like a blanket; birds cawed from the high shadows and were answered by others. Flies buzzed around the amber fur, ignored by this king of all beasts. It came to a small knoll covered with dry, yellow scrub, and looked down over the golden world below. It was his world. Whatever he desired was his, because what he desired he deserved. He was not so much a single animal as a pure force of unfettered nature.

No more did Max August feel the confines of a cold stone cell. Max August was padding through his golden kingdom.

And now he was exploring.

Chapter 29

DECEMBER 30 • 5:00 P.M.

Just before dusk the door to Max's cell rattled momentarily, and then opened to admit three figures. Max was following the sundown through the thick black mat of jungle fronds, and he'd been undisturbed all day. It took several seconds before he knew that he was no longer alone; several more before he could say that his consciousness was back in this one room and time.

He stretched, feeling his kinks give way, and swallowed, tasting his saliva going down; it was all he had eaten all day. But the lion had fed, in the heat of the afternoon, and Max felt no hunger.

The real lion—the talisman—hadn't come to him, he was only now consciously realizing. But that didn't seem to matter, either. It was hard to shake the sense of harmony he'd felt these past few hours, and he'd gotten what he'd needed from his exploration, even if it wasn't what he'd thought he'd wanted.

Ringed round him now were Wolf Messing, his wife, and the hound. Max ran his eyes lazily over Wolf's vexed frown and the dog's savage grin, as he sought the eyes of the old woman. They met his blankly, curiously—but unwaveringly. He held her gaze, and in the end, something dark flashed within their depths, like piranhas in a pool—just before she turned to stare adoringly at Wolf.

The shaman was tapping his fingers. "Not to sleep in my presence, Herr August. Did you not sleep well last night?"

"You know I did." Max's voice was almost amused. He remained where he was on the floor, his legs languidly outstretched.

Messing stepped into the slight bit of brightness that remained of the outside light. "I know you did. Yes. And I am come to tell you why." He chuckled as he took his hand away from his hip, and held it out toward Max, palm up. He then brought his other hand around with a professional flourish and clamped it solidly over the other one, only to lift it again as if it had bounced. But now a chalice stood upon his open palm; the same chalice Madeleine had held.

"I have analyzed your essence, Herr August." He dropped his outstretched hand to his side, and caught the chalice with his other hand before it had begun to fall. With the skill only years on stage could produce, he tipped it toward Max, his wrist high, building the suspense with the time he was taking. A single drop of cloudy liquid appeared on its lip and hung there, sparkling in the fading light. "I have analyzed the energy of your essence, and found you a very ignorant man. You know almost nothing of what you have involved yourself in."

Max looked at Frau Messing. "Do you agree, madam?"

She frowned, perplexedly.

Messing tipped his head back and regarded him from under his heavy brow. "You think to disconcert me?"

"Let her answer the question."

"Do not be absurd."

By the door the three-legged dog growled. Its feral eyes watched Max unblinkingly. Frau Messing rose on tiptoe, as if she might cheer, but wasn't sure; and fanned herself, although it wasn't warm. Messing took a bow, acknowledging his triumph.

"You have no power here," he said with obvious relish. "You have no rights, no means to bargain for them. I had thought you understood, but when I think not, I will teach you. Now, have you any further questions?"

Max got easily to his feet. He brushed the sides of his jeans and straightened his back, taking his time, feeling those kinks loosening, too. He did have questions, of course he did; but he was determined not to forget who and what he faced, as he would have these past four days. The dog was waiting for it; Messing was waiting for it. He wouldn't do it.

He smiled and said nothing.

There was a sudden burst of pleasure in Messing's beady eyes. "You continue thinking of me as a 'worthy opponent,'" he said. "But I have not opponents. Only victims."

Messing saw Max lift an eyebrow. "Cornelius? Pfagh! He has not challenged me for you, no? A wise plan, for once. Might have expected him to be bounded by you, as he's done with that appalling singer. But he knows a fool as well as me.

"He has held you, I now know, tantalized but at bay with his several 'explanations.' He feels he cannot trust you. And with good reasons, to judge by your display of 'heroics' to come to the north Farallon. Yet he does not quit you. No. He is a vain and corrupted man, with a mania for material reward. But he has not been rewarded by the four talismans of Fez. He is an old man, older than me, and he overreaches this time. He has not the power to stop my plan anymore."

Max made no reply, but as a professional talker, he recognized that this denunciation had been the Wolf's longest speech to date that didn't concern himself. If Messing felt such a need to justify his situation, it rekindled Max's hope in Cornelius. Maybe silence was . . . as golden as the lion.

Certainly the shaman didn't appreciate his audience's lack of response. His wife started to clap, mechanically, but he waved her off and kept his eyes on Max.

"Your friend Cornelius has made the 'explanation' that this is a war between wizards, Herr August. Would you like for me to tell you the truth?"

Max stifled a yawn, but without his afternoon of exploration with the lion, he could never have pulled it off. That one had hit home. As it was, he made a show of almost summoning polite interest, and noted that Messing apparently couldn't read him so easily today.

The old man threw his arms wide. "The truth, in fact, is that this is not a war between wizards, but between Devas—also known as Devils, or Angels, or Gods. This is a war, not for men, but for the *fate* of men, committed onto the grand scale; and all of us, even me, are but instruments of their wills. Some of us, however, are more conscious instruments than others.

"These Devas are to man what man is to elementals. Vastly superior, they look on us as we look on gnomes, wondering at our lack of individuality, our repetitive actions, and our difficulty in recognizing those of a higher order that surround us. Sometimes, clearly, we do recognize them; once as beings of light, then as the gods that ride chariots, then as the spirits of nature, now as flying-saucer men. I do not mean we 'recognize' them; I mean we think so. For they come among us as we would come among the gnomes, if we were wishing to affect them. We would do whatever necessary to mold to their realm and not to frighten them, for they are easily frightened. Then, if we became interested enough in these worthless tiny creatures, to wish to direct them, we would choose some among them to work for us, for we would not be suited to their realm to do it.

"This is the final secret of all shamanism, Herr August: there are those below, and those above. We control, and *are controlled.*"

Messing's face was flushed, and his hands trembled slightly. Both his wife and, damnably, the black hound were craning forward, drinking in every word.

"Above man," said Messing, "are the Twin Devas—sometimes known as the Brothers, or the Lovers. Osiris and Set in Egypt. Zeus and Typhoeus in Greece. Wodin and Loki in Germany. Jehovah and Satan in Israel."

Max couldn't let that one pass, though he kept his voice disbelieving and sarcastic. "You're not telling me you work for the Devil, are you?"

Messing lifted his head; a point scored. "Clearly no. The Devil is but one limited superstition, from the many attempts by men to explain the nature of the Brothers.

"I talk of endless, eternal Duality, symbolized in these myths and in others: Yin and Yang, Darkness and Light, Earth and Heavens. Cornelius talked of the fourfold division, and this exists. Yet this clearly is two groupings of two. Four is of the lower levels; two is of the highest.

"So now you are seeing the absurdity of your protector's 'explanation' to you. I do not battle him, and he does not battle me. Rather, my Deva, that men call Naught, battles his Deva, called Essence. And still there is no 'battle,' for the contention between the Brothers is endless. There is no other state of being for Them. Does Night battle Day?

"Yet more," said Messing, gesturing dramatically toward the window, now black with the unnoticed fall of darkness, "sometimes the Day predominates, and sometimes the Night. There are points of turning, and for the Brothers, one approaches. The Millennium. Who rules as we enter the year 2000 sows the seeds for all that follows in one thousand years. It is that for which my Master lusts, and that for which I serve as His agent.

"On Earth, I serve the KGB, and they serve me. But in other realms, we both serve Naught, though only I am so aware."

Messing wiped the sweat from his forehead and upper lip with a white handkerchief he pulled from his left sleeve and turned back toward the dog, an inky blot now in the low lemon light. No words were spoken, but the animal trotted obediently forward and stood just behind the old man, sideways to him. Messing sat down on its broad back. As on the night before, the strongest glow of the omnipresent light surrounded the shaman, but to Max, that glow looked somewhat weaker. He hoped so. But with the whole scene once more lit like a fever dream, it was hard to be certain of subtleties.

Messing had recovered himself and was going on. "Through history, each Millennium has marked a point of turning, as one Brother or the other took command of the centuries. The old world was swept away, either through natural catastrophe or through political change. Each time the Millennium has come close, panic has swept men, and they have feared the end of the world, but that will never happen; this realm endures like every other. It is the form of life, not life itself, which dies.

"The last time Naught took the Millennium was in the sinking of Atlantis and the shaping of the continents as we know them—which may, to you, seem long since. But you perhaps know the analogy of history, in which the fifteen billion years since the creation of the universe is represented by a single year. On such a scale, our galaxy does not appear until one third of the 'year' has gone by. Our solar system does not appear until two-thirds. And man, marvelous man, does not appear until ten-thirty P.M. on 31 December! And then—then, Herr August, the most recent Ice Age ends at four minutes to midnight, and all of recorded history begins at eleven fifty-nine!

"This is more than a pretty arrangement, Herr August. It is a most instructive model, for points of turning ever occur on 31 December—just as the next will occur tomorrow."

"Tomorrow?" Max said through tight lips.

"Oh, yes. Tomorrow midnight, at the second between the years, Naught will take control of myself, and I shall take control of the elements, and we shall shape the remainder of the twentieth century, to ensure the triumph of Decay in the fast-coming Third Millennium!"

He began to laugh.

DECEMBER 30 • 5:50 P.M.

Messing's laugh climbed quickly, out of control, and so all-consuming that he had to turn and take hold of the hound's thick neck to avoid falling over to the floor. The dog moved its head to keep Max in view, but the jock was transfixed far less by Messing's antics than by his plan. The man's obsessed, thought Max with a kind of creeping horror. Really obsessed. It's no wonder I never knew what he'd do next. He's not bound by any rules at all.

After a minute or two the shaman began to gasp for breath. His laughter became strangled, sobbing barks, but it didn't end. That came only when he slumped full across the dog, his mouth wide and slack, beatific. His wife came forward and helped him sit up again, brushing him off; it was seemingly one of her wifely duties, and a routine one. Was nothing in the Wolf's world to be trusted?

Messing rubbed his face and wiped the tears from his eyes as he looked back at Max. A chuckle still danced just beneath the surface of his voice, as he spoke once more to Max's thoughts. "Madness, Herr August. Oh, yes! Glorious! Inimitable! Of all men, I do live in the world of mine own devising, and is it not grander than the world of the herd? The herd is sane; that is its curse. I live as my Master moves me, and the name of Sin is Restriction."

"The name of Sin," said Max brutally, "is whatever you can't do." If he could do nothing else, he would bring this party back to earth and kill out the horror he felt. "And you can't do much, can you, old man? You leave all the real work to your gay deceivers—this bitch, and the Korelatovna bitch, and good old Mr. Xin. Not to mention your zombies."

It worked. The smile dropped from Messing's eyes as if a trapdoor had opened in his skull. He sat up straight, then stood up once more. He snapped his fingers. "Narda!"

Behind him the woman bestirred herself again. From beneath her voluminous skirts she produced a crystal ball, which she held up with a look of childish triumph. After a moment of a gaze so direct and deep as she might have lavished on a child of her womb, she handed it reverently to her husband. Max was reminded of the female gnome with her rock.

"Observe, Herr August," said Messing in exactly the same dramatic tone as he must have used on thousands of volunteers from the audience over the years. "Is it not precisely like those of charlatans?" He laughed again, but harshly.

Max looked at the crystal. The shaman's saffron glow flew into its depths and spun back around forever, while faint shadows shifted and hid. But then, as he looked deeper, the shadows rolled over on themselves, turning inside out, to reveal dull crusts of white light in their bellies. The light grew and surrounded the darkness, and the light and the dark formed two figures. Was it just an illusion, or did the figures resemble—?

No. It was Earl and his wife. Clearly.

Max tore his eyes away. With Messing's powers of mind control it wasn't hard to guess what was happening. But the rest of what he saw around him in the cell—the stone walls, the watching hound, the clothes he was wearing—these were all normal and unchanged. And his mind, as he probed it with that newly won sense of familiarity he had spent the afternoon in obtaining, felt secure. He still felt, at heart, like the lion.

Be honest, he thought. Don't deny anything real.

He flicked his eyes back toward the crystal, and saw Earl and Fern sitting on their couch in their living room.

Earl yawned.

He stretched.

He scratched himself and leaned to his right to pick up his TV remote control. He thumbed it, and sound—"Double your pleasure, double your fun"—came pouring out of the crystal as if sluicing down a long pipe. After Messing's diatribe on the duality of nature, those happy singing voices echoed ominously in Max's ears. Earl settled back with his arm around Fern as the station announced itself, and then, with the subdued clatter of typewriters, "This is the western edition of the CBS Evening News . . . with Dan Rather in New York . . . and Terry Drinkwater in Los Angeles." "Good evening . . ."

Earl put down his remote control and lit a cigarette, then leaned back once more, a grimace of disgust on his face at the sights revealed to him on the television screen. The smoke and Rather's voice spun lazily away.

But suddenly the smoke began to move more quickly, and within seconds it was driving off the red end of his cigarette in a thin, straight stream. Earl exhaled, and that smoke, too, blew abruptly away. He half turned his head to look for the draft, curiosity wrinkling his brow, and then his mouth opened in a silent O. The cords of his neck grew taut, and his thin hands went up toward his face. He stared at something which Max couldn't see, and he screamed. Fern turned then, and screamed, too.

Max moved to his left to get another angle on the room. A figure came into view, and it was the figure of a storm cloud, its lightning glistening and crackling. Small objects in Earl's room began to fly off their tables and shelves in flat arcs. The Christmas tree toppled with a crystallike crash.

The two of them seemed frozen with fear, but at last Earl jumped up and ran for the outside door. Before he made two yards though, he, too, was caught up in the force of the gale. His hands stretched outward, the fingers stiff and twitching, as he strove desperately to reach the doorknob. He could not. And as Max watched in horrified revulsion, the veins in his friend's forehead and nose began to rupture. Earl fell, his eyes bulging from his head. Fern reached for him. Then the television exploded in a frenzy of flat smoke and electronic fire. The windows burst inward, and the room was filled with flying glass. Earl's legs kicked once as he fell across his screaming wife, and then they were swallowed in the cloud.

Max raised his eyes and the expression in them was chilling.

"A small demonstration, Herr August. Very small and insignificant, against the demonstration to come tomorrow midnight. You see now, you have not a place in the contention. You are my prisoner until the end of your little world—which you will see well from this window. Accept that fate, or die as your friends."

"And how do you plan to 'end my world'?"

"You will see. Tomorrow." Messing held out the crystal to his wife, who replaced it in some inner pocket of her skirts. "Come, Narda," he said. "There will be no encore to this evening's performance."

"Messing!" Max's voice cut like a knife. "What is the point of keeping me alive?"

"There is no point, Herr August," said the shaman. "In the end as in the egg . . ." And he laughed.

Chapter 30

DECEMBER 30 • 6:10 P.M.

Max turned toward his narrow window before they'd even left the cell, and looked hard at the night sky. He was already putting the Wolf out of his thoughts as he struggled with the larger question of the Wolf's pronouncement.

Everything is connected, yes. But are we *controlled*? Do higher orders use us as their toys? Is the game over before it begins?

He couldn't believe that; but he couldn't say why. It might have been only that he'd never believed it—that the lion within him had never believed it—but above and beyond that, there was the *way* in which the Wolf had tried to sell it.

Once again, Max thought determinedly, the old bastard spent too much time rubbing it in, and the question is why. Is there something I can still do to upset his apple cart? Or—his eyes narrowed—have I been doing it all afternoon?

Picking at it, he turned back from the window . . . and froze. Not everyone had left the cell after all, it seemed. Just where it had stood before, the black hound was crouched and waiting on its three legs, and it was drooling. Its eyes, bright pinpoints in the diminished yellow glow, were not only intelligent now, but alive with a will of their own.

Immediately Max spoke straight to that intelligence. "Fuck you, dog," he said. "Messing said I'm to be kept alive." But inside he knew that this was on the dog's initiative, not the shaman's. And there was nothing in this empty cell to use as a weapon. This was real trouble. The dog, its eyes fixed on his face, began to creep toward him. Max tried to crouch . . .

. . . but then realized, with a sudden, sick fury, that he was sliding down the wall, instead. He was being entranced again!

The same cottony languor was enveloping his muscles. The same chill was flowing through him, and the beads of sweat which had popped out across his skin at his first sight of the dog felt now like small snowflakes. His breathing was slowing. He struck the floor, and it felt like a pillow.

The dog's lips drew back in something akin to a smile.

But this time, that far corner of Max's mind, that bit that had looked on at his lion trance without being caught in it, stayed apart from this trance as well. He grabbed that little corner and held it grimly. He had to hold on—hold on whatever the cost. For a moment his thoughts dissassociated completely, so that this corner was the reality, and the dog was the dream. He balanced on the knife edge . . .

. . . and then his lips, too, drew back in a stiff smile.

He was beating it!

The dog narrowed its bright eyes in anger as Max lifted first one arm and then the other. It growled and came to a halt. Max looked back across the room at it with eyes as hot as its own. And stood up, slowly. But surely.

Now the hound was uncertain. Max said again, distinctly, "Fuck you!" If not for Messing's example, he might have laughed. For the first time he had beaten a spell—the first time since this whole nightmare began! What the hell. He did laugh.

And the full weight of the monstrous dog came down hard on his chest.

Max crashed back against the wall, grabbing hold of black fur with both hands. His fingers were stiff and one hand was burned, but if he could hold his mind, he could hold this. The white teeth never reached his neck. Instead he whirled and slammed the beast against the wall. The claws came loose from his clothes and flesh, and Max kicked out and felt his boot sink home.

And then, all at once—coming *through* the solid door across the room—a lion! Max's lion! Life-size and aflame!

The hound snarled in alarm and leapt back, but too late. The lion landed on the flagstones and kept coming without a pause. Before the dog could do more than bare its white teeth, golden teeth took it hard and tore its throat open, just that fast. Like a tomcat with a field mouse, the lion shook its prey savagely; dark blood sprayed to both sides. In the lion's flaming light, Max saw the dog's eyes fill with conscious, incredulous horror.

Max had called it, and it had come. It was too much to hope for. But he was not at all surprised.

The lion dropped its burden disdainfully. The dog was limp as it struck the floor, but like another of the shaman's servants, it refused to give in so easily. Its dark head came up for one last, warning bark; but then, the blood in its throat cut that off. With a choking cough the head fell back again, for the final time.

"Lion," said Max, starting toward it.

The creature turned its golden head toward him, and . . .

. . . . .

Max is climbing a winding staircase, around the circumference of a dome. Below him are the rude mud buildings of the city of Kish, clustered and narrow; beyond them, the plains. Only from such a height as he now occupies can he ever hope to see the roofs of houses; and to climb these stairs without sanction is death, for this dome is the crown of the temple.

Sharrum-bani-pal, the high priest, is at his side—an old man, with diadem horned and gilded, and a patriarchal beard tightly woven with colorful beads. The beads catch the light from the torches below as the two men climb in their leftward circle. The men of Kish dare not to look up.

Max—or someone very like Max—is to be trained by Sharrum-bani-pal in the movements of the stars, a skill for which the priest is justly famed. It is even said that Sharrum-bani-pal can reconcile the solar and lunar years, though Max believes this to be one of the myths which must inevitably spring up around impenetrable Kish.

The two men reach the top of the dome, a great circular terrace of lapis lazuli. To one side golden instruments lie beside ancient scrolls on a table of sea-green stone, and the low wall of the terrace is inlaid with the largest jewels Max has ever seen. But Sharrum-bani-pal strides past these things to the center of the circle, and points toward the indigo sky. More stars than Max expects glisten there, but Sharrum-bani-pal's long finger points directly at one precisely overhead. Max recognizes it, for he has seen it, always above, setting neither in flood nor in famine, and he has wondered why that should be.

"Kalbu Rabu," says the priest in Akkadian, his voice hushed; as if, Max thinks, the star could hear. "Kalbu Rabu: the Great Lion."

. . . . .

And then Max was back in Messing's tower, staring at the face of this lion. But in the hungry flames which formed it, it was not just one lion. Now it was a crude fetish, as chalked upon a cave wall; now a noble chariot-beast, stylized in the Egyptian manner; now the centerpiece of a medieval coat-of-arms; now a fat, florid painting of the Renaissance. And now, at last, it was a carving of amber and polished woods, with the letters E.D.W. lightly marked on its underside, and a dark scar along its left hind leg . . . before turning once more to a thing of blinding light and broiling heat, like a lion made of neon tubes and set afire.

Max didn't know how he'd recognized it as his lion before; his head was spinning. But he felt an incredible rush of energy from it, and joy. This *was* his lion; he'd gotten it back. And he was saved from his imprisonment. He had won! Won!

. . . . .

And Max is looking out through lion eyes again, as Madeleine Riggs charges him to send a salamander to a madman, with the call to rise, and to kill. Looking through lion eyes as the Wolf uses his Fire and the diamond-eyed denizens of Air to guard Madeleine's abandoned hotel room; and as the Wolf draws the clouds from above the Farallons to cover Suzanna Ward. Max sees, as if from a great height, his own car tearing through Golden Gate Park. He sees Suzanna step out below, and he feels the fire within him spray downward, a mile or more, to spear the girl and drive his own car off the road. "Yet my strongest link hath e'er been with thee, hadst thou but known," says a voice which may be his own. "I must needs perform as I be charged—yet thou didst live while the maid did die."

. . . . .

And there is another shifting, and Max is watching with the lion among rivers of molten rock thirty miles below the surface of the Earth. The magma is alive with salamanders, crawling, huge creatures far removed from the delicate dancing light Max has seen before. Above him, Max sees clearly, the black bull has gathered battalions of gnomes, in their eerily familiar opposing deployment along a great interface of stone. Farther above, where these slabs have allowed gaps to appear between them, and the rock itself has been all but shredded by the strains of years, the eagle has positioned the naiads; and even in these straitened circumstances, the movements of their slim female forms are bewitching.

Finally, far above the surface of the Earth, the sylphs are gathering as storm clouds once again, shrieking to each other with fierce anticipation.

Now, far out in space, the two planets he saw together (Jupiter and Saturn, he knows it now) are square to the Sun, and the Sun is pulling from below the Earth. The midnight moment comes, and Naught joins the mixture. The lion leads his salamanders upward with the lava. The bull bellows for his gnomes to pull, and hard. The naiads slicken the fault line, and in that sickening instant each slab or rock is released.

On the surface which is San Francisco, the ground lunges twenty-five feet, rippling like waves on the sea. Buildings shake and shatter, their windows raining down as lethal razors in the quickening winds. Fires break out on every hill, fed by the ruptured power lines and gas mains. Thirteen hundred New Year's celebrants die, and eight thousand are seriously injured.

(And a voice that is Max's protests, "It would be a catastrophe, sure. But after all of Messing's buildup, about a war between Devas, it seems almost too commonplace.")

(And a voice which might be Max's answers, "Wait.")

The instant of midnight is gone, and Max sees San Francisco rebuilding. Some people—those who always flee adversity—have moved out, but most remain to pick up their lives with that perverse pride which is the hallmark of the survivor. Camera crews are everywhere, flanked by the anchormen and the President, asking human-interest questions. T-shirts saying "I'm a 25-foot man" are selling briskly.

The elementals, however, have not finished their work; in fact, have never quit. Now another quake, as large as the first, rips the Hayward fault in the East Bay. Death and damage are much greater this time. The man-made islands in the bay, including the Alameda Naval Air Station, simply slide back into the ooze, taking hundreds of people and vital emergency systems with them. The San Pablo Dam breaks, flooding Orinda. San Francisco is hit less severely, but severely enough to collapse the makeshift shelters so many of the survivors have found beds in. The Presidents of both the United States and NBC News escape death only through a miracle; four thousand others are not so lucky.

Now people begin to leave in earnest. Moving vans and U-Hauls fill every passable street, but most are still caught in the third quake. Los Angeles experiences its first damage, and suddenly this is not just a San Francisco problem. Yet most of California bides its time, believing the worst must be over, until the fouth quake drops all the land around the South Bay five feet and rips the low coastal hills apart. A tidal wave spurred on by the eagle surges out of the west, and drowns ten thousand souls while sweeping through the breach. The Imperial Valley begins to fill with water, and the rate of fill increases by the month, as new quakes and the new stress of water weight and tidal motion tear at the long-undisturbed farmland.

Three years have passed, but there is no ending. The Sierra Nevada fault near Bakersfield slips, rattling L.A. again, and the volcanoes of Washington State explode uncontrollably. Again the elementals strike, and most of the San Francisco peninsula sinks, turning that beleaguered city into an island. At last the sea can reach the valley unopposed. The weak rock there gives way, and within twenty-four hours, half the California coast is gone.

And on all sides of the Pacific Ocean, in Australia, Japan, and China, lesser quakes and tidal waves are taking their toll as well. In these, the elementals play no part beyond having produced the initial California changes which trigger the other long-awaited disasters. They have no need.

Science cannot explain any of it.

Now everyone is evacuated from what remains of California in one of the Army's finest peacetime efforts—and barely in time. Just two days after Los Angeles and San Diego are declared officially abandoned, they, too, slide into the sea.

The people are resettled in the interior. A very few travel only as far as the Sierra Madre mountains; most must go at least to Nevada and Arizona, where they cannot see the ocean—and many will not be satisfied until they have escaped the low floor of the deserts to come to rest on the Rockies. The federal budget is thrown away and the U.N. moves in, as all efforts are bent to aid these bewildered victims.

But even now the quakes do not end. Every month, it seems—just as the paranoia and disassociation might be moderating—a new bite is taken from the West. By the sixth New Year after the initial quake, the Pacific has indeed begun to tear the Sierra Madres apart, and stage an end run around them through the Southwest. The lack of revenue and farm produce from what was once a vital part of the economy is causing crippling shortages, and inflation is over one hundred fifty percent annually.

Now begins the resentment, as the residents of the Midwest begin to take their anger and helpless frustration at these inexplicable events out on the strangers who have put such a burden on their good will and torn their lives apart. Crime begins to mount, no one is safe, and the Chinese water torture of each new quake steps up the beat. Easterners, fed up and fearing the possibility of further mass migrations into their territory, begin to sell out and flee to Europe and Africa. But this only spreads the resentment and fear, and fuels it further as the Americans, the ones rich enough to make such moves, begin to buy land and houses at prices unavailable to the man on the street; while those Americans who were men on the street themselves arrive with nothing, and bring the stench of death. The urban and bush guerrillas, their numbers swelling daily, strike hard at the pariahs; the Americans, equally desperate and making their final stand, fight back just as hard.

And, secure behind its forbidding borders and the mightiest military machine on Earth, solidly entrenched on the only remaining undamaged land mass, Mother Russia waits.

The Millennium will soon be upon us.

. . . . .

Max, hardly knowing what was real and what a dream, shook his head and looked around at his cell. He was alone, the lion was gone—but the door, once oak and steel, had been reduced to a ruin of charred embers and pools of gray-black slag. The black hound's one remaining hindleg lay in a rivulet, smoldering with a dreadful stench.

Max kicked the limp body to one side.

"Kalbu Rabu?"

There was no answer. Kalbu Rabu had completed his work, and such beings are not easily held.

Max was dazed and spent. His watch had stopped, and he had no idea how long his visions had lasted, whether a minute or an hour. But that reminded him that the Wolf might come looking for his dog at any time, so he had better make use of this chance while he still had it.

He stepped gingerly across the still-glowing metal, and out through the remains of the door. The stairs wound away from him interminably, and so did his mind as he took them. What Messing was proposing was so *easy*, given enough power, and power didn't seem to be anybody's problem. Not even the strange enigma of his lion could keep Max's thoughts from the epic horror he had seen.

He'd thought he'd known horror in the war. He'd thought he'd looked it in the face, in the past.

But the future was far worse.

Chapter 31

DECEMBER 30 • 6:47 P.M.

Max's legs were rubbery by the time he reached the bottom of the stairs, and he shook himself angrily. You've got to do better than that! he raged. Save the collapse for prime time! He hadn't eaten now for two days, and, though the advent of Kalbu Rabu had filled him with energy, the lion's departure had brought him back to earth. He was hungry, he was cold, he was bruised and he was tired—and he was damned if he'd let any of that affect him.

He forced himself to make good time back through the castle's corridors, within the limits of common sense. It's a popular fallacy that you creep when you want to hide; but by that very definition, it's creeping that attracts attention. Besides, being obvious makes better time.

As he rounded the last turn before the room with the stage and the wheel, he was confronted with an open doorway, from which the yellow haze poured like a sunny morn. He halted to one side of it and dropped to his knees to take a look.

In an ornate chair cut from silver and brass, Wolf Messing lay lank and flaccid, his hands hanging near to the floor and his eyes wide open, staring into the distance. His chest rose and fell almost imperceptibly, but steadily; a slight crust had formed around his slack mouth. From time to time, he crooned.

Beyond him, obscured by his brighter glow, other forms were similarly laid out.

Max wanted to kill him. He lusted to kill him. He knew that there was no percentage in being fancy; dead is dead is dead. But it was inconceivable that the master shaman would leave his body defenseless. The intensity of the glow around his body showed the Wolf to be fantastically alert on some level, if not on this one.

Resignedly Max drew his head back and stood up. There were other ways. He took his three quick breaths; counted five; then stretched out and stepped past the opening. He waited on the far side, but all was silence. The glow remained unchanged. Max nodded once, and went on.

But the door to the talisman room was locked.

As he stood there figuring what to do about it, he heard his name spoken once. Looking further down the hallway, he saw Kalbu Rabu once more, peering out from under an archway. Immediately, he turned and went to join him, feeling his previous lift.

"Good," said Max *sotto voce.* "I thought I'd lost you again."

The answering voice was in his head. "Go now. The Wolf hath

set a psychokinetic to watch o'er the master portal, but thou canst flee through yonder window." Kalbu Rabu nodded toward a shuttered square in the room beyond the archway, flanked by floor-length purple drapes.

"I need you and the other carvings," Max whispered.

"I cannot come, for I be not free."

"I'm your master, aren't I? I free you."

The lion laughed. "I am with thee only 'pon the level elemental. My physical form doth yet bestride the Great Wheel, behind portals which thou couldst never breach, and which I have been charged to protect, not attack."

"Then I'll come back for you, with my friends."

"We shall be gone." Kalbu Rabu pawed the stone in a clear gesture of dismissal. "Haste. Cornelius will know what must be done. Tell him all thou hast learned, and place thy trust in him."

Max wanted very much to touch this thing he'd come so far for, but it was impossible. He could hardly bare to look at it, as bright as it was. So instead, he raised his right hand, palm out. "Kalbu Rabu . . . thanks. What more can I say—except that we'll meet again."

He went quickly to the window. Its shutter pulled back on unrusted hinges, and Max was looking out on the open sea. Waves crashed with the normal phosphorescence of ocean water on black, hulking rocks, twenty feet below.

It was the work of a few moments to braid the curtains into a rope strong enough to hold his weight. Securing it to a heavy statue of Kali, Max climbed into the opening and looked back. The lion was gone. Max nodded and began to lower himself into the free world.

When he felt the cold spray on his ankles, he tried to brace his feet against the sloping rocks; but the rocks were too slick, and when he let go of the drapes, he fell hard. The pain it caused him was the most welcome sensation he had known in twenty-four hours. Looking away from the feebly glowing castle, his only light came from the unchanging stars, so clear that the Milky Way stood out sharply. The air was extremely brisk, the water more so, and it was exquisite.

Carefully Max made his way up and over the boulders, hugging the side of the castle where it nestled among them. When he got beyond the castle's side, he headed back toward the far side of the island, where he had left the *Poseidon*; but avoiding the openness of the basin as much as possible. At the end of his journey, however, lay a not unexpected disappointment. The *Poseidon* was gone. Just a few charred pieces of wood, washed up amongst the rocks, marked its passing.

Max was ready for that. The Wolf must have his own means of transport at hand, and Max had a way to find it—a way he couldn't explain, but knew now how to use. He held his hands to his temples and concentrated on Kalbu Rabu.

Almost at once he felt the chill around him subside. Then, he felt the flow of energy. Finally there was a split second in which contact was made, and he saw his route, in its entirety. He turned his head toward the left. There, on the crest of the basin, a soft glow bobbed—and Max could see it straight on. He scrambled across the rocks after it, his footing unnaturally sure, while the salamander stayed always the same distance ahead. And soon, Max found himself overlooking a closely packed pile of rubble.

But the salamander glided toward those rocks, and then through them. Max laughed, and lowered himself through them as well. Beyond the illusion was a small cove, deeply sheltered by the cliffs. There weren't supposed to be any coves on the north Farallon, of course, but that was a minor matter. This cove held a twenty-five-foot Formula, all he needed and more to get the hell out.

The salamander had vanished.

Wide, easy stairs, cut with the old man and his wife in mind, took him down to the boat, where he cast off and pushed off in less than a minute. By keeping a close watch on each side, he was able to move the Formula out of the narrow inlet silently and without damage. As he entered the flow of the ocean, it required extra care not to wash up against the rocks to leeward; but once past them, he could sit back and let the waves carry him out of earshot of the island. Only then did he hot-wire the ignition and head for the lights of home.

Chapter 32

DECEMBER 30 • 8:55 P.M.

The tide was rising when Max reached Bolinas. He came into the harbor without slowing, throttling back only when he was in clear danger, and let the old tires hung from the dock take as much of the force as he dared. He didn't much care what shape the Wolf's boat ended up in. Luckily the residents of Bolinas were far from the Rod and Boat Club at this hour, physically and probably spiritually.

The door to the club was locked; he broke it down. The one on the other side, leading to the street, he almost broke unlocking. But the van, thank God, was just where he'd left it; his one fear as he crossed the twenty-three miles of sea to reach this spot was that Messing had destroyed his transportation up the mountain. Even now he approached the vehicle with caution, before unlocking the driver's door in one decisive motion.

Valerie Drake sat up from the unfolded bunk in the back. She was awfully damn lucky the light had come on when the door opened.

"What are you doing here?" Max asked roughly.

"That's a fine way to greet an old friend," she answered, rubbing the sleep from her eyes. She was wearing a tight plaid lumberjack's shirt and corduroy jeans, rumpled now, over high leather boots. "I've been waiting here since noon."

"Waiting for me? You don't know how close you came to waiting till doomsday."

She looked at him levelly. "Yes, Max. I do."

"What do you . . . ?" He stopped, halfway into the cab; then finished the motion and slammed the door hard. "Shit!" he exploded.

She came forward and slid into the passenger's seat across from him. "I'm sorry, Max. When I told you there was nobody out there, I thought it was the truth."

"But somebody lied to you. And I can just guess who!"

"Yes, but you have to understand him—"

"Understand him, my ass! I understand a lot of things now, but that'd take some doing. I suppose he did it for my own good, or something like that."

"That's right."

"The fuck! I've had it up to here with old men playing God with me!" He brought his fist down hard on the dash. "And I thought he'd made an honest mistake! I was still trying to warn him of Messing's plan so he could do something about it! But he must know all about that, too?"

"I think so. But—"

"But but but! But nothing! This sucks, Val—first, last, and foremost. You might not believe this—I was nothing much compared to a Big Star or a Big Star's Wizard—but I used to stand on my own two feet. I knew where I was going, and I went there. But ever since I got involved in this goddamned wizardry, I've been nothing but a Ping-Pong ball, going wherever some old asshole smacks me. 'Here, Max, here's all you need to know today. Here, Max, accept my generous protection or get out.' At least the Wolf was straight about what he was up to." He ran out of words for the moment, and sat there seething. "I should take this van and head straight home."

Valerie put her hand on his arm. "And leave him alone to stop Messing and his agents?"

"He doesn't need me. He's had so much experience, remember?"

"But you need him, to protect you from Messing. The shaman will come after you again, very soon."

"I'll take my chances. I've got another ally now, one I trust a lot more. Besides, if Cornelius does beat Messing, I'm safe anyway. And if he doesn't, then we're all of us dead, anyway."

"But he did it for your own good, as you say."

"How? How does it help me? He couldn't have planned what happened out there. He might—*might*—have had some hopes for how it would turn out, but to me it just looks like he tossed me in the pool to see if I'd learn to swim. A pool filled with piranhas. And I don't see that he had any lifeguards on duty in case I sank."

Color flooded her cheeks. "Look, I'm not defending what he did. The whole reason I'm here is that when I found out that he'd lied to me, I felt I had to come down and see if you got back all right. He didn't send me."

"Say that again."

"He didn't—"

"No, I mean about your having to see that I was all right."

Valerie drew back, her hand leaving his arm. "Don't overestimate yourself," she said guardedly. "It's only a normal human reaction."

"And don't underestimate *yourself.* Punks aren't supposed to have human reactions."

The van was suddenly very still as they looked at each other, like jungle beasts come suddenly face-to-face in the tall grass. And then Max reached out and pulled her face toward his. She tensed, resisting, but not vigorously. Their lips met.

Her mouth yielded.

Max pulled back and looked at her again. Her eyes had a look he'd not seen before—a look of almost fear.

Almost, but not quite.

He kissed her again, and this time she returned it. His hand felt the pulse in her silken throat.

Then she drew away and turned her head toward the fogged side window. "Why can't you leave well enough alone?"

He shifted sideways in his seat, following her. "Is it well enough? You, and a man four times your age."

"Leave Corny out of this!" she hissed. "He's a good man, and we love each other—in our way. He's a wizard, and that makes him different. He plays by different rules. But we're good together."

"You and I'd be good together, too."

"Maybe we would. But it won't happen."

"Val, your career's not so important that you have to sacrifice everything to it."

"Shut up, damn you!" She dug her key ring out of her pocket and jabbed the ignition key into the lock. "I'm going back up the mountain. If you're coming, you drive—and if you're not, then get out."

"I thought we—"

"I mean it." Her face was strained and white. "If you think I sleep with him just so he'll guide my career, you're full of shit."

"Hey, that isn't what I meant."

"Drive or get out."

"Listen to me, dammit. I only meant that you put everything second to your career, but maybe now it's time for a change. I didn't mean anything else. All right?"

She said nothing.

"All right?" He reached out and took her hand. It lay limp at first, but then she sighed.

"All right." Her shoulders came down with a shudder. "Okay. But you have to understand. . . ."

"I do. You're living your lifelong fantasy: the life of a superstar. Hot spots, limos, coke, and fans. I understand that. I've done it myself, sometimes." He exhaled his own tension and held her eyes. "But I like *you*, Val—the you that comes from Louisville and thinks up a name like Purina Dog Ciao—and still knows she's living a dream. I don't care all that much for Valerie Drake, the Megastar, with her recording tricks and posters, and special interview rules. If that bothers you, so be it. I've only busted up one ongoing romance in my life, and I didn't like the results. I won't get between you and Cornelius, if that's the way you want it. But I think the you that I like is the one that likes me back, and I'll be looking for more of her." Then he laughed, ruefully. "If Cornelius gets us through tomorrow."

Valerie wouldn't meet his gaze. "Just drive," she said. "Just drive."

Her tone gave him plenty to think about on their long trip up the mountain.

Chapter 33

DECEMBER 30 • 10:30 P.M.

Cornelius's house was brightly lit when they pulled up before it over an hour later. Even as Max killed the engine, the wizard himself appeared in the front doorway and hurried out to meet them, steaming mugs held in each hand. Max looked at Val, and she shrugged; helplessly, he thought. He opened the van door and stepped out onto the dirt. One of the glasses was placed in his hand. Its warmth felt good, and he remembered again how hungry he was.

"Hot buttered rum," smiled Cornelius. "Mead for the conquering hero. Please come inside; I have a fire going."

"That sounds all right," said Max briefly. He was determined to be the older man's equal this time, and not a refugee. For a moment he considered turning to Val and clicking mugs. But it wouldn't be fair to put that kind of pressure on her now.

As he conducted them into the house, however, Cornelius was no longer playing the protector. Now he played at being a butler, guiding Max to one of the deep brown chairs to the left of the fireplace, and Val to one on the right. Between them he placed a small redwood table crowded with plates, a salver of roast beef, potato salad, and steaming rolls wrapped in a napkin, oozing butter.

"You knew we were coming," said Max conversationally.

"Eat. Please. There's more where that came from."

"Fine," Max said. He made himself a heaping sandwich, and

ladled a hunk of salad the size of a softball onto his plate; sat back and took a huge bite; washed it down with rum. The odor of the butter and cinnamon filled the room.

He stretched contentedly. "You're a son of a bitch," he said to his host.

"So Valerie has told me," answered Cornelius imperturbably. "Can I get you anything else?"

Max wanted a reaction. "You can get out and leave the two of us alone."

Val sat forward. "Max!"

"I'll suffer some of your abuse, Max," said Cornelius quietly. Standing between the two of them, the wizard's face was bright with reflected flame. He seemed now neither young nor old, but eternal. "It is true that I tricked you. But there was a valid reason, and I won't suffer you indefinitely."

"Ah, now that's the Corny I came to see." Max took another savage bite from his sandwich and talked around it. "You had a reason. Man, everybody's got a reason. They can be crazy as hell, but they believed sincerely in what they were doing, so please, be understanding." He sneered. "My ass! You're a son of a bitch."

"He's a wizard, Max," said Val desperately.

The Point Man ignored her. "You know what Messing's planning, don't you, Corny? And that he already has all *four* of the talismans."

"Yes."

"Then what the hell are you playing games with *me* for? Why aren't you stopping *him*—if you really can?"

"I can."

"Then why?"

"Because the moment of decision is tomorrow at midnight—and I have only ritual preparations to make for it, tomorrow, during the day." The man in black's eyes rested momentarily on Val, then flicked back. "With two days of spare time, then, I chose to look at you. You wanted to find your lion. You wanted to confront

Aleksandra Korelatovna. You wanted to learn wizardry. And you did not want to sit on my veranda and enjoy the sun. So I wondered if you could accomplish all this."

"You could have asked me. I never doubted it."

"I did ask you, in the most direct way."

"You're still a son of a bitch."

"No, I am a wizard. And so are you," said Mr. Cornelius, sitting down on another of the oversized chairs beside Max. "Could you have told me that?"

Max laughed, but only half derisively. "I'm far from being a wizard. Messing did things out there I can't begin to explain. I may have called my lion, but I'm still not sure what I got."

"You're sure," said Cornelius. "You know."

"Look, let's talk about the end of the world. Forget about me. What are you going to do tomorrow night?"

Cornelius looked him in the eye. "If you'll join me, Max, I'll use your newly won link with Kalbu Rabu. If you won't, it will be no great loss."

"Spoken like a politician. But you forget one thing: I know what that link can mean now. You won't throw away a tap on one of the talismans."

"Max, despite what you and the Wolf believe, the use of talismans demonstrates weakness, not strength. Talismans are like crutches; their powers are always subservient to the wizard's own, and so they are only reminders—just as the Summation of Fez intended. I, however, do not need reminders.

"The Wolf must have *things* to be complete: the carvings, applause, his KGB apparat. This is his weakness. I must have only myself; so when we meet at the time between times, I shall triumph."

"So you keep telling me," Max said. "But what *about* his KGB apparat? They can all of them teleport. I've seen them."

"Teleportation is primitive, Max. Primitive. Those people are as much a side issue to this struggle as—pardon me—yourself."

Max scowled. "It sounds almost boring, the way you put it."

"Not boring. No, not boring at all. But inevitable. And clear."

"Fine—but what about the Devas? Messing does have an ally bigger even than you. You need the Deva of Essence, don't you?"

"Forget about Devas, too."

"What do you mean? Forget gods?" Max put down his mug with a thud, splattering hot rum across the table. "You mean that was all bullshit?"

"No, no." Cornelius leaned past Max and began to make himself a sandwich with the unsplattered beef. He spoke to the meat. "Just as we can act on the elemental level only through elementals, Devas can act on the human level only through humans. To us, they are not beings, but energies; put paid to the human being and you automatically put paid to both the input from above and the output directed below.

"The Deva of Essence will work through me whether I abase myself before him or not; he has to oppose his brother. Conjuring things is a bad business, and another vulnerability to be avoided." Cornelius looked up, and his eyes were finally serious. "Max, if you accept the Wolf's premise that you are a pawn in the grip of great forces beyond your control, you're already finished. But if you accept that the enemy is a man—that the enemies of men are always men, no matter what the gods are planning—then you have a good chance of winning your wars. Hitler used sorcery; where did it get him?"

Max refilled his mug and thought it over. At last he said, "Okay. I felt that, too. But even granting everything you say, I saw Messing, the man, in action. He was crazy, and he was old—but he didn't look weak. So how can you be so *certain* you can beat him?" He stared hard at this other man, calmly eating a roast beef sandwich. "You can't afford to be wrong."

Cornelius chewed and looked at Val. Her eyes were bright; she nodded. He shrugged, got up, and walked to a bookcase between the Plasmatronics on the far wall, where he plucked a leather-bound volume from the stacks, and brought it back to Max. "You do deserve to know," he said.

THREE BOOKS
OF
Occult Philoſophy,
WRITTEN BY
Henry Cornelius Agrippa,
OF
NETTESHEIM,
Counſeller to CHARLES the Fifth,
EMPEROR of Germany:
AND
Iudge of the Prerogative Court.

Tranſlated out of the Latin into the
Engliſh Tongue, By *J. F.*

London, Printed by *R.W.* for *Gregory Moule*, and are to
be ſold at the Sign of the three Bibles neer the
Weſt-end of *Pauls.* 1651.

The book was obviously ancient, though it had been well preserved. The binding was split in only one place along the spine, and that had been mended with skill and care. The page ends were irregular, but only slightly browned. There was no title on the cover. Max opened the book to its title page, which was printed in a primitive woodcut.

At the bottom, in ink all but faded entirely from the page, a cramped hand had signed the book, "Heinrich Cornelius Agrippa." And it was Cornelius's script.

Max looked up, slowly. Mr. Cornelius inclined his head.

Max looked at Val. She said, "A hundred and ten is peanuts."

"I was born in 1486," said the man in black crisply. "I was of the house of Nettesheim, a noble house, but christened with the name Agrippa because such was the custom for babies born feet foremost. From my earliest days I refused to speak German, but insisted upon Latin, which I learned with astounding ease. Only at the age of eight did I turn to modern languages; at the age of twelve, I could speak all major European tongues, and was conversant with all major philosophical schools of the day." He looked at Max inquiringly.

Max waved his half a sandwich at him. "Hey, I'm an old hand at having you rewrite reality, aren't I? Let's hear the rest of it." He slugged down more rum.

"Well, as a young man I followed my family's tradition of scholarly service to the Holy Roman Emperor, but he soon realized that I had too many talents to be moldering away in his libraries. He first made me a soldier, and then a spy. My travels in the latter capacity took me across the bulk of Europe, and I underwent many perilous adventures in the dark and savage lands—of which I'll tell you another time.

"Now this was an era—the early 1500s—with great intellectual ferment, as I told you previously. In my wanderings I encountered the talismans of Fez and their possessors, and gathered together the knowledge of their many occult traditions. In 1509 and 10, at the ripe old age of twenty-three, I wrote my three books of Occult Philosophy, outlining the overall structure of wizardry, as known at that time. These books today are quite quaint, but my purpose then was clear enough—though better expressed in the Latin than this English translation.

"I wrote, 'what I have seen of our modern writers—Roger Bacon, Robert of York (and I go on . . .)—when they promise to treat of Magic do nothing but relate irrational tales and superstitions unworthy of honest men. Hence my spirit was moved, and, by reason partly of admiration, and partly of indignation, I was willing to play the philosopher, supposing that I should do no discommendable work—seeing I have been always from my youth a curious and undaunted searcher for wonderful effects and operations full of mysteries—if I should recover that ancient Magic (the discipline of all wise men) from the errors of impiety, purify and adorn it with its proper lustre, and vindicate it from the injuries of calumnators . . . ' "

Cornelius Agrippa's face shone in the ruddy firelight. "And then there was other knowledge, such as the movement and harmonies of the forty-five planets and moons of our solar system—knowledge known only to myself even today—which I kept to myself for use in private consultation. By the time I was thirty I had become the master mage of Europe, at the side of popes and princes.

"The one bit of knowledge I did not possess at that time—and thus, of course, the most pressing upon me—was the secret of immortality. It was given to me to know so much so early in life; should I not, I asked myself, bend the remainder of my normal span of years to extending that span, in order to preserve that bounty? I worked for weeks, months, and finally years on end at the most abstruse alchemy, and was quite close to success in Scorpio, 1519, when I took it upon myself to accept a student. He was a bright lad—but too bright, as it happened. One day, when I was gone from my house, the wretched lad seduced my wife."

From the corner of his eye Max saw Val tense; he knew the wizard saw it as well. He, himself, let the growing effect of the rum keep him loose and deliberately took another bite of the roast beef. He chewed it stolidly.

The man in black continued after just the slightest pause. "This student then stole the key to my sanctum from my bedroom and went into it. There he found my grimoire, my spell book, left open to the work in progress. The student, unfortunately, read the spell therein aloud, and brought up the demon Belial. The student panicked—knowing more than you do now, Max—and Belial . . . strangled him."

A log broke and fell in the hearth.

"When I returned home, I realized at once that I would be suspected of murder. So I fought fire with fire, and summoned Belial once more. I could control him, and did so as I forced him to return a semblance of life to my student for one hour. Then I sent the youth to the market to buy tomatoes. He walked there, bought the tomatoes, chatted up a village girl, and then died in full public view."

"What did you do to your wife?" asked Max levelly.

"Nothing. I was not monogamous myself, in those days."

"Unlucky student."

"Yes." Agrippa smiled thinly. "That is when I gave up students." He finished his sandwich, allowing the silence of the night to build. Then: "Yet everyone must pay a price for dealing with Belial; I told you conjuring is bad business. The following month I bought a dog to serve as my familiar. I raised it from a pup, training it to be sensitive to the hidden forces, to which animals are more instinctively attuned. But I succeeded too well, and as the dog grew larger, it also grew insane, manifesting an intelligent cruelty which appalled me. It was my first major mistake, and I'm afraid that I compounded it. I was in France, and I ordered the dog to leap into the Saône and drown. It obeyed my first directive, but not the second; although my power was such that it did shatter its hind leg as it cleared the barricade.

"I learned my mistake six months later when the dog, now with a stump where his leg had been, reappeared first in my dreams, and then in the flesh at the side of my archfoe, Cardinal Janus.

"In 1530, I killed Janus, but the dog escaped, as it has ever escaped me, down through the centuries. And now it fights for the Wolf."

"Not any longer," said Max. And then, pulling his ace from the hole, "My lion killed it."

Agrippa reacted as if Max had thrown the dead dog's head in his lap. His voice was electric. "Killed it? *Killed* it?"

"I saw it die."

"Hosanna—!"

Max had never heard that word spoken before; he blinked. The wizard's joy was so intense it was almost tangible, and Max felt nicely satisfied at being the cause. That got him where he lives, he thought, grinning. The old bastard's human, after all.

Cornelius Agrippa's eyes were closed; he seemed to be looking back a long time. Max looked at Val. Her profile was cut sharp against the fire shadows in her hair, and she was staring at her wizard with a face full of shared fervor. Max tried to catch her eye, but she ignored him absolutely. So he sat back in his chair, put down his rum, and looked into the dying fire, trying to pick out the salamanders. He was full now, and more than a little drunk, and the weariness of his past days was finally beginning to creep up in earnest. It was wonderful here by the fire. . . .

"I was right, Max. You did deserve to know." The jock looked up to find Agrippa sitting beside him again. "I was right but without sufficient reason. You've accomplished more than I'd foreseen." The unlined face in the fading firelight was softer, and more humble now. Eternal.

"Max, I have lived a great many years, and I have achieved almost all there is to achieve in my work. I am at the top. And, as has been well said, it is lonely at the top. There can be no one else with whom to share the experience.

"Wizardry comes so easily to me that I have often supposed that it must be, or could be, the same for everyone. And I have always been mistaken. While I live on and on, with a full understanding of life, seeing the ever-present signs of a larger consciousness at work, I also see people chasing after fads: necromancy, spirit rapping, evangelists, newspaper astrologers, est. How is it, I wonder, that people prefer to pay hundreds of dollars for two weekends of personal discomfort, to be force-fed some very basic truths, than seek out all the truths from material which is readily available to them every moment of their lives? Material which *is* their lives."

This side of the wizard brought Max back to full wakefulness.

For the first time since they'd met at QBU, Agrippa was talking straight across to him, and not down. "Maybe because they don't know what they're supposed to be looking for," Max said softly. "Everybody has to start someplace."

"Granted. But is it a start, or an end? If one adopts the idea that one needs to be 'trained,' that one must be submissive to the will of another who cannot and will not demonstrate any clear basis for assuming dominance—! The great Eastern schools demand obedience to a personal master, but the master's goal is to awaken the student to his own sense of mastery—not to entice him into paying more hundreds of dollars for more seminars, ad infinitum, to a series of these 'trainers.' I have yet to meet any graduate of any fad who knew anything more than pop psychology. Certainly they knew nothing of the work of the wise.

"And yet the fads thrive—for the lifetimes of fads—while the Ancient Wisdom remains largely untapped." The man in black shook his head, but a small, wry smile began to turn the corners of his mouth. "One of the minor results is that I am left with few people to talk to.

"Therefore, when I encounter a person who seems able to undertake wizardry, I am always anxious to discover if, in fact, they can do so." Agrippa looked at him sincerely. "You are one who can."

Max looked away; he couldn't help it. As Barnaby Wilde, he'd been handed compliments every day for a decade: the phone calls from fans, the crowds at the window, the recognition, the ratings. He knew how to handle that sort of success. But this was different.

He had lost all the anger he'd come in with, but he took refuge from his feelings in cynicism. "I'm glad to have met your standards," he said. "It seems only fair, since you've never played straight with me for more than two seconds at a time."

"Max, life never plays straight. That is why wizardry is the work of the wise. But you won through, didn't you? Surely, by now, you must realize, as I have had to realize, that one cannot, even with the utmost clarity of expression, take a novice and explain wizardry to him directly. Even the most rudimentary explanation would be too complex for him to grasp. To succeed, one must approach the subject by degrees. This is the true meaning of Being Silent.

"But on the other hand, when someone discovers partial truths on his own, it is better to clarify than not; a little knowledge, you know. Further, it is the tenet of every mystery school that the ultimate goal of creation is the day when every created being will be what we now call a wizard, and will enter the higher realms. Now, as you and I enter the spiritual Age of Aquarius, and approach a new temporal Millennium, we see the preparation for that future all around us. Western society has become more and more accustomed to that which it previously refused to see, and the revelations of Those Who Know have become more frequent. The Summation of Humanity will not come tomorrow night, or in the year 2000, or even in the next Millennum. But it will come, because everything one needs to know to be a wizard, he already knows—including the one last secret *you* have left to discern."

Max sat forward. He waited. But the man in black did not continue, and finally, Max asked, "What is it, then?"

Agrippa brushed imaginary crumbs from his sleeve. "You tell me."

"What?"

"You are a wizard; you can find the secret within yourself, before tomorrow midnight. If not, we'll talk again thereafter—but you're not the man I think you are if that becomes necessary."

Max nodded slowly. "All right," he said. "I accept your challenge. But give me a starting point."

Agrippa said, "It has been called the Innermost Secret. It is known to everyone, without exception, but only those who comprehend it fully may use it fully. It is the final power behind all wizardry." Agrippa stood, and shrugged. "But in truth, it is a 'secret' no longer. I took an oath nearly five hundred years ago, never to reveal any secrets with which I was entrusted. Since then I have read everything I learned then, many times, in open print. This is not to say that the facts imparted to me at my initiation were worthless. Far from it. Merely that the need for secrecy which cloaked them then has been dissipated through evolution."

The wizard's face was a coppery shadow. He said no more.

Max stood up and stuck out his hand. "What time do we get started in the morning?"

Agrippa smiled and took his hand warmly. "Whenever you arise. As I said, I need no elaborate preparations for the Wolf, and we needn't confront him before eleven P.M."

"You are sure of yourself, aren't you?" A yawn started to pry at his jaws. He tried to stifle it, then let it come. "Hey, what do I call you now? Cornelius or Agrippa?"

"Call me anything you want, as long as it's not 'son of a bitch.' "

Max grinned crookedly. "We'll see about that. Good night, Agrippa." He turned toward the fire. "And good night to you, Val."

"Good night, Max," she said properly, behind a proper smile. She stood as he left the room, stretched, and started to gather the mugs and dishes.

"I'll take care of those, Woman," said the man in black. "You need your rest, as well. Don't forget you have a concert in two days."

She laughed. "I don't know how you do it, Man," she said, and turned to kiss him good night. She set her hip against his, snuggling inside his open arms. "But just what do you intend doing with Max, once he learns the final secret?"

Agrippa kissed her ear. "Congratulate him, probably. Why, does it bother you, his knowing?"

"Not his knowing. His doing."

"I've said he isn't necessary to our success. Or"—he looked at her shrewdly—"to anything else we have."

She kissed him again, firmly. "You sound like just another man, instead of a great and wonderful wizard."

"In some things, I am just another man," he said, pulling her close. For a time they clung to each other tightly. Then Agrippa stepped away, and the evening was ended.

. . . . .

Or almost.

Max was waiting for her in the hall. She saw him as she left the room, hesitated, then turned away.

"Val," he said softly. She stopped, and he came up behind her. "I just wanted to tell you—he is a good guy. Strange as he is, I like him. And respect him. And trust him to get us through this."

"I'm glad," she said simply. She did not look around.

"But I still understand why the student risked it."

She reached out blindly and squeezed his hand hard. Then she walked quickly away.

Somewhere in the house, a clock tolled midnight.

The last day of the year had arrived.

Chapter 34

DECEMBER 31 • 6:45 A.M.

The moon, a dying sliver, climbed the lightening eastern sky and grinned back at the waiting wizard. Cornelius Agrippa watched it come, finding both comfort and promise in its inevitable orbit toward the waiting sun, still hidden below the horizon. Those two, more than all the others, still marked the playing out of the endless cord which bound Now to the first Dawn of Time; and no matter what happened under the gaze of the Two Eyes of God, the cord remained unbroken.

It was cold, this dawning of the year's last day—cold within and cold without. The wind which whipped his gray hair and stung his far-seeing eyes had met its last serious obstacle pouring over the Sierra Nevadas on the far side of the state, and had gained only bite from its long journey through the thick Central Valley fog. It had hurled itself over the Berkeley hills and scored the black surface of the bay, to launch itself at last over the man and the mountain which held it back from the waiting sea. The lights of the city far below were weak and wavering, leprous white. The pines on the slopes were bleak.

But you could feel the End in the air, as well . . . that brown and lamplit feeling that tonight would close the books on many things. The feeling of New Year's Eve. There was no way to imagine tomorrow morning, January 1; the year was an old, old man now, and antiquity was all there was.

Cornelius Agrippa thought of Max, and of Valerie. Val was a wondrous woman and what he had with her was very special . . . but her career, which he had molded and therefore could not begrudge, had assumed more of her life than she'd admit. In the days and weeks and months to follow, there was always the chance that she would reach a plateau and elect to remain there. It was her decision, though he would advise strongly against it; but it left hanging the possibility that she would cease to play a role in the affairs which, in the end, concerned him most.

Therefore—and the thought itself warmed him—it was highly providential that Max had shown a flare for wizardry. His temperament was close to perfect, with its openness to experience *and* its hair-trigger control. He would not run the danger of so many mystics, that of drift and passivity, but neither was he so rational that he would live only a half life. He could walk the tightrope, once he learned how not to fall. It was possible that he could walk the cord of Time, just as Agrippa had done.

It was strange, Agrippa reflected, to find this power in an American. Delving into the unknown had always been so alien to their mechanical way of life. The Founding Fathers were wizards—that much, at least, was well known—but they lived at the dawn of the Rational Age. They set out to create a mundane organization, a mechanism of government, which would function despite the erratic nature of man; but one of the results of their generally satisfactory experiment was the *exaltation* of the mechanical, which has made America so unable to accept a *joie de vivre.*

Yet America, with its attempt at universal freedom beneath the organization, was far more able to change herself with the eternal flow of mankind than any other state; her low points were yet higher than many others' high points. The challenge was for America to transcend her dead past, as she once transcended the dead worlds of Europe. If she could do that, she could maintain her ability to lead and to inspire; if she could not, if she were too bound up in the mechanical to adjust to the new waves of power sweeping the world, then she would fall and be replaced, as so many other great states had done before her.

Even with the defeat of Messing's plan, that power would be here, like it or no; but it could be channeled—downward into violence, or upward into consciousness. There would either be a return to darker ages, as Messing's masters hoped, or there would be one more step toward the light.

Cornelius Agrippa stood upon his mountain and wondered if he would still be living when that goal was finally reached. . . .

Suddenly he felt someone standing behind him; the eldritch alarm was exploding at the back of his brain. Lithe as a cat, he swung around, his arms outstretched in a private pattern, and noted without reaction Wolf Messing, crouched over his cane, ten yards away. It should have been impossible; the spells he had cast around this lonely peak should have been impregnable. But the wizard's face betrayed nothing as he asked, in German, "Have you lost your way, Wolf?" His tone was flat.

"Nyet, Agrippa." The shaman spoke in Russian. His eyes were alight, his mouth loose. "Nyet. And Naught. I have come for you." He laughed, that mad laugh, and waved his hand.

Agrippa felt tiny pinpricks sweep across his legs. He leapt aside, catching a glimpse of tiny archers, no larger than his shoes, swarming through the waving grasses. As fast as each loosed one of his tiny arrows, he nocked and fired another. Most of the projectiles failed to penetrate the cloth of the wizard's pants, but those that did stung severely.

He rapped a sharp incantation, and the grass for thirty feet in all directions burst into savage flame. The fire jumped and lashed more swiftly than normal flame, as the shrill cries of the archers filled the air; in less than ten seconds the ground was scorched and bare.

The Wolf spat a Russian obscenity and returned to the attack; the brightening sky above suddenly darkened. No clouds appeared this time, but the air filled with a wounded roar, and hot, red blood poured down from on high. It covered them tenaciously, flooding their nostrils with its metallic scent. Messing, however, had been prepared and was wiping the blood from his eyes even as he lunged forward, slipping slightly in the mud. His hand was empty, but the thrust of his outstretched first and second fingers cut through the wizard's black jacket. His next thrust was never delivered. Agrippa swept his arm out in a dismissive gesture, and the effect was of a blow from an arm three times the size. With a good foot separating the two men, the shaman was flung backward in a decaying arc under the relentless torrent of blood.

Messing landed hard, and slid down the slope in the sepia muck. He struggled to regain his footing, his gnarled limbs working frenziedly, but Agrippa moved swiftly to reach him and pin him with the invisible extensions at his command. It seemed as if he did no more than point at the figure by his feet, but the Wolf was unable to rise. The rain of blood stopped as abruptly as it had begun, as the shaman concentrated his efforts; but so did the wizard. For a long moment the tableau held, as the first of the sun's rays limned them in orange and gray: the two men, alone on the ridge, caked with gore. At the end of that moment it was clear that the Wolf would not rise. A wintry smile stole across Agrippa's smooth features, despite himself.

"There was never any doubt," he said softly.

And in that moment he was struck from behind, with a force unlike any he had ever known in another. His mental alarm was still silent, but the power ripped him sideways and threw him to his face. Desperately he threw up a new defense, but it was too little and too late. His own ribs seemed to clutch his lungs in a wanton embrace; his heart was straining to break free. Through sheer, undying force of will, he turned his head toward Messing, but the shaman lay where he had fallen, too weak to stand. Agrippa twisted farther, and a single gasp, more expressive than the shout of any lesser man, escaped his drawn lips.

Standing over him was Messing's fat wife.

"Yes, Agrippa," she cooed in a voice as low and as knowing as a mother's with her child, "now you understand. It is I who have become your true foe—I, and none other. Herr Messing, with his richly deserved reputation and genuine psychic powers, has been, these past five years, no more than my stalking horse.

"When we first met at Academgorodok, in 1958, it was otherwise; we were master and pupil, at first. Then colleague and colleague. And at last, bishop and queen. But never did more than our initial confreres know of my powers, and they have long since been released from this sphere. Never did you know, and that was our greatest concern. The continuing path of Wolf Messing was too clearly marked, his mind and mine too closely linked. Your probes detected only power—familiar power, if vastly amplified. You attributed it to his advancement, and led others to that same misapprehension—and so, we knew that we would have you, whenever I decided to proceed.

"Now, with the time between Time fast approaching, and the temporary escape of your protégé working against us, I have made my decision. I, and I alone!"

She waved her hands once, and the fat old woman became Mr. Xin of the Chinese Secret Service; twice, and he became—Madeleine Riggs!

"*I, and I alone!*" she screamed, and her red hair flew.

Agrippa could not respond, could not react. His breath was too close in his lungs, his heart beating far too rapidly. There was nothing in this flame-haired woman he could not surmount, given time to prepare—but his efforts had been directed entirely against the man for too long, and it came to him clearly that this was his end.

Lying pressed to the slime, his eyes wide but growing calmer as he forced a final adjustment to the new reality, he saw the woman gesture, heard her chant the spells, and felt the stream of fanged demons coming up from the red netherworlds to claw out the caverns of his mind.

And then he went insane.

Chapter 35

DECEMBER 31 • 7:22 A.M.

Max was awakened by the screams.

Grabbing his bathrobe from behind the door, he ran out into the front room and found Val coming tousle-haired from the far hall, her long legs flashing free of her own hastily wrapped robe. Her face was a mix of sudden awakening and distress. "It wasn't you?" she asked anxiously.

"Uh-uh. It came from higher up the hill."

"It sounded—" she said, but let it die as she threw open the front door.

Outside the wind was picking up. Small clumps of dead grass leapt from point to point, and dust devils swirled along the mountain trails. The sky was the color of a gun.

"He didn't come to bed," Val said as they trotted up the slope side by side. "It happens several times a week. More when something big's coming up. I'll get up and find him at his desk, still dressed, working on a chart or reading Tarot or—"

"We don't know anything yet," Max said flatly. "Let's just have a look."

Val picked up the pace.

When they reached the crest, they found the circle of charred grass, still with a few glowing embers, and the trampled blood. But looking down both sides of the mountain, they could see no human figures.

"You circle around behind the house," Max told her. "I'll take the trees on this side." She nodded and ran off, the wind plucking at her hair and her hem. He stood and watched her for a moment as she grew smaller in the distance, all alone against the vast sweep of land and sea.

Then, with a warning shake of his head, he turned and ran down toward the pines.

But Val was the one who found him. She was stalking doggedly up a steep rise when she heard his voice, and coming over the crest she found Agrippa staggering like a blind man. His whole body was covered in blood; he was singing, or something like it; and his eyes were full of tears. At her approach he jumped like a deer and covered his face with his hands. Her heart was choking her, but she forced herself to get a call for Max out past it, and found that she was crying, too.

They took him back to the house, slowly and with great concern. He would not look at either of them, which left him with only the sky and ground to watch, and his head began to rock up and down, up and down, with the monotonous precision of the truly schizophrenic. Val gentled him into one of the chairs by the fireplace and examined him, while Max built a fire. Despite the blood, she could find no wounds, but the head never stopped its steady sway. He looked older now than Max had ever seen him, older than anyone Max had ever seen.

He and Val moved to the far side of the room by tacit agreement, watching the old man morbidly.

"Messing, of course," Val said.

"But not alone."

She turned sluggishly, her mind bogged down. "What do you mean?"

"I mean there were three sets of footprints in that blood up there."

Val shook her head. "Three? But Messing was the only real shaman—"

"So Agrippa always said. But I don't think he was wrong when he said Messing was his inferior. So he must have been wrong about one of his helpers, because Messing had to have had help."

"Which helper?"

"I'd bet on the Madwoman."

"Because you hate her already." Val squared her shoulders. "My money's on Mr. Xin. Messing's agent to the Chinese . . ."

"Well, we don't know, do we?" Max nodded across the room. "Any more than he knew, poor bastard."

"Corny wasn't supposed to be wrong, Max."

"Tell me about it." He walked back to face the old man. Planted his feet, and forced himself to become calm. Tried to recapture the feeling of breaking the dog's spell. Tried to take control. For a time there was only the crackle of logs on the fire, so like the good time last night. Then: "Heinrich Cornelius Agrippa!"

Nothing changed.

Max spoke to the confidence he had always known within the wizard. "Heinrich Cornelius Agrippa!"

The head began to slow.

Max spoke the name a third time, and the man in black grew almost still.

"What happened to you? How can we help you?"

Agrippa's head stopped completely, thrust forward on the neck now in terrible rigidity. In a normal man it might have indicated an attempt at memory, but there was nothing normal about any of this.

Still he did not speak.

Carefully, choosing each sound and emphasis with all his professional experience, Max asked him again.

Agrippa screamed.

One moment he was absolutely still; the next he was howling, beating his fists on his thighs. Val pushed past Max and held the wizard like a child, rocking him back and forth. Gradually his screams diminished. When she finally released him, he remained as she left him, bent forward; his head began to bob.

"He can't tell you," she said, standing.

"I was close, goddamnit! I know I was close."

"Too close, maybe. I've never known him to be defeated." She shook her head viciously. "What I'm trying to say, he's a wizard—he's above most everything—but he's not God. He's always insisted that he's as human as anyone. If there's any part of him left in there, any part at all, a part that can't fight its way clear of Messing's spell . . . the pain must be enormous."

"All right. Then we'll have to try something else." He took her by the arm and led her into the hall.

But she stopped moving just outside the door. Her beautiful face was suddenly haggard. "What can we do, Max? He was our only hope. The only hope for the world—"

"Shut up!"

Her head jerked as if he'd hit her.

"Now look," he said, "he had better not be our only hope, because I don't plan to wake up tomorrow at the bottom of a crevasse."

"But there's no one to stop it now."

"There's me and there's you."

She laughed, astonished, derisive.

"We haven't got a choice," Max snapped.

"But if Corny himself—"

"I said, I don't intend to wake up in Messing's world of nothingness. Knowing what I know now, I'd rather die tonight, doing my damnedest for the world I want to keep. It's sure as hell better than giving up now, and letting Messing roll on unopposed."

"What makes you think you'll be granted a clean death? You could end up like this," Val shouted, her face red. Within the room, the head of the man in black bobbed.

"Will you help me?" Max asked doggedly. "I have to have your help." He reached up and held her face lightly with his hand. "I know the final secret now, just as he predicted."

"You don't know—"

"I do, Val. I do."

Their eyes locked. She caught her breath. Time hung.

DECEMBER 31 • 8:03 A.M.

"It kept running through my head all night while I slept," Max said urgently. "Energy. Energy enough to stop Wolf Messing, *and* the Devas, *and* the elementals. So what energy that we all share could be that powerful?

"At first, I thought of self-preservation. But that couldn't be all of it. You don't win just because you're forced to it. In every fight there's a winner and a loser, but surely the loser wanted to win, too. Freud could probably work up a case that the loser didn't *really* want to win, deep down: the will to die, as opposed to the will to live. But there must be people who want to win at any cost, and still lose. There must be something stronger than simple self-preservation."

Her hand came up and closed over his, still angled along her jaw line. But she made no move to dislodge it.

"It kept bugging me," he said. "The will to live and the will to die. Essence and Naught: Messing's twin Devas. Osiris and Set. Jehovah and Satan. 'Sometimes known as the Brothers, or the Lovers.' Like Agrippa's Fire and Water. Polarities, with everything else taking place, or not taking place, between them.

"It was nuts. I knew I was just missing it. I could *feel* the power, but I couldn't put a name to it!

"The Air and the Earth appear between the Fire and the Water, I thought. A pair within a pair. A pair of pairs. Duality. Always duality. And always a connection, whether the circuit is actually running or not. On or off. Yes or no. Yin or Yang. Male or female."

His eyes narrowed. "And that's when I got it."

She sighed, but from sorrow or surrender he couldn't tell.

"Sex," he said. "That's the power that's stronger than any other. Because it *includes* self-preservation, but isn't *limited* to that.

"What other power do we all have to satisfy? Hunger, yes. Breathing, yes. Sleep, yes. But those are all self-contained.

"It's companionship; the need for others. That's the power we all *share.* Without sex, we could vegetate—just sit on our asses all day long and breathe and eat and snore. With sex, though, we have to get up and get out. Then comes talking and game playing and everything else—everything that turns individual humans into Humanity."

Max shook his head. "And both Agrippa and the Wolf went all around it, every time. Told me everything about polarity and duality except the part I live with."

But having said all that, he suddenly sighed himself, releasing the tension completely, and his face lost that look of total certainty. "Val . . . it's no secret I've wanted to make love to you, but I would have wanted it differently. I'm no saint, but I'm certainly not using this"—he gestured toward Agrippa—"to get a cheap thrill. If I'm wrong, if there's another way—fine, let's take it. But if there isn't . . ."

"Hold me," she said, and leaned forward.

He took her in his arms. She wasn't trembling, but she was cold. Her soft head cradled in the hollow of his shoulder, and he stroked her hair.

"Corny always left it up to me," she said. "We were both free to choose. He chose monogamy; so did I, without regret. Until you came. But . . ." She looked toward the wizard.

"I know," said Max gently, and led her away from the door, into the early morning grays at the end of the hall. Beside a framed poster of herself at the Albert Hall, she seemed to gain strength.

"I was beginning to want to, Max. You know that," she said, looking into his face once more. "And you're right—about everything. Sex is the secret." She laughed hollowly. "But a girl likes to be courted."

"Val, if we're still here tomorrow morning, I'll buy you every flower in San Francisco."

"You're crazy."

"Sure. Born to be Wilde." He smiled. She crinkled the corner of her mouth; then returned it, rueful but reconciled.

"What do you think we can accomplish?" she asked.

"As far as power goes, I don't really know. Because I don't know any more than I've told you; I don't know what we *do*. But I can contact my lion again tonight, and that'll lead us to wherever the Wolf's got his lair. After that . . ."

Her face grew thoughtful. "We can make a good try for the power. I told you I had a few tricks to help my career, and sex magick is one of them. But Corny already knew where Messing will be tonight."

"I should have figured that. Where?"

"Your old flame's place: the Hyatt Regency. They're having their annual New Year's Eve blowout tonight, with six bands and over six thousand people. It's a 'Time Machine' thing, with a Tea Dance band, a Big Band, a cabaret singer, fifties rock, disco, and something called Space-Age Self-Expression. Total confusion, and the biggest blast in town."

"In more ways than one. The Wolf has an unerring eye for the spotlight, I'll grant him that." Max frowned. "Did Agrippa book a room? They won't let you onto the guest floors without one."

"They'd let me on," she said. "But it's taken care of."

"Well, then. Things aren't as bad as they might be—not by a long shot. Agrippa wanted to get there at eleven, but I think, if you and I are there by ten—"

"—we only have eleven hours to prepare," Val said, taking his hand. "Come on. Let's take care of Corny and get started. But—you should know, Max, that as soon as this is over, I'll want to work to bring him back to us."

"Of course." But now it was his turn to hang back. "I'm—glad you're taking it like this, Val. Any other week, and this would be an impossible situation."

"Punks have no feelings, remember?" But her eyes betrayed her.

Chapter 36

DECEMBER 31 • 8:33 A.M.

They led Cornelius Agrippa back to his bedroom. Val undressed him and put him to bed, her touch gentle and sure. Then she went to a cabinet and withdrew an ornamental Chinese box; from that she took a syringe and a vial of clear liquid. "Thorazine," she said. "Sometimes a party guest goes over the edge." She measured out just over two hundred fifty milligrams and sprayed the excess away. "This'll keep him quiet most of the day." She kept her eyes on his ravaged face as she pressed the needle into his arm.

In a few minutes his bobbing head slowed and his blank eyes began to wander. He lay back and went to sleep. "Help me tie his arms," she said.

When they had finished, she surveyed their work critically, and was satisfied. "He'll be all right without us today. I'll go call a friend to stay with him tonight."

Max was left alone with the wizard. Watching the slow rise and fall of the old man's chest, and no longer having to inspire Val, he had to remind himself that this, too, was real. Agrippa had always been so incredibly vibrant. And solid.

But when she came back, he said nothing of that. She went to the middle section of the bookshelves, which filled the east wall, and pressed a copy of Wilhelm Reich inward. At once, with a muted click and hum, the entire case rotated outward, revealing a low-lit passage.

"Nice," said Max softly. "I've always wanted to see one of those."

"So did he; that's why he built it," she said, and stopped in the threshold. "That bastard Messing!" Her sorrow was rapidly transmuting.

They closed the case behind them; the passage turned out to be a long tunnel—simple, straight, and unadorned—into the heart of the mountain. The walls and ceiling were of some reddish material, not linoleum or plastic, with indirect lighting and vents kept flush. A single-gauge railroad track ran off into the distance, and astride it, waiting for them, was a small, open car made of matte black steel. Two blue-cushioned seats faced each other.

When the two of them climbed in, Max's knees had nowhere to go but between Val's.

She touched a button on the side of the car and it began to roll, gradually picking up speed until they were making about thirty miles an hour through the earth. Max looked at his knees, and at hers, from which her robe had fallen away. Then he raised his head and gave her a look something less than a lover's, but something more than a co-worker's. "So," he said. "Sex magick."

Her eyes were unfathomable; female. "People are at their best when they're exalted," she said quietly. "Witches' circles or Catholic masses, both have the same goal. Exaltation. But the witches affirm what the Catholics deny." She brushed her hair back. "The best sex is always a form of worship."

"Well . . . maybe."

"You'll see. We practiced Tantra, the Hindu form of sex magick; that's what they strive for."

"Why 'magick,' instead of 'wizardry'? And how does Hindu square with his emphasis on the 'Western tradition'?"

" 'Sex magick' is just the common term; don't ask me for the details, because that's not my department. As for Tantra, there is no Western tradition as highly evolved. You don't cut off your nose to spite your face. Tantra works on the special *rapport* between a man and a woman making love, and not just the pleasure. When two people are totally responsive, one to another, each feeling his own sensations and the other's—"

"—you're playing with all the rules. You're in two worlds at once."

"Something like that." She looked at him curiously. "You have come a long way in five days."

Max made no reply.

"Sex is the most powerful force known," she went on after a moment. "That's why so many people are afraid of it—or afraid that somebody else has more of it than they do. But that's just social conditioning. The fact is that everybody has access to as much of the force as they want. Corny always said that the power is there whether you like it or not. The only question is whether you use it or it uses you."

"And by using it, rather than blocking it, Cornelius Agrippa managed to keep from growing old."

"Exactly. Power corrupts, and absolute power corrupts absolutely. If you let the power use you, you may get a hell of a ride, but you'll pay for it in the end because you'll be helpless before it."

"The whole selling your soul to the Devil routine."

"Uh-huh. The wizard's path is conscious control, which means no indiscriminate sex, but no celibacy, either. You do it when the time is ripe, and you make every time mean something. In addition to the pleasure—which only increases as your consciousness expands, believe me—you teach yourself what sort of power you actually have." Despite her not being Agrippa, Valerie Drake had this subject clear in her mind. "The point is to be everything you can be. Whether in bed, on stage, or wherever.

"And that's why Corny said he could overcome Messing and all his friends. Despite his Deva, and his elementals, and his cadre of psychic spies, the Wolf is just as human as you are. So are they all. They know lots of ways to divert you, but not one to beat you, if you know what you're capable of."

The transport began to slow and rolled smoothly to a stop beside a platform overlooking a large room, apparently cut directly from the earth. The eastern wall looked open to the morning sky, but when Max went down and across to it, intending to walk out onto the mountainside, he felt a very subtle but acute sense of nausea. He stepped back quickly and didn't try it again.

"This is his sanctum sanctorum," said Val, joining him in the center of the vast, rough-hewn room. "All of his wizardry is done here, and we'll have everything we need. The one thing you have to remember is that this is just a quick fix. Just like a body builder, we can 'pump you up' for tonight—so that by the time you meet the Wolf, you'll be overflowing with raw energy—but never forget that he has the experience."

"We can get a lot of experience in ten hours," Max said, and took her in his arms. They held each other tightly for a moment, still caught between being lovers and being friends. Then he released her and stepped back.

She walked across the earthen floor and flicked a switch; the circle of heat lamps began to glow. She turned to a cabinet sunk into the clay wall and selected a ten-inch reel of recording tape, which she set in motion on a Studer identical to the one in the house. From the six speakers music began to float—her music, her voice, with nothing but the sounds of the wind behind it. Her song had no tune; it was all sensation, of motion, of pleasure, of love. She sang to herself from one end of the chamber and answered from the other, spinning a web of sensuality. Max had never heard anything to equal it.

This was not Valerie Drake, the Star, with her arrangements and electronics.

This was a woman he'd never known.

She had lit incense while he was listening and poured them both a glass of something golden. "Damiana liqueur." She smiled, handing it to him. "Aphrodisiac."

"I don't need it," he said.

"Oh, yes, you do. We're going to the top, and we're not coming down all day." She reached up and began to undo his robe.

Max took hold of the back of her neck, beneath her warm hair, and kissed her deeply. Then he drained his liqueur in one gulp.

Chapter 31

DECEMBER 31 • 5:07 P.M.

The slopes of the mountain were gathering their shadows, and, with the cooling of evening, clouds were once more rolling off the sea. They spilled across Stinson Beach and Bolinas, to slowly climb the hills. The Golden Gate was an open path to them, and they entered in a long, straight column past the lonely bridge.

On Mt. Tamalpais, wisps of clouds, like wings, were streaming down the landward slopes. The young deer crowded close to their parents at the white things' awesome approach. Far below in Mill Valley, firecrackers went off in a long stream. New Year's Eve was coming with the clouds.

In the circle of wizardry, in the hidden room, Max stroked Val's long, smooth thigh. She was lying with her head resting in the crook of his elbow, gazing peacefully toward the ceiling. She was singing softly, in tune with her recording.

Max breathed in her scent and said slowly, "I see what you mean now. About worship. Not male against female. Or even male *and* female, which is what I always tried for before. But transcendence . . ." He ruffled her hair. "I've had it other ways, but this is the best."

"It gets better," she said.

They kissed and began again.

DECEMBER 31 • 7:00 P.M.

Outside the hundred-yard window there was nothing to see but fog, when Val's tape came to an end. The room was black except for the dull red glow of the heat lamps, and their shifting reflections in the heavy, hanging incense.

"It's time," said Val. Her voice was just as heavy with regret.

Max kissed her. "I'm ready," he said and sat up smoothly. "If I were any more ready, I'd have to explode just on general principles. I feel like I could lick my weight in wildcats, eagles, bulls, *and* angels."

"You're not alone," said Val.

"No," said Max. "I'm not." And he kissed her again, tenderly.

"We need to take the train back up and get a shower," she whispered finally. "But afterward I'm going to put on the sexiest damn dress you or anyone else ever saw."

"Why not? I'm gonna pick one of those tuxes in my closet. After all, we're already celebrating."

DECEMBER 31 • 7:49 P.M.

Max felt, in fact, almost overwhelmingly good. Val had been absolutely right: the feeling of making love shouldn't be kept for a few finite moments, a few times a week. Grabbing hold of it, like he'd grabbed hold of himself within his mind, and keeping hold of it made much more sense when you realized it was possible. The feeling would have to fade sometimes, and have to be brought back—that was human nature—but it wouldn't fade tonight. Again and again throughout the day, he had drained himself utterly, but there had always been more; and the main reason for that, he knew, was Val. Sex always had to be more than casual with him, even under these circumstances. Like she'd said, it had to *mean* something. And this had.

He was swaggering as he showered and shaved, and loving every minute of it.

Tonight's the grand finale, he thought, exploring the contents of his wardrobe with an artist's eye. I came in late; I lost two people; I got taken for more rides than Willie Shoemaker—but I got here. And as long as I'm alive, that spells trouble for the Wolf and his apparat. I have all those scores that have to be settled now, and everybody's IOUs come due at midnight.

Could he beat two shamans, even with his knowledge and use of the final secret? He didn't even think about it. There was no way to know, so no reason to worry.

The tuxedo was cut with that same up-to-the-minute opulence that characterized Agrippa; the one Max chose fit him better than his own. He picked out a shirt straight from an old *Esquire* to go with it, and, expecting there to be watches somewhere, proved himself correct by finding a beautiful Bulova pocket watch in the dresser drawer. The timeless elegance of New Year's Eve was in his blood.

Val was flying just as high. Her tastes had been tempered by the dictates of her image, but these days that didn't hamper her unduly. She wore a resplendent orange crepe de chine with lots of cling and not much else. She all but growled when Max entered the front room, and his grin matched hers. "You are the new year's Eve," he said admiringly.

She opened her bag and took out a shoulder holster full of pistol. "Here," she said. "Present." He hefted it, checked the cylinders, then strapped it on, wondering if you *should* feel this good on your way to what might be your death, and the death of your civilization. He decided it was better than feeling rotten.

The doorbell rang. Val went to a periscopic eyepiece two feet to the left of the door and looked out. Nodded. "It's my friend," she said to Max and opened up.

Ian Farley, bass man for Valerie Drake's band, came in and gave her a peck on the cheek—then stopped dead at the sight of Max August. "What happened to our secret, Valerie?" he asked with a cynical wheeze.

"Max is part of it now, Ian. But there may not be any secret after tonight. Come look."

They went into the bedroom, where Agrippa still lay with his wrists strapped to the bedframe. Heavily sedated, his body twitched and shivered in something like slow motion. His face was covered in sweat.

"Holy fuck," said Ian succinctly.

"Something caught up to him, Ian. I'm not going to kid you—he's in a bad way. But Max and I are going to do something about it. What we need is somebody to watch him while we're gone."

"Of course. I'll . . ." Ian was clearly staggered. "Damn! Mr. Cornelius—!"

Max said from across the room, "Yeah. I thought he was indestructible, too. Listen, we're sorry to have broken up your New Year's."

"Huh!" Ian said. "What's New Year's to a rock band? We did five months on the road this year, and we're startin' all over again tomorrow. Not that I mind," he added hastily. "Hey, all I'd planned to do was sit around and watch Dick Clark work, anyway."

"We thank you anyway," said Val indulgently. She pointed toward the vial and a cluster of syringes on the dresser. "I've been treating him like I'd treat any bad trip, even though he won't come out of it. Give him one hundred milligrams in two hours, and every two hours after that, intramuscularly."

"Don't worry. I know that scene well enough."

"One last thing," said Max. "Don't let anybody—anybody—in until we get back. Not beautiful strangers, not your band, not even us, unless I give you one of these on the bell," and he knocked out the rhythm of "Born-to-be-Wi-i-i-ilde!"

Ian didn't ask any more questions; just bolted the door solidly behind them as they walked out across the dirt to the van. The clouds were solid below them now, as they had been when Max had first arrived, and the stars were solid above. The far horizon was clearly visible where the deep gray clouds met the deep black sky.

Val took Max's arm as they stood on the edge of the slope, looking down off their mountain. "I had a strange trip with Ian and the band here one night," she said softly. "We had all done peyote, and I was out on the hillside looking up at the stars. And then, suddenly, I wasn't looking *up* at them; I was looking *out* at them, as if I were on the *front* of this planet as it plowed through space—like the girl on the front of a sailing ship. There was nothing between me and endless, empty space. No horizon, no clouds, or even air. I was part of the grand design, and there were no limits." She nestled against his arm. "That's what the rest of this night feels like. Valerie Drake—the one you don't like—has to enter that hotel with us, because of her fans . . . but she's not the one who'll be at your side."

"I know that, Val," he said, and turned to face her. "But there's one thing I have to get clear before we start. You said you weren't a wizard; that may or may not be true. Cornelius said I was; and *that* may or may not be true. But I *am* a Point Man, and from here on out, I'm taking command of this operation." He smiled. "All right with you?"

"All right, Max," she said, and kissed him fiercely. "Let's go get 'em."

Chapter 38

DECEMBER 31 • 8:37 P.M.

The fog grew heavy in the pockets of the mountain's winding road, slowing them to ten and then five miles per hour at times. Though he kept silent about it, Max was expecting an attack during one of those times, and he kept his jacket loose around his gun. But in that long half hour rolling down and down, no attack came. It could have meant anything, but by the time they rejoined the freeway, he had chosen the idea that Messing and his unknown aide had considered their danger ended with Agrippa's defeat. Whether that was the truth of it or not, they weren't likely to be so unguarded at the hotel itself.

9:21 P.M.

As Max and Val sped across the Golden Gate, they were swallowed completely by fog; it was pouring through this last chasm at land's end in waves, like the ocean lost to them far below.

Max slowed for the toll, one hand reaching for his wallet, his eyes everywhere, searching for details. There was a dark blue Plymouth, the stripped government model, idling near the edge of the official parking lot; in addition to the Russians, he was belatedly remembering, the FBI, too, had a bone to pick with him. It would be damned ridiculous, but just as disastrous, to get stopped by Hardesty now.

"Take the wheel," he said to Val as they stopped to wait in line, hidden from the Plymouth by the other lanes of cars. She responded instantly, and he scrambled into the dark interior; it was Valerie Drake, then, a woman who meant nothing to the feds, who received a heartfelt Happy New Year from the toll man. The dark blue Plymouth stayed where it was.

Max stayed low and watched the headlight beams of oncoming cars sweep the ceiling of their van as they rolled past the parklike Presidio, and returned once more to the gray blocks and angles of the city.

9:40 P.M.

Traffic was backed up for two blocks in all directions near the Hyatt Regency. Two spotlights split the air, one to each side of the mammoth hotel, with their fluid ovals soaring up the cantilevered sides as high as the revolving bar on top, then diving to the crowds. And crowds there were. The sidewalks were filled with people on their way to the sextet of parties—people dressed in the full range of styles, high to low, past to future, but all with some sort of flash. It looked to be a great night. For somebody.

A policeman stuck with traffic duty was hauling competing streams of cars through his intersection almost by bodily force. He brought Val's quota through, waving them on down Drumm Street toward a series of signs announcing party parking; she took the first turnoff, down a ramp to the underground. "I'm used to limousine service, you know," she said with mock severity. From the depths of the van, Max returned unheeding silence as he consulted his pocket watch.

9:46 P.M.

They were doing all right. They went quickly up the stairs to the street and across. It was a typical winter's night in San Francisco, brisk but refreshing; the fog had not penetrated this far inland yet.

Hip against hip, they walked past the long line of people waiting to present their tickets at the hotel's front doors, and angled toward the VIP entrance. A spotlight caught them, holding on Valerie, while recognition swept through the line. Some of the ticket holders feigned disinterest and others asked for autographs, but she shook her head with a pretty smile and walked on, knowing the floodgates she'd fling wide if she complied.

"There are some advantages to being known mostly by voice," Max said, wondering which among these were Messing's outer guard.

They were admitted through the VIP door by a uniformed security agent. This was normally the side entrance to the Hyatt, where lights were left low and all sound was muted. As they reached the coat check, near plate-glass doors closing off the hall through which the ticket holders were filing, a manager appeared. "Miss Drake. Welcome. Mr. Cornelius is not with you tonight?"

"I'm afraid not, Cyril," she replied. "I don't believe you know my escort, Max August . . . also known as Barnaby Wilde."

"Of KQBU. Yes, indeed." He raised his brows in polite surprise. "I heard your interview the other day . . ."

Max laughed easily as they shook hands. "We made up after. Now it looks like *you're* the one with his hands full."

"It is crazy, isn't it? We expected six thousand, but more have already arrived, and there are two hours to go." He looked around and edged closer. "Frankly, it's a zoo, but fun all the same. The energy is incredible." He laughed. "May I be of any help to you tonight?"

"I wish you could, Cyril," Val said sincerely. "But we've just come for that energy."

Max added, "We might need something later. Can we get in touch with you, or with someone—?"

"Yes, indeed." Cyril pulled a card from his breast pocket and scribbled on it. "Show this to anyone on our staff, and they'll either help you or find someone who can. I may not be available at all times."

"I understand. Thank you."

"All food and drinks are free to you, of course—though if you're hungry, I'd advise eating soon, with this crowd." Cyril was reluctant to leave them. His eyes were discreetly undressing Val, and Max could hardly blame him; it was all Max could do to keep his own eyes to himself. He allowed one hand to brush hers as if by accident, and the look that passed between them was not discreet at all. Cyril mumbled something diplomatic and melted smoothly away.

Val waited until he was well out of earshot, then whispered softly, "What do you hear from your lion?"

"Just give me a minute," Max said. He leaned up against a wall and closed his eyes. He reached in and took hold of the clear center in his mind, seeking those images of Kalbu Rabu's jungle. Val turned to watch the people in the hall.

When she looked back a few moments later, Max was frowning. In another moment he opened eyes hard as flint. "I don't hear anything," he said.

"This is definitely where Corny said to come."

"I know."

"We need the location, Max. The hotel's gigantic."

"I know." He leaned back again, and tried again. His face contorted, and sweat broke out across his brow with the effort; the dress shirt's collar grew tight. Val saw people looking at them now and couldn't suppress the instant mental headline, "Valerie Drake's Lover Has Drug Seizure at Wild Party," as she moved to stand in front of him. It was stupid to think of that now, but it was so deeply ingrained in her. Come on, Max! Tie this up!

He looked up again, breathing heavily. "I can't get him—but I think I know why. The Wolf's figured out how I escaped, and put Kalbu Rabu on hold until he needs him himself. The lion *is* here . . . but that's all I can get."

"Can't you even get a direction?"

"Not yet. We're going to have to search." And not let the mood die, he added to himself. This is no time to falter. "I've *seen* what Messing's planning, and he'll have to let Kalbu Rabu loose before midnight. There's plenty of time left. Since it's certain Messing will be near a stage and an audience, we'll check out the parties."

If she had any doubts, she kept them to herself. "Lead on," she said resolutely.

10:03 P.M.

He took her hand and they went out the glass doors into the crowds. Beside a group of blonde girls dressed in gold—a good omen! Max told himself—was a wall chart of the various festivities. "The Big Band is on this floor, just ahead of us," he read. "Space-Age, Be-Bop, and Cabaret are up one, and Disco and the Tea Dance are up two, on the main floor."

"Shall we trot a fox?" Val asked.

They hurried into the Golden Gateway ballroom to the strains of "In the Mood." This was the largest of the hotel's convention halls, and though the crowds were large, they didn't begin to fill it. Surprisingly half the people there were young, too young to have heard Miller or Goodman in their prime; but the twelve-piece band was re-creating them admirably. As Max and Val circled past the dancers and their ravaged buffet to reach the bandstand, the leader saw them coming and waved with his free hand. He leaned down and spoke from the side of his mouth, keeping his baton dead on the beat. "Valerie, my dear," he said. "Is this social, or would you maybe want to sing?"

She gave him a flattered smile. "Another time, Freddie. We're on a strange and mysterious mission tonight. Do you mind if we have a look around your stage?"

He shrugged. "Why not? Help yourself."

Some of the dancers recognized Valerie as she came up the stage-end stairs. Applause rippled through the room like minnows in a stream, until she had to turn and smile and wave regret; all the while Max was poking behind the blue curtains and peering beneath the platform. There didn't seem to be any extra people there, or any hidden cavities, but he couldn't trust his eyes where Wolf Messing was concerned. He had to touch and feel.

It took ten minutes before he was satisfied. "One down," was all he said. "Let's go."

10:18 P.M.

As they made their way back toward the escalators, the crowds were noticeably heavier. The neatly ordered line of entering ticket holders had melted into confusion; Cyril was fighting hard but looking harried. And on the next flight up the first crack at three parties together had stopped many of the new arrivals before they'd gone all the way to the main floor. Just across from Max and Val when they came off the moving stairs was the Space-Age Self-Expression, but competing waves of revelers, headed in opposite directions, were crossing in front of them. Like gnomes, Max thought, and plunged into them, tacking like a sailboat up and back to get through. Val pressed close behind.

Space-Age Self-Expression turned out to be eight black guys in silver lamé playing synthesized rock. Gold flake balloons hung suspended in the air above the dance floor, until snagged by the dancers and used as imagination required. It was impossible to circle this group, so Max and Val made their way through them, despite the more violent character of their dance. A low buzz instead of applause followed them across the floor; but when it became clear that Valerie Drake wouldn't sing, the crowds went quickly back to their boogie.

Max and Val quickly found nothing and pushed on toward Be-Bop. This time, Max knew the group and did the honors, but the result was the same.

10:39 P.M.

Max, his jaw outthrust, plowed out of the room, drawing protests which he ignored. He made his way to a corner of the hall which was not quiet, but away from the main traffic flow, and tried for his lion again. Again, he had no luck.

They went on for a fast look at the cabaret singer. He was too limber to be the Wolf in disguise, and he had no stage—just tables surrounding a deli filled with those who couldn't get through the evening without a nosh.

They took the back stairs toward the main-floor disco, in an attempt to duck the crowds, but there was no escape now. The three-hundred-foot lobby was absolutely jammed, save for one pitiful space at the far left end to the Tea Dance. Overflowing onto the stairs, people were cheek to cheek and thigh to thigh as far as the eye could see. Sexual vibes struck Max and Val like a hot desert wind; this was the prime party. A huge clock had been hung from the third-floor terrace, and was marking out the time in small jerks.

10:50 P.M.

Pro forma, they looked in the disco, but the dance floor was tiny and filled with glitter people. The DJ alcove was tinier, and filled with the DJ. There was no room for Messing's operations there. And clearly the space reserved for the Tea Dance band was just as impossible; it was collapsing in the crush as they watched. This vast atrium looked precisely like Messing's kind of place, but . . .

Both of them turned their heads toward the rising terrace filled with blank white doors.

Max put his arm around Val and hugged her to him. "Come on. Get out your machete and we'll fight our way to the elevators."

"You think he'll come out on one of the balconies when it's time? Max, we can't search all those rooms!"

"There's only one that interests me."

They stepped into the crowd and were immediately caught up in it. A straight path, or even a controlled tack, was out of the question now. Vast waves of motion surged through the packed bodies; one man reaching into his pocket on the far side of the lobby eventually pushed people aside here. The mood was festive and sensual, but the frustration of an over-packed room was there, too, and it wouldn't take much for the mob mind to shift. Max couldn't help but think just how bad it would get if Messing completed his plans for the quake.

The sound of the Tea Dance was gradually eaten away by chatter as Max and Val made their agonizingly slow progress across the floor. Each forward step required negotiation. But then all at once Max heard another song in his head. The song he knew and hated:

Oo-mm, the storm is threat-nin'
Mah ve-ry life to-day!
Gim-me, gim-me shel-ter!
Ooh, I'm gon-na fa-ade a-way!

It was blasting in his ears, and he was blindly, instinctively, turning to his right as a sharpened edge of blackened steel sliced up along his ribs, just missing in its intended thrust below those ribs and into the heart. Max clamped down on the calfskin-gloved hand that held the blade, caught a glimpse of dark eyes and a moustache that he dimly recalled from the unmoving audience in Messing's auditorium, and forced the arm downward while bringing up his knee. Ten pounds of pressure is all it takes to snap a man's elbow backward; Max gave it much more. The sharp crack of separating tendons was just part of the hubbub. Only those on either side turned their heads, and they were too late. The dark eyes flooded, and the moustache pulled back to reveal clenched, grinding teeth, and then a wave took both teeth and broken arm away. A woman in a pants suit was heading for the bar, and Max was borne away, searching wildly for more attackers.

Whoa chil-dren! It's just a shot a-way!
It's just a SHOT A-WAY!

He had seen that kind of attack in Dao Tiang, or the results of it. A bicycle spoke, long, limber, and all but invisible in fast action, is sharpened to a needle point. The killer crowds his victim on a busy street, slips the needle into the heart and out again in one smooth motion. The victim walks on for another fifty feet, feeling only a pinprick, if that, before finally falling inexplicably dead.

It's just a shot a-way!

"Don't hang back," said Val over her shoulder. "If they separate us, we'll never get back together."

Max stretched out and took hold of her arm. "Make way," he shouted. "Make way; this is Valerie Drake!"

She turned back to him, stung. "Max," she hissed.

"Do it!" he said savagely. And, more loudly, "Come on, buddy. Move it. We've got a VIP here."

Her eyes widened with understanding, and as she looked beyond Max, the crowd abruptly changed to four thousand unknown factors. She twisted forward again, reaching out eagerly. "May we get through? Please? Thank you. Yes, we have to. Sorry. Thank you. Thank you very much. Thank you. Thank you."

The rest of their trip was a nightmare. Even with cooperation, progress was by inches, and there was no way to know if another agent might strike at any moment.

11:06 P.M.

But they came out the other side unscathed. No song had sounded for others in that throng, though Max was certain they were there; the same constraints would have held them back. He guided Val to where they could set their backs against a wall and told her quickly why he'd had to act. She took his arm, but her answering gaze remained steady. If there were ever a woman I could love wholeheartedly, here she stands, Max thought proudly; but then came the unwanted qualifier: if we live through the night.

"The same crack between the years that the Wolf wants to use is working for us—with or without Kalbu Rabu," he said with some satisfaction. "But we'll stay out of crowds as best we can." He stared back at the eighteen terraces overlooking them, and added, "We'll play it close, period. A silencer in here would work just as well."

11:10 P.M.

In front of the elevators uniformed guards were checking room keys before allowing entry. Val showed hers, and she and Max were passed right through. But as the doors closed behind them, a man and a woman who had hurried up began arguing vehemently with the guard about not being allowed to follow. The song began to play in Max's head as he recognized them: two more of Messing's silent audience on the Farallons. He and Val exchanged silent looks as the elevator flew away.

11:12 P.M.

They got off at fifteen and Max retraced the route he'd taken four nights before with Madeleine Riggs. Sometimes those four days seemed like forever, and sometimes like nothing; just now it was the latter. The Madwoman's old room looked like any other outside its closed white door. Hamoto and Hardesty would have gotten all they wanted from it the first day, and the hotel would quite naturally have wanted its rental tonight. Could she and her master have taken it again?

Max knocked loudly. There was no answer.

Neither was there time to disguise what came next. "I hope you and Cyril are real good friends," Max said, and kicked down the door.

The couple tangled on the bed nearly died of heart failure.

Max was already backing out as the man began to get up in a rage. "My mistake," Max said, hands outstretched placatingly. "Wrong room. Just a joke." But he was making certain these two couldn't have been his quarry in hallucinatory disguise, giving the warning song a chance to come. It didn't, and he pulled the broken door almost closed again.

"Let's get to our room," he rapped.

They ran along the terrace toward the red exit sign that marked the stairs, and clattered into the concrete well.

11:16 P.M.

Room 1489 was a large room, almost identical with the one upstairs. Max walked through it and went to the bathroom; when he came out again, he took a flask of Damiana from Val's bag and poured them two glasses. "It's back to Plan A," he said as he handed her hers. "Contact the lion."

Val's answer was calm, but there was something in her eyes . . . "You've tried that already."

"And I'll try it again. Till I get it right." He took his gun from inside his tux and put it into her hand. "I know you don't know about firearms, Miss Drake," he said, "but can you shoot?"

"I can if I have to."

"Let's hope you don't have to. But guard the door." Then: "But not from in front of it." He positioned her in the best spot, alongside the bed, and she sat down there with the pistol on her lap.

"Max, it's 11:19," she said. "We haven't gotten anywhere. Do you think—"

He waved her off. "I haven't got time for that. The game's not lost till the final gun. And sometimes, not even then." He selected a chair well away from both her and the door, tried to calm himself, and resolutely began to probe once more.

11:28 P.M.

But in the end he gave it up. He looked at his watch expressionlessly; looked at Val and shook his head. "Not yet," he said. "I could see the lion's jungle again, but it was my memory, not the real thing. But it'll come." He could also see the tightness of her mouth.

11:29 P.M.

The phone rang. Val jumped a foot off the bed and snatched it up in one motion. It was Cyril. "Miss Drake," he began apologetically, "I'm sorry to disturb you, but a man and a woman were just at the front desk, demanding your room number. Of course, we did not oblige them, but they were very insistent that they were friends of yours. I hope we were right to refuse them."

"Yes, thank you, Cyril. You did exactly right."

"Thank you, Miss Drake. Happy New Year."

She hung up hard, bunched her hands, and began to pace the room. Max poured himself some Damiana and said, quietly, "Val." She looked at him but continued to pace. "Sit down," he said more firmly.

"Max . . ." Her face was taut. "We are running out of time. I haven't—I don't want to undercut the feeling we worked for today—"

"—but you're used to dealing with a real wizard, not a guy who's as much in the dark as you," he said equably. "But will you just listen to me for a minute?"

He waited for her to sit; before his steady gaze she gave in. When he spoke again, his voice was sober.

"I was a Point Man in Nam. You know that. And one day my platoon was tricked by the Cong. All but two of my thirty-five men died on me that day. I swore I'd get even, and, the first chance I got, I tried to do it, to Vietnam, by shooting up a group of innocent people. Thirteen, all ages. I just killed them. Dead."

She half rose. He shook his head.

"Messing hit me with it while I was on his island, and it cut the blocks out from under me, but good. I'd tried to hide it from myself for so long, I went as far down as I've ever been that night. The next day I knew I had to put it aside while I concentrated on getting out, but that didn't change it for me.

"But starting that same afternoon I began to learn—or relearn—the work of the wise. About looking at life on the grand scale, and the way I fit into that full reality. I'd first done that in Nam, too. And I understood, finally"—he paused, wanting to get it just right—"what I did was wrong. It'll always be wrong, and I'll live with it forever. But I know, now, that I'm more than just that one September morning; just as I'm more than just a jock, or a target—or a lover. I'm all those things, and more. I've lived thirty years, and overall I'd have to rate my life a fairly decent one. I made a big mistake, once. A very big mistake. But Messing was wrong; I'm not disqualified forever because of it."

"I would never have thought you were," Val said, coming forward despite him.

"No, but I would have. I'd made Ia Ngu a god—or a devil—and abased myself before it the way the Wolf abases himself before his Deva. I'd do anything not to have to face it. But now I can."

She sat on the arm of his chair, and he put one hand on her leg; but he wasn't looking at her. He was looking into time. "In 1973, I was less than I am tonight. Five days ago I was less. Every day doors were opened for me, by the full reality—but it was up to me whether I went through them or not. Nobody—no god, no devil, and no other man—carried me to this point. It's because I chose to go through the doors I did—because I made mistakes *and* made progress—because I feel most *whole* when I'm out on the point, relying on myself and knowing I can—that's why I am who I am tonight.

"I haven't done all that to fail the world I believe in again. I'm *ready* to get it right this time. And I tell you, the door we need now will open!"

"You sound like Corny," she said. "Maybe you are a wizard, after all."

He shrugged, but not to say she was wrong.

11:38 P.M.

And then his eyes grew wide and his heart began to pound with an alien rhythm. With a strangled cry, he fell back in his chair, and Val, thinking of Cornelius, shouted "Max!" twice. But behind the lids that were falling shut, that for which he had waited so long had come at last. He was seeing through the lion's eyes again, looking at a vast, crisp forest—a forest made of iron. This was not a jungle—nor a river of molten rock. This was . . . a room filled with iron girders.

A motor room.

The motor room to the revolving restaurant at the Hyatt's peak!

"But there's no stage there," a voice he knew protested.

The vision grew clearer and brighter in response. Behind his closed lids, Max longed to close his eyes and blot it out. The light set him aflame, consuming him with its urgent force, before he fell free as an ember, being shaken by Val in room 1489.

"I got it." He tried to speak and found the words hard to form. "I got it."

Chapter 39

DECEMBER 31 • 11:41 P.M.

They raced back to the stairs at the end of the terrace. The only elevator service to the roof was from the lobby; this was the fastest way. They took the cold steps two and three at a time, pacing each other, leaving no breath to spare as they stumbled to the locked red door at the top. Max began to pound on it with both fists, furiously.

11:44 P.M.

After an uncertain moment of no response at all, the door clicked and swung back to reveal a burly maître d' in impeccable evening dress. His face and his tone were scrupulously polite, but there was no give to them. "The Equinox is available only through the elevator," he said, "and I'm afraid we're already overfull at the moment. I'll be glad to assist you to the elevator, and perhaps in an hour—"

Max shoved Cyril's carte blanche into the man's hand, and Val pressed in behind it. "I'm Valerie Drake. Let us pass," she said, even more imperious than Max had dared to be in the lobby. "This man needs your help."

The maître d's face did not change, but he stepped graciously back and held the door. "Of course, Miss Drake. I didn't recognize you at first. What can I do for you?"

She and Max stepped out into the restaurant's crowded foyer of deep red tile and floor-length mirrors. If people were not packed in as tightly here as in the lobby, it was only because the elevator brought them only when the maître d' determined he had the space.

Max said, "I need to get into the restaurant's motor room."

"I see," said the maître d' neutrally. "In that case, I'm sure you'll understand if I check this with Cyril."

"There's no time for that."

"Please, sir. It won't take a minute. My office is right this way." He saw the look in Max's eye and added almost in the same breath, "I'll call immediately."

"Do it, Max," said Val crisply. "It'll take longer to argue about it."

Max nodded shortly. "Let's go."

11:45 P.M.

The three of them went up a short flight of richly carpeted stairs to a suite of offices above the restaurant, Max leading the maître d', Val following quickly. The main office was a wide rectangle, with picture windows on three sides. The view of the city at night was strung breathtakingly from the peninsula to Marin, from Twin Peaks to the Oakland hills. There was soft music playing.

The maître d' walked quickly to his desk. He leaned over it toward the telephone. And Max realized what music he'd been hearing so softly—too late! The maître d' straightened up with a Tokoroff 9 mm in his hand.

"Sit down over there and don't make any mistakes," he said, and his voice was as neutral as before. "You were lucky to get this far, but you cannot get to my comrades."

"You weren't on Messing's island," was all Max could say.

"I'm no psychokinetic, August. I'm a conscious agent, under full-scale conscious cover."

"You're a fool. This lady is somebody; she can't just disappear."

"Sit down, I said. In fourteen minutes this lady will be only one of thousands to disappear."

Val stepped forward. The gun moved slightly, just enough to hold the space between her and Max. "Shoot me now, then," she said. "Let's see what the crowd downstairs has to say about it."

"They won't hear above the chatter. Try me if you like."

"Back off, Val," said Max, turning toward her.

"Max!" Her voice was hot. "To hell with chivalry!"

"Do it, dammit!" he said, and he took her by both shoulders. For a moment his back was toward their captor. His eyes bored into hers. His lips barely moved. "Take the gun." His tux jacket bulged open.

Her hand came up. The weight on his chest was eased. He turned back to the side, toward the stairway, and dropped to the floor, clawing inside his empty coat for diversion. Two shots exploded. Would the darkness follow?

But that was the end of it. With adrenaline clarity he saw the maître d' stumble, the weight of his gun dragging him down. The man tried to fight it, to stay on his feet and raise the weapon again, but his arms fell like a puppet's with cut strings, and his legs went next. He sat down, his legs crossing like an Indian's, and his torso fell forward as far as that position would allow. He was left contemplating the floor like a holy man at prayer. But it was too late for prayers.

Val stood stock still, the gun rigid before her, as high as her chest. Smoke curled through the auburn highlights in her hair. Her face was chalk white, the cosmetic accents to her features bright and tawdry.

Max leapt back to his feet. Took the gun from her hand and slid it back into his holster, all the while turning her toward the windows behind her. The streets below were rivers of flowing light.

"So now you're Number One with a Bullet," he said.

She looked at him, shocked, and saw eyes deep with concern as he gathered her into his arms. She hugged him tightly for a moment, very tightly; then she stepped away. Her eyes were hectic but her color was coming back. "No time," she said.

11:48 P.M.

He went to the dead man's desk and ripped open the drawers. As he'd expected, a set of keys was there, and as he'd hoped, one was marked "MOTOR RM." They ran back down the stairs to the foyer; true to the maître d's prediction no one seemed to have heard a thing. They pushed through the people to the doorway marked "Parties of One or Two Persons," and stepped out onto the revolving wheel.

It was a vast circle, which rotated around the stable center column so slowly as to be almost unnoticeable. Walking onto it was like walking onto any other floor; it was only as the doorway crept away that you realized the difference. Black tables with bright red slicker chairs, all occupied, ranged the outside perimeter beside the three-hundred-sixty degree window. A second level, one step up, filled the inside perimeter; here the tables were blocked into individual booths by mirrored partitions. These tables, too, were flush with men and women who had no cares in the world.

Max led the way along the narrow path between the two levels, dodging the harried waitresses. Halfway around he found what he'd known was there: a bright red door with a neat black nameplate, alone in the curved wall covered with corduroy. Max checked his watch.

11:50 P.M.

Then he checked the diners, drinkers, and help who could see them from their half of the circle. "I need a diversion," he told Val. "I don't want anyone to see me go in here, in case fresh troops show up." Again he turned his back to onlookers, and pressed his gun on her. She flushed, but he cut her off. "Guns don't stop the shamans. I found that out on the Farallons. It'll do you more good than it will me."

She took it and pushed it into her bag, nodded, and tried to smile. "I knew it from the start. You're going to wreck my career." Then she threw her arms around him. "Kiss me now, Max!" she whispered fiercely.

Then she spun away and ran back around the curve until she could see him no more. Before her unending stage fright could catch up to her, she stood in the aisle and sang.

At once people in both directions stopped what they were doing to stare. Valerie Drake! This wasn't on the schedule!

Max faded back against the red nap wall as the tables near him emptied, guests and staff both pushing past to get a look at the show. For a moment he thought Val hadn't gone far enough, and the compression of the people would still leave too many able to look back and see him. But the crowds had grown used to compression; in the end his section was deserted. He slipped the key in the lock and opened the door. Shadows and stench bade him welcome.

It was 11:53.

Chapter 40

Aleksandra Korelatovna and Wolf Messing were in a world of their own making. In a sphere of burnished ebony, they stood straddle-legged on a floating black plate which cut the sphere horizontally in half. In this field of molded shadow the flames of their altars were reflected once in the plate which held them and again as a continuous arc along the half sphere overhead.

The bent figure of the man and the vital one of the woman were robed in the deepest purple. Aleksandra's vestment was cut to display her proud breasts; and Wolf and she, too, had spent their day lost in sex magick. As their limbs moved in snakelike cadence to a rhythm they alone could hear, sparks of crimson and of indigo swept along the swirling folds of their robes.

There was absolutely no sound in the black sphere—not of chanting, not of crackling fire. Reflections there might be, but no echoes. Here was the silence of deep space.

The two figures stood within a great circle, facing a larger triangle, and the single point of contact between the two runes was precisely at the center of the sphere. In this way all of the reflected light in the chamber was focused on that contact. Around the circle, in each of the cardinal directions, one of the talismans stood, and each of them faced that point. The angel and the eagle were closest to it, the lion and bull farther back.

In the heart of the triangle a squat form was struggling to be born.

Wolf silently directed that their dance be brought to a close; the two became still, and watchful. It is good, Aleksandra, the old man thought; and her reply came crystalline into his mind.

Very good, maestro, yes. The Deva is delicious!

It is, isn't it? Nine minutes at most now, until the Summation.

Seven, I believe, maestro.

Wolf Grigorevich Messing let it pass. It did not fit the mood he wanted, and had to have. This woman had taken him over long ago, and he was long past taking offense at her casual disregard for his ego. He was not a realist, but he was a fatalist. She was inevitable.

And still he was the maestro; as long as he stayed within her law. He took her hand now, so soft and warm in his wrinkled one, and looked at her breasts, and wished she gave up more of the Power from their unions. He looked at her face, and wished she'd kept more of the comfortable peasant woman that so many had known as his wife. Perhaps then he would have insisted. He would have made her obey! But this *natural* face with its blue-black eyes was much too decadent for his taste.

His consolation was that she couldn't hear these inner thoughts; but in that he was mistaken. Her eyes swept him, an old man bent and breathing hard, a man no longer a man, and she wiped the sweat from her upper lip and threw it to the floor.

Shall we begin? she queried him. He nodded his assent, and turned back toward the triangle. Within it, something unseen was moving convulsively, the air itself rippling and stretching.

They began another silent chant, in unison.

Coraxo cahisa coremo, od belanu azodiazodore . . .
Das Daox cocasu ol Eanio vohima . . .

Within the triangle the figure began to grow more distinct. It was not only the light which the sphere focused on that point of union, but the energy. The New Year was impossible to mistake now; the ebony chamber was filled with the close scent of mahogany, and the texture of precious deep oils. The light was saffron gold.

Ohyo! ohyo! noibu Ohyo! casaganu! Bajile madareda . . .

Messing capered with the syllables, emoting theatrically.

(Six minutes, thought Aleksandra for herself alone. She watched Herr Maestro from the corner of her eye, and thought, No man should come to shamanism so late. Sixty years gone by before he took charge of his talents! Old fool!)

The squat shape was all but solid now.

NIISO! carupe up nidali! NIISO I A I D A!

In the triangle the Deva called Naught surged forth at last.

In that triangle it was bound to form—but not any form evolution had ever touched. In its realm there was no cohesion, no consciousness or control. Here, forced into a single alien shape at an alien summons, it was a seething mass of rages and terrors—not one thing at all, but many. Their pulpy, fleshy folds, erupting from what might have been their nostrils, were shaped by chaos alone, and they changed, swelling—bursting sometimes with fetid gel, which piled high against the invisible barriers of the triangle beneath—then receding, being swallowed back into the veined mass of pulp which must have been their torso. Like the storm clouds which had dogged Max, they had hundreds of eyes, but these eyes were diamond-like, multifaceted; as the multitude of minds within looked out this way and that, dark burning holes crawled across the facets, leaping into prominence at the right angles, almost vanishing along the edges. They were cold, and wet, and the more they burned, the colder grew the sphere. But they could not escape their triangular prison, so now they cried out:

ZAZAS, ZAZAS, NASATANADA ZAZAS!

These are the words Adam used when he opened the gates of hell, thought Aleksandra. And reaching out quickly, before he could understand or resist, she threw Wolf Messing across the point of focus and into the heart of the horror.

The Deva swarmed instantly over him and ripped free his arm to devour it, as they broke him against the floor.

"ALEKSANDRA!" he screamed, in a voice thin and shrill. That one word, the first audible sound after an hour of absolute silence, echoed in the chamber like a bomb blast. But in Messing's darkening, sparkling mind, her answer was as sharp as a laser.

(The old world ends, maestro. Yin and Yang are too much Order. You and I have called down Naught, but I alone must have it!)

"Aleksandra," he whimpered.

(NOW LET ALL IMBALANCE HOLD SWAY!)

The Deva sucked the old man's head into their heavy folds.

Aleksandra threw her arms wide in ecstasy. Four minutes! Now at last it was hers alone! The years, the long years of scheming, working, waiting 'til she was certain—certain she could call down this temporary shadow of unlimited dispersion, and certain she could withstand them without the balance of that hated man! In this center of Power at the peak of the pyramidal hotel, far from his goddamned crowds, she and she alone would loose the World's Decay. Through her alone would come the destruction of an Ideal, and the deaths of Generations. She would be one of so very few to *make History*!

She spun in delirious triumph and saw Max August leaping for her throat.

. . . . .

Max's watch had read 11:56 when he'd made out the sphere, nestled in the spider's web of iron supports like malignant cancer. There was a slim doorway cut into the side of the thing, through which he could see the Madwoman with her arms thrown wide, and he thought, No Wolf. That's why no stage. But I was right about her being his second.

His best gambit was to hit her hard, physically, before she

could crank up her shaman's defenses; that was what he still did best. He took three quick breaths and broke into a sprint; automatically he began to whisper, "Well, good luck"—but he saw it meant nothing to him now. That time was not this time.

He went in fast, and in his tux, was almost across the black plate before she saw him. He caught one glimpse of the Thing which boiled beyond her, and pulled his eyes away. "Happy New Year, bitch!" he snarled to her alone, as his eager fingers found her throat.

They went down together, her red hair spilling out across the ebony, her face a mask of hate so brutal that he wasn't sure she was the same woman. But the thrill of the contact thundered through his veins, and every cell in his body came alive. This was the Ending! There would be no missed connections, no waking up tomorrow blood-encrusted on the floor. This time, only one of them was going out alive, and that was all he wanted.

Max pinned her to the plate as she raked his face. He stared into her blue-black eyes as he had the first night and saw no surrender now. Deafening shrieks filled his left ear; they had nearly fallen back into the triangle, and the Deva's many limbs fouled the rune's invisible walls just two feet from their heads. Aleksandra shifted toward them suddenly, trying to roll Max to his side and into range.

He threw out one arm and braced himself; longer fingers would have crossed the line. His other hand wasn't enough to hold Aleksandra. She broke free and scrambled away over the polished darkness, her breathing hoarse but strong. Max lunged for her ankle and caught it, but she had no farther to go. At the edge of the circle, her hands fell upon the eagle. Its wooden wings flexed in anticipation—

—and then, the woman and the talisman came together!

She flew at him as he dove aside, with fury made ghastly by the birdlike twist to her face beneath that streaming copper hair. Her eyes were bright and flat. Her hands were up, the fingers lengthened, the nails grown thick. Beneath her robe the shape of her lower body had changed to something plump and bent, and her unseen feet below made the clacking sound of sharpened claws.

In the Equinox the moving platform was gathering speed. Val felt it before any of the patrons, and brought her song to a sudden end, accepting the swelling applause with haunted eyes. A waitress overreached herself and fell across a man's lap. They both laughed.

In the grand lobby seven thousand people crowded together to watch the great clock; two minutes to midnight, it said. The Tea Dance band broke into a waltz to which no one could dance, and boys kissed girls and boys kissed boys . . .

But then the building trembled.

Vast iridescent wings closed over Max's head. Her beak stabbed at his eyes and scored a long gouge down one cheek before he could tear himself free. He knew where he had to go; he didn't have to look. He crouched for a leap across the circle, just as a slashing wing tip cut his feet from under him. He went down hard, taking the impact on his arms and rolling with it. There was one glimpse of the Madwoman as he spun, a quick flash of bird face and wings, and dimly, behind her, the horror she served.

How long till midnight? he wondered crazily. How long? Then his hand struck something other than the floor, and warmth ran up his arm. But no energy this time; he didn't need any. A voice thundered in his head: "Now the portal be wide!" And he was shouting back: "We're in sync!"

And that other mind that was always his mind joined his—not to blot it out, but to complement it, and make it whole. Truths he had always known, taboos he had always feared, crashed and burned as the connections—My God! The Connections!—leapt from one to the other, and found themselves already there. Max August had no name for the amber body he saw surging up off the floor.

In the Equinox people were screaming, shouting, crying to no avail. The restaurant was spinning like a fan, lights streaming by beyond the windows, the noise of its motors a crescendo of pain. The agony filled the natural megaphone of the hotel below; the lobby shuddered like a loosening ratchet. The artificial brook broke out of its walls and spilled down to slick the floor. The clock on the third floor fell and crashed, reading thirty seconds to go.

Val was praying and she knew not to whom.

The Lion is locked with the Eagle, and the Deva looks down over all. The howling of the god-thing tangles with the harsh cries of the bird, but Max is grimly silent—not from heroism, but for control. He cannot hold half of what he's seeing. He cannot comprehend the cues and reflexes which guide his golden limbs in their defense against the claws. He cannot understand the crevasse between the years which yawns around him. There is only one thing which is real for him—the one thing which he's always known, but had to relearn for this time.

He is Max August. Point Man. Wizard.

He is himself now, as never before. He and the Lion are One. He and the Fire are One. He is complete—

—And She is not. She is Naught, decay, and space, at her own command. She and the Eagle are infinity. She can attack him in infinite ways. But infinity cannot swallow the point. Infinity and the point are forever Two.

The relationship between them, the connection and the flow, is as simple and basic as sex. Because they are connected, He has all Power, and so does She. There is no Difference; only Power. But who will give and who will take? Which way will the circuit flow?

The Madwoman sees it, too, and makes the final change. The eagle is gone, and the lion. All talismans are banished, and Max knows too little to return them. There is only the woman and the man again, the challenging, seductive Madeleine and Max.

They are locked in passion's embrace as her nude form caresses his. She means to take him bodily—but it is a mistake, a bad one, and the last one. It brings all the cosmic grandeurs into simple human focus.

"Yin or Yang!" Max roars above the din of Deva and machine. "Yin or Yang! DO I FUCK YOU, OR DO YOU FUCK ME?"

And midnight is within them. One brief second, between times and worlds. One brief second when the Old is dead and the New unborn. One brief second.

He holds her. And

He kisses her.

And those blue-black eyes flash wide with horror. The crimson mouth spreads wide with scream.

And then those eyes are fading. Hot brown points of diamond sparkle in their awful depths, clustering like maggots. She screams again, a mindless thing, but the sound is far inside as her beautiful body grows slack in Max's arms. He drops her to the plate. Her right arm comes up in supplication, but abruptly curves, and bends. It falls back like a fish. Without affecting the soft envelope of skin, incredibly, the bones within are falling apart. She is decaying, and her heart, her stomach and organs bulge upward like mice beneath a blanket, frantically spasming. From the hole which was her mouth, the voices call to Max.

"In the end as in the egg," they scream, and others answer, "Naught."

The brown eyes toast the victor, and her puckering face forms a final kiss of flesh.

Max looks up, and the Deva has vanished, and the sphere has faded, and he is alone on cold concrete with four toppled talismans, and the virgin New Year.

Chapter 41

JANUARY 1 • 3 A.M.

Breath clouds wreathed their vision as Max and Val strode up Sutter Street, two lone figures climbing the corridor of concrete and steel, which touched down at Market Street and ran slowly on to the Embarcadero, where sat the Hyatt. There the street was flush with cops and blue sedans; here there was emptiness, and the clean echoes of footsteps on the crisp night air.

"Was Hardesty satisfied?" Val asked at last, the word clouds catching in her hair. Her slim hand nestled comfortably in Max's light grip. In his other hand he held a suitcase, just large enough for four precious carvings.

"Not at all. There was no way in hell he was going to believe me."

"But he's the only cop who actually knew what you were talking about."

"That's what you think. He knows what he has to know, but he can't get above a cop's framework for it. It's *because* he knows a little something that he won't believe I pulled it off after only six days; he goes by the books he's read. But with no bodies, no Devas, and no black spheres, there was nothing he could do, either for me or to me. If you have a five-point-eight earthquake with fairly limited damage and death, how can you prove there was supposed to have been a ten? And why would you want to?" Max smiled grimly. "No, he's pissed because he's confused; unless he can lay hands on one of the psychokinetics, I expect no thanks from the FBI."

They came to the steeper rise at Grant Street. To their right, a block down, the Dragon Gate leered at them, but neither Max nor Val could see that gate alone. Each saw the other, angrily following Mr. Cornelius. They slowed, and then stopped.

"Come over here," Max said, leading Val into the alcove of the Sutter-Stockton Garage. The mannequins in the store windows watched with toothy smiles, waving encouragement.

Max spread his feet and planted himself firmly on the sloping sidewalk, leaning back against the wall and closing his eyes. There was a feeling of falling backward, out of that firmly braced body, and then there was no feeling at all, only falling.

In free fall, he spoke with Cornelius Agrippa.

"Restored?"

"Yes. Greatly diminished, but restored. My mind is clear, my power sustaining; though not forever, now."

"Death?"

"Five years. I have no regrets."

Silent darkness. And dry, dustless age.

"Max, I relinquish Valerie. My day is done; her life lies ahead of her. So does yours, and you alone know how far. The torch is passed."

"Torch of life?"

"Torch of love."

Ebony space.

"Come see me, today. We will celebrate Today."

"Today and Forever."

"Amen."

He slipped back into gravity, falling not so freely now, being pulled more and more directly toward his form. It looked to be a mannequin; a plastic mask. The plastic eyelids moved upward, hundreds of muscles and millions of blood cells doing their preprogrammed duties, and he looked out at the night and the lovely lady.

They began to walk again, as he told her what Agrippa had said. She squeezed his hand at his news of recovery, and her eyes were shining. "You saved more than you knew," she murmured. "But of course I'll take you now, Max. We've taken each other." They held each other, and there was nothing plastic left in him.

They found themselves before their destination: KQBU, beneath the neon sign. Max let them in with his key, and nodded to the watchman as they crossed Reception toward the studio. Chick Frommer had the holiday fill-in, and was playing new music again. A blonde girl, younger than he, was perched beside him on the counter, filling his paper cup from a flask. His smile when he saw his visitors was bright, but brief.

"Did you hear about Earl and his wife?" he asked.

"I heard, yes."

"Isn't that the pits? What kind of maniac would torture old people like that? It's even worse than the quake, to me."

"To me, too. I'd give anything if death, too, were reversible . . ."

Chick and the girl looked at each other; then at Valerie Drake. The girl said, finally, "Aren't you going to introduce us, Chick?"

"Oh, sure, honey. I'm sorry. I thought you knew . . . Melody Fraser, this is Barnaby—"

His visitor held up his hand then, looking him full in the face. Though he stood in the studio shadows, his eyes seemed to burn with the light of the stars, and the rock 'n' roll record behind them ran out without drawing a glance. A voice like warm wind through a jungle's grass rose to fill the enveloping silence; the man before Chick spoke six words. Short words, but to the point. He said:

"My name is not Barnaby Wilde."

End words

By the time of *The Long Man*, Max has added many skills to his arsenal. One is the Mayan knowledge of Time. Clearly, he hadn't written his *Codex* at the time of *The Point Man*, but here's what it tells us now.

Each Mayan day is made of a number and an image, and each number and image has a meaning. Each Mayan day begins at dawn, not midnight.

Our day	*Mayan day*	*Mayan meaning*
dawn Dec 26, 1980 – dawn, Dec 27	8 Earth	Connecting with the Universal
dawn Dec 27, 1980 – dawn, Dec 28	9 Flint Knife	Being the Unique
dawn Dec 28, 1980 – dawn, Dec 29	10 Milky Way	Personifying Alchemy
dawn Dec 29, 1980 – dawn, Dec 30	11 Sun	Owning All
dawn Dec 30, 1980 – dawn, Dec 31	12 Nipple	Fulfilling Reality
dawn Dec 31, 1980 – dawn, Jan 1	13 Wind	Managing Possibilities
dawn Jan 1, 1981 –	1 Night	Establishing a Private World

When I wrote *The Point Man*, neither Max nor I knew any of this, or even the year I was writing about. Therefore, any correspondences must be coincidence.

Unless . . .

Nah.

About the Author

Steve Englehart is known to millions of comic book readers as the author of such comics as *Captain America, The Justice League of America*, and *Batman: the Dark Detective*. The *Batman* film franchise was generated by his take on Batman and the Joker. His second novel, *The Long Man*, is a sequel to *The Point Man*. He lives in the San Francisco Bay area.